Opulence and Ashes

Also available by Kate Belli

Gilded Gotham Mysteries

Treachery on Tenth Street
Betrayal on the Bowery
Deception by Gaslight

OPULENCE AND ASHES

A GILDED GOTHAM MYSTERY

Kate Belli

CROOKED
LANE

NEW YORK

Copyright © 2023 by Kate Belli

Published in the United States by Crooked Lane Books, an imprint of The Quick Brown Fox & Company LLC.

Crooked Lane Books and its logo are trademarks of The Quick Brown Fox & Company LLC.

Library of Congress Catalog-in-Publication data available upon request.

ISBN (hardcover): 978-1-63910-530-4
ISBN (ebook): 978-1-63910-531-1

Cover design by Nicole Lecht

Printed in the United States.

www.crookedlanebooks.com

Crooked Lane Books
34 West 27th St., 10th Floor
New York, NY 10001

First Edition: October 2023

10 9 8 7 6 5 4 3 2 1

For the tireless advocates of women's rights, past and present.

PROLOGUE

The hungry flames leapt toward the empty sky, seeking something else upon which to feed. There was nothing left, though. The fire had already consumed everything in its path.

The entire structure was engulfed. Anything wooden or cloth had gone up instantly: the furniture, the clothing, the decorative moldings around the doorways, the banister with its intricate carvings. The few keepsakes any of the building's occupants had managed to bring from home were gone in minutes.

The exterior of the building was harder to fell, but the fire did its best, and after a time these elements too succumbed. The glass from windows burst from the heat, the bricks were charred black and crumbled, the roof collapsed.

In a rare occurrence, the building had stood on its own, being banded on one side by a cemetery and having just enough space between it and its neighbor on the opposite side that the firefighters were able to contain the blaze before that building was also destroyed.

Human flesh, too, was spared. Everyone who lived in the building had been able to escape in time. They huddled on the sidewalk in the cold night, shivering in their nightclothes under blankets offered by strangers, tears streaming down their faces as all their worldly possessions were extinguished, ashes raining on their upturned faces like filthy snow.

The fire cared not. It would feed on whatever it was given, animate or inanimate.

And if there hadn't been any people in its clutches this instance, there would always be another time.

CHAPTER 1

New York City

April 1890

The shrill scream was so unexpected, Genevieve grabbed Daniel's hand without thinking.

At the lectern in the front of the hall, Dagmar Hansen paused, allowing his audience to collect themselves. The woman who had screamed was now alternating between deep breaths and nervous, embarrassed huffs of laughter, demurely refusing several nearby gentlemen's offers of water or handkerchiefs.

What good would a handkerchief serve? Genevieve folded her arms crossly. A quick glance over her shoulder had confirmed that the screamer was Irene Tremble, who had been a silly, flighty girl even before she married Leslie Tremble and acquired a surname suitable to her demeanor. It was just like Irene, who had once brought Monsieur Lamont's dance class for young ladies to a screeching halt for an entire hour because she claimed to have spied a mouse and had succumbed to hysterics (of course, nobody else saw the creature, and no trace of it was ever found), to interrupt Dagmar's first lecture. Even the musicians paused, their dramatic swelling chords reduced to a low, soothing melody as Irene composed herself.

Daniel raised a brow at Genevieve in the dim light.

She gave him a tiny head shake and rolled her eyes. It wasn't discreet, but she was past caring if Irene saw.

Genevieve turned her attention back to the image projected just to the left of Dagmar's head and pursed her lips. She didn't let go of Daniel's hand. While Irene Tremble had always jumped at shadows and enjoyed the subsequent attention, in this case Genevieve had to admit the other woman might—just *might*—have been justifiably provoked. Not enough to scream, certainly, but it was true Dagmar had constructed his presentation for maximum dramatic effect. The picture that had so startled Irene was of two young men, surely no more than fifteen years old, in rough jackets and hats, robbing a third, apparently unconscious man, and it had appeared behind Dagmar to the accompaniment of a discordant shriek of sound by the musicians. Most members of the audience had started or winced, as was the intent. Even Genevieve, who had visited the type of foul, garbage-strewn alley pictured, found the photograph unsettling.

"Growler gangs," Dagmar intoned solemnly, "initiate young boys into their ranks early. One way to move up in rank is to commit a robbery, taking advantage of those too inebriated by stale beer to notice their pockets being ransacked." A general murmur of horror swept the crowd.

Genevieve knew, though, that the image was staged. Daniel had prepared her for this and other photographs she might find troubling in advance. Dagmar and an assistant had paid the young men in cigarettes, he'd said, to act out rifling through a drunkard's pockets.

"So, the act itself is not uncommon," Genevieve had said, frowning. "It's just that Dagmar wouldn't be able to photograph any gang members in the midst of thieving, as he would likely be robbed himself, so he staged the image. Is that correct?"

Daniel had eyed her steadily. "Yes."

"Are we ready to proceed?" Dagmar's voice carried clearly over the low hum of the audience members and the soft tones of the musicians. Skirts rustled and throats cleared as the assembled lecture-goers resettled themselves, turning their attention once again to Dagmar's spotlit figure.

"Some of these images are a little troubling, my friends." Dagmar gave a subtle hand gesture to the musicians, whose pace and tempo increased. "But that is why we are gathered here. I took these pictures, and created this slideshow, to expose the horrors under which your very neighbors live their lives. Because, yes, even if you live on Fifth Avenue . . ." The image of the robbery dissolved, slowly replaced by a photograph of the brand-new Huntley mansion, completed at the corner of Fifth and Fifty-Seventh mere weeks prior. Shocked gasps arose all around Genevieve. She glanced at Dewey and Leona Huntley's visibly stiffening backs. "Even if you live here," Dagmar continued, undaunted, "these poor wretches are, indeed, your neighbors." The image dissolved again, this time switching to a pile of newsboys sleeping atop a grate in the sidewalk, huddled together like puppies. The band's piano sounded the treacly opening notes of "Where Is My Wandering Boy Tonight?" A strangled sob sounded from somewhere behind Genevieve's right shoulder.

"These boys lay their heads on the very street only a half mile from where the Huntley mansion stands," Dagmar concluded gravely. "And I do not mean to single out the Huntley family, who are fine, upstanding members of our fair city and who donate generously to this cause." Dewey and Leona sat a little straighter in their chairs, Leona's nose tilting upward. "But let it fall upon *all* our shoulders to help end these injustices."

A grand flourish from the band signaled the end of the slideshow. The lights in the lecture hall rose as Dagmar nodded, acknowledging the audience's enthusiastic applause.

Genevieve felt drained.

She had to admit, Dagmar had performed well. His timing was impeccable, worthy of the stage's greats. She was sure his new charity, the Society to Aid Social Ills, which Daniel had helped found, would raise a great deal of money tonight.

The audience around Genevieve stirred, chattering among themselves as they stood and gathered their umbrellas and reticules. She stayed put, reluctant to let go of Daniel's hand.

"Do we have to go to the reception?" she asked Daniel. The thought of the requisite hand-shaking and hobnobbing was suddenly vastly unappealing. All she wanted was to be alone with her fiancé. "Mightn't we slip out, go to Delmonico's instead?" Now that she thought of it—the private room they could request, the stuffed shoulder of lamb melting on her tongue, the way Daniel's dark-blue eyes would hold hers over his inevitable glass of French wine—Delmonico's was the most appealing idea in the world.

Daniel's face lit up at the suggestion, then he grimaced slightly. "I can't skip the reception entirely; this is partially my project. Why don't we go for a few minutes, then head to Delmonico's?" he asked. "That baked mackerel is calling me."

The lecture room had mostly cleared, yet still they sat, hands intertwined. Daniel seemed as reluctant to move as she felt.

It wasn't that they needed to be furtive with their hand-holding. They were engaged to be married, after all, and discreet displays of affection in public were perfectly acceptable.

One calloused finger slowly slid down the center of her palm, sending a delightful shiver across her shoulder blades. Genevieve responded by running her thumb over the tips of Daniel's fingers. She loved his hands. They were not those of a banker, despite his skill with finances. They were a workingman's hands, though she had only the barest idea of what he had done to gain that roughness.

Something with his former gang, surely. Some of it probably even legal. Much of it not.

And it mattered not, at least not to her. The few things he chose not to disclose to her were only to save her from worry. Genevieve knew, in the depths of her soul, that there was not a dishonest or treacherous bone in Daniel's body.

She closed her eyes for a moment, recalling the feel of those hands gently running the length of her body. When she opened them, Daniel's eyes caught hers and held. Genevieve stared into their depths, her lips involuntarily parting, every sense in her body aware.

A loud throat-clearing started her out of her stupor. Embarrassed, Genevieve looked guiltily to where Dagmar urgently gestured from the doorway.

What had just transpired was *not* an acceptable public display of affection. Luckily, she was fairly sure nobody had witnessed it.

"Come on," she said, rising and tugging Daniel's hand to get him to follow. "We are meant to be feeling bad for orphans, not canoodling."

"Maybe, after Delmonico's, you could stop by the house?" Daniel asked as they followed Dagmar toward the reception area. His voice was deceptively mild, but she could hear its undercurrent of heat.

On the threshold of the gathering, Genevieve glanced over her shoulder, allowing her gaze to match the sultry suggestion lacing his tone. "Perhaps that could be arranged," she murmured, before dropping his hand and plastering on her best hostess face, turning to greet the nearest society matron.

It would be a risk, slipping into Daniel's house late at night. It was always a risk. There were boundaries, propriety, to consider. Even though they had broken that propriety already.

Four times, to be exact.

Moments that had to be stolen, despite their ages, despite their engaged status. Even as Genevieve shook Mrs. Samuel Porter's hand and emphatically nodded her agreement that yes, the plight of the newsboys was simply shocking, flashes of memory and sensation ricocheted through her: the scrape of Daniel's stubble against her neck, the press of his full mouth following.

Genevieve forced her mind back to the present moment, even as her breath shallowed and her cheeks heated. She had to get a hold of herself; surely the entire room could tell what she was thinking.

"Genevieve, I was hoping to see you." Relieved by the distraction, Genevieve gladly turned her attention to her old school friend Prue Nadler. They didn't see each other often, as Prue had married at nineteen and, though also part of high society, maintained a slightly different social circle of friends than Genevieve: that of young mothers.

Not that Prue herself was a mother. It wasn't discussed openly, of course, but Prue had been with child at least twice that Genevieve knew of, and had miscarried both pregnancies.

"How are you, Prue?"

"I am very well." Prue beamed at her, and Genevieve had to admit her friend appeared in much better spirits and health than she had the last time they had met, six months ago at the Allen-Simpson ball during the height of the Season. Then, Prue had been sunken-eyed and drawn, her hair dull, complexion gray. Genevieve had suspected at the time that Prue had been having more female difficulties, but it hadn't been prudent to ask, not in the midst of a ball.

Now Prue's auburn hair was shiny, and she appeared to have gained some much-needed weight, the slight plumpness filling her cheeks.

"Prue, dear, we must be going." Harvey Nadler, broad and squat, suddenly loomed behind his petite wife.

The roses instantly drained from Prue's cheeks.

"Perhaps I can call later this week?" Genevieve interjected.

"I'd like that."

"Now, Prudence." Harvey gave Genevieve a curt nod, took hold of his wife's arm with a grip that appeared harder than necessary, and led her away.

"What are you looking at?" Daniel followed Genevieve's gaze as he joined her side. Their friend Rupert Milton, Earl of Umberland, idled up alongside them.

"Did *you* know there was no liquor at this event?" Rupert's tone suggested this was an unspeakable travesty.

Genevieve ignored Rupert and blew out a breath, watching Prue flash her husband an angry look as Harvey guided her through the door. "I don't know," she answered Daniel as Rupert waved away a footman trying to offer him tea. "Nothing good, I'm afraid."

"What's no good? Whatever it is, it can't be worse than Esmie's feeling, poor mite," Rupert said as he turned to them, shoving his hands in his pockets and rocking back on his heels.

"Rupert, we are not discussing . . . oh, never mind. I'm sorry Esmie still feels so badly."

"She kicked me out of the house, you know. Said my constant popping in and out of our room to check on her was making her seasick. She's likely asleep now." Rupert's wife and Genevieve's good friend, Esmie Milton, was newly expecting the couple's first child and had thus far been continually nauseated.

Indeed, with Esmie so unwell, Genevieve's new sister-in-law Callie having moved to Chicago, and her dear friend Eliza Lindsay in Europe for a whole year, Genevieve had been rather lonely lately. Both Eliza and Callie would be back in a month for her and Daniel's wedding, but it wasn't nearly as much fun to plan the nuptials without them.

Genevieve returned her gaze to the mahogany-framed doorway through which Prue had been led into the night. She *would* pay a call on Prue; she could use another friend.

And she sensed Prue could use one as well.

The back of Genevieve's neck prickled.

Frowning, she swiveled her head left, then right. Was she being watched?

Nothing and nobody unusual stood out in the crowd. Well-heeled men in dark-toned suits and women in light spring dresses gathered in groups, talking in animated voices, some sipping tea. A throng of people surrounded Dagmar, waiting to shake his hand and offer congratulations. White-jacketed staff members of the lecture hall discreetly cleared cups and saucers. She didn't see anybody—

There.

From the far corner, under a curved archway, a man was staring at her.

Genevieve gasped and yanked her eyes down, cheeks flaming as though *she* had been the one caught staring.

Which was ridiculous.

Something about the man's look was entirely discomforting. Though their eyes had locked for only a second, his face held pure malevolence.

Her heart sped up a notch.

Enough. There was no reason for a stranger to stare at her in such a manner. Genevieve squared her shoulders and lifted her eyes, prepared to give the rude fellow her best haughty glare.

He was still there, only now decidedly not looking her way, instead intently studying the informational pamphlet Dagmar had made available to attendees. Genevieve allowed herself to take in his countenance more fully.

Something unpleasant stirred in her stomach.

She was sure she had never laid eyes on the man before.

Wasn't she?

"You've noticed him too?" It was Rupert, not Daniel, who posed the question. He didn't look the man's way but tilted his head ever so slightly in the direction of the archway, his expression serious.

"Noticed who?" Daniel had just finished a conversation with Mr. Samuel Porter and returned his attention their way.

"Don't look now, but there's a man to the left of the tea table who's been watching you for some time. Genevieve too."

"Somebody watching us?" Daniel jerked his head in the direction Rupert had indicated, his eyes narrowing.

Rupert stared at him, dumbfounded. "You'd have made a terrible soldier, you know."

Daniel snapped his gaze back. "The one in the gray jacket? I don't know the man. Genevieve?"

"I've never seen him." The unpleasant thing in Genevieve's stomach churned more. "I'm sure of it. And yet he looks familiar. It's the oddest thing."

Her palms were inexplicably sweaty. Genevieve risked a peek back to the space where the man stood, hoping to reconcile the unsettling dissonance his presence caused.

But the area under the carved archway yawned emptily.

The man was gone.

CHAPTER 2

Daniel frowned at the empty spot under the archway. The man in the gray suit had alarmed both Genevieve and Rupert, and that was enough to alarm him.

But the man was gone. He'd slipped into the crowd and away in the few seconds none of them had been watching.

Which was also alarming.

"Let us leave oddities aside and find ourselves a table at Delmonico's," he said, even as he scanned the crowd for a flash of gray broadcloth.

Nothing.

"We should toast Dagmar's success," he continued, wrenching his attention away from the crowd. It was no use; whoever the man was, he had disappeared. "Mr. Porter said he would hand over a check to the foundation tonight, and I believe he is not the only one. Rupert, you'll join us?" Daniel cast Genevieve an apologetic look over Rupert's shoulder.

Rupert's troubled expression brightened. "Only if I'm not intruding."

Genevieve's nostrils flared in a silent sigh, but she offered a small, lighthearted shrug. "Of course you must come along, Rupert. Esmie wouldn't forgive me if we cast you adrift."

Daniel smiled. He knew Genevieve had hoped they could spend some time alone, as had he. But he consoled himself that they had their whole lives to be alone, and Rupert was as good as family.

Three courses and two bottles of wine later, he and Genevieve dropped Rupert off at his father-in-law Amos Bradley's massive Fifth Avenue mansion, which occupied almost half the block at the northwest corner of Fifty-Fourth Street. It was a hodgepodge of architectural styles, topped with pointed towers and gargoyles, and had been the pride and joy of Esmie's late mother, her effort to outbuild the neighbors who had refused her entrée into the highest ranks of society. They waved at Rupert as he slipped inside.

"Shall we take a look?" Daniel asked, once the crested front door closed behind their friend.

"Oh yes, let's do."

Daniel directed his driver to take them twenty-two blocks north.

Genevieve had removed her gloves at dinner and never replaced them, and her hand was pleasantly warm and strong in his as he helped her down from the carriage.

They stood shoulder to shoulder on the sidewalk, faces tilted up.

"It's beautiful," Genevieve sighed.

Daniel had to agree. Even unfinished, the house was beautiful.

Their house. Or it would be, once it was completed.

They had, of course, hired Genevieve's brother Charles to design it. Eschewing the French petit-chateau style that was so in fashion among New York's monied set, Charles had offered Daniel and Genevieve a long, narrow house modeled after an Italian Renaissance palazzo. The cleaner lines and classical ornamentation suited them, he argued, over the fussy turrets and deep dormers evident in so many other houses on Fifth Avenue.

Daniel agreed. The geometric lines of the large, pale bricks of the lower level were barely visible in the bright moonlight, but he could clearly see the skeletal silhouette of the scaffolding above. One of the horses pulling his carriage snorted softly behind him, the sound carrying in the still night.

It was enough, more than enough, to stand in the velvety darkness, Genevieve by his side, and envision the house in its final state. Daniel could picture them moving through rooms furnished in the way they liked, appointed with objects and art that were to their taste and theirs alone.

"They finished the southern section," he pointed out. "It's coming along."

"That it is. Charles says the construction is on schedule."

Daniel's mind drifted, as it often did when he checked in on the house's progress or approved a necessary shift in Charles's plans, to the two rooms in Five Points he had shared with his family in his youth. He and Genevieve's house, once finished, would be nowhere near as large as most others on these Fifth Avenue blocks, nothing like the looming monstrosity of the Bradley house, which was surely one of the most imposing in a stretch of imposing structures. Theirs was quite modest by comparison: three floors, but with smaller, more intimate rooms. The dining room would be large enough to entertain, but not overly so, and the same with the ballroom. Building a house even this large didn't fully sit right with him, but he and Genevieve had discussed it at length, and they'd agreed that in order to do the most good, to enact the types of changes they wanted to see in the world, they needed to operate within the parameters of society.

And society expected they sometimes entertain.

Not that Daniel minded entertaining, or socializing, nor did he wish to live again in two dim, squalid rooms in Five Points. The tenement in which he'd spent his childhood had been freezing in the winter and broiling in the summer, the only light coming from one small window in the front room, as the rear window faced into a courtyard so narrow his mother could pass a tin cup of spare milk to the residents across, the few times she had milk to spare.

It was simply sometimes hard to stomach that he had so much when others had so little. And that he had so much by a simple twist of fate, by sheer happenstance.

That, and his sister's death.

For a long time he'd considered rejecting his inheritance, giving the money away to a variety of causes, shedding himself of its weight and leaving New York behind forever. Exploring California, or settling permanently in Paris.

By the time he'd met Genevieve, he'd already given up on those notions and decided to devote himself to helping those who came from backgrounds like his. And then she'd dropped into his life like a miracle, full of determination and grace, ready to fight alongside him.

The gratitude made him dizzy at times.

A cab clattered past, shaking him out of his reverie.

"Would you like to walk a ways?" he asked.

"That's a lovely idea. I've been cooped up all day."

Daniel sent the carriage ahead, telling his driver to meet them at the southern edge of Central Park.

"We can say hello to Rupert and Esmie's house too." Their friends had purchased three adjoining row houses and were renovating them to create one large mansion, with Charles providing the design. "I'm British," Rupert had explained, only half joking. "No fancy brand-new house for me. On behalf of my countrymen, I've got a reputation for a love of old and musty things to uphold." Daniel knew the interior of the finished product would be neither old nor musty, and he appreciated Rupert's efforts to retain some of Fifth Avenue's original character.

He kept his hand nestled in Genevieve's as they walked, not speaking much but taking deep breaths of the clear night air. Aside from them, the avenue was almost eerily devoid of people. This was a strictly residential neighborhood, and it was late enough that most of the people behind the redbrick walls of the row houses or the thick stone of the newer, flashier mansions were long asleep. The park was to their right, and its many trees made a low, whispering rustle overhead as a light breeze blew. It wasn't an unpleasant sound, but something about it tonight, how it was layered upon an almost preternatural silence, was unsettling.

Plus, Daniel was reasonably sure they were being followed.

The footsteps behind them were soft, another band of sound in the quiet symphony of stirring leaves and the whisper of Genevieve's skirts.

He paused when they reached the corner of Sixty-Fifth, looking at the facade of Rupert and Esmie's house. "I believe it's almost finished." He kept his voice light.

"Esmie said it should be ready for them to move in in a month, or maybe less," Genevieve said. "That should give them plenty of time to get settled before the baby comes."

He strained his ears. Nothing. If the person behind them had simply been walking on the same stretch of sidewalk, they would have passed by now.

But the footfalls had stopped, indicating the other person wasn't a casual stroller.

"I hope Amos doesn't get too lonely in that big mansion all by himself."

"My guess is he'll spend much of his time in Montana." Esmie's father owned several very lucrative copper mines there.

Daniel looked up and down the street, feigning nonchalance. The shadows were too deep for him to see much. The recessed entrances to the park, various benches, and clusters of trees on the sidewalk all offered excellent spots for hiding, if one wished to remain hidden.

He put his arm around Genevieve and pulled her close, then leaned over to graze his lips over her smooth cheek. She smiled, surprised, and tilted her head up slightly, offering her lovely wide mouth for a proper kiss.

Daniel smiled back and leaned in closer. "Walk a little faster. We're being followed."

Her smile froze.

He casually turned south again and began a leisurely pace, his arm still around Genevieve's waist. Ever so slowly, he increased his pace. Genevieve followed suit, her long legs having no trouble matching his steps.

The emptiness of the night he had been so enjoying was now enraging. Where was the foot traffic, the vehicles? It was New York City, for god's sake; it was never this empty.

Genevieve's back was stiff under his arm, and she stared forward with wide, purposeful eyes. Daniel didn't blame her one bit if she was frightened; they'd had too many brushes with death over the past year.

The scars on his stomach from the knife wound he had sustained twinged in memory.

They were close to the southern edge of the park at Fifty-Ninth Street, which was usually more crowded. His carriage and driver were waiting there as well, the driver a solidly built fellow called Tony. Not quite as solid as his friend and personal secretary Asher, a former boxer who also sometimes drove the carriage, but Tony could hold his own.

If only they could get to him.

The footsteps behind them broke into a run. Genevieve gasped at the sound, and they both began to run as well.

They were still four blocks from Fifty-Ninth Street. They wouldn't make it.

Damn it.

Daniel pulled his gun from where it had been stashed behind his jacket.

"You brought your gun to a lecture?" Genevieve hissed between breaths.

"Didn't you?"

She huffed in response, and despite himself, Daniel grinned, knowing Genevieve was annoyed that she hadn't thought of it too.

Which was unlike her, really. She typically had a small derringer somewhere on her person.

"Get ready to dive to the ground," he murmured. A curt nod was her response.

At once, Daniel pushed her into one of the park's entryways set into the stone wall on their right and simultaneously whirled backward, pointing his gun. The man behind them skidded to a stop so suddenly it would have been comical if Daniel hadn't been so outraged.

Daniel was unsurprised to see it was the man in the gray suit, the one who had been staring at them during the reception earlier. He had been following them so closely that the tip of Daniel's gun nearly grazed the man's white shirt front.

Who was this fellow, and why had he sought them out? Hadn't he and Genevieve been through enough in the past year? Was it old gang business, or a petty thief who had targeted them? Someone with a grudge against him and his money, against Genevieve and her journalistic work?

He didn't care. He just wanted the man to leave them be.

"I don't know who you are or what you want, but get the hell away from us."

The moon was bright enough for Daniel to register bewilderment and, shockingly, what looked like sadness cross the man's face.

"Don't you know me, Dan-Dan?"

CHAPTER 3

Dan-Dan.

Nobody had called him that in over twenty years.

Shock, confusion, wariness, and a tiny, desperate flame of hope all warred for supremacy within him.

Daniel internally stomped on the hope, crushing it before it could take root.

Whoever this man was, this person in the gray suit who was now smiling at him hopefully, there was no way he was family.

"I don't know who you are or what you think this will accomplish. You need to turn around and walk away right now," Daniel said.

The gray-suited man had already backed up a few steps and raised his hands in a tentative gesture. His smile faltered a little, then climbed back up the sides of his mouth.

"You always were so protective. Always so tough. I wanted to be just like you, you know. Join the Bayard Toughs, run with the big kids and the grown men. I dreamt about it for so long." The man dropped his hands, shoved them into his front pockets.

A new flare of alarm shot up Daniel's spine, and he firmed the arm that held the gun.

"Genevieve. Run to the carriage. Now." She could make it fairly quickly, and he would keep his gun trained on this man until she was safe. Daniel kept his eyes fixed on the stranger's hands, waiting for a weapon to be drawn.

Why the hell had he sent the carriage away? Why had they decided to walk? Stupid, stupid.

"I will not," Genevieve said from behind his back, where she had planted herself once it was clear there would be no immediate gunfire. "Sir, please just walk away. My fiancé is a terrific shot, and nobody needs to get hurt tonight."

Daniel gritted his teeth. Of course she wouldn't run. "For once in your life, would you please consider your own safety?" he ground out.

"He doesn't seem much of a threat. You're the one with the gun."

The other man advanced a step. He was a brawny man, not quite as tall as Daniel but a bit broader in the shoulders and chest. A spike of nerve jolted through him, and he cocked the gun, straightening his arm again. The man retreated, yanking his hands from his pockets and holding them higher than he had before, his smile wiped away.

"I don't mean to scare you, Dan-Dan."

Hearing his childhood nickname twisted something deep inside Daniel. "Stop calling me that. You don't know me."

"You're right, I don't. Not anymore. But I want to know you again. I just came back to New York a few weeks ago. I hoped to find some of you still here, but everyone was gone. Then I was at the barbershop, and there was this old paper. It had your engagement announcement in it. I thought nah, that can't be Danny. But it was." The man's grin resurfaced and broadened. "Hello, miss."

Genevieve didn't respond, for which Daniel was enormously grateful.

The man glanced in the direction from which they had come, his hands lowering a bit. "I go there sometimes too. To your house. I watch it going up. It's going to be so grand. Who'd have thought it, back when we were kids?"

Daniel's skin prickled with tension and something else he couldn't quite name. This encounter was making him feel unmoored, as if worlds he hadn't known coexisted were crashing into each other, blurring the boundaries between fiction and reality.

"You need to leave now." He made his voice hard.

"I'm going," the man said, his face finally faltering for good. He took a few steps backward, still facing Daniel, then paused. "Don't you want to know what happened to us? At all?"

In response, Daniel took a step closer. "Go."

His chest hurt. It was as if a fist were squeezing his heart.

The man nodded. "You don't believe me. I don't blame you. I can tell you, if you want. About the others. Stephen, Mary."

Daniel's finger tightened on the trigger. Hearing those names out of this stranger's mouth made his scar twinge again, as though a knife there were being wrenched anew.

This was the cruelest of jokes. Rage blossomed in his brain and radiated through his body. The arm holding the gun shook in response.

The man noticed the gesture and quickly backed away several more steps. "Maybe I'll see you around, Danny. Miss." He tipped his hat at Genevieve, then turned on his heel. Daniel's gut stayed tight as he watched the man retreat.

A few steps away, the man stopped, almost engulfed in shadows. He turned once more, his face catching in the gleam of a streetlamp across Fifth. "I am glad for you, Danny," he said quietly, the smile percolating around his mouth once more. It was sad now rather than hopeful. "Time is a great storyteller, isn't it?"

The man turned then for the last time, melting into the night.

As soon as the sound of the man's footsteps faded, Daniel dropped his hands to his knees. He leaned over, breathing hard, gasping as though he had been underwater for too long. Hell, he might have fallen to the pavement if Genevieve hadn't rushed forward and placed her hands on his shoulders.

"Daniel, are you all right? Do you feel faint? Damn it." She looked helplessly up and down the empty street, clearly hoping someone would come to her assistance.

Time is a great storyteller.

"I'm fine," he managed to gasp.

But he wasn't fine.

As clear as daylight, he could see his mother. The delicate line of her jaw, the dark green of her wide-set eyes. Eyes his sister Maggie had inherited.

His brother Connor had those eyes too.

In his memory, his mother was standing in the doorway between the front room he shared with his four siblings and the room that served as their main living space, where his parents also slept. Her hand was on the doorjamb, and she was looking at him with sympathy in her exhausted, remarkable eyes. Daniel was seven, a bloody scrap of rag pressed against his nose from where a neighborhood kid had punched him during a street brawl. It had been a week since they'd heard the life-shattering news of his father's death—shot down in the First Battle of Bull Run. Daniel had been so proud of his da, serving with the New York 69th. They'd been so sure all the soldiers would be home soon. When Daniel had spotted a group of kids playacting the battle on the street, including one pretending to be a member of the 69th clutching his belly and falling to the ground, a rage deeper and stronger than anything he'd ever felt had overtaken him. He'd launched himself at the surprised boy, and soon every kid in the neighborhood, it seemed, was throwing punches in one direction or the other.

Daniel's mother hadn't cried when she saw his bruised face, his bloody nose. She hadn't scolded him either. He had cried, though. Because his face hurt and his fists hurt and the knowl-edge that he would never see his handsome father again had settled, thick and heavy, around his heart. His mam held him, long and close, until his tears stopped, then she cleaned him up.

"I'll knock their teeth out if they try to play that again tomorrow," Daniel promised fiercely as she stood to leave, meaning it with every bone in his seven-year-old body.

She had paused in the doorway, hand on the jamb, and tilted her head to one side. "We'll see. Time is a great storyteller, it is. Get some rest now."

Time is a great storyteller.

"Daniel, please," Genevieve was saying. Her anxious face was hovering mere inches from his.

He blinked. The night air had cooled further, and Daniel shivered, suddenly more tired than he'd been in months.

"I'm all right," he said, straightening.

But he wasn't.

Daniel stared at the blackness into which the man had disappeared.

It wasn't the only time his mother had said that phrase, the day of the street brawl. It was something she said often. That was simply the time he remembered it best.

And it wasn't even that the man in the gray suit had said the exact thing his mother liked to say. It was a common enough saying.

What had really robbed him of breath was the man's eyes. When illuminated by the streetlamp, they glowed green as a cat's.

★ ★ ★

"Genevieve, do get out of bed. If we don't leave within the hour, we will be late, which would be unconscionably rude. Particularly for a luncheon in your honor."

Anna Stewart, Genevieve's mother, threw open the curtains in Genevieve's room, allowing the bright late-morning sunlight to flood in.

Genevieve rolled over and buried her head in the pillow, groaning inwardly. It was less about the luncheon itself, which would be pleasant enough—it would be attended mostly by women her mother's age who, like Anna, were deeply committed to certain causes, universal suffrage foremost among them. She had known these women since childhood, and they were a lovely, if rather exhausting, group. It was more that she had barely slept and was having trouble peeling her eyes open.

She hadn't gotten home until past three in the morning. After the man who had been following them left, Daniel grabbed her hand and pulled her in silence four blocks down the avenue to his waiting carriage. She hadn't known what to make of his expression; it was thunderous and vulnerable at the same time. Genevieve followed Daniel's lead and stayed quiet, allowing him to process the past few tumultuous moments in peace.

Once in the carriage, she had broken the silence.

"Daniel? Was that . . . was that your brother? Connor?"

Daniel had sighed deeply, rubbing his jaw. "No. I don't know."

Genevieve didn't know what to do with the possibility. She was a riot of emotions, and could only imagine what Daniel was going through. They went back to his house, where Daniel poured them each a bourbon, and reviewed what they knew.

Daniel's long-lost brother Connor had been taken, Daniel had always assumed, by the Children's Aid Society and put on an orphan train to parts unknown. Genevieve knew he had never forgiven himself for not being more present that day, blaming himself that the little ones had been snatched off the streets as though they were dispensable goods to be handed from one party to the next. It was their taking, in fact, that had led to the chain of events that eventually earned Daniel the Van Joost fortune: his eldest sister Maggie's position as a maid at the Van Joost household, her becoming the elderly Jacob Van Joost's mistress, her securing Van Joost's payment for Daniel's education.

Her death by her own hand.

And, in Jacob Van Joost's remorse and guilt over Maggie's death, Van Joost making Daniel his heir.

Genevieve sat close to Daniel on the settee in his front drawing room, leaning against his side with her stockinged feet tucked up underneath her. They were, in fact, in Jacob Van Joost's former house, which had been bequeathed to Daniel with the rest of the man's possessions. It was a large, comfortable row house, with private access to Gramercy Park, but she knew Daniel hated the place and was anxious to be in their new home. He already had a buyer lined up for the Van Joost house.

She sipped her bourbon. "What is the next step? What if that man really is Connor?"

"I doubt he is. It wouldn't take much to find out my family history, not if someone knew who to ask. He's a common grifter."

"But if he's not . . . Daniel, isn't it worth finding out?"

"I've been trying for years to trace my siblings, you know that." Daniel took a hefty drink of his bourbon, finishing the glass. He eyed the bottle on the table but seemed to think better of it. "No investigator has ever been able to find them. I even hired Pinkertons."

Genevieve swirled the remains of her own drink, an act she had watched Daniel perform hundreds of times. There was something satisfying about it.

"If there was something to find, one of those men—I think one of the Pinkertons was a woman, even—would have found it," he continued.

"I'm sure you're correct."

A few beats of silence passed.

"Dammit, Genevieve, that man is not my brother."

"I didn't say he was!"

"Fine. I'll ask Paddy if he can find out anything."

Genevieve nodded, putting down her empty glass. Paddy was the leader of the Bayard Toughs, the gang Daniel had belonged to in his youth and with which he was still affiliated in some ways. The Toughs had a strong information network, and it was possible someone could ferret out information about the stranger.

"He looked at me like he hated me," she said quietly. "At the reception."

Daniel blew out a breath and pulled her closer into his side. "I don't trust it. But I'll see what we can find out. I also have a feeling we may not have to look far. If this man took the trouble to come to the reception, to skulk around our half-built house, my guess is he'll find me again soon enough."

The thought was troubling. As if he could read her mind, Daniel pulled her closer still, the back of his hand lightly running down the side of her face. "No need to worry. I don't think he's dangerous. It's clear it's me he wants to badger, not you."

Genevieve was worried anyway, but allowed the feeling to be pushed from her mind as his lips found hers. And for a long time, she thought of little else.

"Genevieve!" Her mother thrust her head into her doorway again, rupturing her reverie.

Forty-five minutes later, Genevieve and her mother were in their carriage heading for Brooklyn. Her stomach growled loudly, but Anna simply gave her a pointed look, obviously meant to convey that if Genevieve had woken earlier, she would have had time for breakfast. They were bound for the home of Sylvia and Vernon Gloucester, longtime friends of her parents. They had all been active abolitionists in the 1850s, when her parents were newly married. Vernon was a prominent clergyman, Sylvia a renowned speaker and author. Genevieve was fond of them both as well as their daughter Amy, who was two years younger than she.

"We'll make it just in time," Anna grumbled from the seat next to her as the carriage rolled over the East River Bridge.

Genevieve didn't respond as she folded her arms over her chest. It was difficult for her to cross the bridge, and had been ever since Daniel had almost bled to death from a knife wound while on it the previous summer. She kept her gaze focused on where the water met Brooklyn's shore, watching as more and more land became visible.

An unbidden sigh of relief passed her lips once they were on the other side. Other than taking a ferry, the East River Bridge was the only way to get to Brooklyn. She wondered if she'd ever feel comfortable on its span again.

The Gloucesters' house was as graceful and welcoming as always, and once there, Genevieve felt instantly more at ease. Vernon was not present, as the event was for ladies, but Sylvia assured her he sent his best wishes and was looking forward to the wedding.

Genevieve was grateful they sat to eat quickly and was happy to find herself seated between her friend Amy and a pretty woman about her age, whom Amy introduced as Vanessa Albert.

"Mother thought you and Miss Albert might have a lot to talk about," Amy said, leaning over slightly as a red-jacketed footman served a crayfish bisque. "Miss Albert also has a passion for causes that aid the less fortunate. She writes, and is friends with the journalist Ida B. Wells."

"I've yet to meet Miss Wells, though I am very moved by her work," Genevieve said, impressed by Vanessa's connections.

"She is back in Tennessee at present, though she has plans to return to Brooklyn soon," Vanessa responded, spooning some soup.

"Miss Albert runs a mission for Southern women, but has recently experienced a tragedy," Amy said.

"A tragedy?"

Vanessa nodded over her water glass and explained. She had founded the Sunflower Mission House, a settlement home in downtown Brooklyn. It had been established to help young women of color who had been lured from the South to the North with promises of jobs when in reality the jobs were often in the sex trade.

"There were homes and resources for girls of other races, but not for Black women," Vanessa said. A footman removed their soup bowls and replaced them with plates of chicken croquettes a la Victoria. "It took some years, and of course I had the help of many volunteers, the Gloucester family among them, but I opened the mission in 1887. It has been very successful."

Vanessa did not appear much older than Genevieve, and the amount she had accomplished was remarkable. "I'd love to visit it, help if I can."

"Unfortunately, we suffered a terrible fire last week. The physical structure was burned beyond repair."

This was shocking. Fire was an ever-present danger in the city, and an entire structure burning was typically big news.

"Thankfully, nobody was hurt," Vanessa continued. "All the residents and staff were able to escape unharmed, though as the fire happened in the middle of the night, it was a near thing."

"I am so sorry," Genevieve said, aghast. "How awful. What a relief nobody was injured. I must say, I'm stunned I haven't heard of this."

Vanessa smiled politely. "It was covered in the *New York Freeman*."

Genevieve flushed slightly. The *Freeman* was the city's major Black newspaper, to which she did not subscribe. It was an embarrassing oversight on her part, and one she would rectify immediately.

"Tell Genevieve what the fire department isn't doing," Amy said, frowning.

Vanessa hesitated before speaking. "They've ruled the fire accidental, probably from a candle one of the residents had in her room. But all the girls swear they were asleep, no candles. Except one, who couldn't sleep, and thinks she saw someone run from our house and cross the street minutes before she smelled the smoke." Vanessa put down her fork, mouth pinched. "I'm sure you don't want to talk about this sort of thing, though. This luncheon is in celebration of your upcoming wedding." Her mouth softened. "Tell me all about it."

Now it was Genevieve's turn to hesitate. She did not, in fact, want to talk about the wedding much. She was thrilled to be marrying Daniel, but the logistics of organizing a giant high-society wedding were exhausting and, frankly, seemed rather frivolous.

Learning about Vanessa's important cause was far more intriguing to her than flower arrangements for the upcoming wedding. She had been looking for a new story to sink her teeth into, one to present to her editor. The fact that her own paper had not reported on the fire seemed a serious lapse, as Vanessa's mission and the tragedy clearly deserved wider coverage. Plus, there was the mistake of nobody having interviewed the residents of the house in the investigation.

Genevieve's brain was already buzzing.

"Your work is far more compelling a topic," she said under the guests' applause as a lovely, two-tiered cake decorated with pink roses was placed in front of their hostess. "Please, tell me more."

CHAPTER 4

"He's here," Rupert said under his breath as he slid onto the stool next to Daniel.

Daniel smiled to himself, wrapping his hands around his glass.

He'd assumed it would be only a matter of time before the man trying to pass himself off as Connor thrust himself into his path again, and he'd been right. Once they had their mark, con men were persistent.

"Where?" The swill the dive bar passed off as whiskey wasn't as bad as some but still nothing like what he could get at any reputable establishment. The best he could say for it was that it was tolerable.

"Back wall, right side." Rupert had chosen beer instead of spirits. The liquid in his dirty glass looked thin and watery.

He and Rupert had accompanied Dagmar on a photographic mission tonight, this time a stale-beer dive called Hell Gate on Baxter Street. Daniel was there to observe the photographer in action and to help smooth any ruffled feathers Dagmar's bright flash might cause. He'd also thought the grifter would more likely seek him out in a seedier environment than attempt to contact him again when he was with Genevieve.

He had only the grimmest of satisfaction in being correct.

"Perhaps this time he'll tell me what he really wants," Daniel mused. "Get ready, Dagmar's about to shoot."

Dagmar looked Daniel's way as he positioned the mixture of magnesium flash powder above the camera lens and held up a frying pan, off which he would light the powder. Daniel indicated they were ready.

He and Rupert put their hands over their ears and closed their eyes.

Boom.

The sound was deafening, even with his ears covered, and the backs of his eyelids turned bright. Daniel could picture how the flash lit up the dank, enclosed basement space as if it were bright noonday sun, violent in its brilliance. Different sounds immediately rushed in once the echoes of the explosion subsided: a cacophony of aggrieved cries, hacking coughs, and some screams of fear.

Daniel cracked open one eye. A few sparks were still lazily circling overhead, and white smoke clouded the room.

Dagmar's sleeve was smoldering.

Daniel jumped off his stool and batted at the photographer's arm, putting out the nascent fire.

"You trying to blow us up?" A tough-looking fellow with a squashed nose advanced on Dagmar even as he blinked away the afterimage, giving the photographer a rough shove.

"It's for charity," Daniel explained, putting himself between the man and Dagmar. "Let me get you a drink." The squashed-nose man scowled but accepted.

"Give us some warning next time," the tough warned Dagmar and Daniel, "or there won't be enough booze in the world to save you." The other patrons grumbled their agreement as the man eyed Dagmar, who was preparing for another shot, with hostility.

"My apologies," Dagmar said quietly. "I will give a warning before the next exposure."

"That man pretending to be Connor wants money," Rupert said once Daniel had resettled onto his stool, waving smoke away from his face. They had both traveled with Dagmar on several such excursions and knew to expect aggression after the loud, unexpected flash. It was people's shock, though, that created compelling pictures. Daniel didn't love the method but knew it was effective. They had raised more than four thousand dollars from Dagmar's lecture over the weekend.

"I know."

"Don't fall for it, Daniel."

"I won't."

Rupert looked at him sideways. "I know how much the loss of your family still pains you." The words were quiet but hit Daniel like a gut punch.

Of course Rupert knew. Daniel had met his oldest, best friend when he was only thirteen, less than two years after Connor, Stephen, and Mary were taken. When Daniel was seventeen and his older sister Maggie died, Rupert had boarded a steamer as soon as he could. He had been too late for the funeral but had stayed in the States for the remainder of the summer, until the two started Harvard in the fall.

He had been there through Daniel's grief. He knew just how shattered Daniel had been, how long it had taken him to heal.

Had he healed, though? Or simply learned to live with the gaping loss of his entire family?

"Awful lot of fuss for a few pictures." The man calling himself Connor was suddenly at Daniel's side.

Daniel narrowed his eyes. The man had sidled through the crowd unnoticed. This one had a talent for appearing and disappearing at will, it seemed.

He would have to be more careful.

"All for a good cause," Daniel said. He turned on his stool and leaned his back against the bar, eyeing the man. "They raise a lot of funds."

He waited. The mention of money, surely, would provide the grifter an opening. Daniel took a moment to take the measure of this man, the person purporting to be his brother Connor. His hair was lighter in shade than Daniel's but looked just as thick and prone to curl.

And he had those unsettling green eyes.

But the man just nodded. "Riles these guys up quite a bit. Good thing nobody got hurt." His vowels were long and flat, midwestern.

Daniel said nothing, still waiting.

"Hello." The man stuck his hand out to Rupert, who raised an elegant brow in return and did not take the proffered hand. The man's arm dropped. "I'm Connor Lund."

Daniel's own brow lifted. "Lund?"

"Yeah, I was given my adoptive family's name."

Hot temper filled Daniel's throat.

Enough was enough. He was done with this mad charade. Daniel's fists closed of their own accord, and he stepped close to the man, whose eyes widened with alarm at whatever he read on Daniel's face.

Daniel almost hoped the man wouldn't listen to reason. It would be highly fulfilling to smash his fist into this impostor.

The front door of the bar burst open. Cold air and uni-formed bodies poured in, the shrill tweet of whistles rending the night.

"Raid!" yelled several of the patrons.

Suddenly, the place was in total chaos.

Patrons were fighting police, fists flying. Police batons rained blows. Daniel rushed to get to Dagmar through the melee, but an impenetrable wall of bodies had already formed between them. The photographer huddled around his equipment protectively. He caught Daniel's eye and yelled, "Go!" over the din.

"Come on," yelled the man calling himself Connor, pulling Daniel's arm. "There's a back door."

A blow glanced off the side of Rupert's head, nearly toppling him. They had to get out.

"Come on," Connor urged.

The front door was blocked by a sea of blue uniforms. They had no choice. Daniel thrust his chin forward, indicating Connor should lead the way, making a mental note that the man had marked the exits in advance of approaching him.

He could examine the implications of that later.

Connor wove his way through the sudden mass of bodies and Daniel followed, ducking and shoving his way through the raging, yelling crowd. A quick look confirmed Rupert was close on his heels. He glanced back at Dagmar, who was shoving a piece of paper under an officer's nose even as he was jostled on all sides. Dagmar had police permission to be undertaking his work and, once the dust settled, would be fine.

As long as he didn't sustain an accidental blow to the head as well.

Connor pushed open a door that nearly blended in with the rough walls, and they stumbled out into the chilly night. Without discussion they started to run, their feet pounding the pavement, their breath pluming into white clouds.

It was like Daniel was fifteen again, home from Britain for the summer holidays, outrunning the cops as they gave chase after he and his fellow Toughs had stolen something, toppled something, or caused some kind of mischief, all of them sprinting as hard as they could, breathless with laughter.

Because they always got away. They knew the streets better than even the most industrious beat officer, knew the back alleys and hidden courtyards and doorways in the warren of Five Points. Daniel shot a look over his shoulder; nobody was chasing them now, but the feeling was the same.

"Stop," he called, slowing his run to a trot, then halting entirely. Connor and Rupert followed suit.

They doubled over as one, breathing hard, looking down the street and at each other in disbelief. It was cold, the temperature having dropped nearly twenty degrees in the past few days. April always was a tricky month.

"It's just like the time with the apples," Connor said, grinning through his pants.

Cold sweat and the shock of what the man had said tingled Daniel's whole body. He stood tall, his temporarily forgotten anger over the man's con roaring back to life.

"What?"

The man didn't hear the warning in Daniel's tone.

"Like that time we were chased when we were kids," he said blithely. "You know, after Mam died. We stole the apples from that pushcart over on Canal Street? You distracted the seller by pretending to fall and bust your knee, and 'cause I was small, I slipped around the back of the cart and grabbed the apples. We ran back home, laughing like loons. Remember how much Mary loved apples?"

The ground shifted under Daniel's feet. He had forgotten that event, but this man's retelling of it made the memory rush back so clearly it was like he was seeing a series of photographs, each illuminated with Dagmar's flash.

Boom. Falling a few feet from the apple cart, clutching his knee and wailing. He did a good job of it, scraping his knee going down so it really did hurt.

Boom. The frowns from passersby on the street, one kindly lady who'd been sweeping her front step coming down to check on him. That hurt in a different way, so soon after his mother's death.

Boom. Connor, only six, peeking around the side of the cart. Darting his big green eyes between Daniel on the ground and the distracted seller, who was standing with his arms crossed, watching the drama.

Boom. Connor's small hands reaching, grabbing as many apples as he could and stuffing them down his shirt, in his pockets. He had taken a few wary steps away when the seller noticed the bulging shirt and shouted.

Boom. Springing up, bolting down the street, arms pumping, keeping his body between Connor's fast-moving little form and the seller's large one, the terror of being caught combining with the pleasure of moving swiftly and swirling with the knowledge of the apples, all of it forcing hysterical huffs of laughter from his overworked lungs.

The images kept flooding in, an unstoppable tide. He remembered it all now, as if it were yesterday. They'd made it home, the seller having given up after five blocks. Daniel had proudly used his father's knife to cut an apple into neat slices, the eyes of the little ones watching hungrily. Connor insisted on giving pieces to Mary and Stephen first, even though he'd done the hard work of stealing. Maggie had come home during their feast and swallowed at the sight of the fruit but hadn't asked where it came from.

The man calling himself Connor smiled again.

"We came this close to getting sent to the House of Refuge, remember?"

He did remember now. An officer had shown up at their door with the seller, but Maggie had sworn that the seller was mistaken. That the neighbor would confirm the children had been home, with her, all afternoon. The cores of the apples had long been disposed of, and the neighbor lady, whose husband was a Bayard Tough as Daniel's da had been, had been spoken with in advance. The neighborhood would do what they could to keep the boys from getting arrested, generally feeling sympathy for the poor wee ones who'd just lost their mother.

It was a close thing, he recalled. The seller didn't want to give up, said the boys were a menace and should be sent to the House of Refuge, but the officer wasn't willing to contradict the words of the neighbor, especially after several others joined her and swore the children hadn't been anywhere near Canal Street that day.

He wondered now where all those neighbors had been when his siblings were taken by the Children's Aid Society. Why they didn't intervene then, as they had with the cops.

Perhaps they'd thought it was better if the little ones were sent away to live different lives.

Perhaps the incident with the apples was part of that.

Perhaps that was why he had forgotten about the theft, had buried it deep within his brain. Because ever since that day when he was eleven, coming home still dripping from his swim in the Hudson to find Mary, Connor, and Stephen gone, he had known it was his fault.

Daniel stared at the stranger. The tiny flame of hope, the one he had so determinedly stomped out upon hearing this man call him by his childhood name, reignited in his chest.

This time, he let it be.

CHAPTER 5

Genevieve hadn't thought it possible, but somehow the office of her editor, Arthur Horace, was messier than usual. The chair in which she usually sat contained a towering stack of papers held in place with a large, flat volume bound in blue leather. She counted at least five dirty teacups tucked into various crannies or haphazardly placed on shelves.

"Just shift those things to the floor, Genevieve," Arthur commanded, gesturing with his pencil to the pile on the chair. She did as she was told, noting the title of the book as she moved the items: *Game Fishes of the United States.*

"I may do some angling this weekend," he remarked, seeing Genevieve eye the cover. "Trout season, don't you know."

Genevieve hadn't known, either which season it was for which fish or that her editor enjoyed fishing at all.

"How is the wedding planning coming along?" he asked absent-mindedly, eyes on a document on his desk.

Was that all anybody had to say to her these days?

"Fine," Genevieve replied, trying to hide the annoyance in her voice.

"We'll have Miss Anwyll write it up, I suppose," he said, making a note on the paper in front of him. "It wouldn't be appropriate for you to cover your own nuptials." For the past year and a half, Genevieve had covered the society pages at the *New York Globe*, though after some significant successes with investigative stories, Arthur was letting her treat other topics. She had brought in Suzanne Anwyll the previous summer to help with the society column.

Genevieve would far prefer that nobody wrote about her wedding for any newspaper but knew it was useless to argue. She changed the subject to the real reason she was sitting in his office. "Arthur, why didn't we cover the fire in Brooklyn two weeks ago?"

It was a testament to his long career in the newspaper industry that Arthur looked unsurprised by her question, but he did put down his pencil. "Which one?"

"The Sunflower Mission House."

"We did."

"Did we?" Genevieve racked her brain, trying to recall if she'd read the piece and missed it.

"A small mention in the regional section." Arthur shrugged comfortably.

That was why she didn't recall it. It had been a one-line item in a series of one-line items.

"Why didn't we write about it in more detail?"

Unlike her, Arthur did not hide the annoyance in his voice. "Because it took place in Brooklyn, which is of less interest to our readers, and because nobody was hurt. The *Brooklyn Daily Eagle* had more extensive coverage, I believe, as did the *New York Freeman*. I assume you have some point to this line of questioning, other than to question my editorial decisions?"

Genevieve felt color rise to her cheeks but forged ahead. "I believe it may be worth revisiting." She told him about the resident who had spied someone outside the house moments before the fire started. "It wasn't in the article the *Freeman* published," she said pointedly.

Arthur's furry gray eyebrows danced for a moment as he considered. "Are you sure this witness hasn't been questioned by fire officials, and her story dismissed?"

"I'm not; I haven't spoken to her yet. But the mission's founder, Vanessa Albert, feels sure this is worth following up on."

The brows rose, then stilled. "I know Miss Albert's work. It wouldn't hurt to ask the witness a few questions, I suppose. But keep in mind that just because we want there to be a larger story doesn't mean there is one. The fire department isn't what it was forty years ago; they're a professional organization now, thankfully. And if they've deemed this fire accidental, then it probably was."

Three letters and two days later, Genevieve had an appointment with Marla Willis, the former resident of the Sunflower Mission House to whom Vanessa Albert had referred.

"I'm sorry if this is painful to discuss," Genevieve said. She resisted shifting on the hard settee, though it was a remarkably uncomfortable seat. Probing Miss Willis, who was obviously still distraught at the thought of the fire, was equally uncomfortable.

They were meeting in the drawing room of the boarding house in which Marla and three other women from the mission now lived. The mission was helping supplement the girls' rent, as their wages as domestic servants—cooks, maids, and nannies, mostly—were quite low.

"I told the firefighters this, but they didn't seem to believe me," Marla said, her Southern accent light and musical. She was slender and beautiful and sat perfectly straight in a blue armchair. The drawing room was pleasant enough despite the wretched settee, light and airy, with a big bay window that looked to the street. "I have trouble sleeping sometimes, so I was awake, even at that late hour."

"Around two in the morning, you said?" Genevieve checked her notes.

"That's right. I was at my window—we all had our own rooms at the Sunflower House, but here I share with one of the girls—just idly watching the street."

"You didn't want to read a book? Or take up some mending?" Genevieve racked her brain for what else might people do when they couldn't sleep. She herself generally slept like the dead.

"I didn't want to light a lamp. Not because I was afraid of fire, ironically. If I'm around too much light in the middle of the night, it makes it harder to fall back asleep. I was simply looking at the world, daydreaming." She smiled a little at her own choice of words. "Gathering wool, I guess."

Genevieve checked her notes again. "You told Miss Albert you saw someone in the street?"

"Yes." She went to the bay window and gestured for Genevieve to join her. "It's not an exact match, but my room at the Sunflower House looked onto a residential street not too dissimilar to this. Quiet family homes. There was no reason for anyone to be walking around that time of night. The only people I ever saw past midnight, other times I was awake late, were the couple across the street coming home from parties. They were very grand."

Genevieve made a note to potentially speak with these neighbors.

"But this wasn't the Hazelwoods in their carriage. It was a man, and he didn't come down the street. He came from right underneath my window. One moment nobody was there, and then he was. The only place he could have come from was inside the house or through the gate that led to the back garden." Marla blinked back tears as she recounted the rest. How her first assumption had been that one of the other girls had a beau and she wondered how they'd managed to sneak him into the house. How a few minutes later the unmistakable smell of smoke had assailed her nose and how, by the time she opened her door, it was billowing up the stairs like a phantom. The heat of the fire below had already made the floorboards of the upstairs hallway hot, and she realized she had only minutes—if that—to spare. She could already hear the flames crackle and build downstairs. Marla had banged on the doors of the other women's rooms, rousing the house from sleep and ushering all the residents down the stairs and out the front door. "Luckily, the fire was mostly in the kitchen and the drawing room, and we could skirt past it, but just barely. It was a miracle nobody's nightdress caught. We couldn't find Josie and were certain she was trapped up there. It was horrifying."

Marla's eyes were far away, and Genevieve felt certain the woman was not seeing the bright April sky or the handsome brownstones across the street but the bright-orange flames as they leapt and roared, consuming what had been a haven for her in a new, unfamiliar city. What had become her home. "She showed up two hours later. Turns out someone did have a beau after all, but Josie hadn't snuck him in. She'd snuck out." Marla sighed and wiped at her eyes with a lace handkerchief. "Please forgive me. I've told this story so many times, I hate having to tell it again."

The back of Genevieve's neck tingled. "Other than to Miss Albert? Who else have you told this to?"

Marla sighed again and gestured that they return to their seats. "Isaac Conkling, for one. He's the reporter for the *Freeman* who spoke to me. Also Gus Fulkerton from the *Brooklyn Daily Eagle*. The Brooklyn fire marshal, Mr. Keller. I don't know his first name. And someone from the *New York World*."

The tingle shifted to a jolt. "Do you remember that person's name?"

"Jim something. I only remember the Jim part because my little brother is also called Jim."

"Crawford?"

"That sounds right. It may be impertinent to say, but I found him rather rude. You'll forgive me, as it's your profession, but if I hadn't spoken to Mr. Conkling from the *Freeman*, I might never have spoken to a member of the press again. Mr. Conkling was a gentleman."

Genevieve had had several run-ins with Jim Crawford. He was the worst kind of journalist, the sort who only chased disaster for the most salacious details, treating any victims or survivors with disdain. "I know Jim Crawford, and you're not being impertinent, only honest. He's not a very kind person."

Marla's lips pursed at the memory. "No, he isn't."

"And the reporter from the *Eagle*?" Genevieve didn't know Gus Fulkerton, but she'd read the man's piece, and it also made no mention of Marla or what she'd seen.

"Somewhere in between."

"And you told them all about the man you saw?"

Marla confirmed that she had, and Genevieve frowned. She didn't know this Isaac Conkling, but the *Freeman* article had said nothing about possible foul play, and as far as she knew, the *World* hadn't covered the story.

Something was off here.

"What did he look like, this man you saw?"

"It was dark, and I mostly saw his back. I don't really know. But he was big—broad shouldered and tall. Really big."

"Hair color, race, anything else that could identify him?"

Marla shook her head. The poor woman looked exhausted. "I'm sorry, but no. He had a hat, and his coat collar was turned up. It was dark."

Genevieve thanked Marla and took her leave. While she had no information to corroborate Miss Willis's story—yet—some deep instinct she'd learned to rely on told her Marla was telling the truth.

It was time to speak with these other reporters and find out what they were holding back.

★ ★ ★

The glass plate had been blank, but as Dagmar gently moved it in a bin of liquid, images swam to its surface. In the dim light, the faces appeared as if by magic. A crowd of men coalesced, slack-jawed and staring, their stunned, terrified expressions apparent even in the scant light of the darkened room.

Daniel was, as always, fascinated to observe the photographic process.

Though he rarely permitted himself to be photographed.

While he found the process mesmerizing, he didn't quite trust it. There was something about capturing the human face, normally in constant motion, in such stillness that unnerved him.

The first time he had experienced photography was on the eve of his father's departure, when his mother had dragged all five of her children, even Stephen the baby, to the tintypist to get their likeness made. The dour-looking man behind the camera at the cheap studio had frowned at the sight of the smaller children, warning his mother they would not remain still and the plate could be blurred. His mother insisted, determined, but the photographer had been correct. The resultant tintype was a disaster. Daniel could visualize it clearly, even though it had been lost for almost thirty years: Maggie, age ten, barely visible behind the blur that was Stephen, age one, writhing and crying in her lap. Seven-year-old Daniel was to her left, holding Connor's hand and staring at the lens with a wary expression. Connor, only two, had turned his head toward his sobbing baby brother at exactly the wrong moment. His carefully mended and pressed coat was perfectly sharp, but his head was an obscured, faceless smudge. Three-year-old Mary was on Maggie's right in a short plaid dress, and while she had managed to keep still, Stephen's cries were too much for her, and the camera caught the precise second her somber expression crumpled into tears.

Daniel could still see his mam's crestfallen face as she handed over her coins, the photographer's indifferent shrug. They couldn't afford a second plate.

Da had exclaimed over the tintype anyway. "As if any of these wee'uns ever rest," he had said, smiling broadly. "This is how they look in life, moving about, and the picture is all the better for it." He had tucked it away into his inner jacket pocket, promising them it would never leave his person.

As far as Daniel knew, his father had kept that promise. When he was young, Daniel had often imagined the tintype still in that jacket pocket, pressed against his da's slowly deteriorating corpse, deep beneath the Virginia soil in his unmarked grave. The thought, which ought to have been gruesome, was somehow comforting. It would take a long time for the iron plate to return to the earth. Someday maybe someone would find the tintype, long after his da's body was gone.

Maybe it would be returned to them somehow.

Dagmar pulled the plate from another bath.

"All set now," he murmured, setting the glass negative aside to dry. "May I show you some of the new prints?"

Outside the darkroom, Daniel studied a series of photographs arranged on a table. "You're tackling labor conditions too?" he asked, tapping his finger on a picture showing a seated young boy surrounded by piles of garments. Grown men loomed behind the boy, arms folded, adding a distinct air of menace to the scene.

Dagmar nodded, solemn. "The sweatshops are horrible places."

Daniel's eye snagged on what was a quite plain photograph for Dagmar. It showed a long, narrow interior corridor, with four stories of grated doors on one side, facing a wall studded with recessed windows on the other. Rectangles of cold light reflected on various surfaces. There were no people, just the silent emptiness.

There was something about the picture that sent a shudder down his spine. "What institution is this?"

"Blackwell's Lunatic Asylum. I have a few others." Dagmar rummaged around behind him, but Daniel couldn't tear his eyes away from the photograph.

All those rooms. All those cells.

Dagmar's hand slid into his field of vision, placing a second photograph beside the first.

The imposing hulk of Blackwell's towered at the end of a tapering roadway. Daniel counted five stories in one section, a group of faceless, diminutive figures gathered in its shadow. The sight of the asylum, which he had never visited but about which rumors swirled, stirred unpleasant memories.

Rupert imprisoned in the Tombs. His own near detention in the House of Refuge.

"Have you photographed the House of Refuge?" he asked Dagmar now, his curiosity piqued despite his unease.

"I have not."

So many boys from his neighborhood had been sent there. Its presence was both a cautionary tale and a dare, a place of dread and fascination.

Daniel was still unsure if Connor really was his brother, despite his stories. It was somehow painful to accept that a member of his immediate family might still be alive, and could have a presence in his life, after he'd forced himself to grow accustomed to their absence.

He simultaneously did and didn't want to believe it.

"I have others," Dagmar said in his quiet way, slipping back into the darkroom, which was now lit with a kerosene lamp as the plates were developed. This time Daniel followed him, reluctantly dragging his gaze away from the Blackwell's photographs. He pulled the door shut behind him out of habit as Dagmar selected a few prints from a tall wooden cabinet.

These didn't have the same chilling effect as the others, for some reason—a less ominous image of the main building, a rather pedestrian view of the uninteresting grounds, the same view but with some official-looking gentlemen gathered on a path. They weren't Dagmar's most inspired work.

"Let me show you some of the other sweatshop views," Dagmar said, pulling the Blackwell's photographs into a neat pile. "I think they will be very compelling for the next lecture."

Dagmar was right: the pictures would be compelling. Daniel lost track of time as he and the photographer pored over the images, arranging and rearranging them to make the most arresting slideshow.

The scent of smoke was so faint, at first he thought he imagined it.

Competing smells were thick in Dagmar's studio, particularly in the darkroom. The acidic developing chemicals, the dry tang of flash powder, even the hair pomade Dagmar used, crowded the tiny space, filling Daniel's nose.

He paused and focused his attention, holding up a hand for Dagmar to stop speaking.

"Do you smell that?"

Dagmar's head lifted, his brow furrowed. He inhaled a short, sharp series of breaths.

"I do not . . . wait. Yes."

Daniel moved to the darkroom door and placed his hand on its surface. The door was cool, but the scent was getting noticeably stronger. The slightest whisper of worry passed through Daniel's mind.

Fire was always worrisome.

"Could be outside. Still, best we get out ourselves."

Daniel turned the knob and pushed, but the door didn't open smoothly as it should.

"Does this door ever stick?" he muttered, turning the handle and pushing harder.

The whisper increased its volume.

"No," Dagmar said, fear tingeing the edges of his voice. "There is no problem with the door."

Daniel applied his shoulder to the door, once, twice, three times, the loud bang of his actions reverberating through the darkroom, glass bottles of chemicals trembling and clinking unpleasantly.

There were very flammable things in any photographic studio.

Old collodion.

The magnesium flash powder.

Under his shoulder, the solid wooden door of the darkroom grew warmer, and now a sound pervaded Daniel's senses along with the ever-growing smell of smoke.

The snapping, insidious sound of fire.

The whisper in Daniel's head turned to a howl.

CHAPTER 6

"Dagmar, help me," Daniel shouted. He slammed his body into the door again. If he survived this, his entire left side would be black-and-blue.

It didn't matter. The studio was in the storefront of a two-story wooden building downtown, close to the Tombs, as Dagmar's main employment was with the police department. The building's owner, a stout German woman of impeccable cleanliness, often sent the unmarried Dagmar home with bundles of homemade sausages.

Had her cooking caused the fire? Was she even home, or already safely out of the building?

None of the particulars mattered. There was no way Daniel could help Frau Hilde, if she needed it, if he and Dagmar were trapped.

Or if the entire structure went up like a box of matches.

Daniel hurled himself again. The door budged an inch under his assault, but only that. Something was wedged under the doorknob outside, locking them in.

He put his eye to the crack he'd created.

It was like looking into hell.

Through the slim opening, all he could see was fire. Smoke immediately poured through the gap. Daniel pulled back and blinked as his eye watered, the stinging intense.

He looked around the room.

"Is there another way out?"

Dagmar was pressed against the far wall, wedged between a table and a cabinet, seemingly too frightened to speak. He was ghostly white under his pale-blond hair.

Dammit, no help there.

Even a quick glance revealed the answer to his question: no. The jammed door was the only entrance and egress to the small back room.

Daniel redoubled his efforts.

The door opened another inch.

Then another.

Smoke streamed into the room steadily, filling it. He was dimly aware of Dagmar coughing.

Or was it him?

With a massive grunt, Daniel smashed into the door again, cursing its solidity. His left shoulder and hip were already numb.

With a clatter barely audible beneath the roar of the fire, the chair that had been lodged under the door dropped. The floor rose to meet him as his body was suddenly weightless, flying through the now-open door.

Heat seared his left side. Daniel rolled and crabbed backward, away from the flames he'd almost landed in.

Fire was everywhere.

It greedily climbed the walls, licked at the ceiling.

The magnesium flash powder.

There was a jar of it somewhere in this studio.

Just a few grams were enough to create a blinding explosion of light.

If the entire jar caught alight, it could blow the entire building to bits.

Maybe the entire block.

Daniel scrabbled up and rushed to the darkroom. It was getting harder to see, let alone breathe, in the ever-thickening smoke.

"Dagmar." The photographer was still huddled in his corner, racked with coughs and shaking with fear. Daniel hauled him up by the armpits. "We've got to get out; there isn't much time. Where is the flash powder?"

Dagmar could only shake his head, trying to negate the horror around him. Daniel gave the man a little shake.

"*Where?*"

The photographer's eyes darted to the small shelf filled with bottles and jars close to the table with the developing trays.

In the darkroom space, then. The fire hadn't made its way this far back yet, but it was on its way.

A sudden cough hit Daniel so hard he doubled over. Dagmar slid back to the ground.

Fire began to crawl up the doorjamb of the darkroom.

Seconds counted now. There was no time to figure out which of the chemical-streaked, cloudy jars was the flash powder and to calculate whether he could make it through the flames carrying such a hazard, particularly when it was clear he would have to assist Dagmar.

His best hope was to get the two of them out alive before the building detonated.

"Come on, Dagmar." He tried to yell, but the smoke was so thick, his voice was a croak. Daniel heaved his friend up again, eventually dragging him through the flaming doorway into the main studio space.

They were lucky. The outer studio furnishings were sparse and pushed toward the walls. While the walls and furniture were completely ablaze, there was a relatively clear path to the door.

If they could make it in time. It was a miracle the flash powder hadn't already exploded from the heat.

Over the roar of the flames, the shrill tinkle of exploding glass sounded. The windows.

Daniel didn't remember falling, but he was suddenly on his knees. The door was closer but still so far away. Dagmar was lying limply next to him.

His lungs had shrunk; there was no room left for breath. Smoke filled his mouth, nose, throat, and eyes. Heat pulsated from the very floor itself, searing his stomach through his shirt and jacket as he crawled toward the door.

He had to make it to the door. Genevieve was out there, somewhere. Waiting for him.

He couldn't leave her, not yet.

Water poured freely from his eyes. It hurt to breathe, hurt to see. Daniel blinked as a hunched figure emerged from the smoke.

Or was it the smoke itself, contorting and twisting, creating a shape he was desperate to see?

But the form felt solid as it grasped him under the arms as he had grasped Dagmar. Hard, hot floor scraped his knees through his trousers as Daniel was pulled toward the door. He dimly heard men yelling, more glass exploding.

Suddenly there was air, and Daniel blinked again in the bright sunshine. Firefighters rushed around him, pulling a heavy hose toward the building, shouting commands at each other.

"Dagmar," he gasped.

The figure who had dragged him leaned down.

Connor.

"What, Dan-Dan? What did you say?" Connor's face was inches from his, frantic, soot covered.

Daniel managed to point to the building. The entire front wall was aflame. How had they escaped?

"Dagmar is still there. And Connor, the flash powder."

True horror flitted across Connor's face as he realized the implications of what Daniel had said. He rushed away, yelling, and in moments firefighters had taken up the call.

Daniel thought he saw one of the rubber-jacketed, helmeted men carrying another figure through the wall of fire that was the front of the building, but the smoke and crowds were so thick he couldn't be sure. Police had joined the firefighters, and they pushed the onlookers back, away from the building. Panicked cries arose, and the sound of running footsteps combined with the steady rumble of the fire.

Now it was his bum that was getting scraped by rough pavement as he was dragged down the sidewalk, uncontrollable coughs shaking his chest. Beyond the tops of the buildings, a few white clouds floated harmlessly in the pale-blue spring sky.

The last thing that permeated his consciousness was an ear-splitting bang, the loudest sound he'd ever heard. The sky momentarily turned brighter, then everything went black.

★   ★   ★

"I would never have forgiven you if you'd died, you know."

"I know."

Every window in Daniel's office was open, even though the cool spring breeze ruffled the papers on his desk. The various stacks were held in place with a porcelain cup of undrunk coffee, several books of varying sizes, and one of Genevieve's pert white boots.

Daniel smiled at the sight of the boot. It had a little scalloped edge with tiny buttons running up the side and a darker heel.

"So don't do anything foolish like that again," Genevieve said. They were curled up on the sofa, her arms crossed and her stockinged feet tucked under the pale-peach and cream stripes of her silk morning dress.

"Like visit a photographer's studio? I have no intention of it," he replied, feeling the corner of his mouth tug into a broader smile.

"Well, not that. You'll have to get photographed at least for the wedding. Daniel, you know what I mean."

"Like chasing down missing girls, getting shot at by gangsters, or being impaled with a knife by a deranged architect?"

Genevieve harrumphed and folded her arms tighter, looking away from him and out the window toward the pale-green buds dotting the trees in Gramercy Park. Daniel, in turn, pulled her closer to his side, reveling in the warmth of her body against his.

It had been a near thing at Dagmar's studio. He himself had sustained smoke inhalation and had been damn lucky that was all. After Connor pulled him from the burning building, the firefighters had retrieved Dagmar, who hadn't fared as well. In the few minutes between Daniel's rescue and Dagmar's, the photographer had received terrible burns on much of his body. He was expected to recover but would remain in the hospital for weeks.

"Somebody doesn't like the work you and Dagmar are doing," Genevieve said quietly, gaze still on the trees.

"It seems that is the case."

"Will you stop doing it?"

The question was one of genuine curiosity, but Daniel felt sure Genevieve already knew the answer. He inhaled the clean, lemony scent of her hair and answered her with a question of his own.

"Do you think I should?"

She turned her wide amber eyes to his. "I don't know."

Daniel nodded slowly in return.

He wasn't about to be bullied away from his efforts toward reform—efforts at which he and Dagmar had been successful so far and through which they were raising awareness and causing enough public outcry to engender real change—by some coward who feared that change.

He had faced such cowards before and won. He and Genevieve both.

But Daniel also understood her reticence. Since they'd acknowledged their love for each other, life had felt both more precious and more precarious. He had already lost so much, had nearly lost Genevieve on more than a few occasions as well.

How much was he tempting fate if he kept engaging in work that could endanger them both?

She gave a deep sigh.

"Of course you can't stop," Genevieve said. "But I'd feel better if Asher were with you more on these excursions."

"You and me both," drawled a voice from the doorway.

Rupert sauntered into the room, an amused smirk on his face, though Daniel knew the look was manufactured. His friend's eyes showed his true feelings, a mix of apprehension and relief. His whole countenance softened at the sight of Genevieve in Daniel's arms on the sofa, then his nose wrinkled as he took in the mess on the desk.

"I say, is that your *shoe* on the desk, Genevieve? I'm deeply in favor of unusual places to express one's desire, but Daniel does need to work on that desk eventually, and someone shall have to clean it. 'Tisn't sanitary."

The sight of the boot, or rather, the sight of Genevieve taking off her boot earlier, had indeed sent Daniel's thoughts in that very direction, though given the presence of his entire household staff, who were uniformly determined to check on him every five minutes, he had not ventured to make any such proposition.

Genevieve leaned closer to Daniel and sent Rupert a lazily admonishing look. "Nothing untoward happened on the desk, Rupert. I'm merely doing my part to keep the place tidy. All his work was being blown about."

Rupert strode to the open windows and peered out at the park below, his blond hair ruffling a bit as the breeze intensified. "Closing the windows would do the trick nicely, you know."

Daniel did know, but since the fire three days prior, he had relished—no, needed—the feel and scent of fresh air as often as he could have it, even if it did make for a rather chilly environment at times.

"Enough of shoes and what did or did not transpire on the desk," Rupert said, pouring himself a drink from the sideboard and settling into an armchair after giving the desk one last suspicious look. "I agree with Genevieve. Asher, or even one of your friends from the Toughs, should be with you when Dagmar is well and you are able to undertake these photographic excursions again. And of course, I am always available. His prognosis remains the same?"

Daniel nodded.

"And you're not thinking of taking the photographs yourself, are you?" Rupert asked.

"Not at all."

"You always were squeamish around the camera," Rupert said. "I don't quite understand it. I adore being photographed."

Genevieve rolled her eyes at Daniel.

"Dagmar has obviously made someone very angry," Rupert continued. Daniel had told both him and Genevieve about the chair under the door.

"It could be any number of people," Daniel agreed. "Our organization's lobbying at the city level has turned some heads, and the next step is to take our concerns to the governor's office. From there, some actual laws could be passed. For better labor conditions, safer housing . . ."

"Laws that would cut into the profits of many," Genevieve observed. "Remember how low Commissioner Simons and Andrew Huffington were willing to sink in order to keep the money rolling in." They were all quiet for a moment, recalling. The two men had led a secret group of corrupt investors who profited from the construction of substandard tenements. They had murdered several people to protect their assets, including Esmie's mother, and had tried to frame Rupert for the crimes.

"We should all be careful," Daniel said quietly. A stronger wind made the curtains flutter and rustled the papers, trapped under their implements, even more. "Until we can figure out who was responsible for that fire."

Under his arm, Genevieve shivered.

Now *he* was uncertain. Was it wise to continue?

But Genevieve untangled herself from him and marched across the room, firmly shutting the windows.

"We always are," she said in a strong voice, holding up her boot. "Enough moping about, and nobody thinks well on an empty stomach. What we need is some Pont l'Évêque and a good glass of wine. Let's go to Mouquin's."

Daniel doubted cheese and wine, good as it was at the French establishment, would fully dismiss the disquietude that since the fire had settled on his shoulders like a moth-ridden coat. But Genevieve was right: nobody thought well on an empty stomach. He fished her other boot out from under the sofa and handed it over, trying again to block out the crackling sound of fire in his ears.

CHAPTER 7

"And the dresses for Mrs. Stewart and Miss Lindsay will be all set?" Genevieve asked, referring to her close friends Callie and Eliza, who would serve as bridesmaids along with Esmie. She still found it very odd to call Callie by her new last name, especially since it was her own as well, but as Callie had married Genevieve's brother Gavin, she was a Stewart now.

"Yes, yes," Mrs. Brown replied, pinning a bow made of ivory-colored faille onto the edge of her sleeve, right at the elbow. "I've been in touch with the dressmakers both in Chicago and Rome, and both ladies are in capable hands."

Mrs. Brown pulled back and admired her handiwork. From a delicate yellow-cushioned chair in the corner, Esmie clapped her hands together once.

"Genevieve, it is *stunning*," she said, eyes shining.

Genevieve regarded herself in the full-length mirror that graced the dressmaker's main fitting room.

Her wedding dress was almost finished.

She liked fashion as much as the next woman; well, maybe not as much as some. And though her tastes often ran to simpler garments, she did prefer them to be pretty.

But in this gown, Mrs. Brown had created something far beyond pretty.

Esmie was right.

The dress was extraordinary.

It was all she could do to not hop up and down and squeal with delight, but there were still several pins holding the ruffle around the square neckline and the ribbon at the V on her waist in place.

The dress had sleeves with a slight puff that ended at the elbow, a nipped-in waist, and lace and seed pearls decorating the bodice. The sleeves and skirt consisted of alternating layers of silk satin and faille in ivory and pale gold, the warm tones suiting her coloring. A bow decorated the area directly between her shoulder blades, its ends falling down her back almost as far as the modest train that trailed behind her.

It was a sumptuous, gorgeous dress appropriate for the elaborate society wedding Genevieve's mother was insisting they hold.

"Daniel and I don't want a large wedding, Mother. Besides, we planned one before, and it didn't exactly work out," Genevieve had protested when her mother informed her of her plans.

"Nonsense," Anna had said. "Daniel McCaffrey is an entirely different species of man than that pompous little jackanape Ted Beekman. Dear Daniel is entirely too upright for his own good, rather like your father. Besides, he's besotted with you; he won't call off the engagement."

The conversation had taken place in the Stewart family drawing room after a family dinner at which Daniel had been present. He had formally asked Genevieve's father for his daughter's hand, though Wilbur had waved the tradition aside.

"Genevieve is her own woman," Wilbur had said. "She is not mine to give." A moment that moved her to tears when Daniel relayed it to her later.

She had tried all sorts of tactics to convince her mother to scale down the nuptials, including reminding Anna that Daniel didn't have enough relations left to fill his side of the church and that many of the friends and family he would invite were hardly high society.

"Any friends or relatives of Daniel's are welcome to attend," Anna had said in a stout tone as she consulted a fashion magazine for the latest style in wedding dresses. "I do think this shape would suit you, but we should let Mrs. Brown have the last word, don't you think? The woman is a genius."

"His cousin Kathleen, who runs a brothel?" Genevieve had pressed. "His friends in street gangs? Asher the former boxer? Do you really think the families of the 400 will attend once they find out who else is on the guest list?" Genevieve herself was very fond of the people who constituted Daniel's inner circle, but she knew how society worked.

"Oh, they'll come. Caroline Astor will make sure the church is full."

Genevieve had been confounded.

"Caroline Astor? Why would she do such a thing?" The inimitable Mrs. Astor did not take on social favors lightly.

"She owes me," Anna had said in a dark tone.

This made no sense at all, but Anna refused to elaborate.

It had taken Genevieve's father pulling her aside and gently explaining that, for all Anna's toughness and unconventionality, she still wanted to see her little girl married in the most traditional, celebratory way possible.

"You'll understand if you have a daughter someday, Genevieve. Do allow your mother a little grace, for my sake if not hers."

So Genevieve had relented, and here they were. Though as Mrs. Brown's assistants helped her out of the dress, Genevieve once again tried to imagine the Bayard Toughs Paddy and Billy sharing a pew with Caroline Astor.

As with every other time she had tried, she failed utterly.

In the reception room of the shop, Genevieve was pleasantly surprised to find her friend Prue eyeing bolts of fabric.

"We've bumped into each other twice in two weeks; what a treat," she said, and meant it. "I am sorry I haven't called yet. Do you know the Countess of Umberland, Esmie Milton?"

The pleasantries were interrupted by Prue's husband. "You won't spend all my earnings today, I take it," Harvey grumbled, checking his pocket watch. Genevieve resisted the urge to wrinkle her nose. "Miss Stewart, you're here for your wedding dress?"

Why was Prue's husband, a man she barely knew, asking about her wedding dress? Most gentlemen left the particulars of things like weddings to the ladies.

"I am indeed," she said politely. "It is almost finished."

"You will make a most lovely bride," said Prue.

"Marriage is a sacred act," boomed Harvey. His square face, which was rather flushed to begin with, grew redder as he spoke. A few ladies fingering ribbon samples at a nearby counter looked their way. "A holy one. I'm glad to see you're finally on the right path, Miss Stewart, and I'm sure God is too."

Shock reverberated through Genevieve's body. Her mouth opened and closed like a fish, and hot color filled her face. She had no idea how to respond.

"Harvey Nadler, my daughter has not been on a *wrong* path once in her life." Anna emerged from Mrs. Brown's office, where they had been finalizing details of payment and delivery. She was taller than Prue's husband by a good three inches and drew herself up fully, staring down her nose at the man. To an onlooker, she might have looked merely displeased, but Genevieve knew her mother was rigid with fury. "And as for God, well, we know what the Bible says about wolves in sheep's clothing, don't we? Now, if you'll excuse us." She took Genevieve's arm and directed her to the counter to make her good-byes to Mrs. Brown, turning her back completely on the Nadlers.

Stunned silence filled the shop.

After a few moments, Harvey broke the quiet in a too-hearty voice. "I'll be off, then. The carriage will come back for you in an hour, my dear."

Out of the corner of her eye, Genevieve saw Prue being led to one of the back fitting rooms, her face bright with embarrassment.

"Mother, what was that about?" she muttered, once both Nadlers were out of earshot.

"That odious little man had me arrested."

Genevieve and Esmie exchanged a glance behind Anna's back.

"Which time?"

Anna's mouth thinned. "Eighteen eighty-one."

Ah. The time she had been arrested for advocating for contraception by picketing the Presbyterian Hospital on Park Avenue. The arrest that had so shocked Ted Beekman that he had called off the wedding three days prior to the event.

"He's one of Comstock's acolytes."

Genevieve understood. As U.S. postal commissioner, Anthony Comstock had encouraged Congress to pass the so-called Comstock laws of 1873, which restricted circulation or trade of anything deemed "vice," including contraception. Anna and her compatriots had been battling with his New York Society for the Suppression of Vice for years. "I didn't recall he was married to your school friend Prudence. She was always such a sweet girl," Anna sighed.

"Yes, well, it was a small wedding, if memory serves. Many years ago. I don't think we were invited."

Anna sniffed at this, placing the papers Mrs. Brown had handed her in her reticule. "Now before I leave, Genevieve, we must settle the question of the flowers for the wedding luncheon."

"Here and now? In Mrs. Brown's dress shop?"

"You've been evading making a decision for weeks, so yes, here and now."

"Fine." Genevieve succeeded, just barely, in not rolling her eyes like a schoolgirl.

"Orange blossoms?"

"Out of fashion."

"Roses?"

She gave her mother a mutinous look.

"Well, I know better than to suggest daisies," Anna said in a snappish tone. Daisies had been Genevieve's choice when she was planning her wedding to Ted, despite Ted's mother's insistence on roses. "Lilies?" she tried again.

"Too funereal."

"Genevieve, we must choose something."

"I like cornflowers."

Anna greeted this suggestion with an appalled look, and even Mrs. Brown, who was still behind the counter, emitted a small and wildly unprofessional gasp.

"Won't peonies be in season?" Esmie ventured.

Both Genevieve and her mother looked at Esmie, startled.

"I like peonies," Genevieve said, offering her mother an olive branch.

Anna heaved a sigh. "I'll see what Gunter's can do. Enjoy your night with Daniel. Esmie, darling, always good to see you."

"Is Daniel collecting you here?" Esmie asked as they gathered their remaining things. Genevieve had invited her to join them, but Esmie wouldn't hear of it.

"Besides, while the nausea has subsided, I still get so very tired after an outing," she had said. "I shall go home and rest, and you have a lovely time on your own, just the two of you."

"He is coming here," Genevieve said now. "Though it feels wrong to be making merry with Dagmar still in the hospital."

Esmie looked sympathetic. "There's nothing more you can do right now. He's in good hands. Have you heard anything further of this fellow claiming to be Daniel's brother?"

Genevieve hesitated. "I don't know what to think of that man. Connor, I suppose we're calling him, though I don't know if that's his name. He did save Daniel."

"Rather convenient that he was right there," murmured Esmie, pointedly not looking at Genevieve but at some lace displayed under a glass case.

"My thoughts exactly."

She had been waiting to voice these concerns to Daniel himself. There simply hadn't been a good time since the fire. Perhaps tonight she could broach the topic.

As if she had summoned him with her thoughts, the front door of the shop opened and in walked the man himself, shaking an umbrella. Daniel's eyes scanned the interior and lit up when they rested on her.

Genevieve melted a bit, as she did every time she saw the man she was to marry. Judging by the poorly concealed sighs around the room, much of the female population of Mrs. Brown's dress shop felt the same.

Despite her misgivings around the large wedding, she couldn't wait to be married to him.

Esmie passed along a secret smile as she hugged Genevieve good-bye, pausing to say hello to Daniel on her way out.

"I see you've taken my demands seriously," Genevieve said once they were outside, eyeing Asher perched in the driver's seat of Daniel's carriage. She was, as she had suspected, reassured in his presence.

"Hello, Asher. How's Elaine?" Genevieve had gotten to know Daniel's childhood friend and now employee Asher Weber better over the past year, including learning he had a sweetheart.

Asher looked wildly intimidating, with his broad form and scarred, homely face and broken nose, but he had the most beautiful smile. "She's good, miss. Excited about the wedding."

"Are you game for a cocktail?" Daniel asked once they were settled.

"Always."

"Excellent. The Metropolitan Hotel, Asher."

This was a surprise. The Metropolitan Hotel was downtown, and while Genevieve knew it had been very glamorous in the 1850s and '60s, two fires in the intervening years had forced renovations, and it was apparently a shadow of its former self. Even the building's attendant Niblo Theater had been eclipsed by newer theaters farther uptown.

"Why the Metropolitan?"

"Despite Jerry Thomas's passing, they still make the best drinks in the city."

Genevieve surveyed the bar space once they were seated, trying to imagine what it had been like in its heyday. P. T. Barnum and his performers had been regulars here, as well as Mary Todd Lincoln, and former head bartender Jerry Thomas had made cocktails famous with his bartender's guide. Despite fashionable addresses having moved farther uptown, the place seemed lively enough, the bar half-full of patrons, including a slightly intoxicated group of gentlemen streaming into a private dining room with lots of hearty backslapping.

Daniel turned his Manhattan on the table, positioning the drink this way and that. Genevieve watched the condensation gather on the edge of her own glass, a delicate green daquiri she had ordered as it felt summery on this cold, rainy spring day.

He took a sip of his drink, then set it down with a louder thump than necessary. Daniel's smile, usually so effusive and ready—for her, at least—today looked timid, indecisive. His eyes darted around the bar, and his fingers tapped an ungainly rhythm on the table.

A flutter of anxiety rippled in her rib cage.

What was wrong? This behavior was very unlike Daniel, who was usually supremely self-assured.

The image of him jumping from a fire escape in a torn pine-apple-embroidered waistcoat the first time they met rose in her mind. The look of confidence—no, arrogance—that he possessed. Not just in his countenance but in his entire bearing, even in that filthy alley. She clearly recalled thinking the stranger in front of her shared the face of Michelangelo's *David*.

Genevie believed that still, only now she knew its range of emotions so much better: joy, sorrow, fear, worry, anger, mirth.

And now, nervousness.

The flutter grew stronger.

"What is it?" Genevieve demanded. She hated beating around the bush. "Is it Dagmar?" Her hand drifted to her throat unbidden.

"No, I checked at the hospital this afternoon. He remains the same. Genevieve, I . . ." Daniel ran a hand through his hair, which always made it stick up a little. He took a gulp of his drink.

I, what? She thought. The flutter of anxiety was now a drum, beating wildly.

What could possibly be of such import that Daniel was having trouble meeting her eye?

Unless.

Another, decidedly unpleasant memory from her past: Ted Beekman, sitting stiffly in her parents' front drawing room, unable to meet her eye as he broke off their engagement in a stilted, practiced voice. She had been so shocked, she hadn't even been able to respond, had simply watched his pin-striped back retreat out the door and out of her life.

Was she about to hear that same speech again, those halting phrases, see that expression of dread tinged with relief cross another man's face?

It was unfathomable. This was *Daniel*, not Ted, and she knew him better than anyone. Knew herself better, too, than she had at nineteen.

Old insecurities died the hardest, it seemed.

Genevieve took a large drink of her own cocktail, even though it was meant to be sipped. The rum raced into her bloodstream, making her arms and fingers tingle.

Daniel finally looked at her, and the combined longing and hope naked in his expression was more than she could bear.

"I think it's him."

Genevieve blinked. "Who is him?"

"Connor. I think it's him. I think he's really my brother."

CHAPTER 8

A light mist filled the air, softening the details of the surrounding buildings and muting the orange glow of the streetlights. The rain had finally stopped, but dampness hung heavily in the atmosphere.

"Let's walk a while," Daniel suggested, taking Genevieve's arm. Dusk had just fallen, and he was keenly aware of what had happened the last time they had walked rather than taken the carriage, after Dagmar's lecture. But the corner of Broadway and Prince was a bustling commercial district rather than the quiet residential neighborhood in which Connor had followed them that night.

Genevieve was unconvinced by what he had said in the bar, he could tell. She had let him talk, sipping her drink as he spilled onto the table all the pent-up emotions he'd held since meeting Connor.

Mostly, she had nodded. And looked thoughtful.

And a little troubled.

Now she nestled in closer to his side, seeming eager to feel the warmth of his body in the damp, chilly evening.

"You don't believe me," he said.

They walked half a block before she answered. "I believe it is what you believe. I'm just not sure you're thinking entirely clearly about the matter."

"How else could he have known about the apples?"

She shrugged. "Someone else told him the story?"

"But who? There aren't many still left on my old block from those days. Disease or old age or just plain poverty got the old ones, lots of the young ones moved on . . . and it wasn't an extraordinary moment. All us kids stole whatever we could get away with, all the time."

Genevieve's brow wrinkled. It was clear she was unconvinced, and agitated by the idea that Daniel really believed Connor was his brother. They had left the bar after finishing their cocktails, without ordering dinner.

Which was cause for some concern. Genevieve loathed missing meals.

"I feel it strongly," Daniel pressed when she still said nothing. "That Connor is who he says he is. As strong as I've felt anything."

Her only response was to nod again. They passed a brightly lit confectionary shop, its electric lights streaming from the plate glass window, illuminating her face.

Genevieve paused, staring at the displays of peppermints and horehound candy. Daniel stopped with her, earning a hard stare and muttered curse from the man behind him, who also had to stop abruptly to avoid crashing into them.

He resisted the urge to yell an apology in the man's angry wake.

"Do you want to go inside? Do you need a butterscotch? Some licorice?"

Her nose wrinkled. "Licorice is a punishment masquerading as a sweet."

"Genevieve." He gently turned her away from the window and toward him. Her expression was rigid but softened as she looked at him. "It's fine if you're not ready to accept Connor yet. He doesn't even have to come to the wedding. But can you promise to keep an open mind? Maybe try to get to know him before judging him?"

It was obvious there were a million things she wanted to say, hovering on the tip of her tongue. He could see her deciding whether or not to voice whatever was on her mind.

Daniel didn't blame Genevieve her reticence. It seemed an outlandish story, that his little brother, snatched off the streets as a child by zealots and sent far away, could pop back into his life unscathed.

"Of course Connor can come to the wedding, Daniel. He saved your life, after all." Genevieve sighed. "And yes, I will keep an open mind. Know that I only want what is best for you." She laid a hand, encased in the softest of kid leather, against his cheek. Daniel leaned into her palm and closed his eyes, relishing the feel of her touch on his skin, even through the glove.

"Now let us find something to eat. I'm famished."

There she is. Daniel smiled, keeping his eyes closed for a moment longer.

He pulled the gloved hand into his and turned them back in the direction they had come from. "Back to the Metropolitan?"

"No, not tonight. I am not in the mood for old New York," Genevieve said in a slightly rueful voice.

"We'll get Asher and go to Greenwich Village? Tonight calls for a good plate of red sauce at one of those Italian basements, I believe."

"Perfect."

"Tamales, chicken tamales, red hot!" A dark-skinned man in a white jacket approached. A copper canister was strapped to his body.

The scent emanating it from it was delectable.

"What is a tamale?" Genevieve asked, sniffing.

Daniel raised a brow of query at the vendor. He was curious as well.

"Chicken wrapped in corn flour, steamed in corn husks." The man's accent was slightly lilting. He opened the lid of the canister and steam wafted out, warming Daniel's face. Upon being asked, the vendor happily showed them how the contraption worked: the canister had chambers, and a small gasoline lamp in the bottom chamber warmed water above, which in turn steamed the food.

The man handed them a cardboard box each. As they made their way back to carriage, Genevieve peeled back the layers of husks. She looked delighted.

"Oh my goodness. This is quite delicious," she said through bites.

Flavor exploded in Daniel's mouth: the soft chewiness of the corn mash contrasted with the perfectly seasoned meat. "I think this is veal instead of chicken, but I agree. It's wonderful." He made a mental note to return to the area for more on a later date. "Do you still want spaghetti?"

"Yes, this is delightful, but hardly enough for dinner."

Over red wine from a straw-covered jug and bowls of their vermicelli soup starter, Genevieve conveyed some of the leads she was chasing down in her story on the Sunflower Mission House fire.

"I have an appointment to speak with the journalist from the *Brooklyn Daily Eagle* tomorrow, and I hope to speak with the Brooklyn fire marshal as well, but I don't know if he'll see me. I also need to request a meeting with the reporter from the *Freeman*."

Daniel allowed the one harried waiter to whisk away his soup bowl and replace it with a portion of fried fish.

"No Jim Crawford?" he asked.

Genevieve made a face. "Absolutely not."

"I can ask Chief Kincaid to have a word, see if he can ask Marshal Keller from Brooklyn to meet with you, as a courtesy."

"You know the fire chief?"

"A few of the higher-ups in the fire department are old Five Pointers; the ranks are overwhelmingly Irish, you know. He's not what I'd call a friend, more of a friendly acquaintance. He certainly knows Paddy."

Genevieve's eyebrows shot up, and she leaned forward. "Is Chief Kincaid *affiliated*?" she asked in a loud whisper.

"He's not a member of the Toughs, no. But it's in his best interest to remain on good terms with all the gang leaders."

He could see Genevieve mulling this over, thinking of the members of New York's underworld she had come in contact with. There were plenty of others she hadn't.

Spaghetti replaced the fish as he poured them both more wine.

"Speaking of, did Paddy find anything out about Connor?"

"A little. As far as anyone can tell, he's been in town only a few weeks, as he claimed. He's staying at a boarding house on the Bowery, works as a longshoreman when he can." Daniel paused, a pang going through him. Working the docks was honest labor, but it was tough. Connor spoke well enough, seemed like he'd had some schooling. Maybe Daniel could help him find something better.

"Daniel, I've been wondering. Do you think the two fires could be related?"

He set down his wineglass and sighed. He had, of course, wondered this, but decided that it was unlikely.

"The fires happened in two different cities," he said, explaining his reasoning. "Dagmar had no connection to or even knowledge of the Sunflower Mission House; I asked him. Despite what Miss Willis saw, the fire has been ruled an accident, not arson. Not," he continued, when he could see Genevieve wanting to protest, "that I think her story isn't worth investigating. But there were no similarities to the incidents. Nobody tried to trap the residents of the Sunflower Mission, as they did Dagmar and I."

Genevieve visibly shuddered at the reminder, and it took all of Daniel's self-control to not follow suit.

"It's natural for you and me to think there's a connection, and it's odd that Dagmar's studio was set afire while you're investigating a different fire, but unfortunately, there are many fires in our city and surrounding areas. The two are not related." A pair of men speaking loudly in Spanish walked in, distracting him.

"You sound like you're trying to convince yourself," Genevieve said, leaning back in her chair with her wineglass.

Was he?

Daniel was saved from answering by the arrival of the roast chicken and salad.

"Perhaps both our inquiries will yield more information," she said. "I am astonished to say this, but I'm becoming quite full."

Daniel grinned. "That is the point of the table d'hôte: a lot of food for a little money."

She smiled. "It's rather marvelous, isn't it? Even my parents have their favorite Italian place in the neighborhood. My grandmother would be rolling in her grave to see what's become of the Washington Square area, but I like it." Genevieve still lived with her parents on Washington Square's north side, a few blocks from where they sat. "I'll save what's left of my appetite for the sweets and coffee. So, what are your next steps? How do we find out who placed that chair under the darkroom door?"

"I'm going to talk to Connor tomorrow, for starters."

Genevieve's smile faded.

"He was there, after all. Watching the building as he waited for me. We haven't had a chance to speak since that day."

"Haven't the fire authorities questioned him?" Her voice was cautious.

Daniel shifted. It was an unusual feeling, not being synchronous about a matter with Genevieve.

He didn't like it.

"I don't think so, not yet."

Genevieve eyed him knowingly. "You asked Connor to wait to meet with them until after you two had spoken." It was a statement, not a question.

The left corner of his mouth rose almost against his will.

Perhaps they were just as synchronous as ever. She certainly knew how he thought.

"I have."

Her lips pursed slightly, and she looked around the restaurant, which had grown more crowded. Several competing languages could be heard. A woman sat alone in a corner and scribbled furiously in an open notebook, ink staining her fingers, and an elderly couple in outdated and worn but clean clothing beamed at each other as they sipped their wine.

"It's not a good idea, Daniel. You're not a fire inspector; this isn't your area of expertise. I think we should let the authorities handle this."

"I will. I simply wanted to have a chance to speak to Connor first."

She folded her arms. "What about Detective Longstreet?"

Annoyance swirled at the name of Aloysius Longstreet. Why the devil did Genevieve think they needed him?

"It's nothing to do with the police."

"Daniel, someone tried to *kill* you." Genevieve kept her voice low, mindful of the other diners, but it was still knife sharp, almost shrill.

"We don't know that."

She stiffened, her mouth forming an O of shock.

"Someone tried to kill Dagmar, yes." Daniel leaned in, speaking low and fast. Despite their efforts to remain quiet, nearby tables were shooting them curious looks. "But that chair under the door might not have been meant for me. It is possible Dagmar alone was the intended target, and I was simply in the wrong place at the wrong time. Almost nobody knew I was visiting the studio that day."

"Someone knew." Genevieve's voice had gone from shrill to ice cold.

It was as though she had slapped him. "Connor had nothing to do with the fire. Why would he drag me out, at great personal risk to himself, if he meant to kill me?"

She raised a brow. "To gain your trust?"

Daniel leaned back. How could he explain? Genevieve hadn't lost anybody in her life, not really. She was curious and passionate and so smart it was astonishing, but she had also lived, until recent years, a very protected life that had known little hardship. Her siblings and parents were all alive and well; no, they were *thriving*. She had grown up in the comfort of wealth and, frankly, luxury.

But to have all your family ripped from you, as it had been from him? And then to be offered another chance, to be reunited with someone you thought was gone forever? It was nothing short of miraculous.

"It's not just that he knew the story about the apples," Daniel said slowly. He waited while the waiter cleared away their plates, setting down small, sturdy cups of strong coffee and bowls of creamy zabaglione. "There's something about Connor's very essence that feels familiar. His eyes match my mother's. My sister Maggie's. And there's a way he moves, how he hitches his right shoulder up when he's uncertain . . . I had forgotten so much about him. Connor was only six when I last saw him. But now, Genevieve, it's all flooding back."

He stared into the foam that crested his coffee, the drink's bitter but heavenly aroma lazily carried on a tiny plume of steam, willing her to understand.

"If I promise to keep an open mind," Genevieve said, "can you do the same? Can your mind remain open to skepticism, just until you know more? Until we know Connor better?"

Daniel reached past their coffees and took her hands on the table. The gloves were gone, and her fingers were soft, save for the hard calluses on her right thumb and third finger, built from countless hours grasping a pen.

"I can do that," he promised. "I will do that."

But deep inside, he knew his mind was already made up.

CHAPTER 9

"Marla Willis?" Gus Fulkerton, the journalist from the *Brooklyn Daily Eagle*, huffed past her, depositing a file on a secretary's desk without looking at the girl. Genevieve followed him.

The *Eagle*'s offices weren't too dissimilar from those of the *Globe*, the main room a warren of desks in a large, airy building in downtown Brooklyn. One wall of windows looked toward the river, the graceful arches of the East River Bridge visible through the spring mist.

"Yeah, I talked to her," he said. A cheap cigar hung out of the corner of Fulkerton's mouth, its foul smoke itching her throat. The secretary made a face and waved her hand in front of her face. Gus stopped at the desk of a young, nervous-looking man, who handed him yet another file, before weaving his way through the desks back to his own, where they had started.

"Fat lot of good it did me. Dotty gal didn't have anything useful to say."

Genevieve kept her temper in check. She wanted information from this man, obnoxious as he was.

"Marla told me she mentioned the man she saw exiting the premises right before she smelled smoke. That seems useful to me."

"So follow up on it, *Polly Palmer*," Fulkerton said, adding exaggerated emphasis to her pen name. "Smart gal like you. You'll crack the story, sure." He sniggered around his cigar. The nervous fellow across the room leaned back in his chair and smirked, enjoying the show.

This reaction, unfortunately, was one Genevieve was familiar with. While the men at her own paper had mostly learned to respect her, many of her colleagues at other outfits still believed women had no place in journalism.

"Look, Polly," Fulkerton continued, his wooden desk chair creaking in protest as he flung himself into it. "You're a 'reporter,' you're used to rough talk, so I won't mince words. Marla was in the sex trade. Completely unreliable."

"I won't mince words either. She actually wasn't in the trade herself, but yes, the Sunflower Mission exists to help just such women." Marla had told her entire story to Genevieve: How she had answered an advertisement in a small Georgia newspaper to be a cook in New York City. How she'd been ready to leave the rural South and embark on an exciting new life far away. Only when she'd arrived, she'd found that the work was not in a home but rather in a brothel in Harlem. It was a common scam, she later learned, targeting young women not only from the American South but from impoverished European countries as well. The perpetrators counted on the women they lured not having a community or resources to help them, assuming they would be stuck. Rather than submit, Marla had fled, then spent all her money on a room in a disreputable boarding house, until she'd heard about the Sunflower Mission.

"There is no reason to discount what she saw," Genevieve continued. "Her profession, which is that of a cook, by the way, and always has been, has nothing to do with her eyesight."

Fulkerton eyed her over his cigar. "Those kinds of women lie all the time, Polly."

Rage and frustration exploded in her chest. By *those kinds*, did he mean Black women, or sex workers? Probably both.

Probably her too. Probably all women.

There was no speaking to the man.

"I see," she said, holding her back as straight as possible. "You're sacrificing your integrity because of your prejudice. I am sorry for your paper."

Fulkerton's guffaws and the nervous man's giggles followed her out the door.

Genevieve let the crisp wind on the ferry and the bright sunshine, a welcome change after days of rain, calm her spirits on the way back to the office. The small-mindedness of others never ceased to enrage her, but railing at a person like Gus Fulkerton was like trying to argue with the weather. Some people were incapable of change.

Regardless, she dragged her feet as she entered her building's elevator.

Daniel hadn't yet heard from Marshal Keller. She still hadn't received a reply from Isaac Conklin at the *Freeman*.

It was possible there was no larger story to the Sunflower Mission House fire. Perhaps it simply had been an accident. There seemed to be no way to identify the mysterious figure Marla had seen scurrying into the night moments before the fire began.

The elevator door heaved open. Genevieve pulled off her gloves and stepped into the lofty room, sighing.

"Miss Stewart?"

Genevieve swallowed her surprise. Marla Willis was sitting in one of the chairs lined up near the elevator that served as a reception area, apparently waiting for her. Next to her sat a slightly plump, light-skinned Black woman in a dark-pink dress and matching hat.

Marla and the stranger rose as she approached. "We need to talk. My friend Josie here has something to tell you."

★ ★ ★

The scent of char still hung in the air over Franklin Street almost a week after the fire and explosion. Smoke-stained ruins were all that were left of the building that had housed Dagmar's studio.

The sight tore at something in Daniel's insides. The side of the building to the west of the former studio was covered in thick black marks, a pile of still-damp, ruined furniture gathered on the sidewalk. Thankfully, a thin alley on the east side kept the other nearby structures safe.

Frau Hilde hadn't been at home during the fire, he'd learned, but luckily at her butchery business several blocks away. Daniel was making sure she had adequate housing until she was able to get resettled, which seemed a scant service in the face of her loss. All the physical reminders and artifacts she had carried over from her life in Germany, the mementos left by her deceased husband, were nothing but ash now.

And it was his fault.

Despite his insistence to Genevieve that he might not have been the arsonist's target, something deep in Daniel's gut told him otherwise.

It was his money, after all, that had brought Dagmar's work to wider attention. He had provided the financial backing for the glass plates, the chemicals, the lantern slide equipment, the printing of the book that was forthcoming. He knew who to ask for funds, which society matrons would rally their friends to their aid, which power couples would attend a charity auction. It was Daniel, not Dagmar, who knew the ins and outs of City Hall and the governor's office, who knew which city and state representatives to contact, who had the money and power to be heard by those officials.

Dagmar took the pictures, but it was Daniel who made the wheels turn.

Somebody had known he would be in that studio.

Somebody wanted to stop him.

A chill that had nothing to do with the strong April breeze shot across the back of his neck. Daniel shoved his hands into his

trouser pockets and casually looked left, then right, as if continuing to survey the scene.

It was that feeling again, of being watched.

A pair of workers clearing out the remains of the building
leaned on the handles of their shovels and smoked companion-
ably, taking a break.

A dissatisfied-looking woman in a high-necked black dress
pursed her lips as she tried the handle of a millinery shop.

Three young girls with light scarves over their heads giggled
behind their hands as they hurried down the block.

Nothing out of the ordinary that he could see.

But there was so much he couldn't see.

The man alone, nursing his pint in the window of the tavern
on the corner: Was he simply a laborer having a midday bite, or
was he intentionally watching the site, waiting for Daniel's return?
Was the popcorn vendor down the block eyeing him in hopes of
a sale, or for a more sinister reason?

In the bright midday sun, it was impossible to see far into the
blank windows of shops and residences. The dark rectangles
stared back at him, impassive.

Though he hated to admit it, what Genevieve had said at
the Italian restaurant nagged at him. He and Connor had had
plans to meet the day of the fire, yes. But in a bar two blocks
away.

Why had Connor been on *this* block?

The light breeze turned into a sudden gust, tugging at his hat.
Daniel clapped a hand on his head.

"It's McCaffrey, yes?"

A police officer sporting a wide brown moustache approached,
the sunlight glinting off his brass buttons.

So he *had* been being watched.

"You've the advantage over me, Officer . . . ?"

"Jackson."

Daniel waited, but the man declined to say anything further.

Another gust surged. A woman's aggrieved cry filled the street, suggesting a lost parasol or bonnet, but the officer didn't turn his head.

Daniel didn't either.

The prickling on the back of his neck intensified, radiating across his shoulder blades.

"I heard you two were in cahoots," Officer Jackson said finally, tilting his head toward the burnt wreck of the studio.

The man's tone was pleasant enough.

But he stood half a step too close.

There was no way Daniel would step back.

Instead, he arched a brow. "I am an investor in Hansen's work, and it has been aiding my charity's lobbying of state officials for better housing and labor conditions. If those are cahoots, then yes."

Officer Jackson jerked his upper body as if trying to physically dispel what Daniel had said, his apparent attempt at a shrug. "Give 'em better this and better that, they'll never learn. If they want better things, they can work for them."

Daniel looked more closely at Officer Jackson. He looked and sounded as Irish as they came.

As Irish as Daniel.

He turned his attention back to the heaped ruins, matched Jackson's mild inflection. "Hard to afford a better place to live when you make twenty cents a day sewing neckties."

The officer huffed. "My parents didn't take any handouts. They earned their keep, saved their pennies, and we moved out of the tenements when I was a lad. Found a proper apartment on the West Side."

"I'm glad for your parents, but that is simply impossible for some people."

"Nonsense." Officer Jackson spat on the sidewalk to his left, away from Daniel, but the sentiment was clear. "Some are just lazy."

"Hey, Danny!"

Daniel turned to find Connor halfway down the block, jogging toward him and waving one arm, jacket flapping in the wind. He stopped short at the sight of Officer Jackson, then slowed, wariness apparent in his steps.

The officer narrowed his eyes at Connor, assessing. "I'll leave you to it, then."

Connor reached him just as Officer Jackson was departing and watched the tall, blue uniformed back retreat with suspicion. "Friend of yours?"

Daniel shook his head once.

"Okay." Connor sounded doubtful. He waited until the officer was fully out of earshot before speaking again. "So, what's up, Danny? Where we going today?"

The glaring sun was at odds with the brisk breeze, one wanting to pin them in place, the other trying to hurry them along. There were no shadows to hide in at this time of day, not with the sun directly overhead. Every piece of burned wood and charred fragment left from the hollowed husk of the building was brutally exposed.

"Why were you here, Connor?" The question popped from his mouth before he had time to think about it. "The day of the fire. We were meant to meet at the Button Hook on Walker Street." The tavern was as staid as its name, tucked into a block filled with shoe and garment importers and merchants, but staid had suited his purposes that day. He didn't need his little brother hanging about stale-beer joints.

Connor blinked. "The barkeep said they weren't open yet and he wouldn't let me wait, so I came this way. Better than standing around on the corner, right?"

It was a plausible enough explanation, and easy enough to verify. Some taverns shut down between the lunch and evening rushes.

He let his eyes roam the streets again. The laborers had finished their cigarettes and resumed digging. The giggling girls were long gone, the woman in black too.

"Did you see anyone, or anything?"

"No, Danny, no. Nothing. I went into that place there, on the corner, to wait. So I could keep an eye out for you. I was going to catch you when you were done."

Daniel followed Connor's head gesture to the bar on the corner he'd clocked earlier. The man who had been sitting in the window was also now gone.

"I was talking to some other guys—you know how it is, just chewing the fat—when the barkeep said he smelled smoke and went to the window. He yelled 'Fire!' and we all ran out. I saw it was the studio where you were and I ran in, and that's all I know." Connor's right shoulder lifted in the little half shrug Daniel hadn't remembered, but now he did, so well.

Check the story. Was it Genevieve's voice in his head, urging him to remain skeptical, or his own?

"It's good you were here," Daniel admitted. Why did he have to sound so begrudging? He would be dead if it weren't for Connor. "Come on, let's go."

The dissonance of walking down the street with his little brother nipped at him, the years folding in on themselves and layering atop each other. Was it 1890 or 1864? Connor wasn't skipping to keep up like he used to, but his energy was the same, the eagerness of a puppy tagging along on an adventure. He'd always been this way, keeping close to Daniel's heels, desperate to be accepted by the big kids.

Now, over twenty-five years later, Connor still had his hands in his pockets and was bobbing along, a big goofy grin on his face.

It was hard not to grin back.

"So where we going?"

"To the place that was almost our other home."

Connor looked confused, and Daniel smiled to himself, waiting for him to figure it out.

Just as he had when they were kids.

"Oh," Connor said, realization lighting his face, quickly followed by confusion. "Why we going there?"

Why indeed?

"I want to see if it's a suitable subject for Dagmar, once he recovers." It was partially true.

Connor grimaced. "How's he holding up?"

"No progress."

In truth, Daniel wasn't sure Dagmar would want to photograph the House of Refuge. He wasn't actually sure the place needed reforming, as there had been a big, well-publicized effort to make changes just a few years prior. But ever since Connor had reminded him of the apples, Daniel hadn't been able to get the place out of his mind.

All those children, sent away from their parents to live and work. The institution called them wicked and wanted them trained in industriousness and good labor.

Really, what the House of Refuge wanted—what its board of aldermen, what the upper ranks of society who controlled it, wanted—was a supply of obedient bodies to keep the system in place.

Even as a child he'd known that. Everyone in Five Points had.

He supposed there should be some sort of reform for the truly maladjusted child, but he was willing to bet his fortune that the majority of those incarcerated at the House of Refuge were just like he had been. Like Connor. Poor kids, sometimes starving kids. Kids who were just trying to get by.

As their ferry approached Randall's Island, the domes that topped the main building of the detention center grew. The place was imposing, two long wings stretching out from the central building, dominating the shoreline.

The prickle that had assailed Daniel on Franklin Street returned.

He was thirty-six years old, a grown man, in absolutely no danger of being imprisoned by the House of Refuge.

And yet every sense was on immediate high alert.

Something primal told him it would do to keep Connor close, and his wits closer.

Reformed or not, he didn't trust the place.

CHAPTER 10

"Mr. McCaffrey. And . . . ?"

Felix Joyce, the deputy superintendent of the House of Refuge, blinked at Connor owlishly. He was a small, gray man of nervous disposition who seemed more suited to a quiet job totaling figures than running a detention center for wayward children, but Daniel knew appearances could be deceiving.

"This is my associate, Mr. Lund."

Joyce squinted at Connor in the wind, which was much stronger here on the island. "Mr. Ratchford didn't say anything about an associate."

Erasmus Ratchford was the superintendent with whom Daniel had made the appointment to tour the facility. He had pretended he was considering joining the board of the Society for the Reform of Juvenile Delinquents, which ran the House of Refuge. Ratchford had responded eagerly, anxious of having someone of Daniel's social stature and wealth on their board.

He marveled, as always, at the doors money opened.

"Mr. Ratchford didn't say anything about you either," Daniel replied coldly.

Joyce recoiled as if slapped. "He was very sorry about not being able to meet you today. As I mentioned, he is suffering from a bad spring cold. But we have strict regulations about visitors." The gray man twisted his hands once, then made up his mind. "Very well. Mr. McCaffrey, Mr. Lund, follow me."

They trailed Mr. Joyce through a large outdoor courtyard, where a crowd of boys, about ten years old, ran and chased each other. The boys stopped when they saw the men on the path, following their progress with watchful eyes. Joyce either didn't notice or pretended not to, gesturing to the surrounding buildings and describing the functions of each.

"We'll come this way to the classroom. The children aren't in lessons now; those happen in the early morning and evening, after their work hours."

"Lessons after work?" Daniel asked as they stepped into the school building. It looked the same as any other school: rows of wooden desks, a chalkboard. "Won't the children be too tired to absorb their lessons at that time?"

"They get the schooling they need, basic reading, writing, and math. Some geography, and a good dose of moral and religious instruction on Sundays. We believe building a strong work ethic in these boys is our utmost priority. And the girls too, of course." Joyce nodded at a group of girls in aprons who were scrubbing the floor of the hallway.

Daniel smiled apologetically as he gingerly tiptoed down the hall, not wishing to ruin the girls' hard work. Unlike the boys in the courtyard, the girls, who appeared to be anywhere from nine to thirteen years old, did not cease their activities upon the men's passing. They kept their glances furtive, and he heard an explosion of whispers behind him once they were down the hall.

"We must cross the courtyard again to reach some of the workshops," Joyce explained as they stepped again into the bright, brisk day.

Joyce showed them three workshops, where boys were busily engaged in a variety of trades: knitting hosiery or working a large machine spooling wire. In another area, an instructor leaned over a boy, showing him how to properly fit pipe. The inmates smiled at Daniel and Connor as they passed, but their expressions looked forced and wooden. Joyce ushered them through quickly, and in no time they were back in the courtyard.

In the short time they had been inside, the set of boys in the yard had changed. Now about a dozen slightly older lads stood in military-like formation, wearing blue uniforms. As Daniel followed Joyce toward another building, the boys began marching.

Connor nudged him with an elbow and wrinkled his nose, one hand pressing down his hat in the strong wind.

"I didn't know you engaged in military drills," Daniel said, stopping. Joyce had no choice but to follow suit.

"Yes," he said. As one, the boys dropped to one knee and positioned their arms as if holding rifles. "A new initiative just begun this year. We've found it helps with discipline."

"They don't get even toy guns, help them really learn?" Connor asked. He sounded troubled, and Daniel thought he knew why. There was something eerie about the boys moving their bodies in unison but in total silence, going through the motions of warfare but holding only air.

A beat passed as they watched.

"No," Joyce said shortly. "Come along; the boys in the carpentry workshop are expecting us."

Connor frowned, and Daniel gave him a silent headshake. He'd fill in Connor later on what he knew. How almost twenty years prior, the boys at the House of Refuge had staged a revolt. They had briefly triumphed, taking control of the facility.

The revolt had been brutally quashed.

Daniel could still feel the spring air—a light, temperate breeze of May as opposed to the hearty April gust currently buffeting him—that had gently wafted across his face as he read the account, horrified, from the safety of the Harvard campus. He'd been sitting on the grass in the quad, leaning against a tree, enjoying the sunshine and the New York paper; he'd liked to keep up on happenings in his hometown during his time in Cambridge. And there, in black and white, was spelled out the violence that had unfolded on this very island. Boys stabbing officers in the face. Boys attacking shop foremen with branding irons. Boys seizing control of the yard.

The account was incomplete, he was sure. He had wondered then, as he did now, what atrocities had been committed to make the boys held here act in such a way. Over the years the papers had reported on a few—beatings, malnutrition, overwork, isolation cells—but he suspected the truth exceeded even those horrific details.

Shaken, Daniel had read the names of the ringleaders who were punished, both surprised and not to see the name of someone he knew among them: Kevin Grady. Not a Bayard Tough, but one of the Hard Hudsons—a different gang, sometimes allies of the Toughs. Kevin had been a brawny, red-faced, ham-fisted kid, the type you assumed would be a rabble rouser but who was actually fairly gentle, and brighter than he looked. He wasn't a good friend of Daniel's, just one of the kids he'd knocked around with. There were a dozen more just like him.

How was he punished? What had ever happened to him? Daniel didn't know.

Kevin had been only sixteen at the time of the House of Refuge uprising, two years younger than Daniel. He remembered, with great clarity, the feeling of dislocation that had settled on his shoulders at that moment, there in the Harvard yard. What was he doing, in his starched white shirt and black tie? How was it that he, scrappy Daniel McCaffrey of Five Points, was living a life of intellect and luxury, while kids like Kevin were imprisoned? Why was Kevin even *in* the House of Refuge? Something else Daniel didn't know and never would, but he was sure Kevin shouldn't have been there.

His collar had suddenly been too tight. Rage had built and expanded in his chest, but there was nowhere for it to go.

He'd felt like the worst sort of impostor. He had no business in Cambridge. He should be home, in New York.

But he hadn't gone home. Not until years later, after he'd spent over a decade trying to shake his past and rid his nostrils of the scent of his home city, until he realized its futility.

New York was the only place he truly belonged.

Of course the administration wouldn't give the boys toy guns. They'd do nothing to risk even the suggestion of another rebellion.

"Guess it doesn't look too bad," Connor said in a doubtful tone, eyeing the boys. He kept his voice low enough so Mr. Joyce couldn't hear.

But Daniel could tell it was bad. They were being shown a facade. The militaristic uniforms looked new but were too thin, and many shivered in the sharp wind. Several of the youths resembled scarecrows, too thin themselves, hollow eyed and watchful.

"Mr. Joyce," Daniel called as the small man prepared to enter the next building. "You will excuse me, I'm sure. The ferry ride was somewhat long. Would you point me toward the nearest facilities?"

Joyce wrung his hands, brow puckered.

"Mr. Lund can continue the tour while I am gone," he continued. "I know your time is valuable."

"Very well," Joyce said, clearly reluctant. Daniel suppressed a grimace; if Joyce was this sour with a distinguished visitor, one could only imagine how he treated the children. "Do head back to the main office where we entered, and the secretary will point the way."

"There are none closer?" Daniel knew the answer—he was sure the facilities in the workshops for the children were substandard, nothing Joyce would allow him to see—but was feeling ornery and wanted the small gray man to admit it.

Joyce's lips furrowed as tight as his brow. "There are, but the ones in the main office are those appropriate for visitors. I will take Mr. Lund to view the chapel in your absence."

Daniel glanced over his shoulder once to make sure they were on their way. Connor looked over his shoulder too, meeting Daniel's eye and making a face behind Joyce's back. Daniel grinned.

He'd learned long ago, when he was about the age of the boys in the courtyard, that as long as one looked and acted like one belonged in a particular place, one was rarely questioned. He put this into practice as he strolled into the main office and past the secretary, nodding officiously once and walking with purpose, then exited from the side door he'd spotted earlier. Daniel slipped through the side yard and circled back to where Joyce had pointed out the dormitories. He wanted to see the children's living conditions on his own.

The door wasn't locked.

It was worse than he'd imagined.

The year prior, Rupert had been falsely imprisoned in the Tombs. Though that hadn't been Daniel's first experience with the foul, fetid prison, it was his most recent, and the memory of its cramped cells and unbearable scent was as strong as if it had happened yesterday.

The dormitories of the House of Refuge were shockingly similar.

The children's rooms were little more than barren cells, rows of barred iron doors lining several stories of hallways. Bile filled the back of his throat at the sight and smell of overflowing buckets of human waste. One sallow girl in inadequate, ragged clothing listlessly swept the corridor, though after a fearful look in his direction, she doubled her speed.

Daniel didn't need to see anything else. He exited the way he had entered, then looped around the back of the building, peeking across the courtyard.

The boys in their stiff new uniforms were marching in the opposite direction. There was no sign of Connor and Felix Joyce.

Daniel hurried back to the workshops.

As he'd thought, all evidence of industry had vanished. Boys who had been working just a few minutes prior were now idle, and those who were still laboring appeared to be doing so under duress. In one shop, a group of inmates were playing chess with the shop supervisor, the wire-spooling machines still. Everyone who had been knitting or receiving instruction on pipe fitting now appeared bored and restless.

Daniel climbed a set of stairs, anxious to see some of the shops Joyce hadn't included on their tour. Voices floated into the hallway from the first shop he passed.

"Just snatch enough pairs from Otis's shop, we'll make our quota."

"Add that to what he lifted yesterday and we'll beat it." Freshly made men's shoes were piled at the corner just inside the door.

He didn't blame the boys for resorting to theft to meet what were probably impossibly high daily requirements of production. Someone around here was producing something, though—the shoes were evidence of that—and he was sure there would be hell to pay if the shops didn't generate goods. It was probably the older boys bullying the younger ones into doing all the work, and once the younger boys got bigger, they did the same.

The only real evidence of industry he'd seen was from the girls, who scuttled the halls looking terrified, mops and brooms in their hands.

It would be easy to assign blame, but none of this was the children's fault. They were simply trying to survive under an unjust and abusive system.

"Who are you?"

A tall, gangly kid of about fourteen regarded him suspiciously, a pair of shoes dangling from two fingers of each hand. An unruly mop of jet-black hair sprung in all directions above a thin face dominated by a beakish nose the lad would grow into in a few years.

"Just visiting," Daniel said. "How do you like shoemaking?"

The boy snorted. "Better than farmwork."

"Farmwork?" Daniel didn't think there were any fields on the island.

"You visiting someone who lives here?" the boy countered, eyes narrowing. The fingers holding the shoes curled tighter.

"No. I am trying to find out what it's like to live here, though." The boy said nothing. "I saw the dormitories," Daniel continued. "Do those doors lock at night?"

The kid's brows rose and his fingers relaxed. "They showed you the real deal, huh? Of course they lock."

"Where did you work on a farm?"

"Jersey. I tried to run away but got caught, so I'm back here."

Daniel tried to follow the story. "Back here?"

"Yeah. The farm was my placement. Couldn't stand it. I'd rather be inside doing this"—he briefly lifted a pair of shoes—"than outside in all weather, too hot or too cold, digging up rocks or cleaning animal shit."

"Your placement," Daniel repeated, the truth dawning on him. "You mean your indenture? I didn't think the institution indentured detainees any longer." That was what the press had reported.

The boy looked at him with condescension. "Of course they do. Why the hell we in here? They make a pretty penny off us too."

"Robbie!" The bellow came from the down the hall.

Without a backward glance, the black-haired kid stomped away.

Daniel stood alone in the hallway for a few moments. Those in the shops seemed aware of his presence, as he heard the quiet scuffle of footsteps within, but no more chatter.

The reforms made to the House of Refuge in 1887 had been well touted. He'd read about them with interest, as even in Europe he'd continued his practice of taking the New York papers. But it was all a fabrication, window dressing.

He made it back just in time, as Connor and Felix Joyce were approaching the main administration building as he exited. The gray man acknowledged his presence with a curt nod.

"Is there anything else you'd care to tour, Mr. McCaffrey?" Yet another group of boys, the third by his count, marched across the courtyard behind Joyce.

The curtain had been pulled back, and Daniel could see beyond the facade even more clearly now. The children's exhaustion dogging every step. Their eyes glazed with stupor from not enough nutrition and too much work.

This couldn't wait for Dagmar to get better. It was up to him to figure out what could be done to change things, and now.

Genevieve, of course. She would help. Together they could use the power of the press to expose the hypocrisy. He would come back, with her, so she could get a firsthand account of what was really happening on Randall's Island.

"No thank you, Mr. Joyce," he replied. "I've seen enough."

CHAPTER 11

Josie. Genevieve remembered the name. This was the person Marla had mentioned was not at the Sunflower Mission the night of the fire, the one the girls had thought perished. She had appeared on the sidewalk in the midst of the fire, returning from a rendezvous with her beau.

"Josephine Young," the woman in pink said, extending her hand and introducing herself fully.

"Let's head elsewhere to talk," Genevieve said, tugging on the gloves she'd just removed. She didn't have a private office, and she suspected that whatever Josie had to say, it was best relayed out of earshot of the other staff. Alice was already eyeing them with too much interest, her gaze bright and curious. "How about we go to the Viennese bakery down the street, and I'll get us some coffee?"

Josie looked warily around the neat coffeehouse once they were settled at their table, confirming Genevieve's thoughts that the young woman's information must be quite sensitive. She needn't have worried; Genevieve had chosen the bakery because she knew it would be fairly empty at this time of day, after the rush of the lunch crowd. The secretaries, journalists, and other office workers had all gone back to their desks at this hour. They nearly had the place to themselves.

OPULENCE AND ASHES   ☞ 97

"Marla was right," Josie said. "About what she saw." Genevieve held up her notebook and pencil, silently asking if she could make a record of their conversation. The other women exchanged a look.

"Better not," Marla said.

Genevieve nodded and put her notebook away. This *was* sensitive.

Josie waited until the waiter depositing their coffee had departed before continuing.

"There was a man at the Sunflower Mission House the night of the fire," she said, looking up for a brief second from stirring her cup.

Genevieve's mouth dropped open, and her pulse quickened. Josie put down her spoon and met her eyes squarely.

"But he didn't start it," she said in a firm voice.

"How can you know that? I thought you weren't at the Sunflower House that night?"

"I wasn't. But someone was making a delivery to me. There was a mix-up with the dates, and I wasn't there when he thought I would be." Josie looked at Genevieve beseechingly. "Please, I need you to stop looking into this, Miss Stewart. Or Miss Palmer?"

"Genevieve is fine. But even if this man didn't set the fire, he is an important witness. I must speak with him."

"If you do, he will get into trouble." Josie knitted her fingers together next to her coffee cup. "And I will get into trouble. Serious trouble." Her voice had dropped to a whisper. "With the law."

Genevieve's breath caught. "Miss Young, maybe I shouldn't hear any more of this."

"It wasn't a real crime, Miss Stewart. It shouldn't even be illegal," Marla chimed in, whispering as well. Despite the nearly empty coffeehouse, Genevieve leaned closer, just in case. She couldn't think what in the world this was about.

"I'm sorry, I don't understand. Something is either legal or it isn't."

The women exchanged another look.

"You're engaged to be married, are you not?" Marla asked.

"I am," Genevieve said, a little wary now. What did her engagement have to do with anything?

"And you know the kind of work the women at the mission might have been engaged in. What the mission is trying to help alleviate."

"Yes," Genevieve said, still baffled. Was she out of her depth here? Much as she didn't want to, maybe it was time to involve the authorities.

No, she decided just as quickly. The police were already predisposed to not believe these women. They had come to *her*, and they had something important to say. Her job was to listen. Genevieve straightened in her chair.

"Marla said she told you about my beau, Jeremy," Josie said. Genevieve nodded; this was the man Josie had been with the night of the fire. "We aren't engaged, not yet, even though we are very close." Color rose to the woman's cheeks. "And . . ." She looked around furtively, dropping her voice yet again. "Now is not a prudent time to start a family."

Realization dropped like a bright coin. Genevieve colored herself. "I understand."

And she did.

They were speaking of contraceptives.

"That sort of thing can be delivered?" Genevieve was now whispering as well. Contraception, both the items themselves and any written material around them, had been illegal nationwide for nearly twenty years under the Comstock laws.

Again the women's eyes met, as if they were deciding how much they could share. "Yes, from certain providers," Josie said, obviously choosing her words with care. "If they don't have what you want in stock when you inquire, your purchase can be delivered later for a price."

Genevieve felt her color deepen. Though she had now experienced intimacy with Daniel a few times, she had only a limited idea of what such devices were or how they worked. She knew of gentlemen's protectors, of course—it was hard to be a woman of twenty-seven and not have heard of such things—but what might a woman use?

These were not new questions for her. Ever since she and Daniel had begun their clandestine premarital activities, limited though they had been, the specter of an unintended pregnancy had loomed. She'd been far too shy to broach the subject in the moment, which, now that she was ruminating on this in a well-lit café fueled by coffee, seemed ludicrous. She was to marry Daniel, after all, and the man had seen her naked several times now. Shouldn't they have spoken of the consequences of their actions?

Was Daniel using a device and she simply didn't know? Surely she would have noticed if he'd used a French safe. Did he think *she* had some kind of discreet device tucked up inside her?

Genevieve signaled to the waiter for another coffee.

During her first, ill-fated engagement, her mother had tried to speak to her of such matters, which had embarrassed her completely. Now Genevieve wished she'd let her mother talk.

She added a slice of cake for each of them to her coffee order. Hopefully, the portions would be generous. Fortification was needed.

"So you understand why the man Marla saw could not have started the fire," Josie said. "The practitioner for whom he works would only hire the most reliable of people, as the safety of both of them depends on it. He wouldn't risk being caught."

"It is crucial I question this deliveryman," Genevieve insisted. "My mother is an active member in the crusade against the Society for the Suppression of Vice, along with Mrs. Gloucester. Indeed, I am certain my mother knows of the provider from whom you obtained your prescription," Genevieve added carefully. The tables immediately surrounding theirs were still empty, but it couldn't hurt to be too prudent. Many women had been imprisoned for exchanging exactly this kind of information. "I will act with the utmost discretion. Your name need never come up. I promise."

Their pieces of Viennese torte arrived. Thankfully, they were respectfully sized. Genevieve took a large bite.

Another look passed between the women. Josie pulled a folded slip of paper out of her small embroidered handbag and silently pushed it across the table before picking up her own fork and sampling the torte.

Genevieve tucked the note into her own bag.

What had just transpired between them could land both of them in jail.

Well, her mother had certainly spent enough time there, Genevieve thought as she took another bite. The tart taste of raspberry jam exploded in her mouth.

The bail clerk knew her family well.

★　★　★

"Genevieve, is that you?" Anna called from the sitting room as Genevieve removed her hat in the front hallway. "There's a telegram there for you."

It was from Daniel, informing her that Marshal Keller was open to meeting with her, and was expecting her at two PM tomorrow at the station.

Her heart sank. This was the meeting she had been desperate for just this morning, but now it could be dangerous. She couldn't tell the Brooklyn fire marshal about the deliveryman who was trying to meet Josie, so she would have to lie instead and say that her source had been mistaken. She supposed she didn't need to meet with the *Freeman* now either. The information she had from Josie and Marla was too sensitive.

Maybe she could cancel the meeting with the fire marshal, but Daniel had called in a favor. She didn't want to reflect poorly on him.

"Did you find it?" her mother called. "Come join me. There's tea and cake. And I have good news."

Genevieve pocketed the telegram; she'd deal with what to say to the fire marshal later. "What's the good news?" she asked, settling in on the settee beside her mother.

"Gunter's can do peonies, so the flowers for the wedding are finally all settled. Do you want some cake?"

She was full up on cake.

Anna began rifling through a small stack of envelopes. Genevieve hesitated, wondering how best to broach the uncomfortable topic she needed to discuss.

"Mother, do you recall when I was engaged before?"

Anna frowned at an envelope before placing it in a small pile on her left. "We certainly won't be repeating the sugared almonds we planned then. The fairy cakes we've chosen as favors are perfect."

This was the type of detail Genevieve did not care about, but she humored her mother.

"Yes, fairy cakes were a good choice." She eyed the apricot cake on the low table in front of her mother. Maybe she did have room for another slice. "But I'm referring to a different aspect of that engagement."

"The Porters have accepted," Anna beamed, holding one of the envelopes aloft in triumph. She placed it in a larger pile. "I knew they wouldn't be able to resist. Apologies, dear, I'm simply trying to get these sorted. Now, what do you need to discuss?"

Genevieve often marveled at the many facets of her mother. She could be picketing an unjust law one day and planning social coups the next. The woman really was remarkable, even if her formidable energy was sometimes a bit wearing.

"You tried to talk to me about, erm, the wedding night. Do you recall?" Genevieve suddenly needed cake quite badly, and hastily served herself a small piece.

Anna, on the other hand, now set down the envelope she had been studying with care.

"I do," she said, her voice surprisingly gentle. "Is that something you would like to talk about?"

"Yes. I mean, no." Her face must be as bright as a cherry. Genevieve risked a glance at her mother, whose own face held a great deal of compassion. "What I mean is, what if a married woman"—she put a great deal of emphasis on the word *married*—"does not want to have a child right away? What options might be available to her?"

Anna's look changed from compassionate to knowing. "This is an excellent question," she said as she took a sip of tea, back to her usual brisk tone. "We can discuss options, though if you would prefer a professional to do so, I can recommend someone."

"I have heard—that is, someone I know recommended—a practitioner called Pearl Martin. Is that anybody you know?" This was the name scrawled on the scrap from Josie in a neat, looping hand. Genevieve wanted to vet this person before she tried to interview her or gain access to her delivery person. The apricot cake was a glorious soft sponge, and she was grateful for the distraction of eating while having this conversation, even if she was starting to feel a bit stuffed.

"I know her quite well, yes." Anna didn't ask who had recommended Mrs. Martin. Genevieve understood that, like the small slip of paper nestled in her pocket, the conversation they were having, even in the privacy of their own living room, was illegal. "I think she would be a fine resource for you."

The sheen of tears that suddenly covered Anna's eyes was so surprising and overwhelming, Genevieve found herself blinking back tears of her own. Anna put down her teacup and folded

Genevieve into a very un-Anna-like embrace. Genevieve leaned into the solid comfort of her mother.

"I'm just so happy for you, darling. Aside from you and your brothers, my marriage to your father is my greatest joy in life. I hope your marriage to that absolute oyster of a man is just as good." Genevieve laughed into her mother's shoulder, squeezing her harder.

And Anna was right. Daniel *was* an oyster of a man.

"And have children when you're good and ready. You've plenty of time." Anna pulled back slightly and looked her in the eye. "That's what I did."

Nellie appeared in the doorway, bearing a blush of her own. "Mr. McCaffrey is here, miss." All the female staff were a bit sweet on Daniel. Genevieve didn't blame them one bit, enjoying, as always, the small trill of pleasure that zipped across her breastbone whenever she saw him.

"Hello, Genevieve, Anna." He leaned down to kiss both their cheeks. "Is that apricot cake?"

"We didn't have plans to see each other tonight," Genevieve said, leaning back on the settee as Daniel tucked in. "Not that I'm complaining."

"I was hoping to steal you away for dinner again, though I know I did so last night." He sent an adorably beseeching look to Anna. "Could you spare her again?"

Genevieve's mother smiled indulgently. "I'm sure that can be arranged." She gathered up her envelopes. "If you'll excuse me, I must attend to a few things. Lovely to see you, Daniel. Have dinner here next time, will you?"

Genevieve smiled curiously at Daniel as he finished his cake. "What a pleasant surprise. How did it go today?" She meant with Connor, though she knew he had visited the House of Refuge as well. Slight guilt had been gnawing at her all day about their conversation in the Italian restaurant the night before—if the stranger really was Daniel's brother, she ought to behave more charitably toward him.

But there was something about Connor that didn't sit right with her, though she couldn't quite put her finger on what it was.

Perhaps it was simply that she didn't like sharing Daniel's attention, after she'd commanded so much of it in recent months.

Daniel set down his now-empty plate and leaned forward in his seat, elbows resting on his knees, his face intent upon hers.

"I learned some things I wish I didn't know and saw things I can't unsee now. But the truth needs to be known, and the world needs to see. Genevieve, I need your help."

CHAPTER 12

"Where shall we go? Delmonico's? Lüchow's? I don't think I can do Italian again so soon."

They were in Daniel's carriage, rumbling toward his house, the orange light of an early-evening sun streaming through the windows. The days were getting longer, a time of year he enjoyed thoroughly.

He'd had his fill of darkness.

To that end, he had what he knew was a somewhat unorthodox proposition for his fiancée.

"My staff do have the evening off, and Mrs. Rafferty left an entire meal," Daniel said. "Perhaps you would care to have dinner at my house? I know it is a bit of a risk, so I am happy to dine out if you prefer." Being alone at his house together before they were married was very much outside the bounds of propriety, but he didn't think anyone was watching his house or their behavior intently. Genevieve was far too old to need a chaperone, but he certainly didn't want her to feel uncomfortable.

Genevieve's face lit up in response, though, a sight that made his heart glow.

"I would indeed," she said, relaxing into his side. "And a cocktail first, if we may. I'll need time to digest all the cake I had today before I can move on to a proper meal."

"We absolutely may." Daniel pulled Genevieve closer, relishing the coziness of the warmly lit interior. She tilted her face up to his for a kiss, and he was more than happy to oblige.

Perhaps some other activities could occur before dinner as well.

"Daniel?" Her breath was a whisper against his lips.

"Yes?" He moved his own mouth down her delicate jawline, grinning in response to her gasp as he transferred his affections to her neck.

"Are you doing anything to prevent my becoming pregnant?"

His mouth froze.

Daniel slowly leaned back, taking in the sight of her. The woman he was to marry in less than a month.

Genevieve's cheeks were flushed, and her lips slightly parted. His hand had strayed to the back of her head without him noticing, and hair that had been neatly pinned was partially undone, tendrils hanging down the back of her neck.

They would have to fix that before they exited the carriage. It was one thing for an engaged couple to be affectionate in private, another to publicly display the signs of that affection.

"I am."

A deeper color than the flush of kissing infused Genevieve's face.

Dammit, he should have taken it upon himself to explain sooner. It wasn't fair that she had to ask.

Genevieve sat up straighter and braced her arm against the wall as the carriage rattled over a divot in the road, jostling her. "What? I would have seen a rubber, I'm sure."

The shock of the slang term coming from Genevieve's mouth doused his amorous mood as strongly as a bucket of cold water poured over his head. "How do you know what that is?" He tried and failed to keep his astonishment from showing.

Her chin tilted upward. "I read things. And I know people. Married people," she said pointedly. "It was Callie who told me," she added, seeming a bit reluctant.

That wasn't surprising.

"But not when you're thinking, not from her time as an artist's model. She actually told Eliza and me all about gentlemen's protectors when we were still in school. We found the information quite fascinating."

"I'm sure you did," Daniel said, a little flabbergasted at the idea of sixteen-year-old society girls discussing male contraceptives.

But why not? The girls in Five Points had surely known of such things.

"No, I do not use a rubber," Daniel said. He had removed his hat when they'd entered the carriage and now ran a hand through his hair, bemused.

Genevieve looked at him expectantly. "So, what are you using?"

"I . . ." *Spit it out, McCaffrey*, he told himself sternly.

Why were the words so hard to say?

"I don't complete the act inside of you," he finally said, forcing himself to not rush through the sentence. Anyone would think he was a green lad, the way he nearly stammered, rather than a grown man of thirty-six. "Does that make sense?"

Genevieve blinked at him and looked thoughtful. "I know the biology of how children are made. Yes, it makes sense."

Daniel exhaled mightily, unaware that he'd been holding his breath.

"I hadn't noticed you were doing this," she admitted.

"I bloody well hope not. I'd like to think you were otherwise occupied in the moment."

Her thoughtful expression turned a bit devilish. "Yes, I have very much been otherwise occupied during those moments, I believe."

"Good." Daniel blew out another breath and gathered Genevieve back into his arms. "I should have explained earlier. I hope I didn't cause you any worry."

"Not entirely. But you should know I am going to see a woman about getting some kind of method for myself."

Daniel pulled back again, alarm rearing. "That's not safe. Some of those women are watched by the police. You could get in serious trouble, Genevieve. Please, allow me to handle it."

"My mother will be with me. It is someone she knows and trusts. Surely you understand, Daniel. It's my body; I would feel far more comfortable if I were in control of when I do or do not become pregnant."

It was on the tip of his tongue to protest again, but Daniel held back. She was right. Genevieve should be the one who decided something that affected her own body.

"I do understand. But we are in this together now," he finally said. "I can help, if you'll let me." He tucked his chin over the top of her head, messing her hair further. Her own hat had long since been discarded, rolling around the base of the carriage. "Your mother being with you makes me feel better. It's ridiculous we even have to worry about your safety to acquire such items. Such a stupid law."

"Laws are made by people," she reminded him. "They can be undone. Shall we add it to the list of things we're working to change?"

"Absolutely," Daniel said. "But we'll focus on it a bit later, yes? I'd love to resume what we had started."

"Yes," Genevieve said, smiling broadly and turning her face toward his again. "Later."

Some time later indeed, Daniel had the enormous pleasure of regarding his future wife across the small writing table in his bed-chamber. He'd dragged the table in front of the fire for them, and now it was littered with the remains of the feast his cook had left: spring lamb with mint sauce and chilled asparagus partnered with crusty rolls and butter. He'd opened a crisp French white from his cellar, and they had just finished the chocolate éclairs Mrs. Rafferty had left for dessert.

"I don't know why we bother dining out when you have such an admirable cook here at home," she sighed.

Daniel smiled, utterly content. He had donned his dressing gown for their feast, but Genevieve, not wanting to bother with her frock and all its accoutrements just yet, was adorably clad in one of his shirts, her hair a tousled golden mass.

"Is this what married life will be like?" she asked, running a toe up his bare leg under the table.

"I've never been married. We can make it whatever we like. So, yes, if this is what we want, then this is what it shall be."

"We can make our marriage what we like," Genevieve repeated, as though testing the phrase. "I like that idea. Still, I suppose I ought to leave soon," she with a small sigh. "We're not married yet."

Genevieve looked longingly at the vast, now thoroughly rumpled, bed. Daniel followed her gaze. "I wish I could stay."

"As do I. But you're right, it is probably time for you to leave." Daniel stood with reluctance. "We got so carried away, I never did tell you about my day at the House of Refuge."

As he gathered their garments from where they had fallen on the floor—it took a long time to find Genevieve's left stocking, which eventually surfaced under the bed—Daniel filled her in on the events of the day: how he had questioned Connor about his movements the day of the fire and what he had discovered at the House of Refuge.

"The abuses have not ended," he said. Genevieve looked grim as she pulled on a petticoat. "What do you think? Is this something Arthur might let you write about?"

"I don't see why not," she said, tying the petticoat at the back. "I'll speak with him this week. I have news from my day also."

The worry Daniel had felt when Genevieve informed him that she would be visiting a contraceptive provider ballooned into alarm when he heard that the provider's delivery person had been present the night of the Sunflower Mission fire.

"It's not a good idea to meet this person, Genevieve," Daniel said. "We don't know that the deliveryman didn't start the fire;

people do all kinds of nefarious things for all kinds of reasons. Can you promise me not to speak to this man unless I am with you? Please. It would reassure me a great deal."

Genevieve looked suddenly wary. "Is this what married life will be like?" It was the same question as earlier, but now her voice was leaden instead of playful.

"Éclairs daily, you mean?" Daniel strove to lighten the mood. "I would probably have to raise Mrs. Rafferty's wages, and she is already very well compensated, but perhaps she could be persuaded."

Genevieve's face fell further, and instantly he knew it was the wrong tactic.

"No." She was clad only in a chemise and petticoat and folded her arms across her body. The self-protective gesture cut Daniel to the core, any attempts at levity instantly fleeing. "Is this what I have to expect? You, second-guessing my every move? What if the only time I can interview this person is when you're not available? I have to be able to do my job, Daniel, married or not."

"I am only trying to keep you safe. You have a tendency to find trouble, Genevieve. Or it finds you."

"You wouldn't say the same thing to a man."

"You're not a man! You're about to be my wife."

"I can handle myself, Daniel."

"That is not the question. There are situations, places, where I am sorry, but no, you cannot. Not because you are not capable, but because evil men walk among us." He was shouting now, but so was she.

"You think I don't know that?"

"I know you know that, so I don't understand why you won't let me *keep. You. Safe.*" He punctuated the last three words by slamming his palm on the table between them. The dishes jumped, but Genevieve did not. She unfolded her arms and smacked the table herself, once, hard, in response.

The dishes jumped again.

Daniel stared into Genevieve's furious amber eyes, furious himself. They stood facing each other, both breathing hard as though they'd been racing, the detritus of the beautiful meal strewn on the table between them, reduced to scraps of gristle and gobs of crème pâtissière on greasy plates.

Was there no way to make her understand? She held his very heart in her hands. If something were to happen to her, Daniel was sure it would instantly stop beating.

"Do you know how it felt," he said, no longer shouting, "when you were hanging off the East River Bridge? When a madman tried to dislodge you with a knife? Do you know what that did to me?"

Genevieve held his gaze for a silent beat.

"Probably very much what it did to me to see Tommy Meade about to shoot a bullet straight into your head."

Daniel was around the table in a flash. He held her close, resting his forehead against hers.

"And do you know how rare, how precious what we have is?"

She nodded.

"We cannot be cavalier with it. We cannot be cavalier with each other. That is why I want to accompany you when you interview this delivery person. I suspect it is the same reason you remain wary about Connor and his intentions toward me. Toward us."

Daniel heard her slight breath catch.

He waited.

"I'll do my best to wait."

It was such a Genevieve-like answer, Daniel burst out laughing. He couldn't help it.

"That is reasonable."

Genevieve pulled back from their embrace, a rueful smile on her face until she caught sight of a clock. "Gracious, I do need to leave. Help me get dressed." She picked up her corset from the floor and wrapped it over her chemise. "I can't redo this on my own."

Daniel stifled a groan. How was he supposed to tie the laces of her corset when all he wanted to do was *untie* them, lead her back to the giant bed they'd occupied only a short time earlier? Reminding himself that he'd lived through much worse conditions than unfulfilled, raging desire, Daniel turned her around and pulled the laces of the corset together.

"Not too tight," Genevieve murmured. He tied the ends loosely and helped her pulled her rumpled dress back up over her head, then set to work on the many tiny buttons marching up its back.

"You seem to know your way around a lady's garments," she remarked, turning to face him.

"I do, a little," he replied, pulling her close again. She pressed her face into his shirt, which was also considerably rumpled. "I like to flatter myself I'm not entirely wretched to look upon."

Genevieve snorted against his shirt.

Flashes of memory popped through his head, one after another projected like a lantern slideshow: the milky skin and wide eyes of his first love, a Five Points girl he'd known since he was a child, whom he'd sneaked through the back door of Jacob's mansion when he knew most of the servants were away. She'd been terrified of accidentally knocking over a lamp and had held her elbows close until he'd led her through the labyrinth of a house to his bedroom. The bouncing yellow curls and high, feminine laughter of a young heiress in Boston as he had laughingly chased her around his university quarters. The subtle curves and lean lines of Giselle, the mistress he'd kept for a time while in France. There were others, of course, women who wanted to be close to him, women who wanted to be close to his money.

None of them held a candle to Genevieve.

It wasn't self-aggrandizement. He knew he had been considered an extremely eligible bachelor since he'd inherited his fortune, but he had felt no desire to play the game and court any of the countless eager, beautiful women who could have been available to him. He had wanted no part in that. He just wanted to do what good work he could, help who he could with Jacob's money, and live a quiet life. He'd wanted nothing of marriage. Nothing of love.

Until now.

Was this what married life with Genevieve would be like?

Daniel took in the strewn bedclothes, the remains of the lovely dinner scattered across the table, the way Genevieve twisted her hair back into place while giving him a small, secret smile, undoubtedly remembering how it had become so mussed in the first place.

God, he hoped so.

Chapter 13

The midwifery clinic of Pearl Martin was, like most medical offices, discreetly tucked inside a plain brownstone. This particular brownstone, in turn, was modestly wedged between an inconspicuous laundry and a newer, more lavish hotel. It was a nondescript locale and address for what, on paper, was a nondescript business. Professional midwives had practices all over town, often calling themselves physicians in order to compete with the new medical field of obstetrics.

Genevieve wondered how many of the passersby knew that Madame Martin, as the practitioner was known, also dealt in contraceptives and, according to Anna, pregnancy termination.

"Before the quickening, as has always been done," her mother had said as she adjusted her hat before leaving the house that morning.

Genevieve squinted in the bright morning sunshine, taking in the unornamented facade. She'd forgotten a parasol, and the brim of her fashionable hat was too narrow to provide much shade.

"It's on the first floor," Anna said, stopping to close her own sensible parasol.

Was it her imagination, or did a curtain on the second floor of the brownstone twitch, as if someone had quickly stepped back to avoid being seen? Genevieve surveyed the street as Anna continued to fuss with her parasol's strap.

There was nothing out of the ordinary. The avenue was wide, and while it was not as busy as Broadway, a steady stream of New Yorkers flowed up and down the sidewalks on either side. Carriages of all sizes rumbled past. Genevieve stepped back as a young mother with a pram circled around them, nearly colliding with a harried-looking man who frowned at his watch as he dashed by.

More people than she could catalog hurried or strolled past, turning corners or slipping into buildings. Nobody paid them any particular mind.

Genevieve checked the second-floor window again.

The curtain was still.

Her mind must be playing tricks on her. She hadn't arrived home until two AM after her late night with Daniel, and was completely taken by surprise when Anna cheerfully woke her four hours later, announcing she'd managed to secure an early appointment for Genevieve with Madame Martin the night before.

And if there was someone watching them from the curtain, so what?

Maybe it was because they were about to engage in illegal activity, but Genevieve felt unconscionably uneasy. She flinched as the driver of a cab shouted suddenly, shaking his fist after a young boy who had darted across the street.

The distinctive blue of a police officer's uniform was on the far end of the block. She was too far away to make out the man's features, but he wasn't walking away or speaking to anyone or doing any of the other everyday tasks everyone else on the street was engaged in.

He was looking up the street.

Toward her and her mother.

Genevieve flinched again at the sound of the brownstone's front door opening at the top of the steps.

It was Prue. Her friend paused halfway down the steps, obviously just as startled to see Genevieve and Anna as they were to see her. She continued down the last few steps slowly.

"Genevieve, Mrs. Stewart. How nice to see you." There was the slightest tremor in her voice.

"And you, dearest Prudence," Anna said in a kind, reassuring tone. "I hope you are not unwell, though if so, you could not find yourself in better hands. Madame Martin is a wonderful physician."

A slight blush rose in Prue's cheeks. "I am well enough, and thank you for asking. Yes, Madame Martin has been most accommodating."

Anna nodded and patted Prue's arm.

"I apologize I have not called yet; my work has suddenly become very busy," Genevieve said. She *had* wanted to call on Prue, but between the fires and her investigation, she had quite forgotten about her promise.

"I'm not going anywhere. Perhaps tomorrow, if you have time?"

"Let's plan on it," Genevieve said. "If something arises, though, I'll be sure to send a note."

"It must be wonderful to live such a life that something unexpected could arise. My days are quite routine, I'm afraid. I'll have to read something interesting beforehand to make our visit less dull."

"Nonsense, Prudence," Anna interjected. "Genevieve could use a break from some of the excitement of late. Besides, the wedding is just around the corner. You can give her all kinds of advice on the ways of a young wife."

Prue's face turned from red to white. "Of course," she murmured. "You're welcome anytime, Genevieve. If you'll excuse me, I must be on my way."

Genevieve watched as Prue hurriedly walked to the corner. She hailed a cab and then glanced over her shoulder at them before climbing in.

Anna started up the steps and Genevieve followed, checking the opposite end of the block before they entered the establishment.

The police officer was gone.

The interior of Pearl Martin's office and clinic were as respectable and unassuming as the exterior, as was the woman herself. Of medium stature, sporting dark hair overlaid with silver pulled into a neat style, Madame Martin wore a serviceable navy dress and had a pair of spectacles on the bridge of her nose.

To Genevieve's surprise, Madame Martin and her mother embraced.

"Anna, how good to see you. And this is your daughter. I prepared some tea. Unless you'd prefer coffee? Or something cold?" She spoke with the barest hint of a French accent, gesturing toward the tea service laid on a side table in a lovely sitting room.

Genevieve did not know what she had expected, but this elegant woman was not it. She found herself accepting tea, even though she vastly preferred coffee. This was far more of a social visit than she'd anticipated.

"I didn't know you two were so well acquainted," she said, allowing Madame Martin to add three sugars to her tea.

The two older women exchanged an amused glance.

"Well, once you've shared a prison cell together, you become quite friendly indeed." Madame Martin smiled.

Ah, that made sense. "Eighteen eighty-one?" Genevieve guessed. Over a dozen women had been led away in handcuffs during that incident; Genevieve didn't realize Pearl Martin had been among them.

"That's correct," Madame Martin said. "Your mother regaled us all with the details of your upcoming wedding. I was so sorry to hear it was canceled, but it all worked out for the best, correct?

Your mother says you are engaged once again. And the wedding is soon, no?"

"Yes, in three weeks."

Madame Martin beamed. "Wonderful news; congratulations. Now, why don't you and I take our tea to my office to discuss a few things. Anna, I have some of the latest European pamphlets on the question of the vote that may interest you."

Genevieve followed Madame Martin to an equally well-appointed study across the hall, where her hostess settled herself behind a sturdy oak desk. Medical texts and treatises on women's rights lined a tall bookshelf to her left.

"May I speak frankly? Your mother says you would like to prevent becoming pregnant."

Genevieve took a deep breath. "Not forever. But I'd like to enjoy simply being married, to start."

"Very understandable. Is there a chance you could be pregnant now?"

The blunt question was a surprise.

"I . . . I don't think so. My fiancé, he . . . doesn't complete the act," she said, unsure if she was using the correct language.

"Ah, coitus interruptus. Not ideal; only somewhat effective. But as you're so close to being wed, it is less of a concern. Now, let us find you something that will work better until you are ready for motherhood."

Madame Martin proceeded to speak of a whole array of devices women could use to avoid pregnancy, pulling examples out of drawers behind her desk and laying them out neatly. She was so matter-of-fact about the whole endeavor that Genevieve soon forgot her embarrassment and began asking questions and learning words that were new to her, an entire category of instruments that went by a variety of names: pessary, diaphragm, womb veil, lady's shield, French cap.

"Would you use a syringe as well as a device to block the cervix?" she asked, picking up the example Madame Martin had laid before her and examining it curiously.

"You could, though the diaphragm is quite effective on its own."

It didn't *feel* like she was engaging in illegal activity, in this pleasant, nicely decorated office, speaking with an intelligent, interesting woman about basic anatomy and human biology. Genevieve wondered which of her friends knew about such things. Esmie? She had openly wanted to become pregnant as soon as possible after marriage, so perhaps not. Callie, very likely. But she was in Chicago, and this was not the kind of thing one could discuss via letter.

Prue?

Genevieve tucked the thought away for later. With Madame Martin's help, she made a selection she felt would satisfy.

"Madame Martin, before we return to my mother, may I ask you something else?"

"Of course," the older woman said, pausing as she tucked the various samples back into her desk. "Shall I leave these out?"

"No, it is a different matter." Genevieve explained about the Sunflower Mission fire and about the delivery intended for Josie. Madame Martin went pale when she heard her delivery person had been seen.

"That was my nephew, Antoine. He heard about the fire, and we were both relieved he was gone before the authorities arrived. It seemed a near miss, but it appears we were not so lucky as we thought. It is very bad he was seen, very bad indeed."

"Both the woman who saw him and the intended recipient of the delivery are well aware of the sensitivity of the matter," Genevieve started.

"Sensitivity?" Madame Martin interrupted. "The danger, you mean. You have seen how your own mother was treated for simply speaking publicly about these things." She gestured to the items on the desk. "Distribution is a far graver offense. If discovered, I should be sent to prison for a very long time."

"They do understand, as do I. I didn't mean to minimize the risks."

"I questioned Antoine about this fire myself already. He claims he saw no one and nothing."

"Might I please ask him myself? I may be able to jog a memory you could not. Please, as a personal favor." Genevieve was close to begging.

Madame Martin raised one impeccably groomed, thick, dark eyebrow. "But why? You cannot write a story about this, no? Even if Antoine did see something, publicly revealing this would implicate all of us." Her long, elegant hand swept around the room in a gesture meant to include both herself and Genevieve, but also Anna in the waiting room, Marla and Josie in Brooklyn, and the countless other women Madame Martin assisted.

Genevieve couldn't tell Madame Martin she suspected they were dealing with a serial arsonist. Despite Daniel's reassurances, she was certain the two fires had been set by the same person.

She just needed proof. If she found that, had a suspect she could point to, she could leave the name anonymously for Detective Longstreet. Antoine, Josie, Marla, Madame Martin . . . their names need never come up.

Nor hers.

"I asked for a favor, which was wrong of me," Genevieve said instead. "I realize it is I who owe you that courtesy, not the other way around. But I am asking that you trust me, as Anna's daughter. I have a personal interest in knowing who might have started that fire, and frankly I worry they may do so again. I promise not to implicate you or your business in any way."

Madame Martin regarded her over her spectacles for a long, tense moment, lips pursed.

"Very well. Antoine will be here tonight, around eight. If you come then, you may ask him a few questions, but only with me present. I am trusting you, Genevieve."

The relief she felt was surprising in its intensity. "Thank you, Madame Martin. I promise no harm will come to either of you."

Genevieve had no idea if Antoine would be able to help or not, but simply having a lead, a direction to pursue, was calming.

Madame Martin gave a Gallic shrug and sighed. "I am not sure that is a promise you can keep, *chérie*. But I believe you will do your best, and if a fire-starting monster is on the loose, it is our moral duty to try to stop him. Also, I am expecting a delivery this afternoon. When you return, you can pick up the items you ordered."

Genevieve's appointment with the Brooklyn fire marshal was at two PM. She had plenty of time to get there and back before eight.

Her earlier exhaustion was swept away by the momentum of planning. Genevieve was so distracted as she made her good-bye to Madame Martin that Anna poked her side, something her mother hadn't done since she was still in school. Genevieve didn't care; she was too busy thinking about the busy afternoon and evening ahead of her: how she would deflect Marshal Keller, what questions she would ask Antoine, where she could find a quick bite to eat in between.

"Stay calm and follow my lead," her mother hissed quietly as they descended the brownstone steps.

"What?"

"Hello, ladies."

Genevieve stopped short on the bottom step, her breath catching.

The brass buttons of Officer Jackson's uniform gleamed in the clear sunshine. Genevieve couldn't stop from frowning when she saw him; she had had two unfortunate dealings with the man in the past.

She'd recognize his ridiculous giant moustache anywhere.

"Good day, Officer." Anna nodded at the man and continued around him, as though they were simply passing each other on the street. Genevieve hurried to follow suit, then forced her steps to slow.

"Mrs. Stewart, a moment of your time, please."

Anna paused. She took her time turning to face the officer, her brows raised in query.

He tilted his head up the steps. "You've been to see Madame Martin?"

Her mother's brows rose another millimeter, then lowered. "I don't see why it is a concern of the police, but yes. Pearl Martin is an old friend, and provides excellent care for women's needs."

"What types of needs would those be?" Officer Jackson's overall expression was bland, but there was a cruel gleam in his eyes.

He wanted to embarrass them.

Anna folded her hands around the handle of her parasol, which she'd yet to open, in front of her like a club. "How kind of you to ask. I did think I had gone through the change—you seem an educated man; you know what that is, do you not?" She didn't wait for an answer. "So many young men are ignorant of female anatomy. Old men too, for that matter. But where was I? Ah, yes, my monthly courses. I thought they'd stopped for good, you see. But apparently not quite yet. I did experience—"

"Mrs. Stewart, please," Officer Jackson interrupted her. He looked utterly horrified.

"Oh, did you want to know about my daughter's courses instead of mine? She gets terrible pains in her midsection every month, has since her cycle started. Madam Martin was able to offer some wonderful herbal relief. Miss Stewart is getting married soon, and we wouldn't want any affiliated pains to tarnish the day, would we?"

Officer Jackson had two red patches high on his cheeks. Passersby who overheard snippets of Anna's speech gave their group a startled look before hurrying on. One well-dressed boy of about thirteen turned bright red and stared at them over his shoulder with wide eyes.

"Have you no modesty, ma'am?" The officer interrupted again. Instead of cruelly amused, he now looked furious.

Anna blinked at him innocently. "You asked why we were here, sir. I am doing my best to answer your question, Officer . . . ?"

"This is Officer Jackson, Mother," Genevieve said, arching her own brow at the policeman. "He was at the house last year. When you were in Newport, and we had the unfortunate incident with the peeper?"

"That was unfortunate indeed, Officer Jackson," Anna sniffed. "It did take your department so long to catch the perpetrator."

The policeman eyed them both coldly. "I am a member in good standing of the Society for the Suppression of Vice, ma'am. We have our eye on Madame Martin, as she is suspected of dealing in illegal contraband."

Genevieve went cold. Officer Jackson must have been the policeman she had seen at the far end of the block before they entered.

"Surely members of the society, not to mention those of our city's esteemed police force, have better things to do than stop and question women on the street coming from a medical appointment?" Anna's voice was as icy as Genevieve felt. "Or do I need to make your superiors aware of your behavior?"

A long moment passed as the two stared at each other, their mutual dislike palpable.

Jackson broke first. He gave one curt nod, then turned his back on them both, barking at a jaywalker.

Genevieve joined her mother, briskly walking in the opposite direction from the still-yelling policeman. Anna snapped open her parasol with more aggression than necessary.

They didn't speak.

The excitement Genevieve had felt earlier at being able to speak with Antoine curdled, colored by wariness, and her afternoon and evening plans suddenly loomed as potentially treacherous. It was as though she were picking her way across the edges of a frozen pond, unsure which parts were safe to traverse.

She would have to tread even more carefully now. There were more lives than her own at stake.

CHAPTER 14

Early spring was not typically Daniel's favorite season. While he enjoyed the lengthening days and the warming air, spring in New York also meant increased rain, which led to near rivers of mud in some streets. The temperatures varied wildly, and one never knew how heavy a coat one might need. He associated the Easter holiday with childhood memories of being forced to sit through more hours of church than normal in a starched collar, and while there might be cake, there also might not be, if they couldn't afford it.

But today, the city was showing off. Today was the sort of spring day that inspired poets: the sky was a nearly eye-watering blue, the warmth of a gentle breeze was akin to a lover's caress, and fat clusters of bright-purple redbud blooms dotted the tree-lined streets.

The only word for the day was glorious.

Daniel had already been brimming with good feelings before he stepped outside, and now it seemed his cup might truly run over. He was on his way to meet Rupert at his tailor's, where he would undergo the final fitting for his wedding suit. While it would probably not be nearly as exciting as Genevieve's appointment with her dressmaker had been—the groom, he knew, was a visual afterthought in the whole affair, mostly there to punctuate the elaborateness of the bride's costume—he was so delighted to be marrying Genevieve there was an anticipatory spring in his step.

Especially after last night.

He made it five blocks before his good mood plummeted.

Dammit.

Someone was on his tail.

Daniel kept walking, but all his satisfied feelings about the day drained in an instant, replaced with frustrated aggravation.

The indistinct form of a man in a dark coat had been a consistent shadow at his back, appearing as a wavering reflection in shop windows for most of his walk, following just a hair too close.

When he rounded a corner, so did the shadow.

And again.

It was probably a journalist, and not the reputable sort. His and Genevieve's wedding was scheduled to be an enormous, high-profile affair. Daniel didn't really mind, not as much as Genevieve did, but they both were drawing a bit of unwanted attention these days as a result of the early press coverage.

He abruptly turned another corner, this one out of his way, just to be contrary.

The shadow followed.

Yes, it was almost certainly a reporter from one of the city's more gossipy rags. Maybe the *World*.

Daniel suppressed a sigh as he weighed his options.

Confronting the bugger might only give the journalist fodder for an unflattering piece. He didn't want to do that to the Stewarts, not with the wedding so close.

Let him follow. He'd see Daniel through the tailor's front window, then he and Rupert would disappear into the back fitting areas, out of sight. It was irksome, but no harm could come of it.

But what if the shadow wasn't a journalist?

Memory of the searing heat of the fire in Dagmar's studio, of the way the chair wedged underneath the darkroom's doorknob had nearly trapped them, took hold and wouldn't let go.

No, he wouldn't let whoever this was trail him about the city. Even if their motivations were innocent, he had as much a right to privacy as the next person.

And what if they're not innocent?

Though it hadn't been his plan, Daniel had made a fortuitous choice in his last turn. He knew this block well.

Daniel forced himself to keep his pace even and constant, barely allowing his eyes to slide right as he passed the next shop, a butcher's this time. But he still managed to catch the mirage of the figure behind him, gruesomely silhouetted against the hanging display of dripping, bloody hunks of meat.

Without slowing his pace or giving any indication of altering course, Daniel abruptly pivoted and entered a shop in the center of the block just past a narrow alley. The bell above chimed his arrival, and the door made a soft thump as it closed behind him.

At the counter, Giuseppe looked up from his work in surprise. "Good to see you, Mr. McCaffrey. I have some fine new pieces in from Switzerland." Giuseppe Ricci was the finest watch importer and repair person in the city, and Daniel was a loyal customer.

"Today isn't a shopping visit, I'm sorry to say. Might I use your side entrance?"

"Through the back," Giuseppe said, turning his attention back to the eyepiece focused on the delicate inner workings of a watch laid on his counter.

"Thanks. I'll be back next week to pick up the pieces I ordered." Daniel had selected several beautiful pocket watches as wedding gifts for the men of the Stewart family as well as one for Rupert.

Giuseppe barely nodded, waving Daniel back distractedly.

The back was a tiny storeroom lined with shelves and filled with boxes. To his right was the door he'd thought would be there, leading into the alley.

Daniel cracked it open. Unsurprisingly for a watchmaker, the hinges were beautifully oiled and made not a sound.

The shadow figure was there, solid as you like. He peered around the corner, back hunched, waiting for Daniel to emerge from the front, then pulled back slightly as a noisy group of schoolchildren raced past, shrieking.

The figure's profile flashed in his movement. Daniel swore out loud, and the man flinched.

"Connor."

His brother's right shoulder hitched a little, then dropped. "Oh, hey, Danny."

"Why are you following me?" Just saying the words made the back of his neck prickle. Daniel hated being followed.

Connor shrugged. "Was waiting for you, I guess. I didn't get work today, wanted to see what you were up to."

"You were in front of my house." Daniel stated the fact rather than asked. "Why didn't you ring the bell?"

"I dunno." This time Connor shrugged both shoulders. Despite being a grown man, he suddenly looked six again, idly kicking a pebble in the alley. "It didn't feel right. Guess I was a little shy to ring the bell, it's such a grand house." A wistful expression passed across his face, and he gave a short laugh. "Can't believe you and Maggie wound up there. You should see where I grew up."

Daniel's heart twisted, but he quashed the feeling. He hadn't been lying to Genevieve; he really did think this man was his brother.

But that didn't mean he trusted him.

"So because you were shy, you decided to follow me? How is that better than ringing the bell?"

That shoulder hitch again.

"I dunno. Where you going?"

Daniel gave up, sighing. "I am meeting my friend Rupert at the tailor's. You remember Rupert?"

"Can I come?" Connor's wistful, diffident expression turned to an eager one.

Daniel hesitated. It wouldn't be entirely fair to spring Connor on Rupert, the latter of whom shared Genevieve's suspicion of this stranger. On the other hand, it was his fitting, and if he wanted his brother there, it was up to him.

Connor shifted his weight between his feet and looked at him hopefully.

The sun was shining, the temperature was warming, and the memory of the night before all buoyed Daniel out of his irritation.

"Sure, come on," he said.

A wide grin broke across Connor's face.

"I'm sorry I didn't ring your doorbell," Connor said as they exited the alley and fell into step with each other. "That was dumb. But I've seen that lady who answers the door; she's a little intimidating."

"Mrs. Kelly wouldn't harm a fly," Daniel protested. But he supposed his housekeeper could appear that way to an outsider, especially one who wasn't used to a household staff. "Besides, she's from Five Points too."

"Yeah?"

"Yeah. All of my staff are."

Connor's elbow dug into his side for a moment. "Look at you. *Staff.* So fancy."

Daniel hesitated again. It was hard to think about how his life had gone one way and those of his siblings another. Yes, he had spent the latter part of his youth living in luxury and relative comfort, but there had been great loneliness, and loss, and sorrow. Especially after Maggie's death.

He did, and didn't, want to know what Connor had experienced, but the words slipped out of his mouth before he could stop them.

"Tell me about where you grew up."

The look Connor sent his way was a mix of wariness and hope. "You really wanna hear?"

"I do."

"And about Mary? And Stephen?"

The names were like arrows to his heart. "Were you together?"

"No."

"Then just you. Save the others for another day."

Were the little ones, who would now be as grown as Connor, even alive? Dead? He couldn't bear hearing, not quite yet.

As Connor relayed stories of his childhood on a farm in Minnesota, Daniel tried to envision it. He had never traveled farther west than Chicago, though he had read about the beauty of that region. He took it all in: How Connor had been afraid of the cows, at first. How he had been homesick. How he had been afraid he'd forget his mother's face, and those of his siblings, as he had forgotten his dad's.

"I made myself remember, every day. Wrote some of the stories down, even. I never liked school much, but I stayed long enough to learn what I needed to run a farm. The Lunds didn't have any of their own kids, planned on leaving me the place."

"They've passed?"

"Yeah." Connor's voice tightened, but it sounded as if it came from anger rather than grief. Daniel would circle back to whatever emotion was there another day; this was all he could stand to hear for now.

"And your farm?"

Connor hitched his shoulder quickly, then settled it. "Sold it. I never fit in. They were decent to me; I always had enough to eat, warm enough clothes. It was good land, but it had debts. There wasn't much left after the sale, once I took care of those."

"How long ago was that?"

Connor squinted at the sun. "Four years. I spent some time in San Francisco, worked on the docks. Guess I always knew I'd come back to New York someday. It's home, you know?"

Daniel did know.

"We've an addition to the day, I see," Rupert said when Daniel arrived with Connor in tow, looking down his long nose at the other man. Rupert was taller than Connor, but Connor was broader, thicker through the chest.

"Hey, Rupert. Good to see you." Connor swallowed and looked around the fine tailor shop. He tugged a little at the kerchief around his neck.

"Let me get you something," Daniel said impulsively. "To wear to the wedding."

"Nah, that's okay. I've got a nice suit of clothes. Had it for my parents' funeral."

"A necktie, at least. You're the brother of the groom; you ought to have something new."

Over Connor's shoulder, Daniel caught Rupert's shocked look.

"Okay. I guess." A pleased flush graced Connor's cheeks.

Back on the street, after Daniel's fitting, Connor turned to them both.

"Hey, let me buy you a drink, to thank you. And to celebrate." The new blue silk necktie, delicately wrapped, was tucked in a box under his arm.

"I really should be getting on," Rupert started, but Connor threw his free arm around Rupert's shoulders. Rupert stiffened, giving Daniel an incredulous look.

"Come on, Rupert, you can't back out now. I know you're not above a drink in a dive. I know just the place, not far from here."

Daniel stifled a laugh as Rupert reluctantly acquiesced, especially once he saw Daniel was game. Connor was correct: Rupert wasn't above a drink in a dive.

The bar Connor selected was nearby, right off the docks on East Twenty-Eighth Street, its front full of peeling paint with a faded, swinging sign proclaiming it *The Knotty Anchor*. It was packed with longshoremen in shirtsleeves and vests, several with bright red kerchiefs around their necks like Connor. His brother nodded at a few men lined up at the bar before taking over a rickety table near the back. "It's on me. What do you want? The lager isn't bad, I promise."

Daniel leaned back in his seat as Connor moved to the bar to get their drinks. It was good to see Connor enjoying himself, bantering with the bartender, slapping someone he knew on the back in greeting, glancing over his shoulder once to nod at Daniel. It reminded him, again, of when they were young, of how eager Connor had been to show his big brother an interestingly shaped rock, or how he could write his name.

"You really think it's him, don't you?" Rupert said. He turned to find his friend studying him closely.

Before Daniel could answer, a large group of sailors stumbled in, and the noise level increased exponentially. The space around them was suddenly packed with unwashed bodies, each clamoring for their drink order to be heard.

"Just docked," Connor yelled over the din as he squeezed his way through the crowd, setting three less-than-full pints onto the table. "These got a little jostled, sorry."

Daniel nearly fell out of his seat as two sailors shoved each other playfully, one crashing into him.

"Sorry, friend," the sailor grinned over his shoulder before turning back to his roughhousing.

"Maybe we should leave," Rupert called from across the small table, picking up his drink as the same pair shoved against their table, almost toppling it.

"Watch it now," Connor called to the men, who paid him no mind. "What's the matter," he said to Rupert. "Can't handle a little action?"

"Action is fine," Rupert said, standing up and moving closer to the wall. More men joined in the playful shoving, whooping and cackling with glee. They were obviously full of pent-up energy, their pockets full of pay. "Chaos is something else entirely."

Connor eyed Rupert over the rim of his glass, a smirk Daniel didn't like playing on the corners of his mouth. Rupert stared back steadily, his own mouth a thin line of dislike.

Daniel jerked himself away from the roiling crowd in time to avoid getting an elbow to the side of the head. Was he going to have to insert himself between his brother and his oldest friend? They reminded him of a pair of alley cats sizing each other up.

Rupert caught Daniel's eye and jerked his head toward the back door. Daniel pointed back at his half-drunk pint glass. Rupert's mouth thinned further but he nodded, then pointed in that direction and held up a finger to indicate he'd be back in a moment.

"Oy, you men," came a roaring voice. The sailors mostly stilled, though a few gave each other final shoves as though they were schoolboys who had been called to order. The bartender, who bore the weathered skin and broad shoulders of a former seaman himself, stood on the bar holding a stout wooden baseball bat. "If you want your drink, you'll stop that nonsense and line up sensible-like. First drink is on me, but only if there's no ruckus."

The sailors cheered their approval but then formed themselves into reasonable clumps to get their drinks, their former din reduced to a low, genial rumble of chatter.

"See, they don't mean any harm. Bet your friend the earl hasn't been among too many who work the docks before," said Connor, taking Rupert's vacated seat.

"He should be back by now." Daniel frowned at the back of the bar, wondering if the place had indoor plumbing or if Rupert had gone to the alley to relieve himself.

"He's just cooling off. Mad I pointed out how he was scared."

"Rupert is many things, but a coward isn't one of them."

"He's a snob."

"Sometimes. But not today."

"Why are you friends with a guy like that? 'Cause he's a lord?"

Daniel took a long drink of his lager, which, as Connor had promised, wasn't bad. He wasn't going to try to explain his long and complex history with Rupert in this sailor's bar across from the docks.

"I'm going to find him." Daniel pushed himself up from table.

"No, don't go. Hey, I was just kidding. I didn't mean anything."

"I'll be right back, but I want to make sure Rupert is all right. This is too long for him to have been gone."

"Maybe he just left. You know, went home."

"He wouldn't have without saying good-bye."

"Come on, let me get you another drink," Connor called after him as Daniel wove his way between sailors, heading toward the back.

There was a funny feeling in the pit of his stomach he didn't like.

Sure enough, there weren't any facilities in the bar, but there was a back door propped open with a brick. Daniel pushed it open, looking left and right along the grimy alley.

There was no sign of Rupert.

The funny feeling rippled into alarm.

"Where'd he go?" Connor pushed out the door behind him, empty pint glass in hand, surveying the empty alley. "Smells back here. Come back in; I'll get us two more."

Daniel's eyes narrowed. Why was Connor so insistent he not find Rupert?

"Rupert?" Daniel called, ignoring his brother. He walked into the alley, wrinkling his nose. Connor was right: it did smell back here, like stale urine and rotting fish.

"I really think he went home, Danny." Connor looked back through the open slice of bar door wistfully.

The alley was so narrow it could scarcely be called such; it was really more an unpaved walkway between the two buildings. If Daniel looked straight up, a narrow sliver of just-darkening sky was visible, but otherwise the brick on either side climbed upward relentlessly, clammy and damp.

One way opened onto Twenty-Eighth Street. The other angled until two buildings nearly met, in that haphazard way of old structures, with a passage so small only rats could squeeze through.

Daniel took a few careful steps in that direction, eyeing a pile of sodden, useless crates, stacked and slowly disintegrating.

"There's nothing there, Danny. Just junk."

Connor was still standing in the bar's doorway.

A low moan arose from behind the crates.

"Rupert?" Daniel ran the last few steps.

It was Rupert, curled into himself, eyes closed, a trickle of blood running down his face.

"Aw, jeez. He doesn't look so good." Connor was peering around his shoulder.

The pint glass in Connor's hand fell and shattered into thousands of glittering shards as Daniel grabbed his brother's shirt in two fists and slammed him against the brick.

"What the hell did you do, Connor?"

CHAPTER 15

The excitement that had driven away Genevieve's earlier tiredness was long gone. She was still excited, she supposed, but the lack of sleep was making itself known in her heavy muscles and drooping eyelids.

She shook herself in the confines of the cab. She wanted all her faculties about her as she questioned Antoine.

The meeting in Brooklyn with Marshal Keller, so generously arranged by Daniel through Chief Kincaid, had been a useless exercise. Marshal Keller himself was a perfectly nice man, and it was obvious he took his job seriously. He had looked at her kindly through his wire-rimmed spectacles, hands folded over a robust belly, but sternly told her it was her civic and moral duty to share any information about the fire she might have. He had heard Marla Willis's story and wanted to know how Genevieve had come by her additional knowledge.

As she could no longer tell him about what Marla Willis saw, for fear of incriminating Pearl and Antoine, she had lied. Shamelessly.

"I am following up a connection between the Sunflower Mission House fire and another fire at a photographer's studio in New York, that of Dagmar Hansen," she had said. This wasn't, actually, a complete lie, but she had not spoken with her editor about pursuing this line of inquiry.

Marshal Keller's brow had wrinkled. "I thought you had specific information about the Mission House fire. I did interview one of the residents who said she saw a man. Do you know more about that?"

"I do not," Genevieve said, crossing her toes within her boots.

His frown deepened. "I misunderstood, then. So, in what way might the two fires be connected?"

Genevieve had then rambled unconvincingly and, she felt, incoherently, about how both of the fires had occurred at places centered around social reform. Marshal Keller nodded indulgently, but she could tell he was humoring her.

She had slunk away, humiliated, but there was nobody to blame for her embarrassment but herself. She had painted herself into a corner with that meeting and hadn't seen a good way to get out of it.

I should have feigned an illness, Genevieve thought, slouching low in her seat at the memory. The uncaring city rolled passed outside her cab window. *One that lasted for months.*

Genevieve had tried to reach Daniel to tell him about her appointment, wanting to honor her promise to him that she would try to wait until he could accompany her to interview Madame Martin's deliveryman, but she couldn't find him anywhere. He wasn't at home, nor at his club. She checked at her house, and he hadn't left a message. Mrs. Kelly said he had had a tailor's appointment and was meant to meet Rupert, but when she went there, he had long since departed, and by the time she reached her last stop, the Bradley mansion on Fifth Avenue, night was falling.

"Rupert left ages ago," Esmie said when Genevieve found her in the drawing room. It was the one with the paintings of misbehaving cherubs on the ceiling, which always made Genevieve smile. "I have no idea where they are, but Rupert did say he would be home for dinner, so I expect him at any time. Won't you and Daniel join us?"

"I'm afraid I have a late appointment I must rush off to, but let's do so later this week. Are you feeling up to Delmonico's?"

"Am I ever. My queasiness has mostly departed, and I'm constantly ravenous. Do not be surprised if I order two desserts for myself and eat yours as well."

"We'll order as much as you like." Genevieve smiled.

But now she was wishing she had been able to stay.

Between her morning appointment with Madame Martin, the long trek across the East River Bridge to downtown Brooklyn and back, a quick stop for a sandwich and coffee at a café, her fruitless search for Daniel, and now heading back to Madame Martin's, Genevieve was depleted. She had crisscrossed the entire city and its environs all day, and her afternoon coffee had long since worn off.

When she exited the cab at the base of the stone steps of Madame Martin's brownstone, Genevieve instinctively glanced up at the curtain that had moved earlier today.

It was still.

She flinched as the carriage clattered away loudly.

Don't be a ninny.

Was Officer Jackson still lurking about? She didn't see him, but it was fully dark now, doorways and recessed areas near the buildings that lined the wide avenue shrouded in shadow despite the streetlamps.

Park Avenue was by no means abandoned; there were plenty of people still striding down its broad sidewalks.

And yet an uncomfortable prickle traveled down the back of Genevieve's neck.

She hastily made her way toward the warm glow of lamplight visible through the cream-colored curtains in Madame Martin's front window.

"Miss Stewart, Genevieve, this is my nephew, Antoine," Once she was settled inside with some tea, Madame Martin introduced a young man with slick jet-black hair above dark eyes in a narrow face. "Tell her what you saw, Antoine. We can trust Mademoiselle Stewart."

Despite his aunt's assurances, Antoine eyed Genevieve with suspicion, but he spoke anyway. "I did see a man the night I tried to deliver the package to the Sunflower Mission House." Antoine's accent was far stronger than his aunt's. "It was alarming, as usually very few are out at that hour, and as you know, discretion is very important for our work."

Genevieve's heartbeat stepped up a notch. *Two* men had been near the mission house? "Were you able to see his face?"

"*Non.* He was walking away from the house, very fast. But he was quite large, very big in the shoulders." This matched the person Marla had described. "I smelled smoke, heard people yelling as I was approaching the building. You know I cannot be found by the authorities, not with what I was delivering. I ran around the block and pulled the alarm. It was all I could do."

"I understand," Genevieve reassured him. "And nobody was hurt, all the residents got out in time, and the fire didn't spread."

"Yes, we read this in the newspapers. It was a relief. If you will excuse me, I must start my deliveries. I did not see anything else that night."

"Of course. Thank you for meeting me."

"So, Genevieve," Pearl said after her nephew departed. "Was he helpful?"

"He was. The person he described matches what the other witness saw." Genevieve ruminated on this. Two eyewitnesses saw a figure leaving the site of the fire just before its eruption, probably the same individual. They had a rough physical picture of the man but nothing else: no hair color, ethnicity, identifying features. And she still couldn't go to the authorities with the information, as doing so could potentially lead back to Antoine and Madame Martin.

Whatever had happened with the Sunflower Mission House fire, she would have to solve it herself.

Including whether the fire in Brooklyn and that which had almost killed Daniel and Dagmar were related. But without help from the authorities, it would be impossible to round up witnesses from the incident at Dagmar's studio. That fire had occurred during a busy afternoon, when Franklin Street was full of people.

Genevieve suppressed a sigh of frustration. She was too tired to try to unravel these possibly disconnected threads tonight. It would be best to go home, get some rest, and reconvene with Daniel tomorrow.

Besides, the wedding was only weeks away. There was much to do on that front as well.

"I am glad he was helpful. Now, this afternoon I did receive a delivery of the items we discussed earlier today. These deliveries have to be accomplished in person, very carefully, as you know it is illegal to send such things through the mail. It is why Antoine is often so busy." Madame Martin did not bother to suppress her sigh. "You have enough tea, yes? I keep the supplies in the cellar and will be right back."

Thankful she would be on her way to her comfortable bed soon, Genevieve helped herself to more tea, adding three lumps of sugar.

Minutes passed.

She wondered what her family's cook was making for dinner. When she had stopped by her house to check if Daniel had left word, she had told Nellie she would be home late and asked her to put a plate aside.

At the thought of dinner, her stomach rumbled. The café sandwich had been hours ago and, truth be told, not the best sandwich she'd ever had.

Why hadn't Madame Martin thought fit to include cookies with the tea?

Genevieve idly wandered to the bookshelves, taking in the titles. There was some Dickens, she noted, scattered among the anatomy textbooks.

She checked her timepiece. Ten minutes had passed since Pearl had left to get Genevieve's order.

Surely grabbing a few supplies from the basement didn't require that long.

Maybe Pearl was unwell, needed the facilities?

Genevieve selected *David Copperfield*, opened to a random page, and began to read.

All the colours of my life were changing. Soon she was sucked back into the story of David's adventure.

Her stomach grumbled, louder this time. Genevieve checked the time again.

Twenty minutes now.

Something was wrong.

Genevieve ventured into the hallway.

"Madame Martin?"

Silence answered.

She moved down the hall, her footsteps muffled on the thick runner. "Madame Martin? Pearl?"

There was still no answer.

The stairway was on her left, a small doorway on her right. This was probably a water closet. She knocked softly. "Pearl? Are you unwell? May I help?" Genevieve pushed the door open.

She had been correct: a small water closet was within, lined with a dizzyingly patterned red-and-white floral wallpaper. But it was empty.

If this brownstone was laid out like most, the kitchen would be at the end of the hall, and the door to the cellar should be under the stairs.

Genevieve went farther down the hall. Sure enough, she found an empty kitchen at the back of the house, the cooling remains of a roast chicken resting on a scrubbed wooden table in the center of the room and several dirty plates piled in the sink. It seemed Pearl and Antoine had eaten their evening meal before Genevieve's arrival but hadn't had time to finish cleaning. If Pearl had domestic help, and Genevieve suspected she did, they did not live in and had gone home for the day.

Retreating from the kitchen, Genevieve turned to the door at the back of the stairs. It was closed.

Genevieve peered down the hallway she had traversed. She listened hard.

Nothing.

"Pearl?" she tried again.

Her voice echoed through the seemingly empty house.

Maybe she should try upstairs.

No, Pearl had said she was going to the cellar, so it made the most sense to check there first. Genevieve turned the knob to the door. Though it was unreasonable, she half expected it to be locked.

The door opened easily.

The scent of earth and damp filled the hallway. A set of old stone steps led down, and while she couldn't see anything save a stone wall from her vantage point at the top of the stairs, the space glowed with the warm light of a kerosene lamp.

"Madame Martin? Pearl? Is anything amiss?"

Still no answer.

Swallowing hard, Genevieve slowly ventured down the stairs. Halfway down she paused, looking over her shoulder at the open door leading back to the empty hallway.

Was that the creak of a floorboard?

She didn't like this. She didn't like any of this. But if there was a lit lamp in the basement, Pearl had been down here.

Genevieve descended the last few steps. She turned and took in the cramped square room.

Shelves lined most of the walls. On one side were jars of preserved fruit and vegetables, plus one crate of onions, another of
potatoes. The same could be found in the cellar of her own home.

The other side contained deeper shelves. Each had boxes and
crates, some opened, some not. One was piled with books, several
had pamphlets, at least one held what appeared to be pillboxes,
and another contained thin dark-brown bottles of liquid.

Pearl was lying in a heap in the corner.

Genevieve rushed to her side.

"Pearl? Are you hurt? Pearl!" The kerosene lamp stood on a
nearby shelf, and Genevieve used it to examine the older woman
more closely.

Genevieve screamed, the sound reverberating through the
cellar, too loud for her own ears, but she couldn't make herself
stop.

The stout wooden handle of a knife protruded from Pearl's
back. A small circle of blood surrounded where it disappeared,
almost invisible against the dark blue of Pearl's dress.

Genevieve forced herself to stop screaming, replacing the
noise with shaky, hitching breaths. "Pearl, let me see what we can
do. Stay with me, Pearl." She muttered a series of encourage-
ments, praying her mother's friend was still alive. Setting the lamp
on the floor, she carefully rolled Pearl toward her, only to moan
in dismay at the sight of her open, glassy eyes.

She was too late. Pearl was already dead.

Genevieve slumped back on her heels. Why had she waited so
long to search for Pearl? If only she'd found the older woman
sooner, she could have helped. Maybe Pearl would still be alive.

The woman's body was still warm.

Genevieve jerked her hand back. She picked up the lamp,
scrambling to stand. Her thoughts tumbled atop each other like
puppies.

Somebody had been here. Someone had killed Pearl. She
wasn't safe; she needed to leave.

Just as she turned to race to the stairs, a bang echoed through the basement. Genevieve started and couldn't stop a surprised yell from wrenching out of her throat.

"No. No, no, no, no, no." Despite her protests, she knew what she would find as she rounded up the staircase.

The door at the top of the stairs was closed.

Genevieve turned the knob and pushed, but it was useless.

The door was locked.

She banged on the door with both fists.

"Help! Let me out of here, help!"

This, too, was useless.

The house was empty. Antoine was gone, any servants or assistants Madame Martin employed during daytime hours were gone. The brownstone was old and well constructed, with thick walls. She was deep in the interior of the house.

Nobody on the street, none of the neighbors, were likely to hear her.

Genevieve bit her lip and tried to control her breathing.

There were no railings on the old steps, so she couldn't try to kick down the door, as she had done in a similar situation, lest she risk losing her balance and falling down the stairs.

She shoved at the door again, banging her hip against it several times. It didn't budge.

Inhale, exhale. *Think.*

Her mother knew where she was. Daniel would know also, as she had left him messages at his house and the Bradleys'. Whoever had killed Pearl didn't seem inclined to kill her, as they were obviously somewhere in the house and would have tried already.

All she had to do was wait. Somebody would come looking for her, and soon. She had the lamp. She was safe, for now.

Genevieve walked a few steps down, looking back at Pearl's body. Despite her assurances to herself, dread was doing its best to creep into her body, making her hand holding the lamp tremble.

She couldn't slow her breath.

The scent hit moments before she saw it.

The unmistakable smell of smoke.

She looked back at the door.

Pale-gray tendrils crept under the small crack at the bottom edge, curling up insidiously.

Whoever had killed Pearl wanted Genevieve dead too after all.

CHAPTER 16

Rupert groaned again, and Daniel turned Connor toward the mouth of the alley and shoved him in that direction. "Get out of here, Connor." He knelt next to his friend. "Rupert, wake up. What happened?" Daniel didn't bother looking for the assailants. Whoever had attacked Rupert was long gone.

Slowly, and with Daniel's help, Rupert pressed himself to a sitting position. He leaned against the crates, his breath labored and shallow. "God, I feel like death."

"Can you stand? We have to get you to a hospital."

"Give me a minute." Rupert cracked open one eye. "It smells horrid back here."

"What happened?" Daniel repeated.

"Just needed a bit of air," Rupert muttered, shutting his eyes again, arms resting on his knees. "There were four of them, followed me out. Took my money and watch, knocked me about. God, the *stench*." He leaned over and retched into the dirt.

Connor hovered at Rupert's opposite side, ready to help support the injured man. "You heard me, Connor," Daniel said, not looking at his brother. "Go home."

"I didn't do anything, Danny," Connor protested. "Come on. I was with you, inside."

Daniel's chest tightened. He didn't know whether Connor had orchestrated any kind of attack on Rupert or not. All he knew was that Connor had chosen the bar, that Connor was obviously a regular, and that he was friendly with the clientele. That lots of bars like this made a pretty penny out of getting unsuspecting rubes drunk, sometimes even slipping something stronger than liquor into their glasses, and robbing the poor sods afterward.

He didn't know if this bar was that type of establishment or not.

He did know Connor had been very insistent that Daniel not go looking for Rupert right away.

It was enough for him to want Connor out of his sight for now.

"You want to be helpful? Go hail a cab," he growled at Connor. Connor complied, his shrill whistle echoing through the alley seconds later.

Daniel helped Rupert stand, supporting his friend as he limped to the end of the alley, a long string of curses accompanying the short journey. "I feel like I've been on a three-day bender," Rupert groaned as he folded himself into the cab. "My head hasn't hurt this much in years."

Connor stood to one side, hands shoved in his pockets. "I'm real sorry, Rupert. Danny . . . ?"

Daniel shook his head at Connor as he followed Rupert into the cab. It was very probable he was being unfair to Connor, but he couldn't sift through whatever had happened at present. His priority was getting Rupert help.

He watched Connor, his hands still in his pockets and his shoulders slumped, grow smaller on the sidewalk as the cab rattled away. The box containing the tie Daniel had bought him was still tucked under his arm.

"I don't need a hospital," Rupert rasped, leaning his head against the window.

"You should be seen by a doctor."

"Just take me home. All I need is some ice and rest. I feel like a fool."

"You were jumped, Rupert. It's no fault of yours."

Rupert snorted lightly, then winced. "I live in this city. I should know better."

It was dark by the time the cab made its way up Fifth Avenue to the Bradley mansion. Daniel helped Rupert inside, where Esmie and the household staff surrounded them like a flock of concerned geese, clucking their dismay. Eventually Rupert was settled on a long settee in the drawing room under the urinating putto christened Cletus, his face cleaned and a tea towel filled with ice on his head. Esmie flatly refused to allow Rupert a dollop of whiskey for the pain, forcing a cup of chamomile tea on him instead, and placed a call to the family doctor over her husband's vigorous protests.

"He sounds better," Daniel observed.

"I don't know why the two of you can't have a polite drink at your club." Now that Esmie's worry had subsided a bit, she was obviously quite angry. She picked up the tea tray and thrust it at a footman with more force than necessary.

"That's a reasonable question, daughter." Esmie's father, Amos, filled the doorway, eyeing Daniel and Rupert with a less-than-friendly look. "What were you doing down by the docks, anyway?"

"See?" Rupert said to Daniel, looking at him resentfully. His shoes had been removed, and his toes curled in his deep-purple stockings on the settee. "I didn't want to go there; it was Daniel's foolish idea," he finished piously.

"Damn right it was foolish," muttered Amos, chomping on his cigar.

"Father, please," said Esmie in an aggravated tone. "Don't smoke near him." She waved her hand at the smoke lazily circling her father. Amos, who had made an untold fortune in copper mines in Montana, almost always had a cigar in his mouth, sometimes unlit, sometimes not.

Daniel knew Amos hated both New York City and the strict rules around its high society and had wanted no part of it, but he had built his lavish mansion and grudgingly used his wealth to buy what status he could to appease his late wife, Elmira. Elmira had been dead for almost two years now, and while Daniel had assumed Amos would sell the place and return west, it seemed he was willing to stay to be close to his daughter and the coming grandchild.

"You telling me not to smoke in my own house?" Amos grumbled, but he did as requested and ambled away, smoke trailing behind him.

Esmie rolled her eyes. "We can't move soon enough."

Daniel grimaced in sympathy. "I know the feeling."

He was completely sincere. Since Connor's return, Daniel's thoughts had been returning more and more of late to Maggie and the circumstances of their arrival and her eventual death in the big, drafty house Jacob had left him. He knew why it had taken so long for him to decide to sell the place—he'd spent so much time abroad that for years he'd been uncertain if he would ever live permanently in New York again—but now that the decision was made and the sale was underway, he couldn't wait to be rid of the place.

"Speaking of, did Genevieve find you?"

Genevieve had been looking for him? Daniel frowned.

"No, why?"

"She stopped by asking if you were here, but we didn't know where the two of you had gone—you were no longer at the tailor, so she thought perhaps you'd come back here. I would never have dreamed you'd be at the docks." Esmie sniffed, giving both him and Rupert a reproving glare as she handed over a piece of paper. "She left a note in case you returned."

Daniel unfolded the missive.

Dammit.

She had gone to speak with the deliveryman at Pearl Martin's. The midwife's nephew, as it turned out. He supposed that was safe enough, but he still didn't care for the fact that she'd had to go without him. Friend of Anna or not, Pearl Martin and her nephew dealt in illegal goods and services, and that made them dangerous associates.

The appointment had been set for eight PM. According to the ornate gilded clock on the mantelpiece, it was 8:40. She might have come home by now, but maybe not.

"Might I use your telephone?" he asked Esmie, who gestured him toward the hallway.

Heavy emotions swirled inside Daniel as he waited to be connected to the Stewart household. Ever since he and Rupert had set foot in that bar with Connor, the entire evening, and now the night, had gone poorly.

The maid who answered brought Anna to the telephone, who confirmed Genevieve had not yet returned.

"I'm sure there is nothing to worry over, Daniel." Anna's voice sounded tinny through the wire. Daniel could still scarcely get over the new technology that allowed him to speak to someone across town through a device. Telephones remained rare in private homes, but many of the city's very wealthy had had one installed as soon as they were able. "Genevieve and Pearl likely got to talking and she's on her way now."

Daniel thanked his soon-to-be mother-in-law and hung up. While he understood Anna's nonchalance, in this instance it seemed misplaced. Maybe he was overreacting due to what had happened to Rupert, but the fact that Genevieve was still not home was, for him, worrisome.

The need to physically lay eyes on his fiancée was suddenly overwhelming. Daniel made his good-byes and left, heading straight to the midwifery.

★   ★   ★

Coughs racked her ribs painfully. Genevieve had found some rags folded near the preserved goods, and she'd broken a jar of peaches to dampen them, shoving enough under the door to help quell the smoke. Her makeshift barrier was doing a decent job for now, but the cellar was already so filled with smoke it was hard to breathe. She had tied another soaked rag made from a second sacrificed jar of peaches around her nose and mouth, which helped a little, but the cloying scent, mixed with the acrid smell of burnt things, made her gag.

She could handle a bad smell and a sticky face if it helped her not suffocate.

But none of this would help if the door burnt down and fire began licking the walls of the staircase.

The greedy, crackling noise of the flames seeped through the floorboards, the occasional loud pop or crash from above making her wince.

There wasn't any other door to the basement save the one at the top of the stairs.

But there were windows. Two small rectangular windows, each about eight feet off the ground, right where the wall met the ceiling.

It was the only way out.

Genevieve dragged a wooden end table with a broken leg to the window farthest from the stairs, stacking three boxes underneath the legless corner to keep the table upright. Terror and desperation made her whole body shake, but when she firmly pressed both palms onto the table, it held.

She climbed the table, the shaking in her limbs and her heavy skirts making the simple act harder than it needed to be. Frustrated, Genevieve lifted her skirt and untied the rolled cotton bustle she'd worn under her visiting dress, followed by her petticoat, kicking them aside. The style had shrunk in recent years, but she needed to shed as much padding as possible to fit through that window. Her hat followed.

The table wasn't tall enough.

Genevieve's fingers scrabbled at the window latch, pressing and shoving until it finally opened. Fresh air streamed in, and she stood on her toes to get closer to it, pulling her sodden face mask up and gulping greedily between coughing fits.

It was a start, but she wouldn't be able to pull herself through the narrow space if she didn't get higher.

She found a few more boxes filled with pamphlets and stacked two atop the table, once again pressing to see if they would hold her weight.

It seemed they would, but she wouldn't fully know until she was on them. There was nothing to do but try.

Coughing horrifically, Genevieve carefully climbed her makeshift tower. Her heart leapt into her throat when the boxes wobbled slightly—it wasn't a significant height, but if she fell and broke a limb and couldn't climb out the window, she was as good as dead. She grasped the open edge of the window and clung to it until the shifting settled.

There was no way Genevieve could lift Pearl up and maneuver the other woman through the window, but she hated the idea of leaving her body to burn. She really wasn't sure she'd be able to maneuver herself, but it was her only option. And if she could get out, she could raise the alarm and stop the fire before it consumed the whole house, maybe save Pearl's body.

Maybe the alarm had been raised already.

It was going to be a tight squeeze. Atop the boxes, she was about chest high with the window, the ceiling brushing her head. Genevieve yanked the rag off her face and threw it to the ground, relieved to have the sodden scrap of fabric gone.

Slowly, she eased her arms through the small space, then stuck her head through. Her face was in the wet dirt of a back garden, but the clean air tasted heavenly. Genevieve twisted her torso this way and that, trying to fit her shoulders and ribs through the narrow opening.

Small movements were taking an enormous amount of effort, and despite the fresh air, she still couldn't breathe without coughing. Genevieve scrabbled at the dirt, hoping to find something to grab to help pull herself through more forcibly. Her fingers scraped something rough, and shifting her upper body to the left, she saw a small tree growing near the back of the house.

Genevieve stretched, standing on her tiptoes on the boxes. She could just grab the trunk. The window's edge was digging painfully into her lower ribs, and the damp grass and earth were soaking into her dress. An even louder pop sounded inside the house, followed by a great crashing noise.

Whimpering, she pedaled her feet against the interior wall of the cellar and pulled with her arms as hard as she could. The topmost box toppled away, and her feet dangled helplessly for a moment before she pressed them against the wall again, trying to propel herself upward.

She was halfway out. Now it was her stomach that pressed against the window. Genevieve allowed her right cheek to rest in the dirt as her breath alternated between gasps and coughs, and she nearly retched as her body tried to rid itself of the foul smoke it had taken in. She paused there for a moment, shuddering with the effort it had taken to make it this far.

A sudden overwhelming sensation overtook her: that any moment unseen hands would wrap around her ankles, yank her hard back into the basement, and she would be trapped there, the last thing she saw a wall of smoke lit orange by the ever-encroaching flames.

Enough. Genevieve wormed forward on her belly, pulling herself along the grass. Her hips wouldn't fit easily. She squirmed and rolled, kicking her legs, trying to force her body through the too-small space, ignoring the pain of repeatedly banging herself against the unyielding window frame.

An involuntary, hoarse yell of frustration shot from her, scorching her throat on its way out. Finally and painfully, her hips were free, and the rest of her body slid forward until she was fully outstretched on the ground, hacking and coughing.

Genevieve rolled over, chest heaving. The stars were obscured by the steady stream of smoke rising from the brownstone, and the windows glowed eerily from the fire within.

In the distance, she could faintly hear bells clanging, people yelling, glass breaking.

She was so tired. Too tired to shout herself, to try to get the attention of whoever was at the front of the house. Her whole body shook uncontrollably.

She was outside now, away from the fire. That was the important thing.

The yelling grew louder. Men's voices, carrying over the brownstone and into the night air, overlaid by the insistent jangle of alarms.

Somehow, miraculously, Daniel's voice was in the mix, and the sound of it nearly made her weep with joy. Genevieve managed to turn back over, away from the burning building, and half crawled, half dragged herself toward the wall that enclosed the back garden. There had to be a gate somewhere, a way out. Another, louder crash sounded from behind her, accompanied by an uproar of men's voices.

Her ribs and throat felt as though they were filled with broken glass. Each breath was excruciating.

The light of fire illuminated the garden almost as bright as day. There *was* a gate set into the brick, its stout wooden door clearly visible, but it was secured with a heavy padlock.

"Daniel," Genevieve tried. It came out as an inaudible rasp. Her voice wouldn't work.

But as though she had summoned him, Daniel was suddenly there, crouched on the high brick wall of the courtyard. He looked so like he had the first time she'd seen him, when he'd looked down at her from a fire escape, that her mind stuttered momentarily.

Was he really there? Or was her smoke-filled brain creating pictures, illusions of what she wanted to see?

The hellish glow of the fire lit his features. Daniel's eyes scanned the small garden, and she watched the exact moment his fear and determination morphed into an odd mix of horror and profound relief. He leapt off the wall and she was lifted as if weightless, pressed against his firm chest, Daniel's familiar scent filling her nostrils where moments earlier there had been only mud and smoke, just as the wooden gate exploded inward. The flash of a silver axe blade glistened and caught the light of the fire, oddly beautiful and mesmerizing, but Genevieve couldn't watch anymore and closed her eyes against the noise and flurry of motion as what seemed like an endless stream of firefighters filled the space where the gate had been. She felt their quick progress past her and Daniel as the air shifted, then they were moving too, but away from the burning house. Noises continued to assail her: the pressure of water streaming from the firefighters' hoses; the protesting crackle of fire, not wanting to be doused but wanting to feed; the men's shouts as they called to each other in their quest to win, to beat the fire into submission.

"Pearl is inside," she tried to tell Daniel. It sounded like a croak. Her voice still wouldn't work.

"What, love? I can't hear you." He kept moving but put his ear close to her mouth.

"Pearl in basement. Dead already."

His arms tightened around her, and she burrowed her face deeper into him, wanting only to feel the soft linen of his shirt. Genevieve tried to take a deep breath, but her chest resisted, and she coughed again horribly.

She cracked one eye open and was rewarded with the sight of the moon, nearly full.

She was so tired. Surely it was time to sleep. The moon was very bright.

Her one open eye blinked heavily. Daniel's face filled her vision, blocking the moon. His mouth was moving, but she couldn't hear him.

How she loved him. Genevieve tried to say so, but before she could get the words out, blackness descended.

CHAPTER 17

Sunlight was bright behind her eyelids. Genevieve groaned, wishing her mother wouldn't direct the maids to open her blinds in the morning. Or worse, march in and do it herself. Genevieve was a grown woman and could sleep as late as she wanted.

She shifted, willing herself to descend into sleep once more, willing the brightness away. She had been having a lovely dream. Something to do with Daniel and the marble they had chosen for the entryway of their new home. It was a luminescent, pearly gray tone that nearly glowed. Her mind groped for the details, but, frustratingly, they were just out of reach.

Daniel. Marble floor. A patch of sunlight.

If she could get back to sleep, they would return.

It was no use. The brightness was too insistent.

She cautiously blinked her eyes open.

Where was she?

Sunlight was indeed pouring into the room, the curtains open. But the sight outside the window was not the familiar shape of the roofs of the various mews and backs of row houses from her bedroom at home. The sheets were scratchy, and the sharp tang of a harsh cleaner hung in the air.

Realization came forth in a rush: *Basement. Pearl with a knife in her back. Fire.*

"Don't try to talk."

Her father sat in a hard-looking wooden chair next to her bed. He reached forward and took one of her hands in his.

Genevieve searched her brain for the rest, and it complied, the blank spaces between her memories becoming populated, one by one. Wriggling through a window. Daniel on the wall. The feeling of being carried away.

Her throat felt constrained, but she managed to rasp a word. "Daniel?"

"He went to fetch us some tea is all. He should be back any moment." Now her mother was hovering over her opposite side. She, like her father, had tears in her eyes.

"How . . . ," she started, but her father squeezed her hand and shook his head.

"The doctor says you shouldn't strain your throat," he said gently. "You've been here for over twenty-four hours. Gave us quite a scare. We've all been here since Daniel brought you."

As she wasn't supposed to speak, Genevieve experimented with a nod. Her head immediately began to pound.

"The clinic on Park Avenue is completely gone," Anna added, her voice unusually quiet. Gratitude flooded her; her mother had intuited exactly what Genevieve wanted to hear. "The houses next to it had some damage but can be salvaged. We've had word only this morning that they were able to retrieve Pearl. She can have a proper burial now."

Genevieve nodded again, one slow, cautious move. Guilt began to tunnel into her heart, edging aside her gratitude, worming and eating its way into her soul.

She should have looked for Pearl sooner, instead of wasting time in the woman's office reading *David Copperfield*. Two were stronger than one, and together maybe she and Pearl could have prevented the attack.

If she had ventured into the basement earlier, maybe Pearl would still be alive.

"Don't worry, darling," her mother said, sniffling but sounding a bit more like her usual self. "The doctor did say he thought you'd be good as new in time for the wedding."

Unbelievable. Pearl had died and Genevieve had barely escaped death, and all her mother could think about was the *wedding*?

Genevieve tried to speak, but it hurt too much. She opted for staring at her mother mutinously.

Anna jerked back as if she'd been struck. Genevieve's guilt intensified as her mother's mouth crumpled and she rushed from the room, pressing a handkerchief to her face on the way.

Wilbur sighed. "Genevieve," he said in a gently reproving voice.

The guilt compounded.

"We've all been quite sick with worry," Wilbur said, patting her hand. "Even though the doctor said you'd be fine, you did sleep for so long. Your mother has a funny way of expressing her relief, that's all."

Genevieve's eyelids were growing heavy again. How could she be tired when apparently she'd been asleep for a whole day? She didn't want to sleep any more; she wanted to see Daniel. Surely she could stay awake for a few more minutes.

When she blinked her eyes back open, the light had shifted again, the long shadows suggesting it was early evening. Her parents were gone, and Daniel now occupied the hard wooden chair.

He looked nearly as bad as she felt. Dark shadows marred the skin under his eyes, and he sported almost a full beard. He had discarded his jacket and waistcoat and wore only his shirtsleeves, rolled so high she could see the bottom edge of the ink tattoos that circled his upper arms.

Daniel had been leaning forward in the chair, his elbows resting on his knees, a thick china cup filled with something steaming between his hands. When he noticed her eyes were open, he sat up straight, a little liquid jostling out of the cup and sloshing onto his hands.

"Welcome back." A smile of pure relief curled up the corners of his mouth, and Genevieve felt her own lips respond in kind. "Tea?"

The hot liquid laced with honey was exactly what she needed, soothing and coating her scratchy throat. She drank half the cup wordlessly as Daniel watched, his eyes following her every movement as though he were afraid to look away.

"Daniel," she managed, once she'd had her fill. His smile, which had slipped, appeared again, this time smaller and encouraging. He rested a hand on her arm.

"Yes, love?"

It was hard to get the words out, but she needed to say them. "It's my fault. Pearl. The fire."

Real pain spasmed across Daniel's face, and his hand gently tightened on her arm. "It's not. You can't think that."

Genevieve took another gulp of the hot tea. Her throat still hurt, but it was lessening.

"It's only the fault of the madman responsible," Daniel insisted. "Pearl had a lot of enemies. You were in the wrong place at the wrong time."

"No." The fog of sleep was lifting more fully now. The tea was reviving her, and Genevieve pushed herself into a more upright seated position. "Something is happening. The coincidences are too great. You, me."

Daniel sighed, briefly rubbing a hand over his beard. "It's possible. I don't understand how it adds up, though. Why the Sunflower Mission? You'd never met Vanessa Albert before, correct?"

Genevieve shook her head, happy to discover her earlier headache had mostly abated. "Never."

"And your mother?"

She took another deep drink of tea. "Mother? I don't know." Her voice was still raspy, but it was getting a little easier to talk. "She is friends with the Gloucesters, who know Vanessa. Miss Albert doesn't reside in New York full-time, from what I understand. Perhaps she and Mother met had met before, but it wasn't a deep acquaintance."

Her thick ceramic mug was empty. Daniel noticed and took it from her hands. "Let me get you some more, and I'll fetch one of the nurses. Let's see if we can get you home before night falls."

"Really? That would be wonderful." She had been conscious in the hospital for a total of ten minutes and already wanted to leave.

"You haven't any serious injuries; you were mostly here for observation. So, yes, I believe you should be able to leave today."

The thought of a luxurious bath and the crisp, smooth sheets and comfortable mattress at home was motivating. Genevieve spied a clean shirtwaist and green skirt hanging on the outside of a wardrobe door across the room. They were her own, surely delivered by her mother for just this moment. She assumed the dress she had been wearing during the fire was long discarded.

As Genevieve moved the sheets and blanket aside, swinging her legs over the side of the bed and testing the cold floor with her toes, a shadow passed in the frosted glass window at her door.

Two quick, light knocks sounded.

One of the nurses, or Daniel already back with her tea.

"Come in," she croaked, frowning at the sound of her voice. Without the constant influx of tea, she was sounding worse.

Jim Crawford, a rival reporter from the *New York World*, filled her doorway.

Genevieve froze at the edge of her bed.

Tall, gaunt, and pale, Jim Crawford had always reminded her of a caricature of an undertaker, except he had a penchant for suits in light shades instead of black. Today he was in a seasonally

appropriate light-brown color, but it had a sickly yellow under-
tone, giving him a more ghoulish appearance than normal.

He switched on the bright electric light, making his hollow
face glow unhealthily.

Genevieve pulled the blanket up to her chest, trying and fail-
ing to overcome her shock at seeing him in her hospital room.
"Mr. Crawford. Get out of here."

He ignored her, instead pulling a notebook from an inner
pocket and flipping it open, leaning on the doorjamb. Unease
began to tickle her belly.

She would have to push past him if she wanted to leave the
room.

"My fiancé will return any moment, and he will not be happy
to find you in my hospital room." The words came out ineffective
and weak. Genevieve cursed inwardly, hating that her voice was
not up to its full capacity.

A smirk flicked across Crawford's face before it returned to its
usual expression of suspicious distaste. "All for a good story,
Palmer. You know how the game is played. The *World*'s readers
will want to know what one of New York's elite was doing in the
clinic of a suspected purveyor of illegal substances. Care to comment?" His eyes flickered too, nastily, from her face to the raised
bedsheet and back.

Genevieve pulled the sheet tighter, then cursed at herself
again for letting her discomfort show. "I said get out," she said
through clenched teeth. "Mr. McCaffrey will be here any
moment."

She also hated that she had to invoke the presence of a man to
get smarmy Jim Crawford to leave. Her insistence that he go
should be enough, but worms like Crawford responded only to
perceived strength.

And at present, she wasn't at her strongest.

Should she scream, alert the staff? She didn't think her voice
could do it.

"So many fires, Miss Palmer." Crawford dug in his pocket and came out with a toothpick, which he inserted between two canines. "Fire is so pretty, don't you think?" The toothpick rooted and spun.

Genevieve's empty stomach turned.

"Leave. At once." Was her desperation evident in her voice? Good god, how long did it take to get tea? Daniel must have become delayed with some of the hospital staff.

Come quickly, please, she silently insisted.

Crawford's eyes traveled to his notebook. "The mission house fire. The Hansen studio fire. And now poor Mrs. Martin."

Madame, her mind corrected. But Genevieve held her tongue, despite her fury.

He was trying to goad her. She was determined not to give him the satisfaction.

"You've been sniffing around about the first. Your fiancé was present for the second. You were present for the third." The toothpick transferred smoothly to the other side of Crawford's mouth, and his lips stretched around it into a humorless, gruesome smile. "Seems an awfully big coincidence, doesn't it?"

The words were exactly what she had said to Daniel minutes earlier. Genevieve didn't answer but tightened her grasp on the sheet.

"Added to your presence at Ida Gouse's death on Coney Island last year . . ." Crawford's pale brows rose a millimeter. "I know, it was that awful Walter Wilson. Oh, right, you were there when *he* died too, weren't you?" The sucking sound of the toothpick being transferred again was nauseating.

"Seems the kind of thing my readers would want to know," he said again. His hideous smile was gone now, his mouth turned down in a sour grimace. "One society girl who sometimes writes for the papers, around when all these people die. Her fancy fiancé too. How much are you two spending on that wedding? So many pretty, fancy things you're getting as gifts. Be a shame to see any of those go up in flames."

Genevieve's eyes widened at the implied threat. She opened her mouth to shout at the horrid man to get out, get out of her hospital room at once, but only a thin squeak emerged. Crawford took a step into the room, and she gasped, outraged he would dare come all the way into her room, scooting back on the bed almost involuntarily.

The sound of breaking pottery filled her ears at the exact moment Crawford seemed to fly backward. Genevieve gaped in confusion until she saw Daniel flinging the reporter down the hall as if he really were the scarecrow he resembled. Crawford's body disappeared, and Daniel followed it.

She tried to yell his name, but her throat seized again, refusing to cooperate. Genevieve untangled herself from the sheet, which somehow had twisted around her hands to the point of near knots, and hurried to the door. Peeking down the hallway, she saw Daniel picking Crawford up by his shirtfront and lifting him high.

"Stay. Away. From. Her." The words were a forcible command.

Crawford's eyes bulged.

Daniel dropped the reporter, simultaneously shoving him away so Crawford stumbled and fell. He scrambled down the hall to the stairs as Daniel stalked back to the room, kicking shards of the broken mug as he walked. Over Daniel's shoulder, Crawford caught her eye as he straightened, holding up the notebook he'd retrieved in a silent gesture.

The message was clear. He was going to write about her, and Daniel too. And it would not be flattering.

"Are you hurt?" Daniel caught her upper arms and stared intently at her face. "I will kill that bastard if you are."

"No, no," she managed to wheeze. It was all she could say before the hallway and room were crowded with nurses, doctors, and someone from the cleaning staff to clear away the broken tea-cup, for which Daniel apologized profusely.

Three hours later, Genevieve was finally home. The doctor had proclaimed her well enough to leave but advised that she continue to rest for at least a week.

A week? There was no way she could sit still and do nothing for a week. She had to find out what was happening, why it seemed she and Daniel were being targeted.

"What you said before was correct," she said to Daniel. Genevieve had taken a bath and was in a fresh, clean nightdress of her own that was not at all visible underneath a giant quilted wrapper. Her mother had agreed to let Daniel and her visit, perhaps acknowledging that there was nothing alluring about Genevieve's current attire.

Also, Anna was within easy earshot down the hall.

"The Sunflower Mission House is the part that doesn't make sense," she said. "But even Jim Crawford noted it. It must be connected somehow."

At the mention of Crawford, Daniel's face darkened. He had not been home to bathe and looked as disheveled as he had in the hospital but had accepted a meal when it was pressed upon him while she was bathing.

"There's more I haven't had a chance to tell you yet, also," he said.

Genevieve listened with mounting dismay as Daniel told her what had happened to Rupert in the bar by the East Side docks.

She blew out a breath.

"I know," he said.

"I didn't say anything."

"You didn't have to. I know." Daniel swallowed and looked down into his tea mug. She guessed he was wishing it were bourbon, but he insisted on having tea with her in solidarity.

It must be so hard for him, Genevieve thought, *to balance his longing for family against Connor's increasingly suspicious behavior.* "Has Kathleen met Connor?"

Daniel pursed his lips, thoughtful. "I haven't seen Kathleen since Connor showed up," he said. "There hasn't been a moment. I will go this week."

"Shall I come along?" Genevieve was starting to tire but wanted to settle one additional detail before they parted. "And speaking of Connor, when can you and I visit the House of Refuge? It will give me something else to focus on."

"You won't like this," Daniel warned.

"Then perhaps don't say it."

"I don't think it's the best idea at present. We'll go, I promise," he said when it was clear she was ready to protest. "But finding out who is setting the fires takes precedence. Also . . ." Daniel sighed. "Longstreet wants to speak with you. That was why I was delayed coming back with the tea. He found me at the hospital."

"He was there? This afternoon?" This was surprising, both that the detective had come all the way to the hospital to speak with her and that Daniel had apparently diverted him from doing so. Longstreet was usually very tenacious.

"Yes," Daniel said in a grim tone. "They are looking for Antoine."

The guilt that had begun upon her awakening at the hospital intensified. That poor young man.

"I don't want to talk to the police," she said, remembering Officer Jackson and his insinuations. He had been lingering on Park Avenue all morning. Had he still been there that evening, hiding in the shadows, watching her as she returned to the clinic a second time?

Genevieve pulled the wrapper tighter.

"Let's avoid it if we can," Daniel agreed. "And I'll put the word out with the Toughs to keep an eye on the streets for

Antoine. He must need help." He yawned hugely, covering his face with his hand.

"Go home, get some rest," she said. "Tomorrow we'll fight some more." The words were meant to be cheering, but Daniel didn't look particularly cheered.

In truth, she didn't feel cheered either. The faces of those who were gone or displaced flashed in her mind: Marla, Pearl, Dagmar, Antoine.

Someone seemed determined to do them harm. She and Daniel had to act fast, before their names joined the bleak litany.

CHAPTER 18

Boxes and crates were piled everywhere. They were stacked around the periphery of his office, shoved into a corner of his bedroom; some lined the upstairs hallway, and there were even a few nestled next to the dining table. Daniel had to squeeze past them as he edged into the powder room, for god's sake.

"Asher!" he bellowed, after catching one that nearly toppled from its stack near his desk.

His secretary and friend popped his big face through the door and grunted.

"Can't all these boxes go somewhere else? There are plenty of rooms in this damned house; can't they reside in one of the empty ones rather than those in which we live and work?"

Asher regarded him impassively.

"No."

His face disappeared.

Daniel scowled at the space where Asher's face had been. The packing was going slowly, and the entire household was on edge, but he was sure Asher was right.

He couldn't wait to be in the new house. Knowing he was leaving soon was making him particularly restless and agitated, compounded by all these damned boxes and living with half the furniture under white cloths like ghosts. It was unsettling.

There were enough real spirits in this house without creating the appearance of more.

He'd replaced most of Jacob's furniture years before, and much of what was here was not coming with him—he and Genevieve wanted to furnish their new house with things they chose together. But the house was so large the project seemed endless, and objects from long ago kept turning up in unexpected places, churning up memories, some wanted, some not.

Ghosts indeed.

He hadn't seen nor heard from Connor since Rupert's attack at the Knotty Anchor.

"Asher," he called again, less forcibly this time.

Asher's head reappeared in the doorway. "Yeah?"

"Did you send the telegram I asked?"

"Yeah."

Daniel tapped his pencil against his desk a few times as Asher stomped away, before he caught himself and smiled. The pencil tapping was a habit he had picked up from Genevieve.

He hoped he hadn't made a mistake in sending a telegram to Minnesota. Something Connor had said, though, had been nagging at him. Daniel wanted to believe—*needed* to believe—that the oddness around Connor showing up out of nowhere, of him being at the fire at Dagmar's, the fight at the Knotty Anchor, and the attack on Rupert, were not related. But facts were facts, and in his gut he didn't believe he was jumping at shadows.

No harm would come from double-checking.

"Are you *trying* to end your marriage before it begins?" Rupert appeared in the doorway Asher had recently vacated, his outraged tone a poor match for his expression.

Rupert didn't look angry. He looked disappointed.

Daniel didn't have to ask what Rupert was referring to. He knew well enough, and felt suitably guilty about it.

Not guilty enough to not do it, though.

"She'll never know," he said instead. Dammit, he sounded unconvincing even to himself.

Rupert's brows shot nearly to his hairline. "You're jesting, right? This is Genevieve we're talking about here. She's smarter than you, you know."

"What the hell else am I supposed to do?" His agitation and annoyance over the boxes, the damned unanswerable question of the fires, his worry and fear over Dagmar and Genevieve, all collided, ready to explode. "She nearly *died* in that fire, Rupert. When Billy kept tabs on Genevieve before, back when she was on the trail of Robin Hood, it saved her. This is a good idea."

"It's a terrible idea, and you know it. Robin Hood was different. You were trying to protect *me* more than her. And you weren't engaged yet; you didn't know Genevieve as well. You know she would hate the idea of someone tailing her, and if you're not careful, you'll lose her."

Daniel knew this, but having it pointed out was galling. "How do you even know about Billy watching Genevieve, anyway?"

Rupert's eyes slid down the hallway.

Asher. Daniel's anger boiled, close to eruption. Those two were thick as the literal thieves they'd both once been.

"She may hate it, but she'll be alive," he growled.

"And you'll be alone, you bonehead."

"Better me alone than her dead." His growl turned into a roar.

Rupert threw up his hands in frustration. He collapsed into a chair, then flinched in alarm as an unsteady box from the nearest stack shifted, threatening to spill. Daniel sighed, all the fight gone from him at once. He removed the box to the floor.

"Are you really taking all this? I always thought this place was rather sparse, but you must have acquired a decent amount of bric-a-brac." Rupert crossed one long leg over the other, flicking dust off his trouser legs. "Give a fellow a drink, would you?"

Daniel complied, grateful to move away from the topic of him asking one of the Bayard Toughs to keep tabs on Genevieve. The rub of it was, Rupert was absolutely correct. He was risking his entire relationship with Genevieve, but he didn't see another option.

He poured Rupert his preferred whiskey and handed it over, getting one for himself while he was at it.

"I don't mean to stick my nose in where it doesn't belong," Rupert started.

"When has that ever stopped you before?"

"But I've known you a long time," Rupert continued, ignoring him. "These past six months, since you became engaged, well, I've never seen you happier." Rupert tilted his head, pinning Daniel in place with the weight of the years between them. "Though maybe you're less interested in my opinion. After all, you've your brother now." He tossed back half his whiskey in one giant gulp.

Daniel sat up straighter. Did Rupert really think Connor had replaced him? "You can't possibly think I no longer value your friendship."

Rupert raised one sardonic brow. "I don't doubt you value it, no. But is it the same as the affection a true brother can provide?" He waved a hand, as though trying to clear the air of the topic. "Don't mind me; you know I'm very pleased you've regained some family. I never was good at sharing. And no, Genevieve is not the same. While you're irritatingly good-looking, I've no wish to kiss you."

"Rupert, don't be daft."

His friend shrugged. "It's not daft. A sibling is a different animal than a friend."

"It is," Daniel conceded. He'd been so wrapped up in himself, he hadn't stopped to think how Connor's appearance might affect

Rupert. "But you are more than a friend. Connor may be my blood, but I barely know him. You're far more brother to me than he is, and I don't imagine that ever changing."

Rupert was still for a long moment. "It is too bad I've no wish to kiss you, as that was a very nice speech."

Daniel rolled his eyes. "I try to be sincere, and you jest."

"I'm not jesting. You know I feel closer to you than any of my own family. Well, save Esmie, now."

They sat in silence for a time.

"So," Rupert said, crossing his legs the other way. "Have you seen Connor since the, erm, incident?"

"You mean the incident that almost got you killed?"

"Let's not exaggerate. I was knocked about a bit by some toughs, and my wallet was stolen. Hardly a near-death experience."

"It could have been."

Rupert waved his hand again. "Doubtful. My head is far too hard for a small bump to be terribly aggravating. Mostly I'm chagrined I didn't see it coming. So, have you?"

"Seen Connor? No." The whiskey, good as it was, suddenly felt a bit sour in Daniel's stomach. "Not since last Wednesday. My guess is he's around, though. He's good at not being seen."

But I'm better.

Daniel wondered, again, where a farm boy like Connor had learned the skill of obscuring himself in the shadows. Perhaps during his years in San Francisco? Though Connor claimed to have been working the docks while on the West Coast. What need did a longshoreman have for skullduggery?

He was glad, now, he had sent that telegram, even though it still caused him more than a twinge of disloyalty.

"Boss." Asher's broad form was back in the doorway. He glanced at Rupert.

"Go ahead," Daniel sighed. "I know you told him."

Asher didn't look the least embarrassed, the traitor.

"One of the guys says Longstreet and the fire chiefs are staking out Genevieve's office," Asher said. He sounded grumpy and, like Rupert, highly disapproving. "She usually stops in this time of day."

"See?" Rupert said, sharing a conspiratorial look with Asher. "Asher agrees with me."

Asher said nothing, but Daniel knew Rupert was correct.

Why were they ganging up on him? Didn't anyone care that Genevieve had almost burned to death?

Daniel drained the rest of his glass.

"Let's go."

By the time he and Rupert made their way through the thick traffic downtown, Genevieve had arrived at her office. Billy slunk out from around the corner where he'd been leaning, keeping an eye on the door.

"She's in there," he said, hunching his shoulders and shooting Daniel a baleful look from under his hat.

Was nobody on his side?

"I expect Genevieve will be none too pleased to see you," Rupert said, staring up to where the *Globe*'s offices were located. "Perhaps I should wait here."

"She shouldn't have to take on Longstreet and the fire chiefs alone," Daniel said. "I know Kincaid; hopefully, I can help smooth things over."

Rupert looked doubtful but nodded. "*Bon courage.*"

He could hear the shouting the moment the elevator doors opened. Loud voices floated through the closed door of Arthur Horace's office into the main space of the office, where newspaper workers' desks were lined in neat rows. Their occupants weren't even bothering trying to hide the fact that they were, as one, listening to the conversation; they sat, slack-jawed and wide-eyed, staring at Horace's door as if they could see straight through the closed blinds.

"Miss Stewart, you have a duty to share with the police anything you might know about the fire in which you were involved."

Daniel grimaced in disgust. He'd know the self-righteous tones of Detective Aloysius Longstreet anywhere. "Obstructing an investigation is a serious offense, and I know from personal history how you're apt to take matters into your own hands."

"I didn't break any laws." It was obvious Genevieve was trying to keep her voice under control, but he could hear the evident fury under her words. "And being trapped in a burning building is hardly *involved*. I was simply doing my best not to die."

Daniel paused for a moment, hand on the doorknob of Horace's door. He couldn't see who was inside, but if Billy's reports were correct and the fire chiefs were in there as well, he would have to play this with some care.

He had a history with those men.

"You're sure you didn't see anybody? Nobody unusual at all?" another voice rumbled. Daniel pushed the door open as fire chief George Kincaid posed the question.

There were four people crammed into the cluttered, small space. Horace was behind his desk, leaning back in his chair and keeping a watchful eye on the proceedings, his fingers steepled under his chin. Both Chief Kincaid and Genevieve were seated in the wooden chairs opposite Horace, while deputy fire chief Morris Bannon and Detective Longstreet were standing.

Genevieve paused in the midst of taking a breath to speak, giving Daniel a startled look.

"George," Daniel said, leaning forward to shake Chief Kincaid's hand. "Morris." He did the same with the deputy before giving Longstreet a short nod. "What's the problem, gentlemen?"

It was a costly maneuver, bypassing Genevieve to only address the men in the room. Storm clouds gathered in her face.

He didn't blame her; it was a nasty way to operate. But necessary with men like these.

"McCaffrey, good to see you." Morris Bannon greeted him heartily. "Kincaid said you were engaged. Congratulations."

"Thank you," Daniel said, being sure to puff his chest some. "I'm a lucky man, aren't I?"

Genevieve's eyes narrowed dangerously.

"How are you all acquainted?" Horace asked. He wore a patient expression, the exact opposite of Genevieve's building rage, as if he could tell what game Daniel was playing.

"All the way back to Five Points," Kincaid said comfortably. "Danny here was still a young sprout when the fire department turned professional or we'd have had him. His da was a volunteer, God rest his soul. I knew the man well; he helped train me."

"That's right." Daniel maintained an easy tone, though it was a challenge when he could tell he was infuriating the person he loved most in the world. "Now, I'm sure Genevieve has told you all she knows about the fire in Pearl Martin's clinic. She was there for an appointment, you see." He gave the other men a significant look, which Daniel wasn't sure how they would interpret. A pre-marital pregnancy? Generic female trouble? Whatever they assumed, it seemed to work, as they all murmured appropriately.

Except Longstreet. "What ailment caused you to patronize Madame Martin's clinic twice in one day?"

"Now see here, Longstreet," Daniel began, furious himself at the detective's audacity.

"That is none of your business, Detective," Genevieve replied, acid in her voice. "Though I assume you have this information from one Officer Jackson? Would you like to tell everyone why one of the police force was spying on me?"

"Is this true, Longstreet?" Kincaid frowned and twisted in his chair to better look at the detective, just as Morris Bannon chimed in.

"Surely Miss Stewart is correct," Bannon said. "It is no business of ours what the young lady needed from her physician." He was a brash fellow, always had been, and it was odd to see blooms of embarrassment high in his cheeks.

"Physician." Longstreet snorted.

"Midwifery is an old and respected practice," Kincaid said, frowning deeper.

"Must we say words such as that?" Bannon's color was deepening.

"What words should the chief use? Pearl Martin was a mid-wife. She delivered babies and worked with women's anatomy," Genevieve snapped. "As I've told you, Madame Martin went to the cellar to fetch me some medication. When she didn't return, I went to find her. She was already dead." She swallowed. "And while I was in the cellar, someone shut me inside and set fire to the place. I saw nobody, though obviously someone else was in the house while I was there. The thought of which is, frankly, quite terrifying. Indeed, the only person I did see acting suspiciously was Officer Jackson, lurking about the building all day and harassing my mother and myself." Now there were spots of color on Genevieve's cheeks also, but from anger rather than embarrassment.

There was a pause. Horace raised his furry brows in Daniel's direction, as if to say, *What are you waiting for? End this.*

"There is no need for further discussion, gentlemen," Daniel said. "It was a terrible ordeal for my fiancée, but that is the extent of her involvement." He shook hands with the fire chiefs again as they rose, relieved they seemed to agree the matter was settled.

Arthur gave Daniel an appraising look as they too shook hands. "I would still like this story on the nasty business happening at the House of Refuge when you feel up to it, Genevieve," Arthur said. Though he was addressing Genevieve over Daniel's shoulder, Daniel knew the comment was meant for him as well. "It has the potential to be quite explosive, if they still are indenturing those youths. I know you'll do it justice."

Genevieve didn't look at Daniel. "Thank you, Mr. Horace. I already feel up to it, and will do my best."

"Let me walk you out," Daniel offered the visitors.

Genevieve came with them, silent, and Longstreet followed as well, clearly still seething. The detective stomped away once they were on the sidewalk, not looking back once.

Kincaid pulled him aside. Bannon drifted toward Genevieve, asking her about wedding plans.

"Look, Danny, out of respect for you and your da, we'll leave your fiancée alone," the fire chief said. "I'm sure she had nothing to do with the tragedy, but somebody did."

"Yes," Daniel agreed grimly. "Someone did. Did you and the marshal find anything in the wreckage that could help?"

Kincaid shook his head. "Nothing. What of this nephew Madame Martin had?"

"I didn't meet the lad. Genevieve did. Said he went out a few minutes after she arrived."

"That's what she told us too. Can you ask her to keep this under wraps? With this lot, I mean." He gestured with his head at the newspaper office building. "Last thing we need is for the public to think there's a firebug out there, that we're not doing our job. You know it's been a struggle to get taken seriously."

"I do. You and Morris, first Five Pointers to take the helm. You've done us all proud, George."

"Well, we go back quite a ways, Morris and I. And you too. Word of advice, for old times' sake?"

Wariness settled on his shoulders, tensing them. "If you must."

"Oh, I must." Kincaid's brown eyes gleamed at him with intensity. "Quit your dealings with the Bayard Toughs. The old ways are changing. New blood is moving in, and word on the street is Five Points itself may not be long for this world, especially if you reformers have your way. Territories are shifting; it could get ugly."

Daniel blew out a short breath and carefully placed his hands in his pockets. He looked to Genevieve as she stood by the carriage, making polite talk with Bannon, who retained his blush. She was wearing a sage-colored day dress he recognized, one of her favorites.

"I trust Paddy with my life," he said slowly, trying to take in what Kincaid was saying.

"It's not Paddy I'd worry about. Nor any of the Toughs themselves. It's that I'm not sure there will *be* any Bayard Toughs at all once the dust settles. That's what I'm hearing. You don't want yourself—or your gal there—caught in the cross fire."

Daniel nodded thoughtfully, watching the way the sun picked up golden highlights in Genevieve's hair.

He watched her as she said her good-byes to the chiefs, as she took in Rupert standing near the carriage, Asher sitting in the driver's seat, Billy slouched against the building.

As she nodded to herself, adding the pieces up. Watched the realization settle on her face, the knowledge that he'd asked Billy to follow her. That this was how he had known she was having a meeting with Longstreet and the fire chiefs.

She looked disheartened and tired and so sad. He willed her to yell at him. He wanted to yell himself, but what could he say that he hadn't said already?

Could he bear losing someone else he loved, the way he'd lost his family? He just didn't know.

He watched as Genevieve carefully turned her back on all of them, not saying a word, and was swallowed by the pedestrian traffic swirling Park Row.

CHAPTER 19

"I tried to get Suzanne to cancel this party, given your recent ordeal, but she simply wouldn't hear of it," Esmie whispered to Genevieve as soon as she stepped into the foyer.

"There is no need to cancel on my account; this has been planned for weeks," Genevieve assured her. "Suzanne would be devastated." Her friend and fellow reporter, Suzanne Anwyll, had organized the tea in honor of Esmie's impending status as a mother. It was a small gathering of female friends, including Genevieve's mother and a few other acquaintances. She wished Suzanne could have waited until Callie and Eliza were in town, as they would have loved to be present, but they wouldn't be arriving for another week, and by then there would only be time for the spate of planned wedding-related activities: final dress fittings, another ladies' luncheon with all the bridesmaids, plus a formal prewedding dinner party.

"Besides, it is more helpful to engage in regular activities, keep my mind off events of the last week," Genevieve added. She wasn't reassuring Esmie with empty platitudes; she really did feel better when she was busy. It had been a terribly difficult week: the fire itself, recovering from her smoke inhalation, grappling with Pearl Martin's death, the sad event of Pearl's funeral.

The contentious meeting with Detective Longstreet and the two fire chiefs that morning had only compounded her misery.

That, and the way she had left things with Daniel.

Genevieve understood why he had done it, why he had asked Billy to keep an eye on her. But that didn't change the fact that she felt betrayed and disappointed and angry about it.

"Genevieve," Suzanne said. Her lovely gray eyes were lit up behind her spectacles, and a pleased flush graced her cheeks. She seemed happy with her duties as hostess. She was pressing a plate of rhubarb cake with cream into Genevieve's hands. Genevieve took the plate automatically but, for once, didn't want any cake. She looked around the sitting room, taking in the well-dressed women making polite small talk.

Pregnancy was finally agreeing with Esmie, it seemed. She truly did glow, and her face had softened and rounded. She was wearing a center-smocked blouse and boxy jacket in a pretty, smoky shade of blue, one that complimented her fair skin and hair. Genevieve was, in fact, supposed to be writing about the tea party for the paper. It wasn't a major social event, but spring was a quiet season in society until the weddings started, and Esmie's status as a countess made the event of interest to readers.

Genevieve had attended many such parties over the years, and while she was truly happy to be in attendance, she couldn't help but wonder: Was this all Daniel wanted for her? And her father, her brothers?

Genevieve set the untouched plate of cake on a small side table, an unfamiliar emotion rising in her throat. All the men in her life gave lip service to the idea of her boldness, her desire to make her mark on the world in a way that defied conventional expectations. But when it came right down to it, they were all happiest when she didn't push those expectations too far. When she worked as a journalist, yes, but doing *this*. Covering tea parties and weddings and the Newport season, not chasing down jewel thieves or finding the cache of gunrunners or solving the murders of a string of dead girls.

No, they wanted her in a box, pretty to look at, one they could point to and say, *See, here's an educated woman of the 1890s, who has a career and is so very accomplished.* But they didn't really want her to *do* anything.

Anna caught her eye from across the room and smiled, oblivious as she gestured with a fork at Esmie, telling the gathered ladies that when their time came, they needed to choose a midwife carefully.

"Don't listen to these men who think they know better than the women who have been delivering babies for centuries," Anna sniffed, unaware as always of the surprised and uncomfortable expressions of many present. "There is a time and place for this new practice of obstetrics, perhaps, but more and more of the proven and known wisdom—women's wisdom, if you will—is being carelessly pushed aside."

Esmie turned to Genevieve, perhaps hoping Genevieve could restrain her mother (though Esmie really ought to know better at this point), then caught sight of her face. Emsie then saw Genevieve's full plate and frowned.

"What is wrong?" she asked, leaning close. "I can help steer your mother in a separate direction, if you like."

Genevieve shook herself and gave Esmie a distracted smile.

She had identified the unfamiliar feeling: it was despair. How would she and Daniel make this work? How could she make *any* marriage work?

She couldn't focus on the party.

Beside her, Esmie's frown deepened. "Would you like to take a turn outside, get a breath of air? Maybe walk around the block?"

Genevieve barely heard her, barely saw the Anwylls' tastefully decorated sitting room, the back of a discreet footman removing her untouched plate, barely registered Suzanne thoughtfully engaging her mother in a debate over the merits of obstetrics. She was deep in the tunnel of her own thoughts, trying to follow along as they looped and whorled.

Was she being unfair?

A memory arose: Daniel, in his bedroom, his forehead touching hers, whispering how they couldn't be cavalier with each other. Followed quickly by that of him in the gasworks, on his knees, Tommy Meade's gun at his head. This picture was replaced by a memory of Daniel after he'd been stabbed on the East River Bridge, the spreading blood on his shirt soaking into her dress.

She thought of the look on his face as she'd turned her back on him on the street that morning.

Of the hilt of the knife buried deep in Pearl's back.

The fog of her thoughts began to clear, and the despair she had felt so keenly moments before eased a little. Someone was trying to do one of them harm, it was unmistakable. Was it really so wrong of Daniel to want to protect her, as she wanted to protect him? Was she being stubborn to the potential detriment of her soon-to-be marriage?

They would talk, she resolved. The wedding was only two weeks away. First and foremost, she would tell Daniel exactly how much she loved him.

The gentle pressure of a hand on her arm broke through her haze of thoughts.

At some point Anna had replaced Esmie next to her.

Her parents had made their marriage work.

If they could do it, then so could she and Daniel.

"And where is your friend Prudence today?" Anna asked. "Miss Anwyll's and my lively conversation about midwifery reminded me she was meant to be here, but I don't see her."

Genevieve realized with a start her mother was correct. Prue wasn't present.

"Suzanne?" Genevieve called softly. Her friend hurried over, a full cup of tea in her hand that Genevieve eyed warily. Suzanne was known to be a little careless with beverages at times, particularly when she became excited. "Didn't you say Prudence Nadler was meant to come today?"

"She accepted the invitation, yes. But she didn't show, and I've not heard a word. I do hope she's not unwell." Suzanne hurried away again as the butler came by and whispered in her ear, only a little tea sloshing from her cup. A maid swooped down to wipe up the liquid before it could set and stain the carpet.

"Not send a note?" Anna frowned. "Prudence was brought up better than that. I did wonder, though, seeing her at Madame Martin's last week"—Anna glanced regretfully at Genevieve, clearly hoping the topic wasn't too upsetting—"if we may hear news from her soon." Anna's eyes traveled meaningfully to Esmie, indicating that she wondered if Prue was also in the family way.

"Perhaps," said Genevieve. "But you're right, she would have sent a note with her regrets if she wasn't feeling well. I was meant to pay a call on her last week, after we saw her on Park Avenue, but . . ." Genevieve trailed off. Her mother knew why Genevieve hadn't been able to keep her promise.

"She sent me a kind note after hearing about the fire," Genevieve continued. "Asking after my health. That was only a few days ago."

"Well, this ought to be wrapping up soon, and visiting hours will be upon us," Anna said, beaming as two maids set a few prettily wrapped gifts at Esmie's feet. "You should pay her a call today, check and see if she's feeling well. Now, let us see how many wretchedly knitted receiving blankets Esmie will receive. Mine will not be among them; you know I can't knit a stitch. I purchased a lovely gown and bonnet from Lord & Taylor."

*   *   *

Ninety minutes later, Genevieve stood on the front step of the Nadlers' house and rang the bell. Her mother had been correct: it was still calling hours—just barely, but within the acceptable time frame for an unannounced visit.

The stern-looking butler who answered the door didn't ask who she was or what business she had there, just looked down his nose at her as if she should be ringing the bell to the servants' entrance. Genevieve drew her shoulders back and smoothed the skirt of her fashionable afternoon dress, secretly worried her hat was amiss but not daring to lift her hand to check.

She handed over the card she had waiting in her hand. "Would you tell Mrs. Nadler Miss Stewart is calling?"

The butler, who had dark, slicked-back hair flecked with spots of gray, took in her card with cold eyes. He allowed her into the entryway before disappearing.

Genevieve waited. It was unusual, and rude, to be kept in the hall for so long. Perhaps Prue really was sick, but wouldn't the butler have told her right away that Mrs. Nadler wasn't receiving today?

"I'm afraid Mrs. Nadler is not at home," the butler announced disdainfully once he returned.

An unpleasant sensation whirred in her chest at this news. "If she isn't at home, why didn't you simply say so at the front door?" Genevieve pressed.

The butler's look turned even colder as he opened the front door, signaling for her to leave. "Good day, Miss Stewart."

Genevieve didn't budge. If he was going to be rude, she would be rude right back. "When she returns, please tell Mrs. Nadler I'll call again tomorrow."

The butler's dark brows lowered. "I'm afraid Mrs. Nadler will not be home tomorrow."

Her fists clenched around her reticule. "Oh? Has she left town? I am an old friend; Mrs. Nadler and I were at school together," she added, wondering if the butler thought her some sort of interloper. His behavior was very strange.

Something close to an aggrieved sigh escaped his lips. Genevieve had to stifle a gasp; she didn't consider herself snobbish, but this butler was breaking at least a dozen written and unwritten rules of propriety. While she certainly didn't want to endanger anyone's livelihood, she would indeed speak to Prue about it when next they met. She couldn't imagine her friend would want her servants behaving in such a manner.

"She's gone away, to visit her sister."

Genevieve frowned. "In *Italy*?" This didn't make sense at all.

"That's correct. Now, if you'll please." The butler actually grasped her upper arm and physically moved her toward the door, propelling her through and slamming it shut behind her.

She was too stunned, for a moment, to do anything but gape at the closed door.

Prue in Italy? Genevieve remembered Prue's sister, Chastity, a vibrant young beauty who was belle of the ball in their debutante years. Despite her modest name, Chastity had always had a reputation for being wild, and had eventually married an impoverished Italian count. By all accounts, she lived a rather scandalous life abroad. Genevieve was fairly sure Prue's husband heartily disapproved and did not encourage a close relationship between the sisters.

Genevieve had last seen Prue on the steps of the clinic on Park Avenue the previous Wednesday, and had received a note of concern over the weekend. But her friend hadn't been at Madame Martin's funeral yesterday. Was there even a ship Prue could have taken? She would have to check the schedules.

"Miss Stewart?" Genevieve's hand flew to her throat in alarm, startled by the loud, rumbling voice.

It took a moment to place the speaker. "Oh, Deputy Chief Bannon," she said, puzzled. She almost hadn't recognized him out of his uniform.

The deputy fire chief was looking up at her from the base of the steps of the Nadlers' house. He was a tall, broad-chested man with a ruddy face under prematurely bright-white hair and was gazing at her with an expression of utmost seriousness.

Genevieve felt her brow furrow and willed it to smooth out. "What brings you to this part of town?" She internally kicked herself for the question, aware that in the space of a few moments she was, again, possibly sounding snobbish. She knew Deputy Chief Bannon was from Five Points, along with Daniel and Chief Kincaid, and while he had certainly risen in the ranks of New York's society with his prominent position, this expensive neighborhood was occupied only by the city's wealthiest families.

Despite her wish to be egalitarian, something about running into him on this quiet residential street felt odd.

Genevieve peered down the street and sniffed the air. Was there a fire she had missed? She had first met the deputy chief only that morning, though the meeting with Longstreet and the chiefs in Arthur's office already felt as though it had happened a very long time ago.

"I was looking for you."

A flush of surprise flooded her.

Genevieve took a few cautious steps down. Between the firmly shut door at her back and Bannon's imposing figure at the base of the steps, she felt a little trapped.

Which was ridiculous. The sun was bright and warm, the spring buds on the trees were fat and green, preparing to burst into the delicate, early first leaves of the season, and the neat row of large, well-appointed homes here on Madison Avenue were like a trim line of soldiers, chests expanded, proffering security and stability. A pretty nursemaid in a fashionable gray uniform pushed a pram past, smiling up at Genevieve.

"How did you know I would be here?" she asked slowly.

He hesitated. "I knew you had the tea party for the countess, and I asked there first."

Genevieve thought. She and Arthur had been talking about Esmie's party when Longstreet and the chiefs arrived, so it was plausible he had heard them discussing it. And she had told her mother she would pay a call on Prue after the party; perhaps her mother had told Suzanne where she was heading?

"Perhaps you'll come with me," Bannon said. He looked troubled now, in addition to serious. Genevieve's hand, which had drifted to her reticule, flew back to its spot on her throat.

"Did something happen to Daniel?" Panic began to build; she couldn't fathom why else this man she didn't know had ferreted her out. Genevieve ran down the last few steps, suddenly desperate.

"No, no. I apologize, I didn't mean to alarm you. Though it is a matter of some urgency."

Genevieve took a deep breath, trying to calm herself.

"But you'll recall how McCaffrey, er, Daniel, how he said we knew each other, from way back," Bannon said. He shifted his weight and looked away, up the street and down again, before continuing in a lowered voice. "And you must realize we have certain friends in common, from our youth." He stopped fidgeting and fixed her with a significant stare.

Oh. This was about *gang* business. Genevieve was cautiously relieved; she was on slightly more familiar territory here, and the subject explained Bannon's skulking.

"Yes? My fiancé's background is well known. We have no secrets from each other. I am well aware of his past and of his"—she groped for the right word—"friends."

Bannon looked relieved himself. "Good, good. One of those, er, *friends* has information about the fires. He wants to talk to you. He said you'd know who he was."

Genevieve's mind raced. Bannon must be referring to the gangster John Boyle. He was the only person she could think of in New York's underworld who might want to speak with her and not Daniel. If it were anyone from the Bayard Toughs, they would go to Daniel. She and Boyle had a bit of an understanding after last summer's events around the murderer Walter Wilson.

He had made it clear she'd earned his respect after killing Tommy Meade.

"Now?" She had so been wanting to see Daniel, to apologize for her earlier anger. But she also knew it could be dangerous to keep a man like Boyle waiting.

"Yes, now."

CHAPTER 20

Bannon had a cab waiting around the corner.

"It's not safe to talk once we're inside the rig," he said, nodding at the impassive driver. "Some have ears everywhere. I can explain more when we get there."

Genevieve hesitated before stepping in, taking in the view of the calm, peaceful street one last time. She wished she could tell Daniel, or anyone, where she was going. There was no sign of Billy, or anyone else who looked like they belonged to the Bayard Toughs, hanging about. Daniel must have told his associates to back off after her reaction this morning.

She shook herself and climbed into the carriage. It was an ordinary cab, same as hundreds of others that crisscrossed the city daily. And she had been to John Boyle's establishment on the Bowery multiple times, some even on her own. She could do this, and what's more, she could do it for Daniel. If she was able to find out who was setting the fires, then she could help keep Daniel safe. Furthermore, she would tell anything she learned today to Longstreet and Kincaid, despite whatever secrecy Boyle and Bannon made her swear.

Out of the corner of her eye, Genevieve considered Bannon as the cab wended its way downtown. She didn't pretend to know all the labyrinthine ins and outs of gang affiliation and loyalties, so perhaps it wasn't odd that Bannon, who apparently had such ties, was coming to her instead of the police. There was surely much deep-seated suspicion of law enforcement among gang members.

He was almost boyish looking, despite his size, his round face affable now that they were on their way.

The bright day became shuttered as the cab crossed under the elevated train tracks that ran over the Bowery. For many blocks now, the landscape outside her window had shifted, the buildings becoming more dilapidated, the accumulated garbage in piles on the side of the road becoming more frequent. Even in the middle of the day, it was dim here, the shadows thick and menacing between buildings. It was as though the sunlit, green, birdsong-filled day she'd left upon entering the cab belonged to a different lifetime.

"Here we go," Bannon said quietly as the cab turned out from the Bowery and pulled up on Mott Street. Just as she had upon entering, Genevieve paused before exiting the cab.

"Is this one of Boyle's other buildings?" she asked in a quiet voice. The narrow, two-story building was wedged between two larger tenements. She knew Boyle kept an office at his bar, the macabrely named Boyle's Suicide Tavern, about two blocks away.

Bannon's eyebrows raised slightly. "John Boyle operates all manner of properties round these parts."

The cabby, who had given all appearance of ignoring his customers, now twisted slightly in his seat. "Everything all right, miss?" He looked shockingly young to Genevieve, like one of the underfootmen her parents employed, no more than seventeen, perhaps.

Bannon turned a hard, light-blue gaze from the cabby to her, as if to ask, *Well?* He folded his arms across his chest, waiting.

"Yes, I'm fine, thank you," Genevieve reassured the cabby. He flashed her one last look of concern, giving her a final opportunity to speak up before turning his back again.

Genevieve followed Bannon through a tight, debris-strewn passageway between the small building and one of its larger cousins, listening to the carriage clatter away. Bannon opened a side door, though there was barely enough room for it to fully extend, and she followed him again, this time up some dark, narrow stairs. The sound of a baby crying somewhere on the first floor filtered through the thin walls and into the stairway, making her pause for a moment.

Why would Boyle, one of the most successful gangsters in the city, do business in a building as run-down as this, one where a family lived?

Get out, her mind hammered. *Get out now.*

Bannon's bulky, big frame was silhouetted above her. He noticed she'd stopped, so he stopped too, looking down the stairs in her direction. "Everything all right?" he said, echoing the cab driver. His rumbling voice echoed in the empty stairwell.

The crying baby had gone quiet.

Both Marla and Antoine had said the man they'd seen outside the Sunflower Mission House was large and broad. Just like Bannon.

Silly, the other half of her brain, the rational half, chided her. Plenty of men were solidly built, like Asher.

"Miss Stewart?" Bannon's voice held a touch of impatience. "It's not good to keep folks like this waiting."

Genevieve swallowed. She glanced over her shoulder into the darkness of the now-silent first floor, imagining herself bolting down the stairs, back out the side door, racing through the passageway, spilling onto Mott Street and running until she found a cab. Or she could even head to Daniel's cousin Kathleen's brothel, which wasn't that far; she'd taken refuge there before.

Was it suddenly *too* silent?

"It was you they asked for specifically." Bannon had lowered his voice, as if imparting a secret he didn't want heard through the thin walls.

She would meet Boyle, Genevieve decided. He must have his reasons for meeting here instead of at the bar, and he wouldn't dare hurt her, knowing the entirety of the Bayard Toughs would rain down upon his head.

Besides, she had her gun in her pocket. She'd been carrying it ever since the fire at the clinic.

At the top of the stairs, Bannon gestured her into a cluttered room, shutting the door behind him.

Genevieve turned, expecting to see Boyle's familiar bland face.

The chair behind the desk against the back wall was empty.

"But where is—" she started, then stopped, her heart sinking.

Nobody else was in the room at all.

Nobody was meant to be in the room.

It was a trap.

Confusion instantly turned to terror as the truth popped like a soap bubble: Bannon had never said they were meeting Boyle. She had made that assumption, and he hadn't contradicted her. In fact, he'd never said who they were going to meet, just intimated it was someone in New York's underworld. And she had conveniently filled in the gaps for him.

There was no way around the bulk of Bannon to the door. Genevieve reached into her pocket for her gun, drawing it as she took a breath to scream, hoping against hope that whoever was with the baby would hear her and get help.

She was quick, but Bannon was quicker. Before she could finish inhaling, a closed fist was coming directly toward her face, and fast. There was one blazing explosion of pain and then nothing.

★   ★   ★

Genevieve was nowhere.

Daniel ran a hand through his hair, blinking. The insides of his eyelids felt rough as sandpaper.

Where could she have gone? By the evening after the disastrous meeting with Longstreet and the fire chiefs, he had been worried, as she wasn't at her parents' or the Bradleys' by the time he went to sleep. Daniel had passed an uneasy, restless night, not knowing where Genevieve was, but had assumed she was out with other friends, possibly Suzanne Anwyll. Esmie said Genevieve had mentioned paying a call on a friend named Prue; perhaps they had gone to dinner.

He'd also assumed Genevieve remained angry with him, and was taking some time to think through her emotions.

Fair enough.

But now, twenty-fours hours later, Daniel had passed from worried to frantic.

She was *nowhere*.

Genevieve had never come home the night before. Nor had she stayed at the Bradleys', the only other place Daniel could think she might spend the night. Esmie hadn't seen her since the party, and Suzanne said they hadn't been together either. She wasn't at her brother Charles's bachelor quarters. He'd sent a note to Arthur Horace, who hadn't seen her, nor had the few others at the paper Horace had questioned.

In desperation, he'd even checked with his cousin Kathleen, wondering if Genevieve was hiding out at her brothel. He couldn't fathom any reason why this would be so, unless Genevieve had been in some kind of extreme danger and had sought refuge there.

There was nowhere else he could think Genevieve could be.

Nowhere safe, that is.

Why hadn't he kept Billy on her tail? Why hadn't Esmie asked where Genevieve was going after the party? Or Anna? Why hadn't he compelled Asher to follow her anyway?

Daniel knew, though, that he had nobody to blame but himself. Genevieve had been clear she was wary of entering a marriage where her every move was scrutinized, where she wasn't free to pursue her career. She was a damn good journalist too, wasted on the stupid society pieces Arthur still insisted she write sometimes. And what had he done? The worst possible thing: he'd had someone keep tabs on her as though she were an inexperienced child.

It didn't matter that he was simply trying to protect her; Genevieve had every right to be enraged. At first, he had only wanted her to come home so he could apologize. As the hours passed, though, Genevieve's family and friends were certain something more sinister had occurred.

There were no good options.

Either Genevieve had left of her free will and didn't want to be found yet, or a terrible thing had happened to her. Both scenarios were unthinkable in their awfulness, but what other explanation could there be?

"There's simply no other place she could be." Charles frowned. He was at Daniel's house, while Genevieve's parents waited at home, and Esmie at the Bradleys', just in case Genevieve turned up at either. Rupert, though, had come to help Daniel and Charles strategize. Charles had dark circles under his eyes from their sleepless night combing the city. Daniel was sure he had the same.

Rupert was flopped in an armchair opposite Charles. "She could have taken a train to Chicago to be with Callie and Gavin."

"I've sent Gavin a telegram," Charles confirmed. "He'll let us know immediately if she turns up there."

"And what if she went to Paris?" Daniel asked wearily. "London? San Francisco, Shanghai? What if she became tired of New York?"

What he really meant was, *What if she became tired of me?* He couldn't quite bring himself to say the words.

Charles leveled a knowing, sympathetic look his way.

"I think it's time we called the police," he said quietly.

Daniel nodded absent-mindedly. Charles was right: it was time. He hadn't wanted to involve the police before, as he was sure there was a rational explanation for where she had gone. His mind had run through all kinds of crazy scenarios; elaborate, ridiculous mishaps they'd laugh about for years: Genevieve had bought a bun from her favorite bakery on her way home from Esmie's tea and, using the last crumbs to feed some ducks at the lake in Central Park (*Why was she in Central Park?* his brain insistently tried to ask, a question he just as insistently ignored; it mattered not, she was in Central Park), had fallen into the water, after which she was rescued by Mamie Fish, who happened to be strolling by. Mrs. Fish insisted Genevieve come to her mansion for dry clothing, then insisted they all travel to Newport to open the house early, and Genevieve hadn't felt she could refuse, and Genevieve swore she'd sent a telegram explaining all this, but in the confusion and haste she had listed the next house number over and the missive had gone astray, and she was absolutely safe, perfectly fine, the worst that had happened was an unplanned swim in Central Park and some startled ducks, and she'd rather embarrassed herself in front of Mamie Fish. All of society would know about the mishap soon, as Mrs. Fish was quite the gossip, but none of that mattered because it was mostly very silly, and the most important thing was, she was *right here* and *just fine*.

Yes, surely something like that had transpired.

No, his mind insisted in return.

Daniel couldn't delude himself any longer, waiting for any such telegram. Genevieve wasn't cruel. She might be furious at him, but she would never put her loved ones through the agony of this worry on purpose.

His entire midsection was churning with absolute terror now.

They'd already wasted too much time looking in the wrong places.

"I suppose it is, yes," Daniel said. "Make the call."

Charles's and Rupert's eyes met, and Charles silently left. Rupert stood as well.

"You need to eat. I'm going to go and exert my considerable charm on that fabulous cook you employ and attempt to convince her to come work for me. If I am successful, Esmie will shower me with rose petals every morning and evening for the remainder of our life together, so it's worth a try. I'll see if she can send up something tempting for you while I'm at it."

And Daniel was alone. With his anger, his fear, his self-recrimination.

He eyed the glittering decanter of whiskey but decided against it. He would need as clear a head as possible for tonight's search. The Toughs were already fanned out across the city, directed by Asher and Paddy, roaming the Bowery, the Tenderloin, Hell's Kitchen, the opium dens at Chinatown, in and out of brothels and stale-beer dives, anywhere they could think a woman might have been taken against her will.

Daniel would join them, later. After he had spoken to the police. The thought of the simultaneous searches soothed him a fraction. The more people they had looking, the sooner she would be found.

"Hey, Danny."

Daniel started a little at the voice.

Connor was standing amid the boxes in his doorway. He smiled at Daniel uncertainly, and again, Daniel could see the six-year-old his brother had been. He was hunched over, hands in his pockets, fear of rejection written plain on his face.

Why had nobody informed him Connor was here?

"Come on in. Food should be here soon." Daniel didn't have the heart to push away anyone else, not tonight. He wasn't hungry, but Rupert was right: he should eat.

"What's the matter, Danny?" Connor eased into the seat Rupert had occupied. "Your housekeeper waved me back here, didn't say a word. You look awful."

Daniel explained, keeping it brief. He would need to be more thorough for the police soon, and he didn't have the heart to spell out every single detail twice.

"Gosh, that's rough. I'm sorry," Connor said. He had an ankle crossed over the opposite knee and his foot jangled, an irritating, incessant rhythm. "Did you have an argument?" At Daniel's short nod, Connor looked thoughtful. "Bet she's just gone to blow off some steam. Make you worry for a while. You know how girls are."

"It's been over twenty-four hours. Well-bred ladies like Genevieve don't disappear to *blow off steam*, Connor."

"Oh, *well-bred*. Pardon me." Connor hitched a shoulder up, let it fall. "Maybe it's not the worst thing if it ends. She's a looker, but you're too good for her." The jangling foot sped up. Daniel wanted to bark at him to be still. "She's kind of stuck-up, isn't she? You need a good Irish girl, like Maggie."

Daniel snapped. How dare this stranger speak his sister's name?

Because even though Connor was blood, he was still a stranger.

Connor hadn't been there when Maggie let an old man put his hands on her. He'd never had to see that.

Connor hadn't been there when the maid's screams woke Daniel. When he'd run down the hall, already sick to his stomach. When he saw Maggie's body gently swaying from the rope that she'd affixed to a hook in her ceiling, one she must have installed herself, late at night.

No, Connor had been safe in Minnesota. On a *farm*. With parents, even if they weren't blood, but with people who took care of him. Daniel had been alone, in a cold house with a cold man who looked at him with loathing.

Why had the little kids even been alone that day, the day they'd been snatched? Why hadn't Connor yelled, said no, grabbed Stephen and Mary and run back into the house? He'd been six, he knew right from wrong, he knew not to go away with a strange woman.

The fury was sudden and overwhelming.

"Get out," he growled, gripping the arms of his seat to keep from striking the other man.

Connor flinched as though a blow had landed. "Dan-Dan?"

"Don't call me that. Don't call me anything, ever again. Get the hell out of my house." There were few times in his life he'd been this enraged, so much so he literally saw red, and he clenched the armrests tighter.

If Connor didn't leave immediately, he would not be able to control himself.

Some distant part of him knew it wasn't Connor's fault the little ones—and Connor himself—had been taken. He'd only been six. It was Daniel's fault, then and now. But he was sick with acrimony, and Genevieve was gone, and the only person to take it out on was Connor.

He stood, looming over Connor, who leapt to his own feet in response.

"*Get. Out.*" Daniel could hear the shaking in his voice, could see that Connor heard it too.

His brother's fist clenched, and for a brief second he stared at Daniel with a look of such intense fury and hatred, Daniel was certain they were seconds away from beating each other to bloody pulps.

But without a word, Connor turned his back and left.

Just like Genevieve.

CHAPTER 21

Another twenty-four hours gone with no sign of Genevieve. Daniel paused on his threshold. He had barely slept in two days. He'd been awake the entire night before, combing the streets and alleys of the city, darting in and out of saloons, showing a recent carte de visite of Genevieve everywhere he went.

Have you seen this woman? Look carefully. Look again. Are you sure?

He continued all day, trying every department store and shop on Ladies' Mile, asking every flower seller and street vendor. Sometimes he was accompanied by Rupert or Charles, sometimes Asher, or Paddy or another Tough. Sometimes his companion changed, a coordinated transition so seamless he only noticed when the sound of the footfalls next to him shifted. His entire focus, his whole self, was centered on his one goal: he would find her. He had to find her.

They must have walked miles.

And so far, it was for naught. There were no trails to follow. No leads to pursue. Genevieve had vanished, as if the earth had edges and she'd simply fallen over its side into an unknown, endless abyss.

He braced his hands against his own front door and allowed his weight to rest there, exhausted to the marrow. The night rustled around him, trees swaying in Gramercy Park, squirrels settling into branches. Daniel had just come from the Stewart house on Washington Square North, where Genevieve's family was keeping a tense vigil. It had broken something inside him to tell the Stewarts he had no news.

That yet again, he had failed. That Genevieve was still missing.

Anna reported she had checked at the Nadlers', because Genevieve had mentioned perhaps paying a call to her friend Prudence on the way home from Esmie's party.

"Mrs. Nadler isn't even in town. She has gone abroad," Anna had sighed.

"Who told you this? Mr. Nadler?"

"No," Anna said, rubbing her eyes. "It was a terribly distraught-looking maid. I did wonder where their butler was."

The door shifted under Daniel's palms. He quickly stood, blinking, before it opened fully and sent him tumbling.

"Boss?" Asher had beaten Daniel home somehow. "Been keeping an eye out for you," he said in a low voice.

A pulse of hope shot through Daniel's midsection. "Is it?" he began, but stopped at Asher's quick headshake.

"Not that. No news there, though I'll fill you in later on where I went after we split up. Right now, you got company."

Brow furrowed, Daniel wended his way around a stack of boxes to his drawing room.

Longstreet stood before the fire, his hands clasped behind his back. Daniel's heart gave a lurch again, a combination now of hope and fear. Like Asher, Longstreet shook his head.

"I've no news of Miss Stewart, I'm afraid."

Daniel couldn't stop his shoulders from slumping. "Then why are you here?" He didn't try to keep the irritation from his voice.

"Shouldn't you be out there, searching for my fiancée?" Daniel swept his hand at his own front windows before making his way to the sideboard for a drink. He was utterly spent, and needed an hour or so of sleep before beginning the night's search.

Have you seen this woman? Look carefully. Look again. Are you sure?

Daniel swallowed the finger of whiskey quickly, enjoying how it burned its way down his throat. He didn't offer Longstreet a drink. Or the officer who accompanied the detective, the man, he noted with displeasure, called Officer Jackson. The one Genevieve claimed had harassed her and Anna on the steps of Pearl Martin's clinic.

"As you well know, Mr. McCaffrey, the New York City police force has an entire metropolis to protect. So, yes, while we are looking for Miss Stewart, we do have other crimes to attend to." Longstreet's beady eyes stared daggers at Daniel. The detective didn't like him, never had, and the feeling was so very mutual.

Daniel shifted his gaze to the empty crystal glass in his hand. He didn't have the energy to spar with Longstreet tonight. He wanted something hot and quick to eat, a fast bath to rid himself of the stench of the city, and a few hours' rest. That was it.

Longstreet's mouth thinned under his moustache. "I need to ask you a few questions, Mr. McCaffrey."

"What sort of questions?"

"Questions regarding your whereabouts on Tuesday night."

Daniel's head snapped up. They thought he had something to do with Genevieve's disappearance?

"Wouldn't your energies, again, be better spent *out there*, looking for her?"

Longstreet's moustache bristled. "Everyone in Miss Stewart's life is a suspect, I'm afraid. Ladies don't just dissipate into thin air."

Wealthy ladies, Daniel corrected him silently. Poor girls disappeared all the time.

"One did last year," Daniel said instead. "Nora Westwood. I found her, but you all lost her again." He put down his empty glass. One was enough. It was time to end this conversation and move forward with the rest of his night. Food, bath, sleep, search.

"Sometimes when ladies go missing, it's on purpose," Jackson cut in. He stood behind his boss, nearly a head taller, wearing his own moustache, darker than Longstreet's but just as large. "They're hoping they won't be found, especially by the men in their lives." Daniel was surprised at this sympathetic take, but any credit Jackson had due—however begrudgingly given—was instantly canceled when the officer added, "Usually they're not satisfied, if you catch my meaning. Have to get what they need elsewhere."

Daniel's shoulders tensed and his fists curled involuntarily. "Are you suggesting my fiancée left me to run away with another man?"

"Jackson," Longstreet said in a warning tone.

Officer Jackson shrugged a little. "Wouldn't be the first time. Or the last. I've had a few run-ins with that Miss Stewart over the years. She looks like she could use some . . . satisfying."

A stunned silence fell, but it barely lasted a second. Only long enough for Daniel to confirm he'd heard the insult correctly before he flew at Jackson without a second thought. The drawing room erupted with noise: Jackson's pained bellow of surprise, Longstreet's harsh bark at Daniel to stop, the satisfying crunch of Jackson's nose against his fist, the terrific thud of a box of books hitting the floor as Jackson's body teetered backward, knocking into one of the room's many stacks.

"Enough," snarled Longstreet, physically inserting himself between the two as Jackson regained his footing and lunged. "Back off, McCaffrey, or I will arrest you."

Asher burst through the door. He seemed to comprehend the situation in an instant and wrapped his arms around Daniel.

Daniel struggled against his friend's iron grasp, his vision red with fury for the second time in as many days.

"Leave it, Danny," Asher said in his ear.

He nodded once and shrugged Asher off as soon as his friend's arms loosened. Daniel and Jackson sized each other up, panting. Longstreet stayed between then, casting a wary eye between the two.

"I apologize for my colleague's discourtesy," Longstreet said, finally straightening and pulling the hem of his jacket down. He frowned at Jackson, seeming to consider the next best course of action. "If you would be so kind as to answer my earlier question, McCaffrey," he finally said.

Daniel blew out a breath and ran a hand through his hair. He could smell himself, sweat and temper and the long night and day mixing foully. "I was here. My entire staff can confirm it. As you can see, we're preparing for the move to the new house." He gestured to the now-upended tower of boxes, suddenly unspeakably weary.

"If Miss Stewart does not materialize soon, you realize we may have to take you downtown for further questioning," Longstreet said coldly. Daniel only glared back. "We'll show ourselves out."

"What do we know about that man?" Daniel asked Asher as soon as the policemen had left.

"Longstreet? Pain in the ass," said Asher.

"No, the other one."

"Want me to see what I can find out?"

"Yeah."

Daniel didn't trust Officer Jackson. Genevieve had complained about him before, and he did trust her.

If only he could find her.

★ ★ ★

"Daniel."

Daniel sat bolt upright. Rupert was standing in his bedroom doorway, holding a lamp.

"No news," his friend said immediately.

"How long have I been asleep?" All of Daniel's senses snapped awake at once. He swung his legs over the edge of the bed. He'd fallen asleep in his undershorts and a shirt, on top of the blankets, ready to jump into trousers and run out the door if needed.

"Asher said about two hours."

"Is the plan for tonight's search the same?" Daniel squinted at his bedside clock in the dim light. It was midnight. He had coordinated with Paddy, Asher, and Rupert earlier that evening about where they would search next. Daniel felt it was time to give Brooklyn a try.

"As far as I know," Rupert said. He seemed to be waiting for something. Daniel eyed him curiously as he pulled on his pants. Once they were buttoned, Rupert held up a rectangle of paper.

"This came today. Mrs. Kelly is in a state because she forgot to give it to you earlier. Asked me to wake you straightaway."

It was a telegram.

A chill settled in Daniel's bones.

Somehow before he read it, he knew what it would say.

"Turn on the other lamps, will you?" he asked, reaching over and turning on the gas lamp closest to him.

It wouldn't do to read a message like this in the dark.

It was the suit that tipped him off.

Connor had said he'd worn his gray suit to his parents' funeral, not *funerals*.

It had niggled at him, the suggestion that the Lunds had had one funeral. That perhaps they had died at the same time. To quell his doubts, he had sent a telegram to the newspaper office closest to the Lunds' town, asking if there was a record of their deaths, along with a paid response envelope.

Connor's adoptive parents could have died in any number of ways. Outbreak of an illness. A carriage accident. Or perhaps there had been two funerals and Connor had misspoken, or Daniel had misheard.

He opened the telegram, surprised to find his hands shaking. Even though he knew, somehow in his soul, what he would find there, reading the words was still like receiving a blow to the face.

Ingrid and Johan Lund died July 13 1885 in fire, Mantorville. House destroyed. Neither son home during fire. Article coming in mail. Mercy Ennis, Winona Republican.

Whoever had transcribed the message in New York had a spidery, cramped hand. Daniel stared at the crabbed letters, knowing what they said but willing them not to be true.

A fire.

It was too much of a coincidence.

He'd telegraphed the newspaper closest to Connor's hometown of Mantorville, the *Winona Republican*, figuring if the Lunds had died at all suspiciously, the paper would know. And he had been right.

"Daniel, are you okay? It's not Genevieve, is it?"

He shook his head, handing the telegram over. Rupert read it, a crease appearing between his eyebrows.

"A fire," he breathed, a look of horror spreading across his face as he realized the implications. "What's this about *neither* son? Connor had a brother? You think . . . Stephen?"

"I don't think so. Connor said he wasn't placed with Stephen. He offered to tell me what happened to the younger ones, once, but I wasn't ready to hear." Had he missed his chance? There was nothing for it but to wait for the article this Mercy Ennis woman was sending.

"Danny." The yell came from the hallway. Heavy footsteps rushed up the steps, thundered down the corridor. Daniel raced to the door, his heart in his throat.

What had happened? Was it Genevieve?

Asher barreled toward him, his face as full of concern as Daniel had ever seen it. A knot of dread formed in his throat.

"Danny, come quick. It's your house. It's burning."

The house. The house. Oh god, he hadn't thought to check the house.

Daniel pushed past Asher and sped for the door, heart in his throat, racing down the stairs two at a time.

He couldn't believe what a fool he'd been. The house. It was almost finished, but they were waiting on that final shipment of marble from Italy to complete some of the lavatory floors, and work had stopped the previous week. Normally, he and Genevieve would have been by to check the progress, make sure the latest work was in accordance with their plans. He hadn't gone, of course.

The empty, mostly finished structure would be the perfect place to stash a body.

Daniel's mind stuttered over the word, and in his head he pictured Genevieve, bound and unconscious but alive, placed in the middle of the gleaming, honey-colored oak floors of what was to be their bedroom, left there for him like a present.

He didn't doubt whoever had taken her—for he was sure, now, that Genevieve hadn't left of her own will but been taken— was capable of such a twisted gesture. Someone had been toying with them for weeks with these fires.

But *why*?

"Danny."

The cool night air wrapped itself around his body as he dashed out the front door, instinctively turning north to head uptown.

"Danny. *Boss.*" The harsh grunt was directly in his ear. Asher was keeping up with him, pace for pace. "It'll be faster by horse. Come on."

Rupert had already readied the carriage. They jumped in while Asher took the driver's seat and tore uptown.

Daniel didn't trust himself to speak. The city flashed by as Asher expertly wove the vehicle around what little traffic they encountered. Rupert kept silent as well, though he kept his eyes on Daniel as if he were afraid of what his friend might do, his mouth a grim line.

They were getting closer. Twenty-five blocks to go. Twenty. They shot past Rupert's nearly finished house.

Only ten left.

Daniel counted down the streets, planning to hurl himself from the carriage as soon as they reached the corner of Seventy-Sixth.

He thought of the interior of the house, his mind scrolling past the wide, multipaned windows, the marble floors of the grand entryway, the simple interior lines he and Genevieve had chosen, free of overly fussy stucco or gilding. The last time they'd visited, two weeks ago, they had seen the house in its most completed state yet. He had grasped Genevieve's hand, standing in that quiet, echoing entryway, and squeezed it. She had squeezed back.

It was a marvel to him still, that day, that this was his life. That he would be able to exist with Genevieve in a house they had chosen, designed together with Charles, that he was so laden with good fortune. They had grinned at each other stupidly, then raced through the house, calling to each other as they discovered new rooms completed—some wall paneling here, the chandelier they'd chosen there—Genevieve jumping and squealing and clapping her hands at the sight of the giant finished fireplace in the main drawing room, brilliant with sunshine. She followed this by opening her arms and spinning. Daniel had been so delighted by the gesture he'd caught her hands and they'd spun together like children, laughing.

One block to go, and he could already hear the alarms. Smell the smoke.

Asher slowed to avoid hitting a late-night pedestrian, shouting at the man to hurry, but Daniel could wait no longer. He took advantage of the pause and jumped, sprinting.

It was worse than he'd imagined.

Orange flames leapt from the south-facing downstairs windows, where his office and the library were, shooting thick smoke into the street. Three fire trucks were parked in the street, firefighters wielding their hoses and shouting. A small crowd was gathered across from the blaze, huddled in cloaks against the late-night spring chill, watching the activity.

Daniel ran past them all. He got within six feet of his front door before someone tackled him. Two firefighters held him down, yelling over their shoulders for help. Daniel roared and pushed against them.

He didn't care that the house was burning. Genevieve might be in there.

Deputy Chief Bannon's face appeared between the two helmeted men.

"McCaffrey," Bannon shouted over the din. "This is your house?"

"Genevieve might be in there." Daniel broke free from the two men and leapt to his feet, starting for the door again. This time Asher grabbed his arm along with the two firefighters.

Chief Kincaid had joined them. "Get away from the house, Daniel."

"He says someone may be in the house, sir," one of the men restraining Daniel said. Kincaid exchanged a grim look with Bannon.

"Come on," Bannon shouted to the two men. "One more." One of the men raised his arm and a third jogged over, his face damp with sweat from his exertion and the fire's heat.

"Could be a woman inside," Bannon yelled to them. "Mount up."

"It's too far gone," Kincaid protested.

Bannon shook his head. "We have to check." The men ducked their heads and ran into the building. Daniel tried to follow, but Asher, Kincaid, and a third beefy firefighter held him back.

"Let them do their jobs, Danny," Kincaid hollered in his ear. "They've got the gear, they've trained for this. You can't go in there in your shirtsleeves. Come on, don't tire out my men."

Daniel quit struggling, hearing the wisdom of Kincaid's words. They didn't let go, though, as if they knew he would dash into the house the second he was released.

They were correct. He absolutely would have.

A small explosion, followed by a loud crash, rang from somewhere inside. Daniel imagined fixtures toppling, the hungry fire burning all the carved wood paneling to a crisp, the new fireplace charred and black.

It didn't matter. Houses could be replaced. Genevieve couldn't.

What seemed like an interminable time passed. Just as Daniel felt Kincaid's, Asher's, and the firefighter's grips slacken, just as he was readying himself to bolt, four dark silhouettes emerged from the orange light.

Daniel watched the main shape approach, a bear of a man as big as Asher, Bannon's features becoming clear only when he was mere feet from them.

Daniel held his breath.

Bannon shook his head, sympathy written across his face.

Daniel couldn't breathe. What did that mean?

"There's nobody in there, Danny."

Relief poured through him like honey.

"Are you sure?"

Bannon hesitated. "There's no guarantee until it's out. But as sure as we can be for now."

Another explosion sounded, and Kincaid moved everyone not actively fighting the fire back across the street.

Rupert and Asher half carried, half shoved Daniel there.

They kept a wary eye on him once they let go, but Daniel didn't bolt this time.

Instead, he collapsed, his legs giving way.

The was nothing he could now except watch it burn.

Chapter 22

She was so cold.

Genevieve tried to remember if she'd ever been this cold before, but her brain felt fuzzy. Vague images and sounds kept slipping into brief focus before disappearing. She tried to grasp and hold one, but they eluded her over and over. The effort made her head hurt.

Violent shivers racked her body. Why was she so cold? Had her thick down blanket fallen to the floor? Her feet felt frozen.

The elusive memories wouldn't stay put. Were they even real, or had she been dreaming? The shards that emerged made no sense. There was a high, babbling voice countered by a cold, stern one, and a shadowy, foreboding, black-robed figure. The figure in black made her afraid. There was a distant sense of wanting to say something, something important, but being unable to articulate what it was.

Genevieve peeled back her eyes. Blackness met her.

One atop another, other sensations rushed in. The coarse fabric of the sheet below her. The rustling of an oilcloth under the sheet. The scant, scratchy wool blanket above. A hard, firm bed under her back, more like a plank than a mattress. A horrible taste in her mouth, an even more wretched one in her nose.

"Daniel?" her voice croaked. Genevieve cleared it and tried again, panic pressing in from all sides. "Daniel?" she cried again, louder this time.

Where was she? Her brain released another flash of memory, another shard that made no sense: the feeling of being on a boat, rocking gently on the waves, a fresh breeze ruffling her unbound hair.

A memory from Newport?

It was getting harder to breathe, the smell was so bad. What was it?

Where *was* she?

The metallic, clanking noise of keys jangling ripped through the black. Genevieve sat up, fast. Dizziness overtook her and she reached out, into the dark, to steady herself. Her hand hit a stone wall. The scratchy wool fell from her shoulders, and Genevieve shook so hard from cold she doubled in on herself.

A beam of weak light broke in the darkness, then slowly expanded. A door. She was in a room, and the door was opening. Genevieve wrapped her arms around her middle.

The lamplight revealed a broad, hard-looking woman in a brown-and-white-striped dress with a white apron and cap. A large ring of keys dangled from a green cord wrapped at her waist. The woman frowned at Genevieve.

"Awake at last, are you?"

Genevieve blinked in the lantern light. "Please," she managed. Another shiver, more savage than the last. She could barely speak, her teeth were chattering so badly. "Please," Genevieve said again. "Where am I?"

The nurse's—for that was what she must be, with her white apron and cap—mouth tightened into a smirk. "You're in Blackwell's, dear." She looked at Genevieve in disgust. "You'll get a bath in the morning."

Genevieve followed the nurse's gaze down her own front. She was wearing a loose-fitting, cheap cotton dress in a blue calico pattern she didn't recognize. The front was covered with a stain from what had unmistakably been vomit.

Genevieve recoiled, but there was nowhere to go. Confusion pounded her brain along with the throbbing pain in her temples. "Blackwell's?" she gasped. "The insane asylum?" She pushed the blanket back from her knees and tried to stand. What had happened? Where was Daniel? There was some mistake. She needed this woman to know this was a mistake.

"But I'm not insane. Please. Get my fiancé, my parents, they'll tell you. There's no reason for me to be here." Genevieve's knees gave way, and another wave of dizziness overtook her as she collapsed back onto the hard berth.

The nurse's face was like stone. "Sure you're not, dearie. Go back to sleep, and don't be bothering me again."

"Wait," Genevieve tried to call, but the door clanged shut, sealing away the light. Blackness rushed in again. "Wait," she yelled again, but her voice was growing weaker. "Come back, please." She had to explain; they had to listen.

Genevieve's bare feet found the icy floor again as she pushed herself back up. The door was right there; she would pound on it until she had answers, until someone in charge heard her. Whatever was happening, it was a terrible mistake.

The darkness spun around her as she struggled to stand.

"No," Genevieve said, appalled to hear how close to a whimper the word sounded. But her will was no match for whatever had happened to her body. She tried to call Daniel's name again as she felt herself crumple.

★   ★   ★

The next time she awoke, her head was clear. Tired, but clear.

Genevieve remembered.

Not all of it, but enough.

She remembered Deputy Chief Bannon materializing at the base of the Nadlers' staircase. She remembered getting into the cab with him, following him up the staircase on Mott Street. She remembered reaching for her gun, and not being fast enough.

On instinct, Genevieve's hand flew to her hip, to the pocket where her gun should be—she made a habit of ordering pockets in all her clothing, save the most trim of evening gowns. But of course, she wasn't wearing her own clothes anymore. The pocket and its contents were god knows where.

The rest she could surmise. Bannon must have followed her to the Nadlers'; it was the only explanation that made sense, though the why of it was still a mystery. He had knocked her out and must have drugged her. The cold, distant voice she remembered from the figure in black robes would have been a judge, and she feared the nonsensical babbles she recalled might have been herself.

Was that all it took to commit a woman to an insane asylum? The right dose of chloral hydrate to make her half-conscious and nonsensical, perhaps a sum exchanged?

Genevieve's hands knotted into fists.

If it was that easy to do, it should be easy enough to undo.

It was still freezing and dark in her cell—for that's what the room was, she realized with a start. If she truly was in Blackwell's Asylum, this was a cell. But the blackness wasn't as all pervasive as it had been earlier. The sun must be rising.

Genevieve gingerly pushed herself to a seat. She waited, but no dizziness muddled her head. That was good, a good start. If she could move and think clearly, she could figure out a way out of here.

The noise of keys clanged outside her door, and Genevieve scooched to the edge of the bed, slowly testing her legs. She shivered in the thin dress and her bare feet, but kept her stance.

That was also good.

The clanking keys finally reached her door. The harsh metallic scrape of a lock being undone filled her ears, followed by the creak of the door opening.

It was a different nurse this morning, her status recognizable by the same uniform as the previous one. This woman was small and blonde, with red-rimmed eyes that reminded Genevieve of a rabbit. The nurse wrinkled her nose.

"God, you stink."

Despite herself, Genevieve flushed, but she stood her ground. "There's been a mistake. I was brought here against my will. I need to see whoever is in charge."

Another nurse entered, the same one from the night before. "Polly Stuart," she said, glancing at a clipboard. "She came in yesterday, out of her head. Yelled out in the night, brought me around unnecessarily. We might have a troublemaker on our hands."

Shivers still ran up and down her whole body. It was so, so cold in the cell. "My name isn't Polly. Well, sometimes it is. That's my pen name. I'm Genevieve Stewart, and I want to speak to someone in charge."

"Which is it, dearie? Polly or Genevieve?" The larger nurse drawled out the syllables of her name in a fake upper-class accent.

"It's Genevieve, Genevieve Stewart. Polly is my pen name. I'm a journalist; I write under a different name. Now, let me see the person in charge." Genevieve tried to march past the two nurses, but the large one grabbed one side and the rabbity one the other. Both held her fast as she protested.

"Your name is Polly Stuart, and you suffer delusions. You were committed by your own family, dearie, and it was approved by two doctors and a judge. Now come on; normally, baths are after dinner, but we have to wash you before you can eat."

Committed by her family? And doctors? What doctors?

Genevieve thought she remembered a judge but couldn't recall any medical examination. The thought of unknown doctors probing her, mentally or physically, while she was incoherent, was both enraging and terrifying.

"Unhand me. Let me go. Release me now." She couldn't keep her voice from shaking as the two women dragged her down the hall past a grim line of iron doors. Genevieve twisted and pulled against their grasp, but she was weaker than normal, no match for their collective power. When was the last time she had eaten?

The nurses pulled Genevieve, who still struggled as best she could, down a flight of stairs and then into yet another corridor. A sudden, sharp pain shot across the back of her skull as the large one grabbed a fistful of her unbound hair and yanked it backward, never breaking stride. Genevieve cried out.

"Stop your squirming," the nurse barked, shoving Genevieve into a cramped tiled room. "Now get undressed, and don't be all day about it."

There was a large tin bath standing in the middle of the room, surrounded by several other buckets. The rabbity nurse took up a bar of soap and stood at the ready. "Come on, now," she urged.

Genevieve looked at the too-short, threadbare calico dress that covered her body. It was dreadful, cheap and filthy, yet it suddenly seemed the most essential garment in the world. She crossed her arms over her chest and shook her head. "I won't get undressed."

The large nurse narrowed her already beady eyes at her. "You'll remove your clothes or I will."

"You don't smell good, dear," the rabbity one said in a placating tone. "And you've sick in your hair. You need a bath."

There was *vomit* in her hair? Genevieve's skin crawled. She wanted to be clean but was already so cold, the thought of removing her dress and being fully exposed sent yet more chills through her body.

The water wasn't nice and steamy as it would be at home, but perhaps it was lukewarm.

"Enough," the large one growled, taking a step in her direction.

"All right, all right," sputtered Genevieve. Her fingers trembled forcefully as she worked the buttons at the front of the dress. She pushed it down, letting it puddle at her feet, and stared at herself stupidly. The corset and silk chemise she had donned when she'd last been lucid were gone, as were the rest of her undergarments, replaced by a rough linen shift, drawers, and a thin petticoat.

Someone had undressed her, fully.

A shudder more from horror than cold consumed Genevieve.

Someone had taken her clothes, all of them. They had seen her naked and had redressed her.

For the first time since she'd woken, a sliver of real fear poked its way into Genevieve's midsection.

Someone pretending to be her family. A well-administered knockout drop. A judge who could be bought. Incompetent or corrupt doctors.

That was all it took for a woman's life to be stolen. *Her* life.

"All of it," barked the large one.

Genevieve peeled off the unfamiliar petticoat and shift but balked at the drawers.

The large one rolled her eyes and advanced. Genevieve skittered back a step. "All right," she said again, arms crossed over her now-bare chest. The drawers joined the pile of clothes on the floor.

Once she got closer, the bath water did not look particularly fresh. "Is this clean?" she asked.

By way of answer, the large nurse physically lifted Genevieve and dropped her into the tub in one swift motion. Genevieve was so shocked she didn't have time to protest or fight, and further shocked speechless by the icy temperature of the water.

"Wha . . . ," she managed, gasping, before a deluge of water flooded her face, filling her ears and nostrils, even rushing into her mouth. She barely had a moment to breathe before it happened again, and then again. It was like she were drowning; she could barely move for the cold, and it was impossible to catch a breath.

Just when she thought she could stand no more of it, just when she really thought she might drown, the onslaught of water stopped. The rabbity nurse scrubbed at her body and hair with a rough sliver of hard soap. It hurt, but Genevieve was still so stunned by the water's temperature, still so out of breath from the assault of the pouring buckets, she had no energy to protest.

When the nurse had finished her brutal cleaning and there was one final, frigid rinse, Genevieve was allowed to step out of the tub. The thin scrap of fabric the nurse handed over for a towel also didn't look terribly clean, but she had no choice but to use it.

"Here." The large nurse thrust a bundle of clothing into her arms. Desperate to be warm, Genevieve pulled the garments on quickly. It was another pair of rough, cheap drawers and a shift, a dark cotton underskirt, and a thin white calico dress. Both the underskirt and the dress were too short, the dress more so than the underskirt, which stuck out from her hem in a way that would have been comical in any other circumstances. The sleeves were too short also, stopping at least two inches above her wrists.

The rabbity nurse saw her looking. "You're taller than most. But you're here under charity, so what we have is what you get." She compelled Genevieve to sit, then combed her hair so ferociously Genevieve blinked back tears. The nurse then wove her hair into one long braid, tying the end with a scrap of fabric.

"Follow me."

Genevieve accompanied the nurse down another long corridor. She tried to memorize the various turns they took, keeping an eye out for landmarks, wanting to get her bearings.

Eventually the nurse led her into a long hall crowded with women. Genevieve's arms were already crossed over her body for warmth, and she tightened them further. Her heart sank.

She had had little interaction with those considered insane. The plight of the mentally unwell was not among the charities she and her family normally supported, nor even Daniel. They had pooled their efforts to assist the impoverished, she'd rallied behind causes such as women's suffrage with her mother, and she was a generous patron of the arts. It wasn't that she didn't feel the cause important; it was simply not one she had prioritized among the many needs in the city.

One patient smiled but quietly wept, shaking her head vehemently when anyone tried to ask what was amiss, and several others carried on conversations with people who weren't there. One repeatedly tugged her hair and laughed, a high, bitter sound akin to chalk scraping over a slate. Some stared dreamily into the distance, off in their own worlds, while others looked as frightened and bewildered as Genevieve felt.

The windows were open to the chilly morning air, and, like her, none of the other patients were dressed warmly enough. Genevieve's still-wet hair felt like a frozen helmet, and she edged closer to one of the heaters, giving the hair-pulling woman a wide berth.

"Genevieve?"

Genevieve whipped around. The tentative voice had come from another patient, dressed in the same dark underskirt and white dress as hers, hair also in a long braid, sunken cheeked and hollow eyed but unmistakable.

"*Prue.*"

CHAPTER 23

Genevieve gaped, then blurted out the first thing that bounced into her head.

"I thought you were in Italy."

Prue ran her fingers down her braid repeatedly, stroking it as if it were a stole. "No. Not in Italy." She looked around a little wildly, then began humming softly. Genevieve recognized the tune. It was a nursery song.

Concerned alarm crept across her shoulders.

Had her friend *actually* gone mad?

"How did you get in here?" Genevieve whispered. A gray-haired woman edged closer to them, grinning, as if wanting to join their conversation. Genevieve steered Prue a few feet away. "We must speak. I was at your house, looking for you, when—"

"Get in line," a voice barked. It was the large nurse again, accompanied by two others, who poked and prodded and jostled the women into a double line. In the confusion of shuffling bodies, Genevieve lost Prue, then saw her several rows ahead as they were marched into a dining hall.

The women rushed the bare wooden tables, set with simple tin dishes. Genevieve tried to push through the crowd to sit next to Prue; she *had* to speak with her. Bannon had found her at the Nadlers' house, and if Prue was here, and now Genevieve was here, Harvey Nadler was somehow involved with her own admittance to Blackwell's. But again, why? What did Harvey Nadler have against her? And what was Bannon's involvement? None of it made any sense.

She spotted Prue at the far end of the table, the places around her on the long, backless benches already full. Genevieve found an empty seat and craned her neck, hoping to keep an eye on the other woman. She would have to find an opportunity to talk to her friend later.

The meal appeared appalling, a lump of hard, black bread with a scrape of butter, a bowl of room-temperature, lumpy oatmeal smeared with molasses, and a cup of cold tea. A woman with a mass of curly brown hair made a grab for Genevieve's bread, but Genevieve quickly snatched it up herself, immediately aghast at her own behavior.

What was happening? She had been at Blackwell's for less than twelve hours and was already fighting over food, no better than an animal. She tucked her head and tried a bite of the bread, but it was nearly impossible to sink her teeth into. Genevieve glanced around and saw other inmates gnawing on their portions or softening the bread in their tea. Perhaps she could break it apart and the middle would be more edible? She probed at the hard stuff with her fingers, then dropped it in disgust.

There was a dead spider stuck in her bread.

The other patient nipped the bread off the table in a flash with a triumphant look, and Genevieve let it go with a shudder. She averted her eyes from the curly-haired woman applying herself to the spider-bread and swallowed. The oatmeal looked gray and gelatinous and like nothing she could eat.

She knew she needed to force something down. She had to keep her strength up, keep her wits about her. Surely there was someone she could speak with, an asylum doctor or a superintendent or director . . . someone whom she could convince she didn't belong here.

Genevieve took a tentative sip of the tea. It was so weak it was though she were drinking brown water, unsweetened, but she persevered, working up her courage to try the oatmeal.

It was as horrible as it looked, and she gagged involuntarily, eliciting a nasty snigger from the curly-haired patient. Genevieve ignored her and forced the bite down with a slug of tea, then tried again.

She would do this. She could. She had to. She could already see how Blackwell's could wear you down, swallow you up, make you feel hopeless and allow you to sink into despair. How they *wanted* you to sink into despair. Women in despair were likely easier to manage.

Not her. She would find the right people to talk to and convince them she was here by mistake.

And if that didn't work, she would find another way out.

Genevieve steeled herself and took another bite.

★ ★ ★

Daniel stared at the smoldering wreckage of his house as the sky incrementally but relentlessly shifted from deep indigo to pale gray. The fire had been contained, and finally put out, in those predawn hours. It was the time of day Daniel least trusted, and tonight had been no exception. Was the fire really quashed, or was there an unnoticed ember quietly gaining strength in some corner, one that would catch and spread until the brilliant flames again erupted, leaping out of the destroyed windows, disintegrating the entire structure to nothing but ash?

Kincaid had sternly told him to stay put as the firefighters searched the wreckage. Daniel did as he was told.

Was this what would become of his life, of what he had dreamt for him and Genevieve? Had Bannon's earlier search been incorrect? Would they find her charred remains somewhere in the silent, smoking ruins? He couldn't believe it, but he wouldn't rest until they were sure. Until someone could tell him definitively she wasn't there.

The sun was rising but had yet to bring any warmth to the early morning, which remained shrouded in mist. Sometime in the night, barriers had been erected at either end of the block, pedestrians and vehicles ordered away, but the sounds of the awakening city traveled to where he was sitting. Hooves and carriage wheels clattering over pavement, bottles of milk clinking in the backs of trucks, cooks' assistants accepting early deliveries at the servants' entrance, and the chatter of early-morning birdsong filled the air. Less than a block away, life continued its normal pace.

For Daniel, life had shrunk to the square of pavement on which he sat.

Rupert also sat, silent, on the cold, damp ground next to him. Asher stood a few feet away, keeping a wary eye on the street.

Connor was connected to this somehow. Daniel wasn't sure why, or how, but he felt it in his bones. And if Genevieve had been put in that house to die, he would find Connor, and he would kill him, brother or no.

A soot-covered figure emerged from the wreckage. It was Kincaid. Daniel scrambled to his feet, Rupert following. Kincaid's face was impassive as he approached, and Daniel's stomach turned. He found his right fist was clenching and releasing, over and over; he forced it to relax but held his breath as Kincaid stopped in front of them.

Rupert clamped a hand on his shoulder.

"There are no bodies in that house, Daniel." A burr of emotion roughened Kincaid's voice. "It's empty."

No bodies. Genevieve wasn't in there.

Daniel gasped in a breath. His knees wanted to buckle, but he forced himself to stay upright.

"Are you sure?" he managed.

"Yes," Kincaid said. He dropped a meaty hand on Daniel's other shoulder. "Bannon and his boys were right. Nobody was there."

It was hard not to weep in relief. Daniel shook Kincaid's hand, told him to extend his gratitude to Bannon and the rest of the crew. He would have to send something to the firehouse in thanks later.

The lack of sleep was finally catching up to him. Rupert and Asher also looked as though they might drop from pure fatigue and emotion, so Daniel had Asher drop Rupert off on their way back to Gramercy Park, where Daniel wove his way through the piles of boxes to his bedroom. It didn't matter that their new house was destroyed; he would find another place for him and Genevieve to live. He refused to start his new life with her in Jacob Van Joost's old house, the place that had caused him so much unhappiness.

Because he *would* find her.

He didn't want to sleep but knew he would keel over if he didn't get at least a little rest. Dropping his soot-covered clothes to the floor, Daniel fell into bed just as the morning sun, now properly risen, cheerfully streamed through his windows.

His dreams, though, were dark, full of bright, vicious flames. He was in the new house, and could hear Genevieve calling for him, but he couldn't find her. He followed her panicked voice, his own fear rising with the emotion in hers, into room after room, but she was nowhere.

"Danny." Asher's rough voice woke him with a start. Daniel jerked himself upright, blinking, willing the dregs of the dream to dissipate.

It was only a dream. You'll find her.

The shadows on the dark-wood floors had shifted, indicating it was sometime in the afternoon. He hadn't slept the whole day away, then. Good.

"Did you sleep?" he asked, rubbing the last trace of tiredness from his eyes.

"Yeah. Paddy's here. Wanted to tell you himself; he's got information on that police officer."

Ten minutes later, Daniel was in his own office devouring a plate of sandwiches and a pot of strong black coffee. He hadn't wanted to take the time to bathe but was in clean clothes, at least.

"You're sure you don't want one?" He extended the plate to his guest. "Or Mrs. Rafferty can make you something else."

Paddy shook his head. "But some coffee will do."

As Daniel poured coffee for Paddy and Asher, the gang leader filled him in on what he knew.

"Your man is one Brian Jackson, formerly of the Oyster Knife Gang."

Daniel frowned. "A Knifer? On the police force? I've never heard of him; have either of you?"

"No reason for any of us to know him," said Paddy, taking the coffee. "He's younger than you, joined but left while you were away at school, never did much with that lot so far as I know. My sources say he made a lot of noise about finding God. He likes to haunt the dance halls, the Cairo and Bohemia, gives the working girls there a hard time. I've seen the man, didn't know he was police. Sometimes he stands on the corner outside the Haymarket and preaches."

Daniel chewed and swallowed by matter of necessity. The food was as good as always, but for the moment it was purely fuel. Officer Jackson, a former Oyster Knifer. The Oyster Knife gang were the enemies of the gang Paddy ran, the Bayard Toughs. Tommy Meade had been their leader and Daniel's nemesis. Right up until the moment Genevieve shot him, saving Daniel's life.

She had said this Jackson fellow was hanging around Pearl Martin's clinic.

Something didn't add up. Or it did, but not in any way he liked.

He ate the last bite of his sandwich and stood, narrowing his eyes.

"Let's go."

★   ★   ★

The Tenderloin district was bustling, as it was every night, including Sundays, despite the ban on public dancing on the Christian sabbath. The ban was rarely enforced, unless a saloon hadn't paid its "protection" fee to police, in which case it would be subject to raids. The complicity between vice and the police force was an accepted part of New York nightlife, and Daniel wondered where Jackson fit into its complex web. Longstreet, he knew, had made some noise about reforming the force but was not high enough in rank to do much about it yet. Daniel suspected the detective had his eye on loftier prospects.

Asher and Rupert accompanied him, as Paddy preferred to keep a low profile, and together they wove among the laughing crowds thronging the sidewalks. Spring was a quiet time for the city's elite. The parties and balls of the winter season were over; the gaiety and high jinks of the summer season in Newport or other resort areas were yet to come. The Tenderloin, particularly their destination, the Haymarket Dance Hall, provided an outlet of entertainment for all the strata of New York society year-round. Within its walls, members of the Astor 400 rubbed elbows with day laborers, as any man with a quarter would be admitted. Women, of course, could enter for free, though few respectable women did. Once inside, there was drink, music, and girls dancing the cancan. The women working the room would cajole the mostly married patrons into buying them champagne, then joining them on the dance floor and perhaps eventually in a curtained room upstairs. If one wished for male partnership instead, this option was available via the back entrance. There was even an underground tunnel to an adjacent hotel, should one wish for more privacy than a mere curtain.

As they approached the corner of Sixth Avenue and Thirtieth Street, Daniel saw several very wealthy men, pillars of New York society, slipping inside the Haymarket. These men wouldn't dare enter a Five Points opium den, but that was the beauty of the Tenderloin; it was just enough on the fringes of respectability, both geographically and morally, that all types could come and go with impunity. That didn't mean the Tenderloin was safe, of course. Even though the sex workers of all genders who were the Haymarket's main lure were strictly forbidden from stealing from their clients, theft was rampant, and one had to be on guard in any of the saloons in this district.

"Repent! Before it is too late, repent! You, there, I see your wedding ring. Would you forsake the vows you've taken before God, to enter that den of impurity and vice? Turn back, sir, before it is too late for your soul."

There he was. Officer Brian Jackson, in plain clothes, standing atop an overturned fruit carton in front of the Haymarket and cajoling those entering in a booming voice. "Ladies' Mile, where your wives and daughters shop, is but a few blocks south of here. What would they say if they knew of your sins? There is no need to stay here in Satan's circus. Go home, gentlemen, home to those women of virtue, of grace, of tranquil domesticity!"

Jackson was red-faced, a tall, imposing figure on his crate. His eyes gleamed with zealotry, and a trickle of sweat made its way from his left temple toward his cheek. Jackson made no move to wipe it away. Daniel was satisfied to see the man's nose and the areas under his eyes were still swollen from where Daniel had hit him the day prior.

He hoped it still hurt like hell.

Two ladies with bright face paint and stylish dresses sniggered behind their hands at the sight of Jackson before passing under the dance hall's brightly lit sign. Big Tim, the bouncer and manager of the joint, leaned against the doorframe of the entrance. He crossed his arms and frowned in the policeman's direction.

Daniel stopped a few feet away. Rupert stood next to him, but Asher had disappeared into the crowd somewhere. Keeping watch, no doubt, but staying out of sight.

"Officer Jackson? I need to speak with you," Daniel called.

Jackson paused in his ranting, taking in the sight of them. What could only be described as a sneer crossed his face.

"McCaffrey." He spat the name. "You want to finish what we started? Longstreet isn't here to hold me back."

"If you like." Daniel would be more than satisfied to break the man's nose twice.

Jackson scanned the street. He was no fool; he must know Daniel wouldn't come without reinforcements other than Rupert. Big Tim had straightened and was cracking his knuckles and watching the exchange with interest. Daniel knew the bouncer only by reputation but guessed Big Tim would also be happy to see the off-duty officer turned preacher with a broken nose.

"Got more important work to do here than wrangle with the likes of you," said Jackson, seeming to not like his odds. Smarter than he looked, then.

"I know you were part of the Oyster Knife crew," Daniel said, taking a step closer to the crate. "I also know you were outside Pearl Martin's clinic the day it burned, and you spoke to my fiancée and her mother. I think you know more about her disappearance than you're letting on, and if you know what's good for you, you'll tell me what that is, right now."

Jackson looked down his broken nose at Daniel, righteous indignation dancing in his eyes. "I did run with those Oyster boys way back, when I was an impressionable lad. But like I told you, my parents worked their way up. We left Five Points, and I saw the error of my ways. Religion was my savior." He raised his voice again, his words carrying over the raucous, joyful chatter of the passersby.

Daniel ignored his rants. "Why were you outside Pearl Martin's clinic last week? Were you following my fiancée?"

Jackson stared at him coldly. "That stretch of Park Avenue is part of my regular beat. I kept an eye on that whore Madame Martin's place of business, if you can call it that. She was dealing in illicit information and substances, in clear violation of the Comstock Act, and I suspected her of being an abortionist to boot. God sees all, and God passed judgment on her. She deserved what she got, and I am glad of her death."

"You call yourself a Christian, yet celebrate a woman's murder in her own home?" Daniel was nearly shaking with anger.

"The same fate awaits all who do not *repent*," Jackson said, yelling the final word into the night. A small crowd of saloon-goers had gathered, muttering and laughing, rolling their eyes. The sight of them seemed to enrage Jackson further. His face turned a deeper shade of red. "As it does all fornicators." He was screaming now, spittle flying from his mouth, pointing into the crowd. "That includes you, and your fiancée," Jackson said, turning back to Daniel.

Red was beginning to creep into the edges of Daniel's vision again. One more word about Genevieve and he would knock this fool off his carton, and so help him, he would not be responsible for his actions. He could hear Rupert's breath next to him shift, becoming shallower and more rapid, could feel the tension building between the two of them and Jackson.

The crowd could feel it too. There was a murmur, and a wider periphery opened around the crate as people stepped back, a few ducking into the dance hall, shaking their heads as they glanced over their shoulders. Others pressed into the edges, top hats and cloth caps alike, sensing something violent was about to occur, watching it build with greedy, gleaming eyes. Big Tim stepped closer, assessing.

"Where is she?" It was an effort to keep his voice controlled. He was at the base of the crate now, his head level with Jackson's midsection.

"I don't know where your whore of a fiancée is," Jackson said in a low voice. A hush had fallen over the crowd, and his words carried easily in the night. "But I doubt she'll return alive. God has smote her for her sins."

The red consumed him. Daniel's head made contact with Jackson's middle, and the man toppled from the crate. The crowd roared and surged, but Daniel was barely aware of them. The sounds seemed far off; he had focus only for turning this hateful man's face into a mass of blood and bone, all of his pent-up worry and anger and fear and rage flying from his heart into his fists as they pummeled into flesh over and over. He would have killed Jackson, it would have been his absolute pleasure, had Rupert, Asher, and Big Tim not hauled him back.

"If you kill him, you'll wind up in the Tombs for life," Rupert hissed into his ear. "What would become of Genevieve then? Stop, Daniel, stop. Enough. It's enough."

Somehow the words broke through his haze. Daniel shrugged the men off. Miraculously, Jackson was not only alive but still conscious. He struggled to an elbow and spit out a tooth, staring at Daniel with one bloodshot, crazed eye.

"Mark my words, McCaffrey," he said. "God has cast his judgment."

Daniel shook himself and glanced at his bloody fists. Jackson was an obnoxious, delusional fanatic, who bore no resemblance to the model of Christianity Daniel had grown up learning from the local parish priest. He was bigotry and hypocrisy and intolerance wrapped in the cloak of religion; his beliefs were an anathema to the very creed he preached.

And if he hadn't divulged what he knew about Genevieve's disappearance after the beating Daniel just gave him, he must not know where she was.

"We're done here," he said. "But if I see you within one block of Miss Stewart ever again, rest assured I will finish the job, and I will put you where you'll never be found, not even by your god."

With that, Daniel turned his back, allowing the crowd to cloak his way.

CHAPTER 24

Was there a routine at Blackwell's? One of sorts, Genevieve supposed. There were regular meals, if they could be called such. Breakfast was the same hard, black, buttered bread and oatmeal with molasses. She soon discovered the butter was rancid and tried to ask for a piece without. Sometimes she received it, sometimes not. Dinner was the same bread, and prunes, all served with the same weak tea. Inmates stole each other's food at every meal.

Sometimes they worked. Genevieve had first assumed it was the nurses who kept the dining hall and other common areas so spotless, and soon laughed at herself for being so naïve. The patients did all the work, of course, while the nurses kept a watchful eye. As Genevieve was relatively healthy, she was made to scrub the hard stone floors of the entry hall, which, she learned, welcomed new inmates every few days when they arrived on boats from the city. Genevieve dipped a scrub brush into a pail of cold water laced with some astringent cleanser, again and again, her hands turning raw and chapped after a few hours. It was hard, backbreaking work, but a welcome change from the monotony of asylum life, particularly when all they did was sit.

Those days were the worst, the days of sitting. For hours, the entire waking day, a hall full of women who were told to just . . . sit. On hard, wooden benches with no backs. They were not allowed to lie down, to tuck their feet under them, or to walk for a bit to move their bodies. They were not given material to read or permitted to speak to one another. They simply sat, as time slowed to a crawl, the minutes feeling like hours. These sessions were the hardest on all the patients. Genevieve tried to think of good things, bright and clean, during these stretches: her family's faces, the warmth and comfort of her parents' house, the way the sunshine lit the floors of the home she and Daniel were building. It must be almost finished by now. She recalled moments with her friends and strained her brain to remember each detail: Esmie, laughing, falling from a bicycle in Prospect Park. Callie, her face bright with joy, saying "I do" to Genevieve's brother Gavin in the drawing room of the Stewart family home, the answering look of astonishment and love on her brother's face. Eliza proudly telling her and Callie, at the dinner after the wedding, that she was finally going to Italy to set up a sculpture studio.

She spent hours thinking of her favorite meals. If she focused hard enough, Genevieve found she could recall the exact place settings at Delmonico's, could see in her mind's eye the precise location of each gleaming sterling-silver utensil, see how the light caught on the cut-crystal goblets, remember the way the champagne flutes sparkled. And the food itself: silky terrapin soup spiked with sherry, the crackling skin of savory roast duck with herbs, the delightful tart, creamy smoothness of a lemon pot de crème.

Mostly, she thought about Daniel. The way his hair sprang up in corkscrews when it became mussed, how one side of his mouth would quirk up in a half smile she adored, how his eyes darkened when they were about to kiss. The feel of his upper arms under her hands, the way the dark ink there looked between her fingers.

Sometimes, darker thoughts crept in. Genevieve tried to resist these, but it was a challenge. The endless hours of sitting sometimes caused her mind to play strange tricks on her. Once, she was sure she saw shapes in the shadows on the walls, ghoulish figures that morphed and transformed as the sun moved across the sky, the sight horrifying and transfixing, until she forced herself to look away. Another time, a crawling feeling began to creep over her skin, growing and festering, even though she could see nothing. Genevieve resisted the urge to scratch, to claw at her own flesh to make the feeling stop, until she thought she might really go mad.

Prue was in the hall where they sat, but always a few benches away. Even if she were close, Genevieve wouldn't have been able to talk with her, even in a whisper. Genevieve worried about her friend. Prue had a glassy, faraway look in her eyes. Sometimes she rocked a little, humming a well-known lullaby under her breath. Genevieve tried to catch Prue's eye, to give her a smile and nod of encouragement, but was only sometimes successful.

All the patients regularly met with one of the two staff doctors. During her first few meetings, Genevieve tried, desperately, to get the doctors to listen to her.

"My name isn't Polly; please, you must believe me. I'm Genevieve Stewart, and I was put here against my will. My parents are Wilbur and Anna Stewart, and I'm engaged to Mr. Daniel McCaffrey. Our wedding was meant to be Saturday, in Grace Church. I know Caroline Astor. You have to help me get out of here. I want to go home," she had pleaded. The older doctor, a man named Dr. Alba, had the cloudy red-rimmed eyes, shaky hands, and sour breath of a man who abused the bottle. The younger of the two was a nervous-looking fellow known as Dr. Mitchell, with a sharp, pinched face and ice-cold hands.

"You are Polly Stuart," Dr. Alba told her as he looked inside her mouth and peered at her eyes. "You were committed by your cousin Neville Stuart. You have hysteria, and are confusing your last name with the missing lady who has been in the papers. See?" Dr. Alba showed her the paper on which he was making notes, and Genevieve saw her last name was spelled differently.

"But that proves it! Genevieve Stewart *is* missing, or, I am. That's me. I'm missing because I'm *here*. Please, I'm meant to be getting married," she repeated. What day was it? Had she missed her own wedding? Her last exchange with Daniel had been angry. She had been so furious at him for having Billy follow her, and now she wished, desperately, that she had accepted his help. If Billy had been watching, she wouldn't be here now.

Genevieve thought of her wedding dress, of the gorgeous lace and bands of silk, hanging unworn in her wardrobe. Had Callie and Gavin arrived from Chicago, or Eliza from Italy? Did they think she had run away? Did *Daniel* think she had run away, had changed her mind about marrying him? Tears welled, rolling down her face at the thought of how desperate they must be.

Why wouldn't these doctors believe her?

Dr. Mitchell gave her a sidelong glance as he took her pulse. Dr. Alba passed the clipboard with its paper to him when the younger doctor was finished. "You must try to resist confusion of the brain, Polly," Dr. Alba said to her sharply. He shook his head at Dr. Mitchell, as if she weren't there. "The delusions of hysteria can be very difficult to treat."

"Should we give her something?" Dr. Mitchell eyed her in a considering way that set Genevieve's skin to crawling again.

"Not yet. Her delusions aren't harming anyone but herself, for the moment. If that changes, then yes."

Genevieve tried to speak with the superintendent, who toured the facility every few days, but was forced away by the nurses and slapped as soon as the man was out of sight. The sharp crack of the palm against her face was more shocking than painful, but it still brought another set of tears to her eyes. "Try that again and you'll get more than a slap," hissed the large nurse, whom she now knew was called Miss Grismark. The rabbity one was Miss

Bellwether. Very few of the nurses were kind, but those two were particularly vicious, and perfectly capable of delivering a severe beating to any patient they cared to.

"This one says she's getting married on Saturday, in Grace Church," Miss Grismark sneered, leading Genevieve away from the doctors and back to the hallway to await the next wretched meal.

"Ooh, a fancy one. Grace Church, la-di-da," Miss Bellwether said. "She knows Mrs. Astor, she does." They both laughed, the mean, humorless laughs of bullies. By now they were in the hallway with the other patients, several of whom, the crazier ones, joined in. The collective laughter of the insane bounced off the walls and echoed, making Genevieve want to cover her ears with her hands, to scream at them to stop.

"Saturday's in four days, dearie," Miss Grismark smirked. "I'm afraid you'll miss your wedding. Better get used to us, as you're not going anywhere."

The best days were when they got to go outside. This did not happen every day, but all the patients awaited the event eagerly, despite some of the horrific sights that awaited them. Women from the Lodge, a part of Blackwell's where the most dangerous of inmates were kept, were only able to walk tied together by a rope attached to belts around their waists. The rope—and therefore the women—pulled behind them a cart carrying some who were too unwell to even walk. This group screamed and raved, lunged and jabbered, moaned and cried. It was a heart-wrenching and terrifying ordeal to observe.

In the sunshine, outside the dank, dark confines of the institution, were the only times Genevieve felt warm. The rolling green lawns were a balm for her eyes, as were the gray, choppy waters of the East River, surrounding Blackwell's Island on all sides.

The city was so close. She could see it, as tantalizing but distant as a mirage.

Genevieve stared at the pattern of the skyline.

She would get back there, or die trying.

"I found you."

Genevieve whirled from her contemplation of the city. It was Prue, smiling, hands sliding up and down her braid.

"Prue." Genevieve clasped her friend's hands, pulling them away from their motions and squeezing them tight. Prue looked startled, then hummed a bar of the lullaby Genevieve had heard her sing before.

"Prue," she repeated, moving her head until she was looking Prue in the eye. Prue blinked and stopped humming.

"Genevieve," Prue whispered. "What are we doing here?"

"Please, we don't have much time. I need to ask you: What were you doing at Pearl Martin's that day? The day I saw you, the day it burned?" Genevieve was sure that whatever the reason Prue had been at the clinic was some kind of linchpin, a clue, holding this insanity together.

Prue blinked again, a faint flush staining her cheeks. She had lost the round, contented look Genevieve remembered from the night of Dagmar's lecture.

"I was . . . I was getting a contraceptive device." Prue's lower lip trembled, and she looked around furtively, but none of the other inmates were paying them any mind. Miss Bellwether, though, was watching them with narrowed eyes.

"You know I experienced some losses, yes? People gossip." Genevieve nodded. "I felt like the worst sort of failure," Prue continued. "I couldn't give Harvey the one thing he wanted, a child. He said I wasn't a real woman, and I didn't feel like one. All our school friends—well, our married school friends—kept having babies, and I couldn't keep one in my body. Finally, I couldn't take it any longer. I was contemplating terrible things, Genevieve. Throwing myself from the East River Bridge, or under the elevated. But someone recommended Madame Martin to me, said maybe she could help me keep a pregnancy."

Prue swallowed and glanced nervously over her shoulder again. Miss Bellwether had advanced a few steps but wasn't close enough to hear them. Genevieve nodded at Prue encouragingly. "I think we're going back inside soon. What happened?"

"She didn't try to help me keep a pregnancy. Instead, she convinced me to start using contraceptives. It was miraculous, Gennie." Genevieve started, feeling tears prick her eyes to match Prue's. Nobody had called her Gennie since she was small. Hearing it brought such a visceral memory of playing in Washington Square Park with her brothers and a few other children, it was almost as though she were there again, the smell of grass aiding her memory. "I didn't get pregnant again, for the first time in years. I was healthier and happier, and able to envision a life for me and Harvey without children. I started seeing friends again, doing more charity work, as Harvey did his. But that day of the fire . . ." Prue paused, dropping her voice back to a whisper.

"What happened, Prue?" A knot of dread was forming in her throat. Genevieve knew what Prue was about to say but needed to hear it.

Prue swallowed again. "He found out. Harvey. He must have become suspicious, when we didn't conceive again, and he ransacked my things. He found my syringe, my herbs. He was furious, screaming uncontrollably, saying I had emasculated him, made him a laughingstock. I, well, I don't remember all of it. Only that he hit me, many times, until I must have been knocked unconscious. I woke up here. The bruises only just healed."

It was an appalling tale, yet Genevieve believed every word. "Do they know who you are?" She was deeply aware of the privileges of her and Prue's class and wealth, how these factors might give them advantages over these other, poorer women, yet she would use any means available to her if they could help her friend, and maybe her, leave this terrible place.

"Oh yes," said Prue. A hard glint entered her eyes. "They know. Prudence Constance Nadler, admitted by her husband, for reasons of hysteria."

Somehow, this knowledge made Genevieve's heart sink further, though she surprised herself with a small laugh. "I, too, am here for hysteria. But your parents, surely, would help you get out of here, vouch that you are not insane?"

Prue shook her head. "I do not know if they have any legal authority. I'm a grown woman, married for several years now. My commitment here was legal and binding, they say. It is Harvey's right to do so; a judge signed the papers."

Absolute fury threatened to overtake Genevieve. Her own situation was unthinkable, but somehow Prue's was worse. That her own husband had committed her to an asylum, simply because she was preventing herself from becoming pregnant. That it was legal and accepted for him to do so, though Genevieve would wager money had changed hands regardless. At least she was here under false pretenses, not locked away by the person who claimed to love her.

Harvey Nadler. He had a vendetta against her mother, but that wouldn't be reason enough for him to commit Genevieve, would it? Morris Bannon was in league with him somehow. Genevieve remembered one of her last thoughts in the dingy house on Mott Street, following Bannon up the stairs. About how large he was, how broad, and how he fit the description of the man both Marla and Antoine had seen at the Sunflower Mission House. She thought of the fires, of being trapped in the basement of Pearl Martin's house, panicking that she would die of smoke inhalation or get burnt alive. Of Dagmar's wounds, his burned, bandaged body, so wrapped he resembled one of the Egyptian mummies Gavin studied.

The pieces of the puzzle were mostly there; she could feel it. But how they fit together, what the whole picture was, remained inscrutable.

The strident calls of the nurses rang through the soft spring air. "Get in line. Get in line, you, now."

"Prue, what does your husband know of deputy fire chief Morris Bannon?" she whispered urgently.

"You two, Stuart, Nadler, I don't want another word," Miss Bellwether barked. She grabbed Genevieve's arm, her fingers twisting the flesh on its soft upper part, until Genevieve drew in a hiss of pain. Genevieve was taller than the rabbity-looking nurse, probably stronger too, even with the lack of food, but she didn't dare retaliate or fight back. Only a day ago she had seen four nurses gang up on one patient, three holding her down while Miss Grismark held the poor woman's head and beat it repeatedly against the floor. All because the patient, one of those who was truly mentally afflicted, had been unable to stop singing when they were meant to be sitting quietly.

The inside of Genevieve's upper arm throbbed. She would have a bruise there later.

Daniel didn't know where she was, she was sure of it. If he did, he would be here by now, despite the anger with which she'd last left him. According to Dr. Alba, her disappearance was in the papers. They were looking for her. Would he think to check here? And even if he got access to the records somehow, would he know that "Polly Stuart," committed by her next of kin, a cousin called Neville, was actually Genevieve?

She was sure he would figure it out eventually. Genevieve knew Daniel would leave no stone unturned. But it could take time, time she didn't have. It was already a struggle, almost a week inside Blackwell's, to keep true mental confusion at bay. The inedible food, the lack of sleep, the constant cold from the frigid baths—she'd endured that twice now—the way the damp walls kept the interior freezing and miserable even if it was temperate outdoors, all were wearing her down. Genevieve could feel her strength, her will, her mental acuity, ebb with each passing day.

If it took six months for Daniel to find her, would she be the same woman by then?

They were back in the hallway, where they awaited their next meal. The sun was beginning to drop, and along with it the temperatures. Genevieve shivered and folded her arms around her body, searching for Prue's bright head.

She edged her way in that direction, avoiding eye contact with the desperate, mad faces who tried to talk to her.

"I'm getting out of here," she whispered once she was next to Prue. Her friend had been stroking her auburn braid again, and had begun the slight rocking motion. At Genevieve's words, she stilled. "And when I do, I'll get you out too."

Prue's eyes flickered to hers for a second, and for the second time that day, Genevieve's heart sank.

She knew the look in Prue's gaze, knew it and feared it. It was the emotion she fought against every minute of every hour of every day that passed.

It was hopelessness.

CHAPTER 25

Genevieve tipped back the ugly straw bonnet they gave the inmates for their time outdoors and turned her face to the sun. It had been a series of beautiful days, and she wondered if the timid warmth outdoors would translate into a less chilled atmosphere indoors, but she wasn't holding out much hope. She suspected it would remain unbearably cold inside until the summer, when the cells would transform to being unbearably hot.

Not that she intended to stay here long enough to find out.

Two days of outdoor time in a row was a treat. Perhaps the nurses, too, wanted to savor the fine spring weather? Genevieve gave the river an assessing eye.

It was calmer today.

Genevieve made her way to Prue again, who was standing closer to the river's edge. They weren't allowed to get too close, of course. She was pleased to note that her friend was not humming the lullaby under her breath; truth be told, it was a trifle creepy.

"Prue."

Her friend offered a dreamy smile. "I was thinking of what it might feel like to drown."

Genevieve's mouth went dry.

"I don't think it would hurt, do you?" Prue turned her attention back to the river. She started stroking her braid again, and rocked a little from side to side.

"Yes, I do," Genevieve said in a firm voice. She turned Prue back toward her and forced the other woman to meet her gaze. Prue shifted her brown eyes, not wanting to look Genevieve in the face.

"It would hurt a lot," she pressed, resisting the urge to give Prue a small shake. "I am getting out of here, Prue. I promise. And I will get you out too. You can't be shut in here against your will. There are avenues, recourses. Daniel is a lawyer, my father is a lawyer, we will go to the papers. Harvey won't be able to bear the bad publicity, if it is known he committed you for pregnancy losses. You will be free again. Please trust me."

Sunshine sparkled on the river at Prue's back. Genevieve didn't tell Prue that she too had been considering what it would feel like to move through those gray depths. Not to die, though.

Genevieve wanted to live.

"Please, Prue, does Harvey have any dealings with deputy fire chief Bannon? A large man, very tall, broad, prematurely white hair? Does any of that ring a bell?"

The dreamy expression slowly melted from Prue's face, replaced by one of confused sadness. She was focused on Genevieve, though, and that was good.

"I don't think so. That man doesn't sound familiar. Harvey's a terrible snob, you know. I don't think he'd be friends with a firefighter, chief or no."

Genevieve chewed her lip, remembering what her mother had said about Nadler. That he was a follower of Anthony Comstock.

"But he thinks himself rather a moral man, correct? My mother said he supported the Comstock laws."

Prue pursed her lips and looked at the river again, but not, Genevieve was relieved to see, with the desperate, hunted air of a few moments earlier.

"You're lucky, Gennie," she finally said. "You were lucky to not marry Ted Beekman. I'm sorry my family snubbed you after your broken engagement and didn't invite you to my wedding. We should have."

Genevieve waited. She had learned, during her work as a journalist, that sometimes silence garnered the best results.

"I didn't really know Harvey when I married him," Prue continued. "I was only nineteen, after all, and we weren't allowed to spend very much time together while we were courting. He seemed like all a girl in my position could want. He was wealthy, came from a good family; he was already thirty, well established. When we courted, he was charming, if a bit stiff." A lovely breeze wafted in from the river, picking up pieces of their hair and sending small strands flying. Genevieve pushed hers away impatiently.

"It wasn't until we had been married for some time that he revealed his true colors. There is a reason some thirty-year-old men choose to marry nineteen-year-old girls." Prue smiled ruefully. "He is obsessed with purity, with the souls of fallen women, as he called them. He believes there is a natural hierarchy between the sexes, between races. Blacks wanting equal rights was infuriating to him—I sometimes wonder if he wished Lincoln hadn't emancipated those poor enslaved souls, though of course he knew he couldn't say such a thing publicly. There were constant rants about how the poor should work themselves up; that if someone couldn't pull themselves up by their bootstraps, it was their own fault." Prue sighed, nudging at the grass with the toe of her shoe.

Genevieve checked behind them. They were relatively alone. The nurses were huddled in a group by the main building, chatting among themselves. The other inmates, those deemed trustworthy enough to be on the lawn unaccompanied, dotted the grounds. Some examined leaves or acorns, some walked in circles, some simply sat on the earth and admired the sky. The woman closest to them was called Vanda, a pretty young girl with large, dark eyes. She did not seem to speak any English. Gene-vieve thought perhaps her native tongue was Hungarian, though she couldn't be sure. Vanda seemed perfectly sane, simply scared and unable to communicate. Genevieve wondered if perhaps Vanda's lack of English was the entire reason she had been committed.

"Harvey's real feelings about other people went so far beyond what I was taught to believe, how I was raised to have respect for all of God's creatures, that I did not know how to address them. I tried to argue his points, gently of course, but that didn't go well at all. I tried to ignore him, but that also wasn't successful. Finally, I pretended to agree with him. It was a way to keep the peace, you understand. I wonder how many marriages are made up of such deceptions."

Genevieve wondered too. It sounded like a miserable existence.

"I had some of my own money, of course, from my parents. As we have no children, I turned my attention to charity work for the impoverished, a cause rather close to my heart, learned from my family. I did this anonymously, behind Harvey's back," Prue said. Her eyes had regained a little sparkle.

"That was rather rebellious," Genevieve said. And she meant it. Harvey Nadler seemed a controlling and unforgiving man; it must have taken quite a bit of scheming on Prue's part to carve out some important work of her own.

"Yes," said Prue. "It rather was."

"And you will be again," Genevieve insisted. "Once you're out of Blackwell's, you can file for divorce." A parade of rebellious women Genevieve was lucky enough to know marched through her mind: Eliza, devoted to her art, wresting figures from marble through sheer strength and artistry; Callie, who had worked as an artist's model, doing what she needed to survive when the world turned its back on her; her mother, who had fought and protested and championed the needs of women everywhere for decades now. Even Esmie, who could have stayed safe in her shell, had broken free of her own shyness and insecurity and was living as rich and full a life as anyone.

It was nearly physical, her longing to see them all.

"I don't know, Genevieve. Once Harvey had me committed, I'm not sure I have legal rights to my own money anymore. The money my parents left me, that should have stayed mine alone. Not that it has been for years." The sparkle dimmed from Prue's eyes. "That was all he ever wanted me for, I see that now. The money I brought, my status as a virginal schoolgirl, and the potential for a baby. He got two out of the three, I suppose."

Genevieve crossed her arms over her chest, even though the sun was warm.

"It wasn't even enough, my money," Prue continued, bitterness clouding her features. "He always wanted more. You know he skims off the top of the donations to the charities he manages? All those boards he sits on, the Society for the Suppression of Vice, the Society for Reform of Juvenile Delinquents—they're all just avenues to make money for him."

Connections Genevieve previously hadn't been able to see were lining up in her mind.

"The Society for Reform of Juvenile Delinquents?" she asked. "That runs the House of Refuge?"

"Those poor children," Prue said. "Harvey makes thousands off of them."

Genevieve's breath caught. *The indenture program.*

"How so?"

"Companies submit bids for the boys' labor. Harvey is the middleman, and he takes a cut. A large one. It's still cheaper for the businesses to use the boys and give Harvey some money than hire working men, so everybody wins."

"Except the boys."

Prue nodded sadly. "Yes. Except them."

Morris Bannon had been in Arthur's office when her editor had said they were planning to expose the indenture program. Bannon and Nadler were clearly in league with each other. Was Bannon getting a kickback from Nadler? It must be a great deal of money, though, for a man who devoted his entire career to fighting fires to start setting them.

But Pearl Martin hadn't been embarking on an exposé of the House of Refuge, nor anyone at the Sunflower Mission House. Genevieve shook her head as if to displace a fly. There were so many threads to untangle, she couldn't keep track of them all.

"Why were you both at Dagmar's lecture?"

"Harvey liked to stay apprised of people like Dagmar's work," Prue said. She looked a little embarrassed. "Your fiancé's too. He used to quote the Bible: 'Be sober, be vigilant; because your adversary the devil, as a roaring lion, walketh about.'"

"And Daniel, Dagmar, those like them, were the lions?" Genevieve spoke slowly, but her mind raced.

"Yes." Prue shrugged a little. "Not just them. Anyone promoting social reform."

It clicked. One piece of the puzzle did, at least. She had been so busy looking at the individual trees, she had failed to see the forest. There were no personal connections between the Sunflower Mission House, Dagmar's studio, and Pearl Martin's clinic. Each might not have even known of the existence of the others. But they were all trying to engender *reform*.

Just as she had told the Brooklyn fire marshal. Only she had made that up, to keep his attention away from Marla and Antoine.

Was Harvey Nadler so extreme in his beliefs that he would have the businesses he was against set on fire?

A sudden commotion distracted Genevieve from her thoughts. Patients were yelling, nurses running. "River runner!" one of them shouted. "River runner!"

Vanda raced past them, looking neither left nor right. Only once she plunged into the river did she fearfully glance over her shoulder. When she saw the nurses in pursuit, she began moving more quickly, pushing her body against the currents, heading deeper and deeper into the murky water.

All the patients were gathered on the river's shore now, some desperately calling for Vanda to come back, some encouraging her to swim for it. Genevieve overheard Miss Bellwether telling the other nurses she would fetch the guards from the workhouse. "They have a rowboat," she called as she ran, skirts raised high.

The remaining nurses tried to corral the other patients back to the building, but the women were having none of it. Genevieve, too, resisted the hand on her arm, straining to keep her eyes on Vanda. The woman in the water was up to her shoulders now, her head bobbing.

"No," Genevieve said. Vanda's head bobbed once more, then disappeared. A murmur rose from the gathered patients. It popped back up momentarily. She could just see Vanda's dark hair masking her face, her open mouth and outstretched arms.

Genevieve pushed the nurse's hand off her and ran to the river. That woman was drowning, right in front of their eyes, and she couldn't stand by and watch it happen.

"Polly, stop right there," came a harsh voice, but Genevieve ignored it, moving as fast as she could. She was a strong swimmer; she could help.

A force hit her back and sent her flying. Genevieve barely had time to lift her hands to protect her face before she slammed into the ground, grass and dirt filling her mouth. The pressure on her back increased; the nurses must be piling on top of her to hold her down. It was all she could do to turn her head to gasp a breath.

She could see nothing from under the press of bodies but heard the patients crying out in hope. "She's over there, just there!" The boat must have come.

The cries of encouragement continued, then tapered off, and finally there was silence. From under the nurses, Genevieve could only hear the slap of the oars on the river, the faint sound of bird-song. Finally, the weight on her back lessened, and she was hauled upright by Miss Grismark, who held her upper arm in an iron grip.

The other patients were being herded back to the main house like so much livestock. They were mute, ashen faced, heads bowed.

Miss Grismark shoved Genevieve into their midst, and she fell into step with the rest of the inmates.

Genevieve wiped some grass off her face but didn't look back at the river. She didn't need to. She knew what they'd found.

⋆ ⋆ ⋆

They were running out of time.

Daniel knew it, and suspected that the group gathered in his front drawing room knew it too. In addition to Genevieve's parents and brother Charles, her brother Gavin and his wife Callie had arrived from Chicago. Genevieve's dear friend Eliza had also arrived, right on schedule, her boat from Italy having docked four days prior. Rupert was standing near him, while Esmie, red-eyed and puffy faced, was sitting nearby.

Genevieve had been missing for over a week. The police had absolutely no leads, and he and the Bayard Toughs had had no luck either. And while he didn't regret a single blow he'd landed on Officer Jackson's smug face (though not so smug now), he was already in a precarious position with the police, and now could be arrested at any time.

"I don't understand. You're not saying you'll stop looking, like the police?" Anna clutched Wilbur's hand. Both of Genevieve's parents were pale; they looked as though they'd aged a decade in the past week. Daniel knew he didn't look much better.

"Of course not," he said quickly. "I'm only saying we seem to be retreading the same ground. I simply don't know where else to look. She's not in any hospitals, the police have no record of a woman matching Genevieve's description, and despite the flood of tips coming in for the reward money, apparently none of them were worthy." The Stewarts hadn't wanted to go to the press at first, and Daniel had agreed. Foolishly, they had all assumed they'd find Genevieve quickly. How could they not, with the entire police force and one of New York's biggest gangs combing the city for her?

But as days passed, they had rethought the idea. Somebody somewhere in this city must have seen something, and if altruism wasn't enough to make that person come forward, Daniel was convinced cash would. Arthur had run several articles, including a handsome engraving modeled on Genevieve's photograph, with the promise of a hefty reward for information.

Half the tips were nonsense. It was exhausting and wasted valuable time trying to sort the wheat from the chaff. To make matters worse, the police search had thinned in recent days. Earlier that afternoon, Longstreet had intimated to the entire family that they assumed Genevieve was dead and were now searching for her body rather than hoping to find her alive.

"I'd get your affairs in order, McCaffrey." Longstreet had pulled him aside afterward.

"What were you thinking, saying such a thing to Genevieve's family? She is missing, not dead."

"It's best they prepare themselves. You know as well as I do that if she hasn't turned up by now, she likely won't. Unless you know more than you're letting on?"

Daniel released a frustrated breath but said nothing.

"I liked Miss Stewart," the detective said in a grudging tone. "I'm sorry for this. But you know I'll have to take you in for more formal questioning. Especially after the stunt you pulled with my officer. You're lucky he was out of uniform, or you'd be in front of a judge right now."

"She's. Not. Dead." It was all Daniel could do to keep from unleashing the same rage on Longstreet that he had on Jackson. How dare the man speak of Genevieve in the past tense.

Longstreet gave him a pitying look. "I'm just waiting for a judge to sign the paperwork. Could be as early as tomorrow. Please don't be tedious and try to hide from me or my men." The detective's words about Genevieve sounded sincere (*She's not dead*, his mind blared), but there was a distinct glint of satisfaction in his eyes at the prospect of arresting Daniel.

Daniel couldn't remember ever being this tired. And yet as the days passed, the less capable of sleep he became. Time was blurring together, one long interminable stretch of moments, day or night, where Genevieve was still missing. How long ago had their house burned down? Five days, six? He wasn't sure.

"And my imminent arrest may impede my abilities to search for some days." Daniel reminded the assembled family. He ran a hand over his face. The thought of being locked up in the Tombs and not out there, relentlessly hunting for Genevieve, was enraging. "But I don't think that's happening until tomorrow."

"We'll keep going if Longstreet comes for you," Rupert said quietly. "Don't worry about that."

"Ridiculous, that you might be arrested," Anna said. "Anyone who knows you knows you couldn't harm a hair on Genevieve's head. And that terrible Officer Jackson deserved to get punched."

"Mother," Charles said in a warning tone.

"Don't you *Mother* me, young man," Anna said, nearly vibrating with indignation despite her own obvious exhaustion. "I know that awful man, and I know his type. He's just like that wretched pigeon-faced Harvey Nadler; he's another one of Comstock's, mark my words."

A tingling began at the base of Daniel's skull. "What do you mean, just like Harvey Nadler? One of Comstock's what?"

"One of his acolytes," Anna said. "That horrid Harvey Nadler is also, the one married to Genevieve's sweet friend Prudence. I can smell their kind a mile off. You know Nadler had me arrested."

"We know, Mother," Gavin murmured.

The tingling in Daniel's skull intensified as he sat up in his chair. "Anna, I know you visited the Nadlers and were told Mrs. Nadler, Prudence, was out of town," he said slowly, thinking it through.

"Yes."

"But did you get an answer as to whether or not Genevieve tried to call?" Daniel wasn't sure what he was getting at, but for Anna to connect Jackson to a household Genevieve had said she might try to visit the day she disappeared . . . could it be something worth exploring further?

"Oh." Anna's face fell, and she looked crestfallen. "No, I suppose I didn't. I assumed that if Prudence wasn't there . . ." Anna trailed off, a blush rising in her cheeks. She wilted a little in her chair. "I was so distracted."

"Of course," Daniel said. "It's completely understandable." The tingling was now running down his arms. He quickly explained the situation to the visitors: how Genevieve had mentioned visiting the Nadler house, but now they needed to double-check whether she had actually done so. "We should pay Harvey Nadler another visit," he concluded. "One he can't dodge as easily."

As leads went, it was awfully thin. But it was something new, a stone they'd thought they'd turned over that was actually undisturbed. A subtle feeling of anticipation rippled through the group.

"Tonight?" Gavin rose, his brow lowered and dark. He looked ready to tear Harvey Nadler apart for information on the spot. Charles stood too. Both Stewart brothers were tall, Charles leanly muscled from years racing sailboats in all but the most dangerous weather, Gavin from his own athletic pursuits of fencing and boxing, not to mention years of arduous fieldwork in Egypt. Daniel was glad to have them here, glad they were on his side.

The search parties could use the fresh blood.

"No, we want to make sure he's home. I'll have someone keep an eye on his place tomorrow, let us know when he's definitely in." He wasn't sure it would do to show up on Nadler's doorstep with Rupert, Asher, and the Stewart brothers looming behind him, but he would cross that bridge when he came to it.

"Eliza and I will be searching also," Callie said as she too stood. She raised her chin. "I know my way around the dance halls after last winter."

Gavin stared at her. "You will do no such thing," he said.

"Genevieve is our closest friend. Women may tell us something they don't feel safe telling men," Callie said. Eliza joined in the argument, stating that they were perfectly capable of asking questions at dance halls and they knew how to keep themselves safe. Charles crossed his arms and watched, raising an eyebrow at Daniel.

Daniel grimaced back. Personally, he felt it was a fine idea for Callie and Eliza to join the search, but it wasn't his argument to have.

"Mr. McCaffrey." His housekeeper, Mrs. Kelly, edged in, handing him a letter that had arrived with the evening post. "You asked us to keep an eye out for anything from Minnesota." There were circles under her eyes as well. His staff adored Genevieve.

Daniel murmured an excuse and left the various Stewarts to sort out who would be searching where tonight. He retreated to his study and considered the sealed envelope carefully.

Something important, clarifying questions about his past, his family, was inside. Was he ready for whatever information it contained?

"Once more unto the breach," he muttered, and tore the envelope open.

CHAPTER 26

TRAGIC FIRE CLAIMS TWO LIVES

Ingrid Lund, 62, and Henrik Lund, 67, were both killed on July 13 when a fire destroyed their farmhouse in Mantorville. Neither of the Lunds' two sons, Dennis and Connor, both aged 24, were at home when the fire occurred, being away on business in St. Paul and LaCrosse, respectively. According to Connor Lund, his parents were not meant to be at home that evening but had planned to attend a church social in nearby Kasson, which included an overnight stay at the home of Ingrid Lund's sister Martha. Services will be held at Augustus Lutheran Church at 3pm on Monday, followed by a reception in the parish hall.

Daniel read the article again. Then a third time.

Though it was probably the last thing he needed, he poured himself a finger of bourbon from the sideboard and settled into his chair, reading the article yet again.

Two brothers, then. Dennis and Connor. Not Stephen, according to this. Daniel wasn't sure if he was relieved or disappointed. He checked the byline: Mercy Ennis, the same woman who had responded to his telegram.

Connor hadn't shown himself since the day Genevieve went missing, when Daniel had kicked him out. He couldn't help but wonder if his brother was lurking in the shadows regardless, keeping watch, biding his time. For what, he wasn't certain. But if history was any indicator of Connor's behavior, he would pop up soon.

Who was Dennis? Connor had said the Lunds had no children of their own. Was he another refugee from a large city, like Connor? What had become of him? Connor had said he'd sold the farm, by which he must have meant he'd sold the land itself, and any remaining livestock, as the house was destroyed. Why hadn't this other brother wanted the land? Daniel imagined rich farmland in Minnesota might be worth quite a lot.

It was disturbing that Connor had never mentioned an adopted brother, especially one his exact age.

There were too many unanswered questions, and Connor himself, it seemed, was the only person who could answer them.

Finding a pen and a scrap of paper, Daniel scribbled out another query to Mercy Ennis in Winona, Minnesota. He'd have one of the footmen deliver it to the telegraph office first thing in the morning.

"They're going to the Tenderloin." Gavin huffed into Daniel's office and crossed his arms, glaring down at him.

"Callie and Eliza?"

"You have to convince them to stop."

"I think trying to talk the ladies out of doing something is a fool's errand, and presumptuous to boot. We are not their keepers."

Gavin bristled. "Callie is my wife."

"Yes, your *wife*. A grown woman with her own mind. Not your child, nor yours to control."

Gavin gaped at him for a moment, clearly at a loss for words.

"I know what you're thinking," Daniel continued. "If I had compelled Genevieve to stay home, perhaps she wouldn't be missing. But I tried, and all it did was sour things between us. What was I going to do, keep her behind a locked door forever? Smother the very spirit I love most about her?" He sighed and rubbed his eyes. "They want to help, Gavin. And I think Callie is correct; perhaps there is a woman who saw something but who doesn't feel safe talking with a man."

"Esmie's not going," Rupert reported. He appeared behind Gavin, leaning against the doorframe. "But only because she's pregnant, and the nausea still comes and goes. It might turn off any potential witnesses if they were vomited upon."

Gavin glowered at him, crossing his arms tighter.

"Come on, we can drop off the ladies on our way uptown," Daniel said, heaving himself out of his chair and shaking off his exhaustion as best he could.

There was no time to be tired, not when Genevieve was out there somewhere. And not when tonight might be his last night to search, if Longstreet's threat of arrest was as imminent as he claimed.

Daniel rubbed the sides of the telegram message he'd written, the thick paper smooth under his fingers.

He would hand off the note before he left with strict instructions for it to be sent as soon as the office opened.

Just in case Longstreet was quicker than he thought.

*   *   *

An older woman with scraggly gray hair tried to hand Genevieve a scrap of fabric to dry her face. Genevieve shook her head, using her own underskirt to mop at her face and hands, even though the resultant dampness made her colder at night. The gray-haired woman, like many others, had violent sores on her face, and all the inmates shared the same rag as a towel.

She didn't know what infection the sores constituted, only that she didn't want it.

Watching poor Vanda drown had left Genevieve feeling weaker than usual, and nauseated. The mood at dinner had been mixed, with some patients excited by the action at the river, feverishly discussing it, and others, like her, left subdued and shaky, glancing at each other in silent horror.

Despite her best efforts, Genevieve couldn't force herself to eat, and she made no objection when the same woman with curly hair from her first meal snitched the prunes off her plate. Now, shivering uncontrollably in bed under her thin, scratchy blanket, Genevieve couldn't stop the image of Vanda's bobbing, sinking head from repeating in her mind.

Crossing the river had been her plan. She'd swum the East River before, when she and Daniel had been trapped on a small spit of land called Duck Island, all the way uptown, escaping gunrunners. She wondered now, realistically, if she could make it from Blackwell's to the city. The memory of the cold water sluicing over her head, the leaden feeling of her arms, the near delirium she had experienced on her previous journey was daunting, and not an experience she wanted to repeat. She'd been mentally preparing herself to undertake it regardless, but as her body shook from the cold, Genevieve tried to assess her own physical condition.

The swim from Duck Island had been almost a whole year ago. She was weaker now. It was astonishing how quickly it had happened, after only a little more than a week of bad food and little sleep, but a swim from Blackwell's would be treacherous, longer than the distance from Duck Island, and she wasn't sure she could make it in her current condition.

Vanda's sleek head slipping under the dark-brown water flashed in her mind again. Genevieve shuddered harder. She would reassess in the morning.

The next day dawned as all her days at Blackwell's had: the sound of a key scraping, her door creaking open, stumbling to the facilities, the long wait in the cold hallway for breakfast. Would they be allowed outside again today? She doubted it.

Genevieve's suspicions were confirmed once breakfast was over.

"Polly Stuart," Miss Grismark said, narrowing her already-beady eyes in Genevieve's direction. She had given up trying to correct the nurses over her name. "You're to come with me. Doctor's visit."

"But I'm not unwell," she protested, following the nurse out of the dining hall. "There are others who are truly sick."

"Not for you to decide who gets seen. You tried a runner yesterday; doctor has to examine you."

It was also useless to protest that she had only been heading into the river in an attempt to save Vanda.

It was Dr. Mitchell today. Once in the examination room, Genevieve tried the same approach. "Doctor," she said as he checked her pulse. "There are women with sores on their faces. Open ones. They are far worse off than I and ought to be seen to prevent the spread of further illness, do you not agree?"

Dr. Mitchell eyed her the way he always did, as if she were a specimen in a jar he was considering for dissection. She fully expected to be ignored, but to her surprise, the doctor turned to Miss Grismark.

"Nurse, is this true? Are some of the patients exhibiting open wounds on their faces?"

Miss Grismark huffed and folded her hands in front of her. "Just poor hygiene, Doctor. Some don't want to wash."

"All the same, they should be seen. Please fetch the worst of the cases and bring them to me. You may wait in the hallway with them until I am ready."

As Dr. Mitchell turned to fetch his stethoscope, the nurse sent an enraged glare toward Genevieve. She would pay for speaking up later.

A folded newspaper was sticking out of Mitchell's bag. Genevieve longed to snatch it, to have something to read, to occupy her mind for just a few moments. What was going on in the world? She stilled her itching fingers but craned her neck, looking over Dr. Mitchell's shoulder as he leaned too close to listen to her heart.

The date on the upper corner of the paper was visible.

It was Saturday, May 17.

Her wedding day.

The shock of seeing the date in black and white stilled her. She was meant to be walking down the aisle of Grace Church this morning on her father's arm. Daniel was meant to be waiting at the altar, beaming at her, his dark-blue eyes shining with love. Callie, Eliza, and Esmie were supposed to be standing there too, and she would be holding peonies, as she and her mother had agreed.

To think, she had fussed and argued over *flowers*. When all she should have been thinking of was how lucky she was, what a charmed life she led, how graced by good fortune she had been to know Daniel's love for even a day.

A shuddering breath, hot on her neck, snapped Genevieve out of her self-recriminations. Dr. Mitchell was still listening to her heart, or, she realized, purporting to. His head was too close to her chest, and he gave another deep, audible breath. Instinctively, Genevieve started to recoil, but she stopped and forced herself to stay put, thinking furiously.

Swimming away from Blackwell's was out of the question now. But perhaps there was another way off this island.

At Genevieve's stillness, the doctor's breath quickened. She noticed a thin sheen of sweat appear on his forehead. Slowly, he dragged his eyes up from her chest, taking in her face. Genevieve made herself stare back, keeping her face as neutral as possible. His tongue darted out like a lizard's, giving his lips a quick, involuntarily lick.

I can use this.

Genevieve leaned a little closer, her breasts getting closer to the doctor's face.

"Thank you for agreeing to see the other patients," she murmured. "I could tell the first time we met you were the smarter of the two doctors." Dr. Mitchell's eyes flew back to hers, a sly hopefulness in his muddy brown gaze. He had a scraggly little beard cut into a goatee, probably in an attempt to disguise his undisguisable weak chin.

"You believe me, don't you?" she whispered. "I could see it in your face. You know I'm telling the truth about who I am."

Dr. Mitchell's eyes then dropped to her mouth. Genevieve ran her top teeth over her bottom lip, softly, as though she were thinking. He watched her every move, his breath growing more rapid.

"I know what your chart says, miss," he said, still breathing hard but averting his gaze. He tucked his stethoscope back in his bag. "It is important to avoid confusion of the brain."

Genevieve ran a hand up his arm. "My family will pay for my return."

She deliberately didn't use the word *fiancé*.

Dr. Mitchell snapped his head back. Greed now entered his eyes, both for the money and something else. He swallowed and licked his own lips again, that disgusting tongue flicker. Genevieve held herself still, refusing to flinch. She kept her hand on his upper arm, lightly shifting her fingers in small circles. His eyes darted to the door and then back to her.

"I'll need more than money," he finally whispered.

The oatmeal she had forced down roiled in Genevieve's stomach, but she could play this game.

She had to. It might be her only chance.

"Anything you want."

"Anything?"

Genevieve opened her eyes wide and nodded even as her stomach lurched again. She kept the motion languorous. Of course, she would do nothing at all with this odious little man, but that was to worry about later. The most important thing right now was to get him to agree to help her.

Dr. Mitchell eyed her mouth again and began to lean toward it, his hot, foul breath blowing in her face. There was no way she could kiss him. Panic began to press at her from all sides, but a loud, strident knock at the door forced the doctor to jerk back.

"I told you to wait in the hall," he said angrily as Miss Grismark threw the door open.

"The patients you wanted to see are here, Doctor," she said. The nurse passed a cold eye between them, as if she knew exactly what had been about to transpire.

"Shut the door," Dr. Mitchell said in a firm voice. "*Nurse.*"

Miss Grismark's mouth tightened, but she did as she was told.

"There's no privacy here," Genevieve whispered. She now ran a hand up the doctor's thigh. He gasped and started, a visible quiver running over his body. "Maybe . . . on the boat? That's how we'll leave, isn't it? You'll take me back on the ferry? My family is very, very wealthy," she said in his ear. She slipped her hand from the top of his thigh around to his outer hip, her fingertips sliding up the inside of his jacket, resting on the fabric of his shirt.

"I had nothing to do with your commitment," Dr. Mitchell said. He gasped again as Genevieve let the tip of her nose brush his neck, just under his right ear.

"Of course not," she said in a soft voice. "It was an unfortunate misunderstanding. You will be the hero for seeing the truth, for setting me free." Genevieve pulled back and looked at him encouragingly.

She could tell he liked that vision of himself. Should she remind him she was a journalist, could get his name in the papers?

The doctor's gaze sharpened. Genevieve held her tongue. Maybe she had gone too far.

"If you refuse me on the boat, or there's no money, I'll make sure you're sent right back here," he warned. His voice had taken on a nasty, threatening timbre. "I'm in charge here, and I can have you committed so fully, you'll be here until you die."

Genevieve's heart flipped. Try as she might, she couldn't keep the sudden fear off her face.

Dr. Mitchell smiled thinly, satisfied. His whole body jerked forward, and he licked the side of her neck, quickly. She did flinch now, her shoulders stiffening. Dr. Mitchell's eyes narrowed in desire, and she realized he enjoyed the thought of her being afraid.

"The ferry leaves at five. Be ready when I send for you," he whispered. "And remember what I said." He settled back into his chair and refound his stethoscope before calling out, "I am ready for the next patient, Miss Grismark."

CHAPTER 27

By two in the afternoon the next day, Billy sent word that Harvey Nadler had returned from lunch at a restaurant and was at home. Earlier in the day, Daniel and Charles had decided they would make the visit, much to Gavin's very vocal protests.

"You're too hotheaded," Charles had said, rolling his eyes at his brother. "You'll pick up Nadler by the shirt collar and shake him, and then he'll be too rattled to tell us anything. I've seen you do it a thousand times."

Gavin looked sulky. "Not since I was at university," he said. "Well, not much."

"Besides, you should stay here with Callie and our parents." Charles lowered his voice a little, glancing at the ceiling to where Callie, Eliza, and Genevieve's parents still slept. They were in the Stewart family dining room, which was laid with a sumptuous breakfast. Daniel was forcing himself to eat some toast. "Today might be hard for them." He shot a quick look at Daniel as he poured more coffee.

Daniel busied himself adding sugar to his coffee. Normally, he drank it black, but he felt he needed the jolt of sweetness today. The sugar reminded him of Genevieve, who heaped plenty into hers.

He understood what Charles meant.

He and Genevieve were meant to be getting married today. Daniel had been so wrapped up in the search that, for the past week, he'd quite forgotten about the impending wedding, but when he'd woken today at dawn, the image of Genevieve walking down a church aisle in a white dress was the first thing that had filled his brain.

Ruthlessly, he had shoved the thought aside. He didn't have time to dwell on the what-should-be; it was a luxury he could not afford. He and Genevieve would still marry. Maybe it wouldn't be at Grace Church, maybe it wouldn't be in front of all of New York society, but it would happen.

A stab of guilt had prodded him, though, as he realized *someone* had been thinking about the wedding. Someone would have had to go through the laborious motions of canceling the plans, notifying the two hundred invited guests. Whoever had done that work—he guessed Anna and Wilbur, with the help of their staff—had kept the particulars from him this past week.

"I'm coming with you, and that's final," Gavin groused, finishing his coffee in one gulp. "Genevieve is my sister."

"If you come, you have to stay in the carriage," Charles warned.

Now Daniel and Charles stood on the Nadlers' front step, Gavin glowering at them from the sidewalk. He had refused to stay in the carriage but agreed not to come inside and physically intimidate anyone. Not yet, anyway.

Callie and the elder Stewarts had encouraged Gavin to accompany Daniel and Charles. All three, and Eliza, looked as tired and frustrated as Daniel felt. Callie had said the women's late night had been fruitless.

"Nobody had any information," she reported sadly. "Though many had heard that Genevieve was missing and knew that the wedding today was canceled. The chorus girls we spoke with, in particular, seemed truly distraught over the story and wished they could help. I think they liked the idea of the big wedding, the rich fiancé . . ." She glanced with regret at Daniel.

"If any of those women knew anything, they'd have told us," Eliza confirmed, yawning and reaching for the coffeepot. It was lunchtime now, but the ladies had just woken up. "Some have been following the news about Genevieve closely."

This was good. The more people who knew of her disappearance, the greater the chance somebody would come forward with some kind of information. It was essential to keep the fickle public interested, he knew. They were lucky Arthur would continue to run stories, and the canceled wedding made good fodder for the other papers too.

The ghoulish Jim Crawford hadn't printed anything damning about Genevieve's disappearance yet, but Daniel suspected it was only a matter of time.

Or perhaps he knew Daniel would kick his head in if he did.

"Please take Gavin," Callie had insisted in Daniel's ear before they left. "If you don't, he'll stay here and stomp around and curse, upsetting everyone."

A tall man with hooded eyes and a sneer answered the door to Daniel's knock.

"Mr. McCaffrey and Mr. Stewart for Mr. Nadler, please," Daniel said as he and Charles handed over their cards.

The butler gave each card a haughty glance, then frowned at Gavin on the sidewalk.

"Mr. Nadler is not in," he said, starting to close the door.

Daniel planted his palm against the door. "He is. And we need to speak with him."

The butler pushed, but Daniel pushed back, never breaking eye contact. "Mr. Nadler is not receiving visitors," the butler said. The pressure of the shutting door under Daniel's arm lessened. He quickly looked over his shoulder and saw that Gavin had advanced two steps up the front stoop. Gavin stared at the butler, cracking his knuckles.

Daniel chose not to point out that the butler had changed his story about Nadler's presence in the house. "We will not take much time."

The butler hesitated.

"Just myself and Mr. Stewart," Daniel pressed, sending a warning glance to Gavin.

The butler must not have liked the look of the three men gathered in front of the house, plus Asher in the driver's seat of the carriage. He relented, pulling the door open and instructing them to wait in the foyer.

After a few moments, Harvey Nadler strode toward them from the back of the house. There was no sign of the butler. "My apologies if you were kept waiting," he said. "Please, come back to my study."

Daniel didn't know Harvey Nadler, or his wife. He only knew what Genevieve and her mother had told him about the couple. Nadler was a short, rather rotund man, with a balding head and neatly trimmed gray moustache and beard. He led them to a dark-wood-paneled office.

Morris Bannon rose to shake hands as they entered.

"Morris," Daniel said. He stopped in surprise. "You know Mr. Nadler?" Billy hadn't mentioned Nadler having a visitor.

Bannon leaned forward to shake Daniel's hand. "Harvey is a great help with our widows and orphans charity," he said. "He does a great deal for displaced youth. We've been discussing the particulars of the next ladies' bazaar fund raiser."

"Have you now?" Daniel asked. Bannon's unexpected presence had thrown him off-balance; the firefighter's large form was incongruous in Nadler's rather cramped study. "Where are the ladies?" He meant the question in partial jest, but as soon as he said the words, the oddity of the situation struck him.

"They'll do the actual selling of the items, of course," Nadler said as he took a seat behind his desk, gesturing Daniel and

Charles toward leather armchairs facing him. "Baked goods, sewn fripperies, ribbons, that kind of thing. It's generally better if we do the heavier lifting, so to speak. The business part: securing a venue, renting tables, you know. A lot more goes into organizing these events than many realize."

Daniel introduced Charles to both men as they sat. Nadler's explanation didn't sit right with him; in his experience, the women who ran charity fund raisers and bazaars knew exactly what they were doing and marshaled their volunteers and resources with the skill of generals.

"My own wife, of course, is abroad, visiting her sister. I know it is the weekend, but we are rather busy today." Nadler gestured vaguely to the stacks of papers and files on the wide mahogany desk. "What can I do for you?"

"Perhaps you have heard that my fiancée Genevieve Stewart, your wife's friend, has gone missing."

"A bad business, that," Bannon put in from his spot on a red leather sofa behind him. The back of Daniel's neck prickled as he glanced over his shoulder.

He didn't like not being able to see Bannon and Nadler at the same time.

"So she hasn't turned up, then?" Bannon continued, concern on his wide face.

"She has not," Charles said in a quiet voice. Charles's mild, soft-spoken manner often lulled people who didn't know him into thinking he was weak, but Daniel knew Charles had a spine of steel, like all the Stewarts. "Our mother was under the impression that Genevieve was coming here the day she disappeared, hoping to pay a call on Mrs. Nadler. Can you tell us if she did?"

Nadler steepled his fingers under his chin. "I apologize for my inability to be of service, but as I mentioned, Mrs. Nadler is abroad. She departed well over a week ago."

"That doesn't answer the question, Mr. Nadler," Daniel said, as pleasantly as he could. It was as though he could feel Bannon's eyes boring into the back of his neck. He resisted the urge to twitch; it was making his skin crawl. "Mrs. Stewart, Genevieve and Charles's mother, says Genevieve did not know Mrs. Nadler was out of town. I'm asking if she stopped by."

The room was silent for a beat too long.

"I'm sure I don't know," Nadler said in a too-hearty voice. "I'm not in the habit of keeping track of who comes to call on my wife, particularly when she is not at home." Daniel thought this rang untrue; Harvey Nadler seemed exactly the type of man who would keep track of who sounded his bell. "Let me ring for Percy."

Nadler pulled a discreet bell rope behind his desk. A heavy tread sounded in the hallway, and seconds later the tall butler opened the study door. "Sir?"

"Percy, did a Miss Stewart come to pay a call on Mrs. Nadler? This would have been . . ." He looked inquiringly at Daniel.

"A week ago Tuesday. The sixth."

"Tuesday the sixth. Mrs. Nadler would not have been at home," Nadler added.

"I do not believe so, sir," Percy said, not looking at Daniel or Charles.

"You don't believe, or you aren't sure?" Daniel said. "You were mistaken earlier about whether Mr. Nadler was in."

Percy's jaw clenched visibly, and he stared at Daniel with hate-filled eyes.

"You must forgive our little subterfuge," Nadler said. "I've been having problems with solicitations lately. Percy has strict instructions to say I'm not at home to all but a few select visitors."

"Problems with solicitors? I'm surprised to hear it."

"I'm glad you're not similarly afflicted. Now, Percy, did Miss Stewart come to pay a call or not? Apparently, the young lady is now missing."

The butler's dark eyes held no empathy at the mention of a missing woman. "No," he said in a cold voice. "Nobody has tried to call on Mrs. Nadler since she went abroad."

Another still moment passed.

Percy was lying. Daniel could tell.

He just didn't know why.

"I'm sorry, Daniel." Bannon's voice behind him nearly made Daniel start. "I've got to get to the station soon. I'm sure you understand, but Harvey and I really do need to get back to the widows and orphans now. You almost created a few more the other night, you know, the way my men fought that fire. Not of my family, of course. I haven't got a wife. Never met the right girl." Daniel stared at Bannon; the man was almost babbling. "McCaffrey here's house burnt down a few days ago, I'm afraid," Bannon said to Harvey.

"Troubles upon troubles," Nadler murmured. "I shall pray for you, Mr. McCaffrey. Percy, you may see our guests out."

And with that, he and Charles were dismissed. There was no choice but to follow the butler's tall, thin back out of the room.

Daniel wished they'd brought Gavin inside after all. The man was hiding something, and a vigorous shaking would do him some good.

★ ★ ★

Miss Grismark had had her revenge. When it was time to go to the dining hall for lunch, the large nurse pulled Genevieve from the hallway and set her to cleaning stone floors again. By the time they had met with Miss Grismark's satisfaction, the meal was over. Prue slipped her a hunk of the dry black bread later.

Genevieve was annoyed to have missed lunch, as she wanted to keep her strength up for her coming escape, but a bypassed meal wasn't the worst the nurse had in store for her.

She was washing her hands after using the facilities when Miss Grismark stepped out of the shadows.

Genevieve turned to the door, but the nurse was quicker. In a flash, Genevieve found herself pressed against the hard stone wall, one of the nurse's meaty hands wrapped around her throat.

"Think you can get me in trouble with the doctors, Polly?" Miss Grismark's foul breath was directly in her face. Genevieve gagged. The nurse jolted Genevieve's head forward a few inches, then slammed the back of her skull into the solid stone. Stars sprang into the corners of her vision. "I will make your life a living hell."

A stronger wave of nausea than earlier surged. Genevieve pushed against Miss Grismark's chest, but the other woman was as tall as her and much broader. In response, the nurse squeezed her neck tighter. Genevieve gasped. It came out like a croak.

There was no room for air. Memories of being trapped in the midwifery clinic basement, barely able to breath, were suddenly all-consuming. Panic encircled her rib cage and added to the sensation. Genevieve batted at the nurse with her hands and feet but could tell she was losing steam.

The nurse pulled her forward again.

No. If Miss Grismark banged her head against the wall again, Genevieve knew she would pass out.

She might miss her chance to leave with the doctor.

"Miss Grismark?"

Genevieve barely heard the other woman's voice. She tried to call out, but there was no room left in her throat.

The nurse stilled.

"Miss Grismark. Dr. Mitchell wants Polly Stuart straightaway." Genevieve recognized the voice as Miss Bellwether's.

The grip on her throat lessened. Genevieve sucked in a greedy gulp of air.

"What for?" Miss Grismark growled over her shoulder.

"I don't know. But he wants her, now." Miss Bellwether sounded anxious.

Miss Grismark turned back to Genevieve. She let go and pushed her to the ground, where Genevieve crumpled, the stone floor cold on her cheek.

Rancid breath filled her nostrils again as Miss Grismark crouched low. From where she lay, Genevieve saw wicked delight fill the nurse's eyes.

"Until next time."

CHAPTER 28

Dr. Mitchell was waiting at the entrance of the asylum when Miss Bellwether brought her there. Genevieve forced herself to calm her hitching breath, even though it hurt her throat to do so. The van that would take them to the ferry was waiting.

"Very good, Miss Bellwether. Thank you," Dr. Mitchell said, moving to take the arm the nurse wasn't holding.

Miss Bellwether didn't relinquish her hold on Genevieve.

"We didn't receive any notice from the superintendent about this patient going to the mainland, Doctor."

The doctor's eyes narrowed. "Are you questioning my authority?"

"No, Doctor. But typically there are papers."

"Are you saying I didn't follow procedure?" His voice dropped, carrying a distinct current of threat. The doctor's grip on Genevieve's arm tightened.

Miss Bellwether's cheeks colored, but she held her ground. "I'm sure you did. However, the superintendent—"

"Superintendent Wicks is not here today," Dr. Mitchell snapped. In his ire, small flecks of spittle flew from his mouth and landed on Genevieve's face. She didn't dare wipe them off. "Nor is Dr. Alba. I have telegrammed my associates at Bellevue; Miss

Stuart is to be seen at once. She is coming on the boat with me, and once on shore, she will be secured for observation, and once my colleagues there have determined she can return, she will."

A frown passed across Miss Bellwether's forehead.

"Bellevue, sir? But we have noticed nothing amiss with Miss Stuart."

"*Miss Bellwether.*" Dr. Mitchell lashed the words like a whip. The nurse flinched.

The orderly driving the van hunched lower in his seat at the sound of Dr. Mitchell's sharp voice. In any other circumstance, Genevieve would feel sympathy for the nurse; she obviously knew something was amiss but clearly felt she couldn't directly contradict the doctor.

Today, though, she offered an internal prayer of thanks for Dr. Mitchell's bullying ways.

"Do I need to show my very thorough knowledge of procedure by filing a complaint against you?" he continued through clenched teeth.

Miss Bellwether's look shifted from puzzled concern to sullenness. "No, sir," she muttered, nearly thrusting Genevieve toward the doctor.

Dr. Mitchell helped Genevieve into the back of the van before climbing into the front next to the driver. As the horses started and began the surprisingly pretty drive toward the ferry dock, Genevieve wiped the spittle from her face. Out the window, she saw Miss Grismark at the entrance of the asylum, hands planted on her hips, watching the van's retreat. The cupola-topped octagonal structure grew smaller and smaller as the road wound its way through the lush, verdant spring lawns, graceful enough to beguile one into thinking they were on a country estate rather than an island full of misery.

The smell of the river had been a constant presence since her arrival at Blackwell's, one that intensified as the van slowed to a halt at the dock. Dr. Mitchell escorted her past the indifferent crew to a smelly, tight cabin lined on either side with wooden benches. Further forward, through a narrow passage with a door she assumed was the head, was a cramped room that contained a dirty cot.

A cold thought arose. Was that where they had laid her on the journey over?

Once they were out of sight of the crew, Dr. Mitchell pulled her close and nuzzled her neck. Genevieve contained a shudder of revulsion.

She was so close to freedom. It was just on the other side of the river.

"How long do we have?" she asked.

The doctor ran his hands up her arms and across her shoulders. "It depends on the currents. Could be anywhere from thirty minutes to an hour or more. So we should get started."

"What about the crew?" She could hear the men's cries to each other as they prepared the boat to launch, the shudder of the engine as it was fired with coal.

Dr. Mitchell gave an annoyed glance at the door to the deck. "You're right. Let me tell them you're quite disturbed in the mind and it is crucial we be left alone, so as not to agitate you." He looked pleased with this bit of trickery.

"Good idea."

More sounds carried as the doctor left the cabin: him calling to a crew member, an answering voice, the rhythmic slap of waves against the sides of the small ferry as it left the dock. Genevieve stumbled and nearly fell as the boat progressed, unprepared for its sudden rolling motions. She held a wall for support and looked around the cabin wildly.

There had to be something in here she could use to overpower the doctor.

Her plan was risky, but it was the only one she had.

Everything was latched into its proper place, as a well-appointed cabin should be. Sailors were a tidy lot, at least on their own vessels. There were some lines, an extra fender. Genevieve quickly considered the line, but it was too large and thick to unwrap in time. She stumbled to a row of cabinets fitted above the benches. She noted a bottle of rum strapped down within one, a series of tin cups cleverly slotted into a wooden grid in another. Nothing useful.

She would have to rely on her own strength.

The door handle turned. Genevieve clicked the cabinet shut and sat on a bench.

Her heart was hammering.

"All set," Dr. Mitchell said, smoothing his tiny beard. He closed the cabin door and, to her dismay, locked it.

Genevieve chewed her lower lip as the doctor sidled next to her on the bench. He placed a hand on the side of her face and leaned toward her mouth. Her mind raced. How was she going to do this?

The boat lurched over a particularly large swell, throwing both of them off-balance on the hard wooden bench.

That was it.

"I see a cot there," she said, tilting her head forward and pitching her voice low and throaty. "I think that might be more comfortable."

Dr. Mitchell's eyes lit up. She stood and held out one hand, bracing herself against the cabinets as the ferry rolled again.

The doctor took her hand, so eager he was close to vibrating. She gestured for him to lead the way.

It was better to be behind him, so he couldn't see what was coming.

Genevieve followed Dr. Mitchell for a few slow, lurching steps. She too was shaking, but for different reasons.

He was two steps away from where the cabin narrowed dramatically into the small passage they had to pass through to reach the space with the cot. The boat rolled again, and the doctor stumbled slightly.

Now.

Genevieve pulled her hand out of his and in one quick motion shoved the doctor with all her might in the direction of his stumble, right into the corner of the wall containing the head. He hit his face, hard. Blood immediately spurted from his nose.

The doctor yelped in pain and covered his face with his hands. Genevieve wasted no time. She grabbed him by his jacket and whirled him to face her, shoved his hands away from his face, and punched him as hard as she could in his jaw, followed by another to his already damaged nose. There was a satisfying crunch, and the doctor fell in the passageway in front of the head in a heap.

She stood over him like a hunter over her prey, panting, her body shaking from the surge of effort. Gavin and Charles had taught her to box when she was young, and Genevieve knew how to land a hit.

Now what to do with him?

After a moment, she dragged the doctor by his ankles away from the door to the head and opened it. Despite the narrow vents letting in fresh air, the small privy smelled horrible, containing a wooden seat with a hole in its center and a stack of papers for use.

It was a challenge to haul the doctor into the head. He was smaller than her, but his body was still dead weight that was difficult to move. The ferry continued to roll horribly; Genevieve's body was still trembling, and her right hand and arm were beginning to ache from the force of her punches. After pulling him back to the head, she was able to position herself over his body and lift him upright. Their chests briefly pressed together, so close an approximation to what Dr. Mitchell had wanted that Genevieve involuntarily gagged again—the smell from the head didn't help—and then quickly shoved him onto the toilet seat.

Another moment's rest to catch her breath. The front of her dress was covered in blood from Dr. Mitchell's nosebleed. Once her breath slowed, Genevieve propped the doctor up against the wall, but she knew he might topple over anyway with the motion of the boat.

No matter.

She retrieved the bottle of rum. It was about one quarter full. Genevieve poured it over the doctor's shirt, pausing for one small, panicked second as he stirred and moaned. Dr. Mitchell settled again, not quite regaining consciousness. She muttered another prayer of thanks and tucked the bottle next to him, before firmly closing the door.

But her job was only half done. How to get off the boat without alerting the crew?

Bracing herself against the cabinets again, Genevieve made her way to the cabin door. Luckily, the lock was a simple latch and didn't require a key; she worried Dr. Mitchell would wake if she tried to rifle through his pockets. Genevieve turned the latch and slowly crept up the few steps but crouched low, cautiously poking her head above deck.

The river breeze felt miraculous on her face. She listened, hard. The paddle on the ferry churned; the water hit the sides of the boat in a soothing, rhythmic sound.

She couldn't hear any voices.

Emboldened, Genevieve allowed herself to stand a little taller. It was either pure luck or Dr. Mitchell's design that there were no other passengers on the ferry tonight. She assumed the crew were heeding the doctor's warning to stay away and were either at the bow of the boat or in the wheelhouse.

The city was tantalizingly close. She studied the shoreline, taking in the outlines of the buildings. It seemed they were headed to the Twenty-Sixth Street docks, near Bellevue. She couldn't wait for the ferry to dock; if the crew discovered her, they would restrain her until she was imprisoned again, especially with the blood on her dress. A sailor or two might believe Dr. Mitchell had drunk too much rum and passed out on the privy, but any doctor or police officer who examined him would be able to tell the bruising and swelling on his face were due to blows.

There was only one way off the boat. And she would need continued luck on her side.

Staying low, Genevieve crept toward the stern. She didn't dare glance over her shoulder at the wheelhouse, dreading the thought of making eye contact with a crewman who happened to look her way. Her whole body tensed, waiting for the rough cry of *Oy, you there. Stop right there*, the rushing pound of feet on the deck.

It didn't come.

Crouched again, Genevieve positioned herself on the starboard side of the stern, closest to the city. Another piece of luck: the paddle that propelled the boat through the water was positioned in the midsection of the ferry, on the port side. Still, she would have to jump well clear of the wake, if she could.

You can do it, she whispered to herself. It wasn't dark yet, only just nearing dusk, she guessed around six thirty in the evening.

Without allowing herself to think too hard about it, Genevieve climbed the wooden railing and flung herself as hard as she could away from the boat. The wind intensified in her face, sending her braid and skirts flying, and then the shocking smack of cold water hit before she was submerged.

Genevieve dug into reserves of strength she wasn't sure she had as she kicked her way to the surface, following a shimmer of light she could see dancing atop the water. She gasped and spat as her head emerged, frantically looking in all directions to get her bearings.

The ferry continued chugging south. The noise of the paddle and the lapping sound of waves drowned out anything else she might have heard, like the yells of a crewman who saw her leap into the water, but she didn't want to wait to find out if she'd been seen.

Her heavy skirts dragged at her, the river trying its hardest to pull her under. Genevieve swam toward shore, focusing all her

attention on kicking as forcibly as she could. The water tasted
foul and her body began to shake again, this time from cold. The
Thirty-Fourth Street ferry terminal was a bit south, she could
see, but it was far too commercial and busy for her to swim to;
ferry passage continued well into the night. Instead, Genevieve
headed toward one of the smaller piers extending into the river.
She was, again, extraordinarily lucky it was a Saturday evening.
Most of the commercial river traffic was done for the day, the
various vessels safely docked or moored. If it had been earlier in
the day, she most assuredly would have been spotted by another
boat, or worse, hit by one.

The swim seemed to take forever. Her limbs were so tired,
and she was trembling so hard. Genevieve forced herself to keep
going, even when it would have been so much easier to allow the
water to slip over her head, to let herself be folded into its dirty
brown embrace. At least then she could rest.

It was Daniel, of course, who kept her swimming. She could
hear his voice in her ear, so clear it was as though he were swimming next to her. *Just a little farther, love. You're almost there. Don't
stop; I'm waiting for you.* Memories of him filled her vision, laying
atop the view of continuous water and distant docks and tall
buildings she actually saw. Daniel in his shirtsleeves in a snow-
storm, standing over the body of Ernest Clark. Daniel in a spotless white suit, standing in the sun on the lawn of her parents'
cottage in Newport. Daniel bare chested, in his bed, his eyes
alight with love and desire.

With a start, Genevieve realized she was nearly there. The
proximity of the docks propelled her to swim harder, and she
tried to pick the one that looked the most deserted.

Slipping around a covered pier—not a wise choice, who knew
who might be inside—Genevieve chose a short, open dock as her
destination. Several fishing boats were tied to it, bobbing peace-
ably in the waning light. She reached the closest piling and clung
to it, shuddering, oblivious to the barnacles scraping her hands.

She listened, again. Voices carried from the streets, as did the faint sound of carriage wheels on pavement, but the dock itself and its attendant vessels were quiet. Genevieve pulled herself to the ladder at the end of the dock and slowly hauled herself up. The river poured from her dress as she ascended.

Night air wrapped itself around her body. Genevieve wrung what water she could from her braid and her skirts. The night was fairly temperate, a good mid-May evening, but there was always a brisk breeze by the water, and her teeth chattered.

Genevieve hunched into herself as she walked into the city. She had to get the institutional dress off, not only because it was dangerous to be walking about in a wet garment but because she couldn't risk someone recognizing its significance. She hurried farther west, away from the river and the commercial buildings. A few blocks south, she found what she was looking for: a residential area. Even better, on Thirty-First Street, there was a vacant lot between buildings, like the gap in a child's smile after a first lost tooth, and strung across the backs of the exposed buildings were clotheslines.

Shirts, trousers, sheets, dresses, petticoats, and bits of toweling fluttered, ghostlike, in the half-light of dusk. Brighter lights were shining from the windows in the surrounding houses and apartments. Genevieve hugged the brick edge of a building as she studied the lowest hanging line, hoping it bore the fruit she needed.

There. A woman's light-gray dress hung damply in the center of the line, its hem a foot from the earth. Genevieve crept behind the line. It was probable she wouldn't be seen, given the ever-darkening purple sky, but it was best to be careful. In a quick motion, she tugged the dress from its pins and hugged it close, hurrying across the lot to where a small section of the recently demolished building still stood. Huddling behind the low, jagged brick wall, Genevieve peeled off the Blackwell's dress and petticoat. The dress she'd stolen was a bit damp still from its washing, but not nearly as sodden and heavy as the one she discarded.

Genevieve pulled the new dress over her head. It seemed to be a maid's uniform, both too short and too wide, and a bit ridiculous without a petticoat. She glanced at a clean petticoat on the far side of the clothesline with longing but decided not to risk it, instead scuttling just close enough to yank down a single wool stocking. She fashioned the stocking into a belt, pulling the dress a bit tighter around her waist so the garment less resembled a nightdress. Genevieve then pulled her wet hair out of the hateful braid—vowing as she did so to never braid her hair again—wrung it out, and twisted it into a knot at the nape of her neck, securing it with the scrap of rag from Blackwell's.

It wasn't ideal, but it would have to do. She already felt a little warmer, her shivering having lessened now that the river-soaked dress was off her body.

Genevieve waited for a family to pass on the sidewalk before she stepped out from behind the wall. She kept her head down and her shoulders hunched, quickly walking down Thirtieth Street, heading west, then turning south down Third Avenue.

Daniel's house was only ten blocks south. She would go there. Even if he wasn't home, his staff should be. They knew her, they would let her in, put her by the fire. They would find Daniel if he wasn't in. Telephone her family.

The thought of all these mundane, simple pleasures—a fire, warm food, her loved ones close—brought tears to Genevieve's eyes. She was so close, so close. The sidewalk was crowded with pedestrians enjoying the mild spring night, and even though she heard only good-natured voices and laughter, terror dogged her every step.

What if one of the nurses passed her on the sidewalk? What if someone called her out for appearing so strange, for wearing a stolen dress? Was the specter of Blackwell's imprinted upon her somehow, recognizable to the bare eye? Genevieve flinched at every group she passed, especially those comprising giddy young men, fully expecting someone to see her, to stop and yell, *There she is; there is the crazy woman who escaped from Blackwell's Insane Asylum! Quick, lads, grab her before she gets away!*

She folded her arms tighter around her body and walked faster. Only three blocks to go now.

Genevieve focused on making short distances, muttering the blocks off under her breath at every corner. "Twenty-Second Street. Twenty-First." At the corner she turned right, then left again down Gramercy Park East. She passed the newish apartment building at a near run, startling one of its residents as she emerged with a small dog on a leash.

Daniel's house was just down the block.

The familiar terra-cotta exterior came into view. Genevieve ran harder.

CHAPTER 29

Daniel descended from his carriage, staring up at the shadow of the ugly terra-cotta mansion that was his house. Ugly to him, at any rate. He had never liked it, never liked the huge, sweeping staircase that felt more foreboding than grand, the thickly paneled walls that made him feel encaged, the ostentatious wall sconces and dark carpeting.

Another unsuccessful afternoon of searching. He was painfully aware of the passage of time, of how long it had been since Genevieve had gone missing, of how he expected every minute to feel the hard clap of a hand on his shoulder, to turn and see Longstreet behind him with a warrant for his arrest. It was forthcoming, he knew. He also knew that, as he had nothing to do with Genevieve's disappearance, he wouldn't spend too long in the detective's clutches, but even an hour of not being able to devote his singular attention to finding Genevieve was too long.

Hell, even a minute was too long.

He resented his own body, its physical need for food and sleep, as these too were impediments to time spent finding her. He was only stopping at home for a quick bite and a change of clothes, as he was rather afraid he smelled. It was already dark, they'd made no progress with Nadler, and Daniel couldn't think what else to do but continue combing the streets until he found something, some piece of evidence that would point him in the right direction.

They were planning to extend their search tonight. New Jersey, Connecticut, Long Island. Maybe even upstate.

Daniel sighed, shoving his hands in his pockets. His head bowed of its own accord, and he fought back tears with a deep breath.

The truth was, Genevieve could be anywhere by now. There was no evidence she was still in the area at all. If she had been taken against her will, as he assumed, she could be across the country. Hell, she could even be across the Atlantic.

"You McCaffrey?"

Daniel jerked his head up. A young man, a boy really, who looked no older than seventeen, stepped out of the shadows of the park across the street and into the lamplight.

"Who's asking?"

The boy took a few steps closer, joining Daniel on the sidewalk. He too shoved his hands into his pockets, mimicking Daniel's stance.

"Name's Colby." The boy thrust his head back. He was a tall, lanky fellow, all knees and elbows, in a coat that had seen better days, as had his top hat and the soiled kerchief around his neck. God, he looked barely old enough to shave.

"Okay. What is it, Colby?"

The lad shuffled his feet a little. "I think I seen that missing woman. The one you're supposed to marry?"

Every sense was instantly on high alert. Daniel's hands came out of his pockets, and he straightened to his full height.

"What do you know?" The question came out as a growl, and Colby took a narrow step back.

Dammit, he didn't want to scare the kid. But if he had to pick this boy up and shake him as Gavin had wanted to do to Nadler to get information about Genevieve, he would.

"There's a reward, right? And I don't have to talk to any coppers? I found you because I don't like them. Been waiting over there a spell." Colby jerked his head at the opposite sidewalk. "Figured you'd come home eventually."

"You figured right. Yeah, there's a reward. It's big. Tell me what you know, and we'll see about the police. I won't connect them with you unless I have to, I promise." At the young man's hesitation, Daniel continued. "I don't like 'em either."

Colby blew out a breath, seeming to think it over. Daniel waited, though he was itching to grab this kid by the shirtfront and threaten him with violence. Finally, the kid nodded.

"I drive a cab, see? And about a week ago I was hired by this guy, had me pull up a few doors down from a place on Madison Avenue."

"Madison and . . . ?" Daniel prompted.

"And Forty-First."

A spike of energy shot through his midsection. Nadler's house.

"There's a lady on the steps of this one house, see? I think it was your girl. Pretty sure it was, anyway. She was in a green dress? The guy told me to wait around the corner, then showed up with the girl. Real pretty, and she smiled at me when she got in the cab. I remembered that."

"She got into your cab?" Daniel was almost bouncing on his toes now. This was it. This was the break he'd been waiting for, he could feel it. Genevieve had indeed been wearing a green dress the day she disappeared, the sage-colored one he liked so well. That detail had been in the papers, and anyone could fabricate a sighting of a tall blonde woman in a green dress, but nobody but family and trusted friends knew that she had been planning to pay a call on Prudence Nadler.

"Yeah, with the guy."

"The man who lives in the house on Madison?" He would tear Harvey Nadler from limb to limb.

"I don't know who lives in that house; I didn't see neither of them go in. I mean the guy who hired me. Down at Union Square. He hailed my cab. Another driver tried to pick him up, but he waved that guy away, pointed at me. Then we drove uptown, see? He had me go real slow up Madison. Then we stopped when he saw your girl, and like I said, he told me to go around the corner. She was on the house steps."

Daniel digested this. "So they came around the corner together, and she got in your cab willingly? You didn't see a gun, or a knife?"

Colby shrugged. "I didn't see nothing. Just the two of them got back in the cab. She smiled at me, so I don't think there was a gun or something." Daniel thought the young man still looked troubled.

"What happened next?"

"He had me go to Mott Street. I didn't like that. She looked like a lady; she had no business on that block. But I don't get paid to interfere with what customers want. I just take 'em where they ask. I don't think she wanted to be there, though."

Daniel's pulse quickened even more. "Why do you say that?"

"She got out and then just stood there, looking at this house like she didn't want to go in. I asked her if everything was all right. The guy gave her a look, and she said yes."

"That was it? And you left her there?"

Colby shifted uncomfortably. "Well, yeah. Like I said, not my place to interfere. She said she was okay. Nobody was hurting her or nothing. The guy paid me extra, and they went inside. I waited a few minutes, just in case, but they didn't come out. I thought, who knows, maybe I had it wrong and she was a fancy girl, see? And I forgot about it. But then I saw the picture in the papers a few days ago, and I thought nah, she wasn't no fancy girl. I think she was *this* girl, your girl. But I didn't want to talk to no cops. Took me a few days to find you."

The young man sucked in a deep breath, as if all that talking had winded him.

"Saw there was a reward," he said again.

Daniel nodded absent-mindedly, his mind racing. "Once we know your tip is good, the money is yours. Can you take me to the house on Mott Street?"

"Not right now; I gotta get back to work."

"I'll pay you. Tell me what you make in a night, and I'll triple it."

The kid shrugged. "Okay." He gestured back across the street. "Cab's next block over."

"Wait," Daniel called. His mind was racing; he'd want backup if he was heading into Five Points. He needed Asher, Rupert. Maybe some Toughs. "This man who hired you? What did he look like?"

Colby turned back to him. "Big like a bear. Strong. He had white hair, but he was young. Not like me young, like you young. Thirties or forties, maybe? White hair but not a real old guy, see?"

Daniel did see.

Morris Bannon.

What the hell did Bannon have against him and Genevieve? What was he doing with Harvey Nadler, besides pretending to care about widows and orphans?

"Head inside," he told Colby. "Through that door under the stoop. I need to get some friends; they'll follow us. There will be something for you to eat, if you want."

The kid shrugged again, but in surprise this time, a little jump of his shoulders. "Yeah, okay. I could eat."

Daniel watched Colby ring the bell of the servants' entrance, then nodded at the footman who answered it after the young man looked at him in question. Colby disappeared inside, and Daniel took a deep, clearing breath.

His heart felt as though it was going to pound right out of his chest. After over a week, he had a lead. Something to chase.

And a name.

Morris Bannon.

Untangling the why of Bannon's involvement would have to wait. First, he would chase down this house on Mott Street, chase down the deputy fire chief. He would find Genevieve.

As Daniel turned toward the house to begin making the telephone calls and dispatching the necessary messages to those he needed—*Asher, Rupert, Paddy, Billy, Gavin, Charles*, his mind recited—the sound of running footsteps filtered through his plans.

Frowning, he paused at the base of his stoop. Nobody ran in Gramercy Park. It wasn't a running kind of neighborhood.

It must be the police, coming for him at last. He wouldn't go, not quietly. Not when he had the first real lead on Genevieve since her disappearance. This Colby character would speak with them too, whether he liked it or not, and Longstreet would have no choice but to investigate the house on Mott Street and question Bannon.

The footsteps grew louder. Daniel squinted into the gloom. He descended the few steps he'd climbed and waited on the sidewalk, holding his ground. He wasn't going to cower inside his house. He wasn't afraid of Longstreet.

Whoever was running passed under a streetlamp, and Daniel saw with a jolt it wasn't an officer at all.

It was a woman.

A woman in a misshapen, light-colored dress that flapped around her. A woman running with an ungainly lurch, nearly a limp, tripping over her own feet and almost falling, before righting herself and continuing her desperate, wavering stride.

His body knew before his mind. Daniel's feet began their own run, toward the woman who was still halfway down the block. He'd traveled several feet, heart in his throat, before his head caught up with his heart and a single cry, equal parts joyous and anguished, ripped from his throat.

"*Genevieve.*"

CHAPTER 30

Daniel caught her just in time. After over ten days of little food or sleep, being choked by Miss Grismark, knocking out Dr. Mitchell, and swimming the East River, Genevieve's strength left her. Her legs buckled, simply unable to take another step.

But Daniel was there, and swept her up before she hit the pavement, murmuring to her as if she were a child, telling her she was home, she was safe, he would never let anything happen to her ever again. Genevieve melted into his embrace, allowing herself to be carried up the front steps of his house.

"Asher, Mrs. Kelly," he bellowed. Genevieve peeked over Daniel's shoulder as he carried her up the grand curving staircase.

"Asher's still out," Mrs. Kelly's voice answered. "Who's this lad in Mrs. Rafferty's kitchen?" The housekeeper's body followed her voice, appearing at the bottom of the steps. She burst into tears at the sight of Genevieve, burying her face in a handkerchief. *It's okay, Mrs. Kelly*, Genevieve wanted to say. *Please don't cry, I'm home. I'm fine.*

But she found she couldn't speak. She was simply too tired.

"Call the Stewarts, let them know she's back." Daniel's voice was exceptionally tender. Genevieve closed her eyes and rested her face on his shoulder.

"And then call the police, tell them Miss Stewart is here and we must speak."

"Sir, the police are already here." Genevieve's eyes snapped back open. A worried-looking footman had joined Mrs. Kelly at the bottom of the stairs. "They just arrived, sir. Saw them pull up out front." He had no sooner finished the words than the doorbell rang.

Mrs. Kelly and the footman stared at each other.

"You can open the door," Daniel said.

Mrs. Kelly did the honors.

"McCaffrey," Detective Longstreet called as he walked through the door, his eyes scanning the corners of the entryway and the front rooms. A pair of hearty-looking officers followed. "Come out. We have a warrant for your arrest."

"I'm afraid you're rather late to the game, Longstreet. As usual," Daniel said.

The detective's mouth dropped open as he took in the scene on the stairs.

"Miss Stewart? Is that you? Are you well? Unhand her at once, Mr. McCaffrey."

To Genevieve's surprise, she was able to find her voice after all. "No," she said. It came out as a croak. She cleared her throat and tried again. "No, Detective Longstreet, I am not well, nor do I wish for Mr. McCaffrey to put me down, until it is in one of the guest rooms where I can rest."

"Bugger that, you're going in my bed," growled Daniel. "It's by far the most comfortable."

Longstreet blinked.

Daniel continued up the stairs without waiting for the detective to reply. Longstreet uttered a small curse, then followed them. "Wait here," he barked at the officers.

Genevieve felt Daniel use his foot to nudge open the door to his room, and moments later she was lying atop Daniel's wide, soft bed, on the burgundy-patterned down quilt that had become familiar to her over the past few months. A fire already crackled in the fireplace across the room. A deep sigh of relief escaped her.

The bed smelled like him.

"You're damp, love, you can't stay in this," Daniel said quietly, untying the stocking around her waist and looking at it quizzically before dropping it to the floor. "Mrs. Kelly," he yelled again over his shoulder.

Behind Daniel, Longstreet stood in the open doorway, his arms crossed. "I need to speak with Miss Stewart, McCaffrey."

"Only if she cares to. And only once she's comfortable."

Mrs. Kelly pushed past the detective, her hands fluttering over Genevieve helplessly.

"Will you call the Stewarts again and ask them to bring some of Genevieve's night things, and some clean clothes? And in the meantime, can you rustle up a nightdress? Perhaps one of the maids'?"

"Of course, sir."

Mrs. Kelly shooed the detective out of the doorway. "Out, you. We have to get Miss Stewart put to rights, then you can ask all your little questions."

"I need to know where she has been these past days. It's been almost two weeks," Longstreet said indignantly as Mrs. Kelly closed the door, but he allowed himself to be shooed. "Much police time and money has been spent trying to find her."

"And a lot of good that did, didn't it? Poor lamb found herself, it seems." Their voices faded as they moved away from the door. Genevieve felt a weak smile cross her face at the housekeeper's protectiveness.

"Let's get this off you," Daniel whispered as he gently pulled the still-damp dress from her head. She slid under the covers and removed her institutional chemise and drawers, still clammy from her swim. Daniel piled another blanket onto the bed, and Genevieve reveled in being warm for the first time since she'd woken up in Blackwell's.

"I looked for you everywhere," Daniel said. He was kneeling next to the bed, staring at her with hungry eyes. Even though she was nude under the blankets, there was nothing sexual about his look. It was more the gaze of a ravenous man who had been presented with a feast: awestruck, grateful, and a trifle disbelieving.

Was she even deserving of such a look? After she'd been so harsh with him for simply trying to keep her safe?

"Daniel," she whispered. "I'm so sorry."

His eyes widened in shock. They were bloodshot, she noticed, and underscored with deep shadowy pouches. "What on earth do you have to be sorry for?"

"That I was foolish enough to let myself get taken, and to put you and my family through so much worry."

"Genevieve," he said firmly. "This isn't your fault. None of what happened is your fault. The only fault lies with those who took you. It was Bannon, wasn't it?"

She nodded. Daniel's jaw clenched, and his hands made fists atop the blankets. "I just found that out, minutes before you came down the street," he said. "The cabby who took you to Mott Street found me and told me. He's in the house now, or was. He may have run out when the police arrived."

"Bannon and Nadler," she said. "Prue is there too. Daniel, we have to get her out. There are so many women there for no reason. We have to get them out."

Daniel's hand felt cool and soothing on her forehead, as if she were a child with a fever. "Out of where, love? You weren't in jail, were you? The police were looking for you; there was no record of you having been arrested."

A knock sounded at the door, and Mrs. Kelly stuck her head through. "I've a clean nightdress for you, dear. And Mr. McCaffrey, that detective is chomping at the bit. Asher has returned; should I have him throw the officer out on his ear?"

"No," Genevieve answered. Both Daniel and Mrs. Kelly looked at her in surprise. "Let me put this on, and then he can come in. I can tell you both at the same time," she said to Daniel.

Eyes troubled, he nodded his agreement. In minutes, Genevieve was clad in the nightgown—also too short, but clean and soft and delicious against her skin—and Detective Longstreet was in an armchair in front of the fire across the room from her. Genevieve had the bedclothes pulled up to her chest, and her wrists stuck out from the ends of the plain white garment, but she felt covered enough to be in his presence. Daniel sat on the edge of the bed protectively.

She told them everything. About how Bannon had persuaded her to take the cab with him to Mott Street, how he had overpowered her before she drew her gun, and how she had woken up, apparently days later, in Blackwell's Insane Asylum as Polly Stuart. She told them both about Prue Nadler, and what Prue had said about her husband Harvey harboring hatred for social reformers, and how he profited from the House of Refuge and other charitable institutions. She told them about the terrible conditions at the asylum, how many women, like her and Prue, were committed against their will when they were obviously mentally sound. She told them about Vanda drowning herself, and how she'd tricked Dr. Mitchell into thinking she would perform sexual favors to secure her release. Neither man interrupted her during her story, for which she was grateful, though she did notice Daniel closing his eyes and taking deep, controlled breaths at parts of her tale, particularly when she spoke of being drugged by chloral hydrate and how she'd had to navigate the doctor's advances.

"I jumped off the boat, and managed to swim to the piers around Thirty-Sixth Street," Genevieve said. Mrs. Kelly had brought a tray with chicken soup and strong, sweet tea with lemon, which Genevieve was just finishing. She was starting to feel insurmountably tired again. She noticed Daniel doing the closed-eye, deep-breaths motions again.

"I'm afraid I stole that dress," she said with regret. "I know which clothesline it was; I will pay the owner for it. I was soaking wet and needed something dry. Well, drier." She glanced at Detective Longstreet, half expecting to find him frowning at this admittance of theft, but he didn't seem fazed. His eyes were bright, fixed on her face. "And I walked here. That's it." Genevieve handed the tray to Daniel and leaned back.

Mrs. Kelly knocked again. "Miss Stewart's family are here, sir," she said.

"In a moment, Mrs. Kelly," the detective said. "We are in the midst of a police inquiry."

The housekeeper harumphed, folding her arms under her ample bosom and fixing Longstreet with a beady eye. "They've not seen their girl for these many days, while you lot chased your own tails, and you're asking them to wait longer?" Her Irish brogue, which was usually rather muted after an adulthood in New York, was growing stronger as she became irate.

"I'm sure they don't want to interfere with police business," Longstreet snapped. "Just a few more minutes," he added in a softer voice.

"I saw Morris Bannon at Harvey Nadler's house earlier today," Daniel said once Mrs. Kelly had retreated again. "I don't know how Genevieve and I became targets for his crimes, other than our interests in reform, but it is clear they are both in some way behind both these fires and Miss Stewart's kidnapping and wrongful commitment."

Longstreet stood. "I can see you need your rest, Miss Stewart. And I have some men to question. McCaffrey, I know you feel targeted, but I need you to stay out of this. If even a fraction of Miss Stewart's story is correct—" Genevieve bristled under her blanket. Longstreet saw it and held up a hand. "Do not take umbrage, Miss Stewart. It is a lot to take in. Harvey Nadler is an upstanding member of society and is on the boards of several charities and institutions. Deputy Chief Morris Bannon has a spotless reputation. Yet somehow you claim the two of them decided to commit arson, murder Madame Martin, attempt to murder Dagmar Hansen, bribe a judge, and have you unlawfully committed to Blackwell's? You cannot blame me for feeling it necessary to pursue these claims with extreme caution. Though"—Longstreet tugged his jacket down and smoothed back his hair—"I daresay many of them will be easy enough to prove. However awful the institution may be, it does sound as though the asylum was possibly also taken in by the ruse. I wouldn't be surprised if there was a notice of an escaped inmate called Polly Stuart awaiting me at the office. I'll let you rest, and be in touch soon."

Longstreet started for the door but paused, his hand on the handle. "I mean it, McCaffrey," he warned. "Let us handle this."

Daniel didn't take his eyes off Genevieve's face. "You don't have to worry about me, Detective," he said. He winked at Genevieve, but his eyes were filled with a deep rage that countered the playful gesture.

She didn't mind. She was enraged too.

Mrs. Kelly had been hovering outside the door.

"Another minute more, please. I have a few more things to discuss in private with Genevieve," Daniel said.

The housekeeper harumphed again but closed the door.

Genevieve waited.

"What we don't know is why," Daniel finally said, picking up one of her hands to hold between his. He rubbed at her fingers. "You're still cold," he said with worry.

"I'm not. Well, maybe just my hands. Keep rubbing them; that feels good. And isn't money the why?"

"Probably, yes, Yet there is something else, a piece I don't understand but I feel must be related."

Genevieve continued to wait.

"Connor," he said finally. It sounded as though it pained him to say his brother's name. He told her about how Connor apparently had a brother called Dennis, and how their adoptive parents—he assumed Dennis was also adopted, anyway, unless Connor had lied about the Lunds having no children of their own—had perished in a fire.

"Could it be a coincidence?" Genevieve asked, though it sounded weak even to her own ears. "I'm sure there are plenty of fires every day, in New York and Minnesota."

Daniel shifted on the bed, still rubbing her hands. It really did feel delightful. It was also making her even sleepier.

"I don't think so," Daniel said quietly. "But it's not for you to worry about. Right now, just focus on getting some rest. Do you feel up for seeing your family?"

Genevieve nodded. "For a few minutes." She allowed herself to be tucked deeper into Daniel's bed.

"I'll get them."

Bare minutes later, Genevieve was surrounded by her parents, brothers, and Callie. She could barely keep her eyes open long enough to take in each face and tell them she loved them. Her mother's hands had replaced Daniel's, and she fell asleep feeling safe, warm, and more grateful than she had ever been in her life.

★　★　★

Daniel waited at the doorway until Genevieve fell asleep. Her brothers and Callie headed toward where he stood. Everyone's eyes were bright with happy tears.

"You don't mind if we stay a while longer, do you, Daniel?" Anna asked.

"Of course not. You're welcome to spend the night; I've plenty of room."

"I believe Wilbur and I shall, for propriety's sake," Anna said. "Thank you." Wilbur took the seat Longstreet had recently vacated. He smiled distractedly at Daniel but kept his eyes trained on Genevieve, who was now sleeping soundly in Daniel's bed. "We'll take her home in the morning, once she's rested."

Daniel understood. As much as he didn't want to let Genevieve out of his sight, they weren't married yet. "I'll tell Mrs. Kelly to make up a room."

Gavin and Charles and Callie were still clustered in the hallway as Daniel gently closed the door.

"Come with me," he said to the brothers.

He led them to his study, where everyone took seats. Daniel hesitated at Callie's presence.

"Don't start," she warned. "If Gavin is here, I'm here."

Daniel filled them in on what they knew about Bannon and Nadler.

"I knew it." Gavin thumped his fist on the arm of his chair. "I knew that son of a bitch deserved a thrashing."

"What is the next step?" Charles asked.

Daniel hesitated. He'd been wondering that himself. "I've got to sleep," he admitted. "But I won't believe Genevieve is out of danger until Nadler and Bannon, at least, are located. Longstreet asked—well, told—me to stay out of it. I'll give them tonight. If they can't find the men behind this, I'll do it myself."

Gavin nodded. "And we'll be with you. Go get some sleep. Charles and I can take turns staying up, if it makes you feel better."

Daniel hesitated again.

"Go on," Charles added. "Asher is here also, and the footmen. She's home, Daniel. Get some rest. I'll take first shift while Gavin escorts Callie home."

"Why don't I get a shift?" complained Callie.

"Because you need to be able to help tend to Genevieve tomorrow," Daniel said. "Anna wants her back on Washington Square, and she's correct; that's the place for Genevieve to recover. Anna may be up all night, and someone needs to be alert tomorrow."

Callie's mouth twisted, but she agreed, sighing.

Gavin clapped Daniel on the shoulder as he departed. As Daniel was heading upstairs, Charles caught him and shook his hand, pulling him into a half embrace as he did so.

"We'll find them, Daniel," his soon-to-be brother-in-law whispered in his ear. Daniel pulled back slightly and stared Charles in the eye, hearing the quiet vehemence in the man's voice. "We'll find them, and we'll make them pay."

CHAPTER 31

Longstreet and the police hadn't found Bannon or Nadler overnight. The detective delivered the news in a sour voice, looking as tired as Daniel had felt the night before.

"Neither are home, and nobody we've questioned thus far knows where they are. It's just one night, McCaffrey. These things take time. Don't go charging all over the city expecting to handle this yourself."

Daniel was disappointed but not surprised. Checking with the detective this morning had been a formality. He knew the responsibility to find the men who did this to Genevieve was his and his alone.

"Blackwell's Insane Asylum did indeed admit a patient called Polly Stuart ten days ago," Longstreet admitted with some reluctance. "Who escaped via the ferry yesterday evening. The judge who signed the commitment papers is being brought in for questioning later today. There is no sign of the doctor who helped her escape, though the crew on the ferry did find him unconscious in the head. They carried him ashore, where he woke up and fled." The detective spread his hands wide. "I've got men on it."

Daniel's priority was not Dr. Mitchell, though he would gladly beat the man bloody and throw his body from the East

River Bridge if the opportunity arose. He was hunting bigger prey.

Morris Bannon, specifically.

He recalled, not for the first time, how Bannon had lumbered out of his own burning house, delivering the news that Genevieve was not within, and how he'd watched Daniel double over in relief. And the bastard had known all along where Genevieve was. He'd probably even set the fire himself.

Daniel's carriage rattled along the cobblestones toward the West Side. He was on his way to question someone who might have an idea about Bannon.

The hunt had begun.

It was another bright, beautiful spring day. Fat clusters of flowers decorated the trees as they rolled their way through the city, white and every hue of pink dancing against a relentlessly cheerful blue sky. Their sweet smell wafted through his vehicle's open windows, the whole city perfumed for a few short weeks. He inhaled deeply and drummed his fingers on his knee, thinking.

In his pocket was an answering letter from Mercy Ennis in Minnesota. It had arrived in the late Saturday post, but with Genevieve's appearance, nobody had thought to give it to him until this morning. He'd had to read it twice to confirm it said what he thought, then he'd carefully folded the letter and tucked it away.

The information would keep for now.

Asher pulled the carriage to a stop on Bleeker Street, in front of a neat, dark-blue row house with lace curtains in the windows. Paddy was waiting out front.

"He's in there," Paddy said as Daniel and Asher joined him on the sidewalk. "Saw me through the curtain."

The words had no sooner left Paddy's mouth than the door of the row house opened. Fire chief George Kincaid invited them inside.

The good smells of a Sunday lunch cooking permeated the air. Kincaid had them sit in his front parlor. "I can guess why you're here," he sighed. "Police already came this morning. Scared my wife half to death. A bad business, this," he muttered, shaking his head. "I can't wrap my head around it. Morrie Bannon, an arsonist and kidnapper."

"George, do you have any idea where he might be?" Daniel pressed.

The chief sighed again, deeply, and gazed out the window. "None. He wasn't married. Joined the lads at the pub for a pint now and again. He's well liked by those under him."

"Can you tell us anything you might not have wanted to tell the police?" Paddy asked. He had chosen to not take a seat but stood near the door.

Kincaid eyed Paddy speculatively. "I know what you're asking."

Paddy returned the look with a hard one of his own. "Well?"

"He was an Oyster Knifer, sure, way back. In and out, though. Before your time, Danny, though Padric here might have known." Paddy folded his arms in front of his chest and shook his head. "Wasn't ever serious with him; said they got too rough, they had more than enough numbers and didn't need him. That's what he told me."

Bannon, a former Oyster Knife gang member. Same as Officer Brian Jackson.

They were getting closer to the truth. Could there be a tie between religious zealots like Nadler, so determined to impose their standards of morality on everybody else, and gang life?

Money. The answer popped into his brain like an electric light being switched on. Just like Genevieve had said.

Of course. Vice always made money. Did these moral crusaders really want to see what they railed against brought to an end? If true reforms happened, what was left to rail against? The endless donations would cease, and the grift would be over.

So which gang was Nadler affiliated with? The Oyster Knife gang had disbanded after Genevieve killed their leader, Tommy Meade. Most members had been absorbed into John Boyle's network, so far as he knew.

"And you're a Hard Hudson," Paddy said to Kincaid. It was a statement, not a question.

"Well, I was. Still am, sort of. You know. I have to stay on good terms with everyone."

"What did you mean when you told me territories were shifting?" Daniel asked.

Kincaid pursed his lips. "New blood moving in, taking Tommy Meade's place. But with new territories. They've forced out some of the Hard Hudsons over in the Tenderloin and tried to take on Ming Li's outfit. Haven't had as much success there; Li is pretty well entrenched." Kincaid glanced at Paddy, who stayed impassive.

"John Boyle?"

"Nope, not Boyle. Don't know who. If anyone knows, it's Padric here."

Paddy frowned. "Nobody calls me that."

"Eh, I knew your mam."

"Don't be taking liberties."

"What do you think of all this, Paddy?" Daniel asked.

"Heard some tell. Different territories, wasn't my business. They took up on the west side of the Tenderloin, weren't causing us no trouble."

Now Daniel frowned. "But Meade held no sway in the Tenderloin; he was a Five Points man. His old territory and properties are Boyle's now, right?"

Paddy nodded shortly. "And Boyle keeps himself to himself, least where Bayard Toughs are concerned. Had no gripe with him neither."

Daniel leaned forward in his chair. "What if the Oyster Knifers didn't disband after Meade died? Maybe some did, joined

Boyle. But maybe some regrouped under whoever is in charge of the leftovers. Maybe it's these who took the Tenderloin real estate from the Hudsons, tried to take some from Ming Li. Maybe Bannon was in league with this new outfit, and whoever they are, they're in league with people like Nadler. Does that sound correct?"

Paddy and Kincaid exchanged a glance. "Seems that way, yeah," Paddy said.

"So where's this new outfit's headquarters?"

★ ★ ★

The full moon shone directly into Genevieve's open bedroom window. Despite her experience with a peeper climbing through the window the year before, she preferred to let the night air in while she slept, especially in these temperate months.

Even more especially after being locked in a cell on Blackwell's.

She rolled over in bed and stared at the moon. It stared back. She rolled in the other direction and watched the peculiar patterns the moonlight created dance across her bedroom wall.

Finally, she flopped onto her back and sighed.

It was no use. She couldn't sleep.

Her day had been lovely and restful. She had left Daniel's house in the morning with her parents. Once home, she had indulged in the longest, most luxurious bath of her life, soaping herself and her hair many times over. She had changed into a loose cotton day dress and rested by the fire in her front sitting room all day, again with the windows open to let in the bright spring air. Nellie had brought her tray after tray of delicious food, and she'd been perfectly content to simply spend time with her loved ones. Rupert and Esmie had come to call, as had Eliza, and they had passed many happy hours together with her family.

And of course, Daniel had visited. When he'd first arrived, she'd raised her brows in question at him.

He had minutely shaken his head.

Nobody had been arrested, then. The men who had committed her to Blackwell's against her will, who they assumed had killed Pearl Martin and had tried to kill her, Daniel, and Dagmar, were still out there somewhere.

She had been able to put the thoughts aside for most of the day, but here at night, her mind turned the events over and over, probing them from different angles.

She could think of one person who could have answers. Someone she should have seen weeks ago.

Genevieve threw off her blankets and quickly dressed. The house was still and quiet as she tiptoed downstairs, avoiding the second-to-bottom step, which creaked.

"Where the hell do you think you're going?"

Her hand flew to her heart in surprise.

Charles came out of the front sitting room, frowning at her.

Genevieve raised her chin. "None of your business," she whispered.

"Whatever it is, it can wait until morning."

"Actually, it cannot."

"Don't you think you should wait and speak to Daniel?"

Genevieve hesitated. "I honestly don't think I'll be in any danger. Trust me, Charles. I know the hell you've all been through, I'm not about to do anything that reckless again."

"Sneaking off in the middle of the night to an unknown destination isn't reckless?"

"Dammit, Charles, I know what I'm doing. The person I'm going to see doesn't care for Daniel, and I don't think will talk to him. But he might talk to me. And no, I can't see him during the day."

A look of understanding dawned on Charles's face. "Fine. But I'm going with you."

"No, you bloody well aren't."

"Try to stop me," he said in a cheerful whisper.

"If you're that concerned, loan me a gun. I lost mine."

"Ah, when you last went off by yourself to solve a crime. That gun?"

"You're a dunderhead," Genevieve blurted in a furious whisper, then clapped her hands over her mouth. *Dunderhead*? Was she six years old?

Charles covered his own mouth to contain his hysterical laughter. "Come on," he finally said. "Let's get this over with. The dunderhead has a gun."

As they slipped out the front door and made their way down the front stoop, Genevieve tried to wheedle the gun from Charles. "It will make me feel better to hold it. Besides, I'm a better shot."

"Are not."

"Am so."

"I taught you to shoot."

"Sad, when the student surpasses the teacher. Come on, at least let me see what you've got."

Charles handed the piece over to her, smiling, and Genevieve looked at it with approval.

"Will you get the carriage, or should we find a cab?" she asked.

"Oy. Where are you going?" It was Billy, skulking in the park across the street.

Genevieve sighed. She should have known Daniel would leave someone to watch the house.

"We're going to see John Boyle, and you can't stop us. And keep your voice down; my parents are sleeping," Genevieve hissed in a loud whisper.

"Don't forget Gavin. He'd tie you to a chair rather than go along with this," muttered Charles, who then eyed her with speculation.

"Don't even think about it. I've got the gun now, remember." She held the weapon aloft as proof, careful to not point it at anyone. Unfortunately, at that exact moment her neighbors the

Wellingtons rounded the corner. Mrs. Wellington caught sight of Billy, and the weapon, and gave a small screech, rushing to their front door.

Genevieve waved a cheery hello with the gun. "Hello, Mr. and Mrs. Wellington! No worries; all is well. Apologies for the canceled wedding!" They gave her an appalled look and scuttled inside.

She laughed, feeling a bit mad.

Maybe she *was* mad.

"Boyle?" Billy said, keeping a nervous eye on the gun. "Why you always pointing a firearm at me, miss?"

"That's where Daniel has gone, hasn't he? It's the only explanation that makes sense. Bannon wouldn't risk himself just for Nadler, nor would Nadler risk himself unless they both were in danger of significant financial loss." She had thought and thought about this, and was sure Daniel had come to the same conclusion. "Boyle has a lot to lose if reformers succeed in getting the brothels and dance halls and opium dens shut down. Nadler also makes a lot of money off the same institutions staying open. They both have reason to try to intimidate us. I want answers, and Boyle will have them. You can come with us, or stay here."

Genevieve started walking toward Fifth Avenue to hail a cab. She didn't care if either man followed her or not, but seconds later Charles was by her side.

"Hey, you gonna let your sister do this?" Billy's voice floated behind them.

Charles smiled thinly. "You heard her."

"They're not at Boyle's."

Genevieve stopped. She turned, slowly, and took in the deserted stretch of Washington Square North. Then she carefully raised the gun and pointed it at Billy, whose hands flew in the air.

"Where are they?"

CHAPTER 32

Daniel walked slowly up West Fortieth Street, hands stuffed in his pockets, his hat pushed back away from his forehead. Paddy and Asher were with him. They had spent the remainder of the day strategizing back in Five Points at the tavern that sometimes served as the unofficial headquarters for the Bayard Toughs. Kincaid, of course, had wanted no part of whatever gang war was about to be unleashed, and had politely shown them the door, assumably returning to his peaceful Sunday lunch.

About halfway up the block, he stopped in front of an elaborately decorated stucco facade. The brightly lit sign above the doorway proclaimed the establishment as *The Painted Serpent*, written in bright, curving script.

The place didn't look exceptional in the least. They had passed no fewer than a dozen similar-looking dance halls on their way here. Women in bright dresses with plunging necklines and plumed hats navigated around them on the busy street, some entering the building, others heading elsewhere. There were far more men coming and going from the Painted Serpent, and just like the clientele at the Haymarket a few days ago, they seemed to come from all social classes and income levels.

"Was Adoo's Theater before this," Paddy said. "They couldn't keep it up; this place took it over." Daniel didn't know either establishment; he didn't spend much time in the Tenderloin.

"Maybe we should have brought Billy," Paddy said thoughtfully. "He's surely been here. The lad does enjoy a good set of legs."

"I like Billy where he is," Daniel said. They'd left him to keep watch on the Stewart house on Washington Square North. He wasn't the brightest, Billy, but he was loyal as they came and could be mean as a snake if the situation called for it. Plus, Daniel suspected he harbored a soft spot for Genevieve.

The men flanked the entrance, waiting for a quiet moment. As soon as there was a break in pedestrian traffic, they moved as one.

Asher and Paddy quietly felled the bouncer stationed at the front entrance. All three men casually entered the dance hall and fanned themselves out, as was the plan. The patrons paid them no mind as they weaved their way through the crowd. It was a lively spot, the music loud, and a line of girls danced onstage. Like at the Haymarket, Daniel assumed there was an upstairs area for private encounters.

He didn't care what people got up to upstairs. He only wanted to know where the person in charge might be.

Paddy caught his eye from across the main room and shook his head. Daniel agreed that whoever they were, they weren't here. Sometimes the head man held court at a table, gambling and drinking and keeping an eye on things. He didn't see anyone who fit the bill. There were some high rollers, men flashing money, but they didn't exude the air of authority of a boss.

On the other side of the room, Asher straightened up from speaking with a young woman and nodded to Daniel. The girl took Asher by the hand and guided him behind the stage. Daniel and Paddy followed. There was a staircase tucked back there, leading down.

The stairs led to a large, dimly lit room flanked with curtained areas and a small bar on the far end. Nobody was tending the bar, but next to it was a wooden door, guarded by a beefy man with a shining bald head and one gold hoop earring, like a pirate from a storybook. Noises floated out from behind the curtains, women's soft, encouraging voices, men's groans of pleasure.

Asher leaned down and whispered into the girl's ear. Up close, she was older than Daniel had assumed, which was something of a relief. The woman looked behind her at Daniel and Paddy, her bright-red lips pursing in displeasure.

"I don't do three at once," she said.

"What's behind that door?" Asher was obviously repeating his question, now loud enough for Paddy and Daniel to hear.

"The painted serpent herself," the girl smiled. "Best in the business. Now, I can do one at a time, while you others wait at the bar. Which one of you will it be? You first, big fellow?" She started toward a curtain.

Daniel stepped to the bar and rested an elbow on it, his right hand, the one not facing the pirate guy, resting on his gun.

Asher let himself be led.

As soon as the woman slipped behind the curtain, Daniel said, "Any chance of a drink?" The pirate fellow scowled in his direction.

Once the man with the earring was distracted, Asher turned and took two shockingly fast, long lunges toward him, knocking the pirate out in one swift blow to the face. Even Daniel, who was expecting the move, was surprised at its ferocity.

The music floating down from upstairs masked some of the noise of the man's body falling, but not all of it. The woman poked her head out from behind the curtain and gasped. "Stay there," Daniel said.

He stepped over the body and turned the handle of the wooden door, gun drawn and raised. Paddy and Asher were directly behind him, weapons at the ready.

His gut told him that behind this door were answers.

The door slowly creaked open.

Daniel wasn't sure who or what he expected to find, but it wasn't the sight that greeted him.

"Hi, Daniel."

It was a voice that sometimes haunted his nightmares. High and girlish, with a constant, underlying titter.

Sitting atop a wide, gilded desk was Nora Westwood, the girl he'd tried to rescue from Tommy Meade the year before. The girl who, it turned out, hadn't wanted rescuing. The room was so bright and garish after the dim curtained space, it made his eyes water. She swung her legs like a child and laughed that obnoxious giggle that simultaneously set his teeth on edge and made his skin crawl.

And next to Nora, with a gun pointed straight back at Daniel, stood Connor.

"You two know each other, yes?" Nora laughed behind her hand again, eyes dancing. As she spoke, Bannon's huge form suddenly filled the doorway, his own gun pressed to Asher's temple.

Paddy's eyes darted back and forth. Seeing Daniel had Connor covered, he turned his weapon to Bannon.

Daniel nodded. "We do indeed."

"Hey, Dan-Dan," Connor said. His green eyes, so like Maggie's, were luminous, shining with an emotion Daniel couldn't quite read. Triumph? Mixed with a touch of regret?

Daniel nodded again. "Hey." He then asked the question that pressed on him from all sides, the question that had blazed bright in his brain ever since he had received Mercy Ennis's latest letter.

"Where is my brother, Dennis?"

★ ★ ★

Genevieve had been in some dive bars before, but never this type of dance hall. Any other time, she might have stopped to gawk at the row of women dancing on the stage. They were quite athletic, performing all manner of high kicks and hip swivels, in the tiniest costumes she'd ever seen. There was less fabric on them than a bathing outfit.

"This way," Billy said, leading them to a cleverly disguised passage behind the stage. Inside the passage was a staircase leading down. Billy paused, glancing back at her and Charles. "Have your wits about you. The bouncer wasn't at the front door—not a good sign."

Sounds from the band upstairs echoed throughout the large, shadowy basement room. A thick red-and-black patterned carpet covered the floor, and a series of red velvet curtains with gold tassels lined either side of the room. A man with a short, pointed gray beard stepped from behind one of the curtains, putting on his jacket. He didn't look at them as he hurried back up the stairs. A few moments later, a woman in a violet dress followed.

Billy carefully made his way to a closed wooden door next to an empty bar at the back of the room.

A woman's head poked out from behind another curtain.

"Don't go in there," she hissed in a whisper, her eyes wide. "There's trouble. Get back upstairs."

Fear spiked from Genevieve's stomach to her heart. Billy thought Daniel was behind that door. If there was trouble, that meant Daniel was in trouble.

Charles pulled a gun from the back of his waistband.

Genevieve gasped. "You cheater."

He just smiled tightly at her, giving a flick of his light-brown eyebrows.

Billy had drawn a gun as well.

Genevieve swallowed. At least they were well armed.

Suddenly, a man with a gold hoop earring flew out from behind one of the curtains, knocking Billy's gun out of his hand and raining blows on his face. Billy instantly fought back. At the same time, another set of footsteps came running down the stairs.

Charles whirled toward the noise, but the man barreled at them, taking advantage of the two seconds it had taken Charles to shove Genevieve behind him. The man plowed into Charles's midsection. Genevieve lost her breath as her brother's body slammed into hers, sending both of them into the closed wooden door.

The man drew back for a punch, and Charles surged forward, releasing Genevieve and knocking his opponent down. They wrestled for Charles's gun, rolling over each other on the carpet. Genevieve gasped in a breath. There was no way to shoot either of the attackers without endangering Billy or Charles.

She turned instead and flung open the wooden door. Her mouth dropped open at the sight that greeted her.

It was a lavishly decorated office. Bright-blue wallpaper with a twisting snake design adorned all the walls, topped with gilt-edged mirrors. It was like being inside a kaleidoscope, or a carnival fun house.

A fun house primed for death, that is. She wasn't sure she'd ever seen so many firearms in one space.

Connor caught her attention first. He stood next to a woman seated atop a desk. Connor's gun was pointed at Daniel. Daniel had a gun trained on the woman. Bannon nearly filled half the room. He had a firearm pressed to Asher's head, but Paddy had a gun pointed at Bannon.

And now she pointed her weapon at Connor. If he fired at Daniel, he'd be dead before his bullet found its home. Connor flicked a glance her way, acknowledging her presence.

Genevieve had never met the woman on the desk but knew who she was right away.

"Nora Westwood," she breathed. She ought to know; she had stared at the young woman's photograph long enough. They had searched long and hard for Nora, at her own father's request, assuming she had been taken against her will.

But she hadn't. Nora had left home willingly, and had wreaked havoc on the lives of every person she touched.

Nora clapped her hands gaily. "We're all here, wonderful. It is lovely to meet you in person, Miss Stewart. I see you brought reinforcements, but I also see my men are taking care of them quite handily." She laughed, a tinkling sound like shattered glass that grated on every one of Genevieve's nerves.

"You can see we're at quite an impasse," Nora continued. She acted entirely unfazed that Daniel had a gun trained on her, or that any of the men in the room could blow each other to bits at any moment.

As she spoke, the fellow who had attacked Charles squeezed into the office. He had an arm around Charles's neck from behind. Genevieve winced. Her brother was pale, and a trickle of blood ran from his nose and around his mouth. "Ricky's got the other one down, miss. He's clearing out the rest of the curtains now."

The "other one" must mean Billy. Genevieve bit her lip.

"You took over for Tommy Meade," Daniel said to Nora. His gun never wavered an inch.

Nora laughed again. "I wondered when you would figure it out. Isn't it funny? Nobody suspects a showgirl. At first I only had to pretend I was the emissary from the new boss, telling these boys what to do. And they did it! They'd become used to me because of Tommy, you see. They simply assumed I was the new boss's girl. But then slowly, to trusted companions, I revealed there was no new boss. Or there was, but it was me, all along! Ta-da!" She flung her arms in a wide arc. Everyone in the room flinched at the sudden motion, which made her laugh again.

"They'd already been following my orders. I'd gained the boys territory and money, way better than they'd had with Meade. There were naysayers, but we took care of them. Morris here was a huge help," she purred, smiling in Bannon's direction. "It was really very easy."

"You never gave up your loyalty to Meade," Daniel said to Bannon. "Leaving the Knifers, that was an act. You're an Oyster boy, through and through."

Bannon huffed his agreement. "And proud of it," he said. He spat in Paddy's direction.

"What was your stake in targeting reformers? What threat was the Sunflower Mission House to you, or Dagmar Hansen?" Genevieve asked.

Nora rolled her eyes. "The Sunflower House was Harvey's pet peeve. I didn't care if he wanted the place burned, so I told Morris to go ahead."

"But how did you meet Harvey Nadler?" Genevieve asked.

Nora looked at Genevieve as though she were stupid. "Not a very good reporter in the end, are you? I've known Harvey since I was small. He's good friends with my father, don't you know."

Genevieve blinked. It still didn't add up for her. How had Nadler known where Nora Westwood was? She'd disappeared a year ago.

"He came here," Daniel said. "You opened the Painted Serpent and saw Harvey Nadler in here one night. Maybe even emerging from one of those curtains. He couldn't reveal your whereabouts to your father without incriminating himself, and you, what? Blackmailed him?"

Nora laughed again. "He was here all the time, was Harvey. Like so many of those holy types, they practice exactly what they preach against. Some of my best customers. Blackmail, no, nothing so crass. We entered a mutually beneficial partnership." She sat straighter on the desk. "He hides his greed behind his little causes, but it's all about the money for him, same as it is for me. I'm just more honest about it."

Daniel's eyes narrowed. "And the indenture program at the House of Refuge is his biggest source of income, isn't it?" He glanced quickly at Bannon, then back to Nora.

"When my editor mentioned I was working on a story about the indenture program, you were there," Genevieve said to Bannon. "In Arthur's office. With Longstreet and the fire chief. But you killed Pearl Martin before that meeting. Set her house on fire with me inside."

"That was Harvey too, after he realized Madame Martin had been giving his wife her little devices." Nora shrugged. "I didn't have a problem with Madame Martin myself. She provided a good service. But Harvey did insist, and a good partnership is all about give-and-take. We didn't know you would be there. That was a bonus."

"And Dagmar was getting close to exposing Nadler's grift," Daniel said.

Nora nodded thoughtfully. "I suppose he was. Neither of us liked him, or that project. I'm sure you must realize, I really loathe you, Mr. McCaffrey. Setting fire to your pet project, that was my idea. And I very much hoped you would be in that studio when it burned to the ground. I really did. But . . ." She sighed, cutting her eyes at Connor. "Another disagreement ensued."

Daniel's gaze stayed on Nora, but he spoke to Connor.

"So it was you. You did set the fire at Dagmar's studio."

Connor offered a sad smile. "Guilty."

"Why save me, then?"

His smile twitched. "I got sentimental."

Genevieve's arm was getting tired. There was an energy at work between the two men she didn't understand.

"I'm going to ask my question again. Where the hell is my brother, Dennis?"

Her arm almost dropped in surprise.

Dennis?

CHAPTER 33

Nora rolled her eyes. "This obsession with a brother you haven't seen in over twenty years is quite tiresome, Daniel."

Daniel ignored her, though he kept his gun aimed directly at her heart.

"Seems like you know where he is," Dennis finally said.

"I'd like to hear it from you."

Dennis nodded. "He's in Minnesota. On the farm."

Even though Daniel had known this would be the answer, a wave of intense grief rose within him.

"How'd you figure it out?" Dennis asked. "Thought I had you fooled good."

"You did," Daniel said quietly. "I believed you. I thought you were Connor. He told you all about his life in New York, didn't he? About our family. Stories from our childhood, like with the apples. You had a whole lifetime to study his gestures."

Dennis smiled. "He got himself a little notebook and wrote down everything he remembered, soon as he got to the farm. Said he never wanted to forget his real family. The Lunds picked us because we looked so much alike, like brothers. Only a few months apart in age. I never did have a family here. Was an orphan from the get-go. I liked Connor's stories."

"But you didn't like Connor all that much, did you?"

Dennis's smile faltered. "We were like oil and water. He was the good one. I wasn't. The Lunds liked him better. That was hardly fair, was it? He'd had a family. He'd had siblings. I never had any of that. Why should he get liked best?"

In the periphery of his vision, Daniel saw Genevieve's arm trembling slightly from the effort of holding her gun trained at Dennis for so long. *Just a little longer, love.*

Daniel nodded at Dennis, as if the man's ramblings made perfect sense. "You didn't mean to kill them, did you?" he asked quietly. Mercy's letter had explained so much. Two adopted brothers, she explained, so close in appearance they were mistaken for twins. One known for his exploits, the other the darling of his adoptive parents' eyes.

Records indicate the property was left to Connor Lund, but both he and Dennis disappeared soon after the funeral and haven't been seen or heard from since. It was well known in town that Connor was the more responsible of the two. The taxes on the Lund property continue to be paid, assumably by Connor, though the land is left untended. It is believed Dennis may have gone to find his fortune out west, as he often claimed he would. Connor's whereabouts remain a mystery.

Dennis blinked a few times. "They were meant to be out of town. Connor and me, we were supposed to come back here. Home, to New York. We'd talked about it since we were kids, since we met on that train. But all the money was in the farm, and the farm was going to Connor. He changed his mind." Dennis swallowed. "I thought if the house was gone, maybe he'd sell. Come with me after all."

"When did he confront you?" Daniel kept his tone low. He tried to tune out the rest of the room. "After the funeral?" he guessed.

Dennis swallowed again. "It was an accident," he said. "We fought, and he fell, and there was a rock in the ground, and . . . it was an accident."

Another wave of grief. Daniel did his best to ignore it. He could mourn his sweet little brother's sad, useless death later. "He's buried on the property?"

A nod from Dennis. "I didn't sell it. Borrowed a little against it and went out west, like I said. Made enough to come here."

Their eyes locked. For a few beats, it was as though they were alone in the room. "I wanted to find you," Dennis said. "And Maggie. I wanted a family."

Daniel nodded, once. "I understand," he said.

And he did. Even though, once he'd received Mercy's letter, he suspected that the man he'd come to believe was his brother was actually Dennis Lund, the confirmation of this fact made his heart contract.

It was like losing Connor all over again, twice in the space of minutes.

"And you had Rupert jumped in the alley?"

Dennis's mouth quirked up a little. "Sorry about that. I don't like that guy. And I'm sorry about your house." He blinked a few times, his brow contracting. "I got a little crazy, you know?"

Daniel remembered running through the streets with this man, breathless with laughter, feeling that a fragment of his heart he hadn't known was missing had slotted neatly back into place. How he'd ignored Rupert's warnings, and Genevieve's, his own gut, in order to keep that fragment from loosening again.

"I understand," he said again.

"Imagine my surprise when one of the boys told me there was a man down on the docks asking around about Daniel McCaffrey," Nora said. The spell between Daniel and Dennis broke, and the reality of where they were rushed back in. "I had them bring him in, and I couldn't believe my luck. A look-alike for McCaffrey's long-lost brother. Dennis here wasn't opposed to making a buck, so he started to work for me." She ran a hand down Dennis's arm and gazed at him fondly. Daniel suspected their relationship was more than just business.

"So you were after money," he said to Dennis. Just like he'd suspected from the start.

"In the beginning, yes," Nora said. "But you proved so much more interesting than mere money. When it was clear you actually believed Dennis was Connor, that's when the real fun began." She smirked. "It was my idea to burn your house down. Dennis here just lit the match."

Daniel shifted his attention back to Dennis. He stared into the man's green eyes again.

They really did resemble his sister's, and Connor's. It was remarkable.

"Well," he said to Dennis. An entire battalion of feelings warred within him: regret, sorrow, loss, and, surprisingly, gratitude. "It was nice being your brother for a while. So thank you, Dennis."

And he smiled.

Dennis smiled back.

Nora snatched the gun from Dennis's hand. "It would be so poetic if you were shot by your long-lost brother—oops, not really." She laughed. "But I'm afraid I simply can't resist killing you myself. If it weren't for you and Miss Stewart here, my Tommy would still be alive." Nora cocked her head, her gaze quickly flitting around. "It doesn't look like we'll all make it out of this room, does it?"

Daniel stared at Dennis, who was looking down, breath coming in hard, fast pants. Genevieve redoubled her stance.

"Shoot him and you're dead," she said softly.

Another click sounded in the room. Ricky, the pirate-looking man, now had a gun pointed at Genevieve. "And so are you," he rumbled.

Nora looked delighted. "I cannot imagine a more fitting end," she murmured. "Let's play, shall we?" With a maniacal glint in her eye, she swung the gun up and pointed it at Daniel.

A blur of motion passed before his vision as he ducked. The air moved above the crown of his head as two shots sounded in quick succession.

Daniel dropped to his knees and tried to see the entire room at once. Several things happened at the same time. Nora screamed; Bannon lurched and shouted, firing a third shot that seemed to graze Asher's ear. Paddy rushed Bannon's legs, toppling him into Genevieve, who kept hold of her gun even as she went down under a heap of male bodies. The man holding Charles must have loosened his grip in the confusion, and Charles elbowed him in the gut before diving into the fray after his sister.

Almost simultaneously, the wild trill of police whistles filled the air, followed by screams and yelling. Blue uniforms rushed into the office and began grabbing bodies, hauling people up and handcuffing them indiscriminately.

Daniel saw Genevieve being pulled up and back by Charles, then he dropped all the way to the carpet where Dennis lay on his side.

He met Dennis's one exposed eye and took hold of his hand.

Dennis smiled weakly, a stream of blood steadily pouring from his mouth. It stained his teeth red.

The blur of motion had been Dennis, stepping in front of Nora's gun. The second shot had hit him square in the chest.

"It was nice being your brother for a while too." Dennis's voice came out in wheezing, labored gasps. Daniel was dimly aware of police officers shouting. He could hear Longstreet's voice in the mix, and Nora screeching. "Connor was right about you. You are the best big brother in the world."

Longstreet held back the officer who tried to haul Daniel to his feet.

Daniel stayed there, lying on the carpet next to Dennis. He held his hand until he died.

Chapter 34

In the end, there were still peonies. Genevieve still wore her gorgeous gown, and the wedding guests enjoyed an elaborate six-course meal, as had been planned.

But the ceremony didn't take place at Grace Church. Daniel and Genevieve married three weeks after the incident at the Painted Serpent on the broad lawn of the Stewart family cottage in Newport. It was highly unusual, getting married outside, but Genevieve said she wanted the ocean in the background as they said their vows. Only family and their closest friends were invited, and Genevieve remarked that she was pleased she didn't have to wonder what Caroline Astor might make of being seated at the same table as Paddy.

Caroline Astor didn't make the cut. Paddy did.

The meal was provided courtesy of Delmonico's, who sent two of their chefs to Newport just for the occasion.

It remained a constant source of amazement, the things money could buy.

Take their burned home on East Seventy-Sixth Street. The entire house was being rebuilt, from the ground up. Much of the original plan would remain in place, though Daniel and Genevieve had discussed a few tweaks. After a week in Newport following the wedding, they returned to the Stewart townhouse on Washington Square to prepare for their honeymoon. The new house ought to be done when they returned in the early autumn, but Daniel knew it was likely there would be unforeseen delays. In the meantime, he and Genevieve had decided, at Wilbur's suggestion, to make the Stewart family house their temporary home, rather than his mansion on Gramercy Park.

That house was sold. Daniel had put the few belongings he wanted into storage for the duration. It hadn't amounted to much: some of the art he'd bought abroad, his books and other personal items. Everything else he gave away or, if the new owners were interested (they were interested in rather a lot), he left behind.

What an enormous relief, to leave it all behind.

It was as though for years, a huge stone had sat upon his shoulders without him realizing it. He hadn't understood the weight of living in that house, not fully. Now that it was gone, he felt lighter and freer. He hadn't felt this unburdened since childhood.

Not since his siblings were taken on the orphan train, he realized.

That was a long time to be carrying such a weight.

"Darling, do you think I'll need two bathing costumes, or three?" Genevieve called from one of the bedrooms.

They were alone, apart from a few staff members. Anna, Wilbur, and Charles had all remained in Newport. Gavin and Callie had returned to Chicago, but not before they shared exciting news.

"We are returning to New York," Gavin had announced, holding Callie's hand.

"Oh! I had rather thought it would be different news," Anna said, obviously not sure whether to be elated or disappointed.

Gavin and Callie exchanged an amused look, Callie's clearly saying, *I told you so.*

"All in due time, Mother," Gavin said. "Columbia is starting an Egyptology program, and they want me to run it." Wilbur ordered champagne, and they toasted Gavin and Callie's imminent return as the sun set over the ocean.

"Two should do, I think. If one is still drying, you can wear the other," he called back. They had designated two empty bedrooms as packing stations.

They were departing for Italy in two days, on the same boat as Eliza, and would drop her at her studio in Rome once they landed.

Eliza had protested, shocked. "I can't accompany you on even part of your honeymoon," she said. "You'll want to be alone."

"We have an entire ocean liner to share," Genevieve said. "And we would love your company. Besides, Rome is only our first destination, and you can show us the sights. We'll be by ourselves for the whole rest of the journey." After Rome, they would continue south, touring Pompeii, Naples, the Amalfi area, and then Greece and the Aegean Islands. They would be gone all summer.

Genevieve swept into the room where Daniel was sorting his own clothes for his valet to pack. "Though I've read that on very secluded islands, one can sometimes forgo a bathing costume altogether . . . ?" She smiled suggestively.

"I love that idea," Daniel said, pulling her close and dotting her neck with small kisses.

He still wasn't sure he believed his good fortune. That Genevieve had survived her ordeal at Blackwell's, that they all hadn't died in the basement room of a cheap dance hall run by a two-bit gangster.

Of course, Genevieve had written about her experience. Arthur had published her explosive series of articles, "Ten Days in an Asylum," in the *Globe*. Already politicians were calling for reform, and hearings were being scheduled. Daniel had forced himself to read it all, even though it was among the more painful experiences of his life. *She lived it*, he thought grimly. *The least I can do is read it.*

He was so enormously proud of her. The series of articles would save lives.

As he read them, though, it took much of his willpower to not head to the Tombs and kill Morris Bannon and Nora Westwood where they rotted in their cells, awaiting trial. Not to mention that rat Dr. Mitchell, who had disappeared.

Daniel hoped the bastard smelled the stench of the privy in his dreams.

At least he didn't have to worry about Harvey Nadler. The coward had jumped off the East River Bridge rather than face arrest.

"Are you sure you can stand being gone so long?" he asked, holding Genevieve close. "We can still shift our plans. Three months is a long time."

"Of course," Genevieve said, sounding surprised.

"It will be hot."

"We can handle it," she said with a wicked smile that made his blood sing. "I've nothing but the lightest of dresses."

"We could stay longer . . . ?" he teased.

"And miss the birth of Esmie and Rupert's baby? Never. Three months is perfect. Besides, I need to be here to testify in the fall."

The wheels of justice moved slowly, but they were turning. It gave him hope.

He passed the hope on to Dagmar, who was slowly recovering.

"We will be a part of it, Daniel," Dagmar said from his hospital bed when Daniel visited. He was horribly scarred on much of his body, and while his voice retained its musical accent, it came out much raspier than before. "I will be strong enough to return to work soon. The House of Refuge, the asylum at Blackwell's—we will document all these places. We will shine our light on them, and they cannot survive the light."

"When I return," Daniel said. "You keep getting stronger. And then, yes, we will take them on together."

"Oh!" Genevieve said now, bringing him back to the present. "While you were seeing Dagmar, Prue called. Look what she gave me as a wedding gift."

Prue hadn't been well enough to attend the actual wedding, having been released from Blackwell's only days prior. It had taken weeks, but with her husband dead and with Daniel's help, they and Prue's parents had been able to secure her freedom.

Genevieve waved the gift from Prue in the air, a lovely lightweight lavender wool shawl, thin as a whisper. She wrapped it around his neck and pulled him closer. "Prue made me promise to not get into any more trouble." She grinned.

Daniel rested his forehead against hers, inhaling the scent that was part fresh grass, part lemon. It was wholly Genevieve. "And what did you say?"

She pulled her head back and met his eyes. "I told her we can't get into too much trouble on a boat."

Daniel grinned back and picked up his wife in one quick motion. She threw back her head and laughed.

His *wife*. His brilliant, beautiful wife.

"Depends on what kind of trouble you mean," he said.

"I think you'd better give me an example."

Daniel whisked her down the hall to their bedroom, and proceeded to show her just what kind of trouble he had in mind.

ACKNOWLEDGMENTS

The late nineteenth-century investigative journalist Elizabeth Cochrane Seaman, aka Nellie Bly, was always my inspiration for Genevieve Stewart, even back when Genevieve had a different name and the first Gilded Gotham mystery, *Deception by Gaslight*, was a different genre. I've always known that Genevieve, like Bly, would spend time in Blackwell's Lunatic Asylum, the psychiatric institution for women that was located on Blackwell's Island, today's Roosevelt Island (while the term *lunatic* is not one in use today, it was the accepted term at the time). The island housed the asylum, an almshouse for the poor, several hospitals, and two penal institutions. Bly became famous for having herself committed to the asylum in September 1887, then writing about her experiences in a series of articles for her newspaper, the *New York World* (the newspaper of the same title in the Gilded Gotham books is fictitious). These articles were then released in a book titled *Ten Days in a Mad-House*.

I relied heavily on *Ten Days in a Mad-House* to recreate Genevieve's time at Blackwell's Asylum. Many of the harrowing experiences Genevieve lives through were directly taken from the book: the torturous, freezing baths, the spider-infested food, the days of sitting, the abusive nurses, and more. I could find no accounts of a woman escaping from the institution, though apparently at least one male prisoner did manage to escape the island via boat. Stacy Horn's book *Damnation Island: Poor, Sick, Mad & Criminal in 19th-Century New York*, an excellent resource on the institutions housed on Blackwell's, was another useful source.

While my academic field is art history, there are times when I teach women's studies, as my scholarly research sometimes takes me in that direction. I remind my students that the types of restrictions on women's rights I describe in this book were not, in fact, so very long ago. Unmarried women were not legally allowed access to birth control until 1972, after the Supreme Court decision in *Eisenstadt v. Baird*. Indeed, parts of the Comstock Act of 1873, discussed at length in this book, have never been fully repealed, and as of this writing the act is being newly revived as justification to restrict women's access to certain reproductive medication. On the Comstock Act, as well as methods of nineteenth-century birth control, I consulted Amy Sohn's book *The Man Who Hated Women: Sex, Censorship and Civil Liberties in the Gilded Age* and Amy Werbel's *Lust on Trial: Censorship and the Rise of American Obscenity in the Age of Anthony Comstock*.

The photographer Jacob Riis and his lantern slide lectures, the latter of which became the 1890 book *How the Other Half Lives: Studies Among the Tenements in New York*, serve as the basis for Dagmar Hansen and his project. Vanessa Albert and the Sunflower Mission House are based on the real Black reformer Victoria Earle Matthews and the White Rose Mission she founded. On Black life in nineteenth-century New York, I also consulted Carla L. Peterson, *Black Gotham: A Family History of African Americans in Nineteenth Century New York City*. Terry Golway's book *So Others Might Live: A History of New York's Bravest, the FDNY From 1700 to the Present*, provided information on the history of the New York City fire department. An article in *The American Journal of Legal History* by Alexander Pisciotta, "Treatment on Trial: the Rhetoric and Reality of the New York House of Refuge,

1857–1935," was a useful source on that subject. Any errors on these topics are mine alone.

Deep thanks are due, as always, to my agent, Danielle Egan-Miller, and the entire team at Browne & Miller; this series would not exist without their efforts. Also thanks to my editor Faith Black Ross at Crooked Lane Press for being a stalwart champion of these books, and to the rest of the crew at Crooked Lane who make sure the Gilded Gotham series gets from my laptop into readers' hands. Designer Nicole Lecht once again provided a gorgeous cover.

Writing a book is both a solitary endeavor *and* takes a village, and I couldn't do any of this without the support of my family and friends. Much gratitude goes to Christine Gillespie, for always listening, and to Celeste Donovan, both for always listening and for being an extra set of eyes on the final edits. I remain eternally grateful to Marc, for giving me the time and space to sit at my desk, and to Roy, for helping me remember to step away from it. Lastly, none of this would be possible without those of you who have enjoyed these characters and give your valuable time to inhabit their world with me for a while. Thank you for choosing to do so.